Lose Yourself In Great Reading!

It gives me great pleasure to welcome you to "The People's Friend" Feel-good Fiction Special Vol 2.

Like last year, with summer fast approaching, we want to create something that you can really treasure and enjoy in the months ahead, whether you are travelling to sunny climes, or simply relaxing at home.

It is the perfect publication to have to hand while you are sitting in the garden, with a clear blue sky and warm sunshine.

Once again, the remarkable "Friend" Fiction Team have been lost in piles of manuscripts, selecting the fabulous fiction you will find within these pages.

I don't think it's any exaggeration to say they have done a wonderful job curating the tales within.

Turn over and you will find 44 truly amazing stories, packed with drama, romance, adventure and holiday thrills.

Throughout your magazine, you will also find compelling poetry – perfect for those little moments of mindfulness and calm

It all adds up to hours of great reading!

Our Illustrations Editor has also been hard at work creating the stunning artwork you will see alongside the words.

We hope you agree that it is a very special and thoroughly enjoyable package.

Enjoy every page, and have a truly fantastic summer.

Stuart

Stuart Johnstone, Editor.

What's INSIDE

The People's Friend Feel-good Fiction

Holiday FEVER

- 8 Someone To Lean On by Meg Stokes
- 10 A Clifftop Discovery by Jackie Morrison
- 12 Go Team Taylor! by Kate Blackadder
- 14 Hit The Road by Audrey Mary Brooks
- 16 Streets Of Paris by Charmaine Fletcher
- 19 **LONG READ:** Stargazing By The Sea by David Balmer
- 27 According To Plan by Beth Watson
- 30 Paradise Found by Jacqui Cooper
- 33 Without You by Eirin Thompson
- 34 Surprise Me! by Marie Penman
- 36 Sit Back And Relax by Sheelagh Mooney
- 38 **POEM:** The Sea by Bridget Baldock
- 40 **POEM:** Body Beautiful by Ros McKenna

Dreams of ROMANCE

- 44 In The Nick Of Time by Fiona Thomson
- 46 Seas The Day by Charmaine Fletcher
- 48 Her Heart's Desire by Sharon Haston
- 50 Throw In the Towel by Stefania Hartley
- 52 Turn Of The Tide by Anne Pack
- 55 **LONG READ:** Forbidden Love by Alison Carter
- 63 The Last Scoop by Becca Robin
- 66 Let's Dance by Jackie Morrison
- 69 Picture This by Chris Sutton
- 70 A Sight To Behold by Fiona Thomson
- 72 Coming Back To The Cove by Sally Waterbury
- 74 **POEM:** Salad Days And Strawberry Nights by Angie Keeler
- 76 **POEM:** Magic! by Ros McKenna

106

46

86

www.thepeoplesfriend.co.uk   www.facebook.com/PeoplesFriendMagazine   twitter.com/@TheFriendMag

CONTENTS

27

63

Cosy CRIME

- 80 Elsie Investigates by Becca Robin
- 82 The Guest List by Alison Carter
- 84 Isabella's On The Case by Sharon Haston
- 86 All That Glitters by Sally Waterbury
- 88 Double Exposure by Joanne Duncan
- 91 **LONG READ:** School For Murder by Liz Filleul
- 99 Seaside Sleuths by Kate Finnemore
- 102 Out For A Duck by Alyson Hilbourne
- 105 A Small Fortune by Alison Carter
- 106 Sting Like A Bee by Charmaine Fletcher
- 108 Pick A Pocket Or Two by Alyson Hilbourne
- 110 **POEM:** Wish You Were Here? by Laura Tapper
- 112 **POEM:** ¡Y Viva Espana! by Sharon Haston

Sunshine DAYS

- 116 All At Sea by Tess Niland Kimber
- 118 Moments Like These by Marie Penman
- 120 Fit For Purpose by Helen Yuretich
- 122 Intrigue In Ibiza by Val Bonsall
- 124 The Grass Is Greener by Rebecca Holmes
- 127 **LONG READ:** Life At Smithy Cottage by Melissa Banks
- 135 At Close Quarters by Louise McIvor
- 137 **POEM:** The Remedy by Susan Batten
- 138 A New Chapter by Katie Ashmore
- 141 Home Healing by Jane Ayres
- 142 A Fair Bit Of Drama by Joanne Duncan
- 144 The Whole Picture by Margret Geraghty
- 146 **POEM:** Steady Sailing by Emma Peterson

If you like this Bookazine then you'll love our weekly mag, 3 weekly Special and our fortnightly Pocket Novels…

Available in newsagents & supermarkets

£2.50 £3.99 £4.99

Published in the UK by DC Thomson & Co Ltd, Dundee, Glasgow and London. © DC Thomson & Co Ltd, 2025. Registered Office: DC Thomson & Co Ltd, Courier Buildings, 2 Albert Square, Dundee, Scotland, DD1 9QJ. Distributed by Frontline Ltd, Stuart House, St John's St, Peterborough, Cambridgeshire PE1 5DD. Tel: +44 (0) 1733 555161. Website: www.frontlinedistribution.co.uk. Export distribution (excluding AU and NZ) Seymour Distribution Ltd, 2 East Poultry Avenue, London EC1A 9PT. Tel: +44(0)20 7429 4000. Fax: +44(0)20 7429 4001. Website: www.seymour.co.uk. EU Representative Office: DC Thomson & Co Ltd, c/o Findmypast Ireland, Irishtown, Athlone, Co. Westmeath, N37 XP52. For advertising queries, contact lee.rimmer@canopymedia.co.uk or call 0204 5532900. For subscription queries, contact shop@dcthomson.co.uk or 0800 318846/01382 575580 (UK) +44 1382 575580 (International), www.dcthomsonshop.co.uk/pfd. Editorial communications to "The People's Friend", 2 Albert Square, Dundee DD1 1DD. While every reasonable care will be taken, neither D.C. Thomson & Co., Ltd., nor its agents will accept liability for loss or damage to any materials submitted to this publication. The People's Friend is a member of IPSO (the Independent Press Standards Organisation), which regulates the UK's newspaper, magazine, and digital news industry. We abide by the Editors' Code of Practice and are committed to upholding the highest standards of journalism. If you think that we have not met those standards and want to make a complaint, please contact readerseditor@dcthomson.co.uk or Readers Editor, The People's Friend, DC Thomson & Co Ltd, Courier Buildings, 2 Albert Square, Dundee, Scotland, DD1 9QJ. If we are unable to resolve your complaint, or if you would like more information about IPSO or the Editors' Code, contact IPSO on 0300 123 2220 or visit www.ipso.co.uk.

Holiday
FEVER

It's the time of year when thoughts turn to getting away from it all. These stories will put you in the mood for long, happy days filled with sunshine and smiles.

Someone To Lean On

Savannah wanted to enjoy her holiday without anyone's help . . .

BY MEG STOKES

If Savannah hadn't been so acutely aware of the tour group around her, she would have cried.

The carousel continued round and round, but there was still no sign of her blue suitcase with its fancy, colourful luggage tag.

"Still no sign of it?"

The young tour representative, Hannah, had come up behind her.

Savannah shook her head.

"Look," Hannah said, "I'll sort it out with the airline, but we've really got to go now.

"The coach is waiting and everybody wants to get to the hotel. You can always buy the basics and don't worry – it'll turn up."

Savannah turned, with a last, despairing look at the empty carousel. Then, disappointed, she followed Hannah out into the warm, Egyptian morning where the coach stood, idling.

What a perfect start to the holiday, she thought, as she climbed aboard.

How could this happen when she had planned everything to the nth degree – as she did with everything in her life?

"That happened to me once," an older woman with ash-blonde hair said, as Savannah sat down next to her. "But everything turned up eventually.

"I could help you buy some things later, if you like . . ."

Savannah leaned back and closed her eyes as the bus moved forward and the woman's voice faded slightly in the roar of the engine.

She would go out later and buy some things for herself, she thought.

She didn't need any help. She had only chosen the tour because it saved her having to organise trips to sites herself, but she had no intention of becoming part of a group jostling around the Valley of the Kings or Hatshepsut's Temple.

"Wouldn't you be better staying with us for a while, love, instead of going so far away?"

Her mother's voice came back to her.

"It's not like the separation was a shock, Mum," she had answered, "and I'm fine with it. Nick wants some space – I understand that. I really don't need looking after."

"You sometimes make it hard to help you, Savannah," her mum had responded.

The coach slowed down and Savannah opened her eyes on to the sparkling blue water of the Nile.

I don't need any help, she thought as they pulled up in front of the hotel. I'm fine on my own.

• • • •

Luxor market – a 15-minute walk from the hotel – was very unlike the market of Savannah's hometown.

Wooden roofs covered the lanes and the stalls on either side were hung with colourful rugs and bags, shoes and souvenirs.

Jewellery sparkled in the lights and the air was redolent with spices.

For a while, Savannah wandered up and down, shaking her head and sidestepping merchants as they tried to persuade her to buy their goods.

Eventually, she moved towards a stall which sold clothing, picked up a top and asked how much it was.

But the merchant seemed intent on haggling with her over the price and she began to feel panicked.

Everything was so strange.

The smell of the spices, so pleasant and enticing earlier, now felt cloying, making it hard to breathe.

She thrust the top back into the merchant's hands and stumbled away.

At that moment, she felt a hand take her elbow.

"Come on, Savannah," the ash-blonde woman from the tour bus said. "It is Savannah, isn't it?

"I thought you'd come here. It's all very overwhelming, especially if you're not used to haggling.

"I know a store a few streets away where you can get everything you need. I'm Liz by the way."

Savannah felt herself being led out of the market and towards a large store further into the town.

"You'll probably have to buy clothes a bit different from the sort of things you usually wear," Liz said as they entered the store, eyeing Savannah's neat and tidy skirt and blouse.

At dinner that evening, Savannah wore a loose, embroidered top and a flowing, cotton skirt that felt soft against her bare legs.

Colourful sandals had taken the place of her black court shoes.

She didn't know how she felt about her rescue from the market. Grateful, obviously, to Liz but cross with herself that she had needed rescuing at all.

It was only a market, after all. Surely she should have been able to cope without being rescued like a child?

Liz hadn't mentioned the panic attack and Savannah was grateful about that, too.

There was still no news about her luggage, but she had been able to buy what she needed and, she had to admit, she loved her new clothes.

They made her feel freer somehow, if one can say that of clothes.

The alabaster workshop was uncomfortably warm.

The male workers wore jalabiyas and sat in a row, the alabaster stone in front of them as they carved bowls and vases.

Above and behind them were posters showing diagrams of the age-old craft.

The tour group stood and

watched for a while before carrying on into the shop where the alabaster goods were for sale.

At first, Savannah hadn't wanted to join the tour group for this trip, but then she had thought that a piece of alabaster as a present for her mum would be nice, so here she was.

It was very warm in here.

She moved slowly along the shelves, picking up pots and dishes and running her hands over the smooth, cool surface of the alabaster.

Suddenly she was aware of black spots in front of her eyes. She blinked rapidly and struggled to focus before she felt herself slipping away.

The pot in her hand fell from her grasp and she heard it hit the ground with a smash, before everything went dark.

When she came to, there was a circle of concerned people above her.

She struggled to sit up and then was helped to a seat in the corner of the room, while the owner of the shop fetched cool water for her to drink.

"It is hot in here," Hannah said once they were on their own, "but have you been drinking enough water? You really must drink plenty in this heat, you know."

"I thought I had been," Savannah said, annoyed with herself yet again.

Rescued twice in two days. This was getting ridiculous. She knew that in the publishing office where she worked she had a reputation for being self-assured and super-efficient.

What would they say if they could see her now?

When the rest of the tour group went to the Colossi of Memnon, Savannah stayed in her room and rested.

"Are you having a good time, darling? I didn't expect you to call."

Her mother's voice sounded a little anxious.

"I'm fine, Mum – just having a day's break. It's very hot here."

"Well, it is Egypt in the summer. You must make sure that you're drinking plenty of water."

Savannah sighed.

"Nick came round yesterday and mowed my lawn," her mum said.

"Oh, did he? I thought . . ."

"You thought he wouldn't come any more because of how things are between you and him?"

"I suppose I didn't think about it at all really," Savannah admitted. "How is he?"

"Quiet and rather pale, I thought. I made him stay for dinner."

"That's good. Mum, what did you mean when you said that it was hard to help me?"

"Goodness, did I say that? Well, I suppose I meant you've always been so independent.

"Independence is a good thing, of course, but it's not a weakness to lean on other people when you need to – to accept help.

"You've never been very good at that, you know."

No, Savannah thought. She knew – or she was beginning to.

• • • •

The Karnak Temple complex was one place that Savannah didn't want to miss and she decided to join the tour the next day.

Standing in the vast Hypostyle Hall, she allowed the rest of the group to move on.

She was amazed by the vast columns around her decorated with hieroglyphics and evidence of Egypt's history.

"Amazing, isn't it? I never tire of seeing it."

Liz came to stand beside her and spoke in a whisper, aware that this was what the space required.

"Are you feeling better today?" she asked.

"Yes, much better, thank you. I think I've just let myself get a little run-down," Savannah replied.

She placed her hand against a pillar, feeling the coolness of the ancient, sandstone carving beneath it. "My husband and I have just separated," she heard herself admit.

"I'm sorry. That must be hard," Liz said,

"Yes, it is." She took a deep breath. "I don't know quite how I feel at the moment, Liz.

"I wonder if I could have done things differently, if it was my fault. My mother says I'm too independent."

Liz gently laid a hand on Savannah's arm.

"It's a fine balance, isn't it?" Liz's voice was quiet. "We're told it's a good thing to be independent, yet it can be quite isolating, can't it?

"Perhaps we forget that it's also a good thing to be able to lean on somebody when we need to.

"Is your husband somebody you could lean on?"

"Oh yes, he is, but maybe I don't lean on him enough," Savannah said with a small smile.

They stood quietly a little longer, then they began to move slowly out of the hall towards the tour group.

"Are you coming to the light show this evening?" Liz asked. "You have got to see Karnak by moonlight."

"Yes, I'm looking forward to it."

It was strange, Savannah thought, how she now felt part of the group she had initially intended to shun.

• • • •

The Mortuary Temple of Hatshepsut is cradled by the cliffs of Deir el-Bahari.

Its three magnificent terraces shimmered in the early morning sunlight as Savannah got off the coach.

The tour group began to walk up the causeway, flanked by the falcon statues of Horus.

"This is awesome," Savannah said, looking upward as they climbed.

"Isn't it?" Liz said. "Hatshepsut was only the second Egyptian queen to reign in her own right. Now that was a truly independent woman!

"Of course, she had to appear to be male in order to rule as pharaoh, so you'll see the fake beard and masculine garments in any depiction of her."

"That's fascinating," Savannah said as they continued to the top of the incline. "You know so much."

"Egyptian history has always been a passion of mine," Liz said with a smile.

• • • •

"Oh no!"

A wail broke out behind one of the columns as Savannah was examining the relief scenes on the wall.

When she turned the corner, she recognised a young woman as being part of their group.

She was leaning against a column and staring at her digital camera in disbelief.

"Oh, hello," she said as Savannah appeared.

She grimaced and held out her camera.

"The memory card is full. I can't believe it. There has been so much to film and it now tells me it's full and I don't have a spare."

Savannah smiled and pulled her bag off her shoulder. She delved into her bag and pulled out two memory cards.

"Well, it's your lucky day because I have plenty of spares. That's what comes of being super organised!

"I'm Savannah, by the way. I don't think we've spoken before."

• • • •

Later, back at the hotel, Hannah told Savannah that her luggage had arrived.

"You'll be pleased to get back into your own clothes, I would imagine," she said.

But Savannah wasn't too sure.

She had found the loose fitting garments she had been wearing to be comfortable and unrestrictive, so she might go shopping when she returned home.

And maybe it was also time to speak to Nick.

Hopefully, it wasn't too late to learn to lean on each other.

A Clifftop Discovery

Could some miracle reunite Julie with her lost ring?

BY JACKIE MORRISON

FINDING herself back in Cornwall was a surprise to Julie. She'd vowed never to return after that first disastrous holiday here.

To be fair, their family holiday ten years ago had been fun: the vast beaches at St Ives, the surfing at Newquay, the stunning fishing villages of Mousehole and Mevagissey and the hidden coves they'd revelled in finding around Porthcurno Bay.

That's what had caused the problem though.

Julie couldn't fathom why Adam wanted to go back.

As Julie looked through her flower shop orders for the coming week, she rubbed at the back of her left hand where her wedding band shone.

It sat alone on her finger, because ten years ago she'd lost her engagement ring somewhere in Cornwall.

"It'll be different this time, you'll see." Adam was enthusiastic that his bribery of a boutique couples' hotel would enthuse Julie.

"I'm not sure we'll find a lot to do. We've seen all the gardens, lots of the beaches, and there are shops here. I don't need Cornwall."

"We haven't seen it all, Julie! We had the kids with us last time, remember? All of our activities were focussed on keeping them amused. And we haven't seen all the gardens, not at all."

"I'll give it a try," Julie whispered. She had that sense of doom that came over her whenever a programme set in Cornwall came on the telly.

Whatever it was – drama, travel show, comedy – she'd switch channels as quickly as possible, heart thumping just like it had when she'd noticed her ring had gone.

She'd thought about her engagement ring many times over the years. She wondered if it wallowed deep in some drain at the cottage they'd rented, or if it had fallen off in a supermarket, or on the street. Imagining it on someone else's finger made her wince.

When they'd been dating, Julie was still in horticultural college and Adam finishing up his engineering apprenticeship. All their early earnings had gone on the deposit for their tiny flat.

Somehow though, Adam squirrelled away money until the day he proposed in the local park.

Cherry blossom trees sent down pink confetti as Julie said, "Yes!"

On Julie's small hands, the engagement ring looked dainty, and just right.

When Adam explained he'd had the original gold and central diamond from his grandma's ring refashioned, adding the small diamonds into the new setting to resemble a flower, Julie had cried at his thoughtfulness.

A dainty daisy shape moulded in gold and diamonds. It suited her to perfection.

It even seemed to foretell that one day she'd have her very own flower shop.

Julie had been precious about the ring. When she opened her own flower shop, she'd worn it under her fingerless gloves, relishing the feeling of knowing it was always with her.

Arriving at the boutique hotel was a revelation to Julie.

They'd never been so extravagant with their holidays before but, with the teenage twins staying with their grandparents, Julie and Adam appreciated the opportunity to celebrate their anniversary as a couple.

A worry niggled at the back of Julie's mind. She hoped Adam hadn't planned anything secret.

She didn't like surprises. Over the years, she'd been nervous that he might try to present her with a replacement engagement ring.

She told him many times, the ring could never be replaced, and not to even try.

The last time she'd said this, Julie wished she could take the words back when she'd seen how hurt Adam looked, his dark hair falling over his blue eyes. The ring, with its connection to his grandma, was an emotional loss for him, too.

Adam worked his magic by listing the gardens they were going to visit, and Julie thought the short break might turn out ok after all.

She was so lucky to have a husband as thoughtful as Adam.

Adam was more inclined to favour a city break, or a visit to the theatre, so she wasn't the least surprised when he'd said that, today, they were visiting a theatre at the edge of the world.

The approach had given nothing away, even when they'd made the walk down from the car park.

That first view of the Minack Theatre perched on a rocky outcrop at the edge of the sea made Julie gasp with delight.

They learned that Minack, from the Cornish "Meynek", means a rocky place.

For Julie, the biggest surprise was yet to come, for as they looked down to where the theatre had been carved from rock, there were sub-tropical gardens abundant with colour.

Meandering pathways and steps surrounded with

glorious floral displays, led tantalisingly towards the terraced open-air theatre with an archway framing the sparkling turquoise sea and white fringed beaches of Porthcurno Bay and beyond.

It was impossible to explain how instantly uplifting it was.

Winding their way down paths and steps, they explored the plants and the story about Rowena Cade and her gardener Billy Rawlings who carved and built this extraordinary place mostly by hand.

Julie paused now and then to acknowledge a stunning piece of foliage or sniff a bright flower.

Pinks and lemons were scattered through with purples and the upper terraces strewn with contrasting layers of succulents in gold and red, purple and green.

Adam spotted something too.

"Look, love, the flower beds have names on them. They're named after people in Shakespeare plays!"

So, Adam, had managed to incorporate some of his favourite things into this day out too!

"Oh, they must be filming the performance later, I saw a film crew over there." Julie called to Adam, who immediately whisked her in the opposite direction.

"Let's take some photos from the stage. You'll look good there with your dress, love."

Julie, for once, was inclined to believe him. She loved how the periwinkle blue picked out her eye colour, and the dress was cool in the summer heat.

The warm breeze from the sea beyond gently whipped her golden hair around her bare shoulders.

She'd worn little dangly silver starfish earrings she'd bought in the fishing village of Mevagissey and with her gladiator sandals, she felt smart but comfortable.

The moment Julie glanced through the stone arch though, her stomach plummeted. She looked over to the secluded coves where the tide rippled onto soft white sand, and she imagined her ring a thousand leagues under the sea.

They'd visited those beaches with the children the year she'd lost her engagement ring.

When she turned back, she thought Adam was tying the laces of his trainers and the camera crew were setting up for later.

Then, Adam reached for her hand.

"Julie, will you say yes all over again, please?"

Adam held out his hand where something sparkly glinted in the sunshine.

Julie felt unsteady on her feet.

What was he doing?

"Julie, it's the most amazing story! Please say yes, so I can get up?" Then he leaned towards her, saying in a stage whisper, "They're filming us for a segment. Please say yes, love – look!"

Julie looked closer, screwing her eyes against the glare of the summer sun.

It was a delicate golden ring with a floral setting in diamonds. Her heart quickened. It couldn't be!

"It was found, Julie! It is definitely your ring – look!"

Adam held the ring out for her inspection, and there inside the band were the initials A & J, 2010 in a cursive engraving.

"Oh!" she gasped in disbelief.

"Do you think you could give me a hand, love, my knee isn't what it used to be!" Adam laughed as he fell forward, taking Julie in his arms.

"Come sit down and hear all about it. It's a miracle it was ever found. The news team want to tell the story!" Adam said, energetically.

Julie sat on the stone terraced seating, a cushion of springy grass beneath her, and twisted the ring on her left hand, getting used to the comfort of it.

It still fitted her finger perfectly.

Julie was amazed to discover that Adam had hooked up years ago via email with a local metal detectorist team who regularly went out on weekends to seek treasure.

Having given them note of all the places they'd visited on their Cornwall family holiday, Adam hoped against hope that the ring would turn up one day.

Of all the places Adam had imagined the ring might be, he never thought it would turn up where it did.

It hadn't been the detectorists who'd found it.

Megan was interviewed alongside them, the film crew jovial.

"The last thing I expected walking my dog was to find a diamond ring!" Megan laughed heartily.

A dinner-lady in a local school, Megan had been out on a regular dog walk to the sea when she'd found something surprising on the approach path to the beach.

Hundreds of feet had likely walked that route over the years and the ring had been pressed and buried, deep in earth and grass, until uncovered perhaps by a large rainfall and uprooted by Megan spaniel, Dizzy.

"It looks a lot cleaner today!" Megan laughed.

"That's a wrap!" the young reporter smiled.

"That's a yes!" Julie called out, throwing her arms around Adam.

"I can't believe you had metal detectorists looking for this for years and it was found by Megan and Dizzy!"

It hadn't taken long for word of Megan's exciting find to reach Terry, the main detectorist, and together with the inscription, it had made identification easy.

We found it! Well, Megan found it! the email had said.

With their anniversary on the horizon, Adam had wasted no time planning the last-minute secret getaway whilst Alan spoke to the local press.

Julie smiled as Dizzy, the clever young dog, clambered to be patted and was then led away to have his photo taken under the theatre's arch. The hero of the story.

Julie's cheeks were rosy with joy, as she looked into the blue eyes of her husband, the same eyes that had looked earnestly into hers as he'd popped the question in the local park in their youth all those years back.

"What a day! What a holiday!" Julie beamed.

"It's not over yet." Adam said, "We've got complimentary tickets for the evening theatre performance. It's an adaptation of Agatha Christie's short story 'The Jewel Robbery' at the Grand Metropolitan.

"Oh, we shouldn't tempt fate!" Julie cried, "My ring! I'll have to sit on my hand all evening to be sure it stays put."

Adam took hold of her hand.

"Well, your ring was never stolen, it just went on an extended holiday in Cornwall! Even so, maybe I should hold on to you all night."

The couple were oblivious to the crowd that filed in behind them, settling in for an evening of drama to the backdrop of the sparkling Cornish sea at Porthcurno Bay.

The couple's own drama had played out perfectly.

When the two came together to kiss, Julie's hand on Adam's shoulder, diamonds sparkling, it was the perfect moment after a 15-year search came to a successful fruition.

Go Team Taylor!

Without Susie, this family holiday didn't feel the same . . .

BY KATE BLACKADDER

Set in 1971

SUSIE walked into the room.

"What's up?" I asked.

"We've been waiting for you, Freckle Face."

She's my big sister. I can call her what I like.

"Mandy!" Mum said. "OK, team, decision time. Where shall we go on holiday this year?"

That's my family – Team Taylor. The four of us, tight as a drum. Especially on our caravan holidays.

That Saturday in March 1971, the day things began to change, we sat round the kitchen table.

We should have been drinking hot chocolate with a swirl of whipped cream on top.

It's tradition when we're planning our summer hols.

Well, I thought it was, but Mum forgot and made a pot of tea instead.

There were chocolate digestives though.

"St Andrews again? Good old Kinghorn?" Dad said. "Or how about Dunbar for a change?"

He put a leaflet on the table.

We'd gone to a caravan site in St Andrews twice before and Kinghorn three times, so I pounced on the leaflet.

The picture of Dunbar was like a book cover – blue seas and red cliffs and yellow sand. Very Enid Blyton!

"Dunbar! Dunbar!" I chanted.

Susie raised her hand as if she was in class.

She had that skulky, slithery, sidley look again.

She looked down at the table.

"Count me out this year. Christine has asked me to go with her family to France. To a hotel in Brittany."

"In where? A what? You can't go." I spluttered tea and crumbs over the formica. "Mum, tell her."

Dad and Mum sat back and I waited for them to let Susie know that going on holiday without Team Taylor was not allowed.

But instead they exchanged glances.

"That'll take some thinking about," Dad said. "When are they going?"

"The second week in July," Susie mumbled.

The week that Dad had booked to get off work, a week that couldn't be changed.

"Mum," I wailed.

She patted my hand.

"There's no harm in discussing it, dear. Susie's sixteen and we know Christine's family."

"We'd have to contribute to the cost, of course. A hotel will be dear."

"Christine says you wouldn't." Susie had a silly big smile on her face. "The hotel's gorgeous.

"She showed me a picture. It's got a swimming pool and a balcony."

"There'll be a flight though." Dad looked worried. "We can't let them pay for that."

"Her dad's driving all the way," Susie says. "Her mum says they want me to be company for Christine, give them some time on their own."

So who was going to be company for me?

I stared hard at the Dunbar leaflet, trying not to cry. The minute I saw that picture I'd imagined me and Susie exploring.

Searching around those cliffs for caves and secret passages, maybe finding treasure or escaped convicts like the Famous Five.

We could be the Famous Two.

And what about the things we do in St Andrews and Kinghorn?

Susie trying to teach me to swim. Dad making a bonfire on the beach and cooking sausages. Getting choc-ices for pudding. Our sandcastle competitions.

Palling up with the children of other caravanners to play rounders. I couldn't do that without my big sister.

All these things rushed through my head but what did I say?

"What about our shell collection?" I burst out, waving my hand at the windowsill and its accumulation of finds from all the beaches we'd been on.

"You can pick up shells even if I'm not there, Mandy Pandy." Susie looked from Mum to Dad and back again.

"So, can I? It'll be good for my French," she wheedled.

"How? You'll just be talking to Christine." I snorted. "On the balcony."

"Shush, Mandy," Dad said. "Susie, Mum and I will speak to Christine's parents."

I jumped up as fast as my bad leg would allow and banged the door as hard as I could when I left the room.

Five minutes later, as I knew she would, Mum came through to my bedroom.

It's really our front room but after my accident, when I couldn't climb the stairs, they had a bed put in here.

They kept asking when I'd like to move back up but Susie said she liked having our bedroom to herself.

Mum sat on the bed.

"Do you want to ask a friend to come with us, Mandy?"

"Why?" I could feel my lip wobbling. "Do you and Dad want time on your own, like Christine's parents?"

Mum stroked my hair.

"We just thought you might like to have company of your own age."

"We're Team Taylor! I don't want someone else coming. Anyway, I don't have a best friend."

That was true.

I'd been off school for six months and when I went back everyone had shifted around and I didn't fit in anywhere.

Mum looked sad.

"I probably will get one when I go to high school," I said then. "But that's not until after the summer holidays."

"Dunbar sounds lovely, doesn't it?" She kissed me on the forehead. "We'll write tonight and book a caravan."

Later I overheard her talking about me to Dad.

"It's hard for her but she'll make new memories in a new place."

I didn't want new memories. I liked my old ones.

• • • •

Dunbar wasn't blue and red and yellow that first evening.

There was a fog – Dad said it was called a haar – over the water.

It made everything gray. You couldn't even see to make a bonfire.

Mum put out cold ham and heated up a tin of beans and we played board games that didn't need four players and then we went to bed.

I couldn't sleep. It wasn't the same without Susie to giggle with. Every time I sat up and looked out everything was still gray.

"Go to sleep, Mandy," Mum said several times.

And I must have done eventually because I woke up and there wasn't a haar anymore and the caravan was empty.

If Susie had been there we might have had a pillow fight, but she wasn't so I went to the door and looked out.

Mum was sitting in a deckchair, her face tipped up to the sun.

From somewhere there came the smell of sausages cooking on a bonfire.

I didn't wait to put on my slippers and the grass was cool under my feet.

"There you are, dear," Mum said. "Didn't want to wake you."

"What's the time? Where's Dad?"

"Nine o' clock." Mum pointed to the beach. "Making sausages for breakfast as a treat.

"And he went to the shop for rolls to put them in." She indicated the plate on the picnic table.

I sat on one of the other two chairs. Three altogether this year, not four.

"What do you think Susie will be having? What do they eat in France for breakfast?" I asked.

"When I was there we had croissants and café au lait – that's milky coffee."

"You've been to France?" I stared at her.

"With friends from college. Long time ago."

I got the feeling Mum regretted telling me.

"Not nearly as nice a breakfast as morning rolls with hot sausages inside," she added.

I didn't think so either, although I had no idea what a croissant was.

"There's Dad," Mum said. "Scoot and get dressed, Mandy. After breakfast he'll go exploring with you."

"But what will you do on your own? You can come, too."

I got up carefully. I knew the knack of getting out of that chair.

It was the wobbly one Susie had fallen out of last year. I think we laughed for ten whole minutes.

"I'll stay here." Mum smiled. "I don't get the chance to sit in the sun very often."

"I could stay with you," I offered.

"Thank you, dear, but I look forward to hearing about your adventures."

Dad put the sausages on the table.

"Team Taylor breakfast coming up!"

I knew they were trying to cheer me up but how could we be a real team when a quarter of us was missing?

It was quite fun exploring with Dad though.

He doubted if we'd find stolen jewels, or boys kidnapped by their cruel uncles, but he knew the names of all the wee things that scuttled about in the rock pools and he didn't mind me filling his jacket pockets with shells.

When we got back, there was a woman and a girl with fair pigtails sitting in our deckchairs beside Mum.

The girl was in the one I'd sat on, the wobbly one.

"You'll never guess who's staying next door!" Mum said. "Jane. We were at secretarial college together – haven't seen each other since we left."

"And this is Elizabeth. She's eleven."

Mum looked meaningfully at me but I turned my head away. I didn't want a friend. I wanted my sister.

Then I saw that Elizabeth had one of her arms in plaster.

"What happened to your arm?" The words were out before I could stop myself.

"Fell off a swing," Elizabeth said. "What happened to your leg?"

She must have seen me limping across the grass.

"Knocked over by a bus."

It's not funny falling or being knocked over, believe me, but we found ourselves grinning at each other.

"Dad." I tugged at his jacket. "I want to show Elizabeth my shells."

"I collect shells, too!" Elizabeth said.

She tried to stand up but got tipped out of the chair, fortunately not from high up like a swing, and not on to her broken arm.

I think we laughed for ten whole minutes.

• • • •

"We called ourselves the Famous Two, do you remember?" We're reminiscing during one of our regular phone chats.

Elizabeth splutters with laughter.

"We didn't find any hidden treasure but I'll never forget anything about that holiday."

I smile although she can't see me. Having Elizabeth as a friend is better than any treasure.

Maybe our spectacles are rose-tinted after 30 years but we remember a week of golden sunshine and so much fun.

We made a housie in a cave, decorated with shells and seaweed, and had picnics in it.

I finally learned to swim under Jane's instruction.

We took night about staying in each other's caravans so we could play Snap and talk as long as we wanted, and we cried when we had to say goodbye.

I made so many new memories.

Susie had a great time in Brittany but she said she'd missed me so I seized the moment and said I'd move back upstairs to our bedroom.

I don't think she was that pleased but Mum and Dad were glad to have their front room back.

She'd brought us all presents and mine was a huge white shell, which took pride of place on the kitchen windowsill in Mum and Dad's house and now in my own.

Team Taylor went back to Kinghorn the following year, but after that Susie was all grown up and doing her own thing.

"So what are you doing for holidays this year?" Elizabeth asks.

We've come full circle.

"We're going with Susie and her lot, and Mum and Dad to St Andrews," I tell her. "Three very fancy caravans."

We try and holiday together once a year.

Dad cooks sausages on a barbeque now and awards marks to his grandchildren's sandcastles.

Mum still brings potato salad but she's not allowed to do anything else but sit in the sun (or inside if there's a haar!).

Susie and I have changed our name so we're not Taylors anymore, and we have all these lovely additions to the family.

We're a bigger team, but still a team. Still tight as a drum.

Hit The Road

Emma was sure she'd packed everything the family needed for this trip . . .

BY AUDREY MARY BROOKS

RIGHT then, are we ready?" Nick asked. He had pushed the picnic chairs into tiny gap between at the top of the pile of luggage and the roof of the car.

It was a good job they had a four-by-four.

"We really need to get started if we're to be there before dark. I did want an early start."

"There's no point in making an early start," Emma said, forcing a pillow down the side of the box of groceries. "Everyone will be making an early start. All the queues will have gone now.

"Just let me check my list and we can go."

"Again? You've been checking that list for a week. Anyone would think we were moving house, not spending a week in a holiday cottage."

"Precisely, Nick. It is not a hotel. Happy Holiday Lets might not think in the same way as we do."

"I'm certain they don't think in the same way that you do, Em. No-one does."

Emma sighed.

"I mean that they might forget the basics. It's a big company and they own a lot of properties. We need to be prepared," she said.

"Be prepared? We're going to Wales, not Outer Mongolia!" Nick protested.

"You said yourself that all the main supermarkets are only a couple of miles away and one of those is open twenty-four hours a day.

"We could even have our own online shopping delivery there if we wanted – the same day."

Emma ignored this remark and checked down her list.

The list was actually three pages in a notebook plus some bonus Post-its: yellow for "Yes, we must take it", blue for "Bound to forget if I don't put it on a Post-it" and pink for "Possibly, if there is room in the back".

Emma insisted that Nick go down the list with her to double-check. "Have we got the walking boots?"

"Do we really need the walking boots and the wellingtons?"

"Of course we do. Remember the year when we didn't take the walking boots? We all had to go out and buy new ones, and then Mae got blisters because she hadn't broken them in.

"The next year we took the walking boots and forgot the wellingtons. Of course that was the week of the only flood that particular area had had in forty years."

"So have we got them or not?" Emma rolled her eyes.

"Yes, we have walking boots, and the wellingtons, and the flip-flops, and the slippers.

"We also have the summer shoes we only wear for best, and the summer shoes we wear for best if it's been raining. We are all wearing our travelling trainers because you made us.

"We have two large holdalls full of shoes. And, before you ask, we have every type of outfit for every type of weather in all four seasons."

Emma checked they also had every type of coat for every type of weather piled on the top of the suitcases and bags.

"Will you please get in now?"

"When I've got the picnic for on the way. We are not stopping at services because it costs a fortune. I also need to check that we all have our water bottles and sweets to suck.

"Speaking of water bottles – do you think we should take hot water bottles? What if we have a cold spell? What if they turn the heating off at night? Cottages can get very cold at night."

"Em, we are not taking hot water bottles! I absolutely refuse to put them in."

"Have you taken the key to Mrs Rodgers next door? Does she know how to work the burglar alarm? Does Mae have Honeybun? You know she won't sleep without Honeybun."

"Yes!" Nick said.

"There's no need to get snappy, Nick, I'm only asking. Right, I think we're ready now," she said, loading the picnic bag into the car at the front with her.

She would have to sit with her legs sideways, but that was normal for any trip.

"Finally. Are we all ready in the back?" Nick shouted out as they all strapped in.

"Yes," came the reply.

"Good. Then off we go to Llanfair-pilly-gilly-something in Wales."

"Don't listen to Daddy. We're going to Abersoch!"

They'd only just turned the first corner when panic filled Emma.

She snapped her head round to look at who was strapped in the back and make sure no-one had been left behind.

"What? What is the matter, Emma?" Nick asked nervously, slamming on the brakes in an emergency stop.

There was a yell from the back and a pack of nine toilet rolls landed on Nick's head.

"Nothing. Nothing at all. Everything is fine."

Emma sighed. Everything was fine.

Reuben was in the back, alongside his sister Mae, rocking Honeybun.

Beside them was Ernie the dog, and her father – Grandad John. All was well.

Nick shook his head and drove on again, slowly.

Grandad decided to add his take on it all as he tried to move the dog to one side because his leg had gone to sleep.

"I can't understand why we need all this stuff, Emma. Your mum and I used to travel all round the world

with just a small suitcase each."

"What's it like abroad, Grandad?" Reuben asked.

"Hot and sunny, and you only need a small suitcase."

"Too hot and sunny for you, Reuben, and too expensive," Emma added firmly.

"Don't listen to your mum, Reuben. You need sunshine. Vitamin D is very important."

"Not as much as you'd get in Spain, Dad," Emma said.

Honeybun appeared over Emma's shoulder and Mae announced, "Olivia has gone to Florida to see Mickey Mouse and Moana."

"Finlay has gone to Mexico," Reuben added.

"Well Olivia and Finlay are very lucky children. They also have parents with more money than sense."

"Finlay's dad is a doctor."

"Doctors have a lot of sense," Grandad commented. "It takes years to become a doctor, and you have to be top of the class at school, get ten out of ten in all tests, and pass all your exams.

"Mind you, doctors have money, too. In fact, they have as much money as they have sense."

"Yes, thank you, Dad!"

"I spy with my little eye, something beginning with 't'," Grandad said.

There followed a very long list of things they could all see.

"We give up, Dad, what's the answer?" Emma asked.

"Too much luggage!"

They stopped at the service station for lunch, in order to eat their own picnic.

Then they stopped at the services after that for them all to use the facilities they all now needed.

Eventually, three and a half hours later, they arrived at their destination. It was a smart, fairly new property, built in a cottage style.

There was a key safe and Happy Holiday Lets had sent Emma a code for it.

She punched it in, but the key safe would not open. She tried several times to no avail. Nick climbed out of the car to help her.

"It won't make any difference if you put in exactly the same code Nick – it still won't work."

"Sometimes it needs a man's touch," Nick said, pressing the numbers in firmly.

Nothing happened.

"I rest my case," Emma said, finding the phone number for Happy Holiday Lets.

"Why can't we get in yet?" Mae whined, peeping through the letter box of the cottage.

It was a hot day, and they'd all climbed out of the car. Nick had set up the picnic chairs in the small front garden.

Grandad was sitting reading a book, Ernie the dog still on his lap.

Nick and Reuben were playing football on the grassy space opposite.

Emma had single-handedly dumped most of the contents of the car onto the front garden around her father in order to find the sun-cream which she had packed in a bag that turned out to be underneath everything else.

"Mummy I need to get in. I need the toilet."

"You'll have to hang on a little longer, darling. Just a few minutes. The lady will be here very soon."

Emma was getting desperate. She decided she'd better ring Pam from Happy Holiday Lets. They had been messaging backwards and forwards. They must have tried every code under the sun, but still, they couldn't get in.

Pam said they had a spare key in the office, and she would bring it over, she was only 30 minutes away. That was nearly an hour ago.

Emma's phone rang. It was Pam.

"Hi, Emma. Where are you? I can't understand what the problem is. Have you gone for a walk?"

"No, we're here, waiting outside. Where are you?"

"Waiting outside? You can't be. I'm inside, looking out of the window. There's no-one here."

Emma felt rather warm, even though she was standing in the shade.

"I think there might be a problem, Pam."

• • • •

"The wrong cottage! We are at the wrong cottage!" Grandad said, reluctantly standing up for Emma to take his picnic chair.

"It isn't my fault, Dad, it's Happy Holiday Lets's fault. They sent me directions to the cottage. It's just that they sent me the directions to the wrong cottage. The right one is only about ten minutes away."

"It is not ten minutes away, Emma, it's about an hour away by the time we've packed all this lot back into the car again."

Emma muttered something about "we" being her and Nick.

Her dad helpfully pointed out that he had a bad back, one that had been made worse sitting with the dog on his knee for four hours.

The neighbour in the cottage next door had kindly let Mae use the bathroom.

Eventually they were on their way again.

"I'm hungry," Reuben said.

"I'm hungry too, lad," Grandad John said.

"I'm starving," Nick added.

"Don't even think about stopping for chips," Emma said.

They stopped for chips.

"I told you it would be an hour," Grandad said.

It was indeed an hour before they reached the right cottage, and early evening.

Pam had left the key under the mat.

They took their chips inside and ate them before they did anything else.

Afterwards, Emma instructed everyone to help bring their belongings in, including her dad. It was getting dark. They had emptied the car and played hunt the vacuum cleaner.

They'd had to use that when Grandad spilt a packet of cornflakes all over the floor.

Why hadn't Emma brought a full packet?

Why hadn't she sealed the half-full packet up with Sellotape?

Cornflakes were the only cereal her father ate. Now she would have to go to the supermarket.

Emma had washed the pots – there was a dishwasher, but she'd forgotten to put in tablets and Happy Holiday Lets hadn't provided them.

They hadn't provided laundry products, either, and Mae had spilt blackcurrant juice all over herself and Honeybun.

Why hadn't Emma thought of laundry products?

There were more moans later that evening when they discovered that the TV didn't have a streaming service included.

They were going to play a board game, but it seemed Happy Holiday Lets didn't keep any of those either. Emma had not included them.

Grandad came to the rescue by initiating a game of charades.

Emma started to make a list of the things they would need for next year's holiday that she'd forgotten this year. It was a very long list.

She made a note in capital letters that said: DO NOT USE HAPPY HOLIDAY LETS.

Much, much later and totally exhausted, Emma and Nick fell into bed.

"I was thinking it might be better to go abroad next year, Nick – we'd only need the bare minimum if we go full board. It would save all this kerfuffle every time."

"Go abroad? Are you mad, Emma? Certainly not – that's for people with more money than sense!"

Nick suddenly shook, rocking the bed.

"What is it? Are you all right, Nick? Why are you shaking? Are you shaking with laughter?"

"I wish. No – I'm freezing.

"Why didn't you put the hot water bottles in?"

Set in 1976

Streets Of Paris

Gina was beginning to feel overwhelmed all alone in the city . . .

BY CHARMAINE FLETCHER

As Gina gazed about the tiny Parisian avenue, its undulating cobbles and patchwork of shops resembling several others she'd passed before, the scene began to blur.

Hopelessly lost and aware that tears threatened, Gina stood still, just as her mother had instructed her when she was little.

"If we're ever separated or even when you're older and lost," she'd said.

"Don't worry; find a quiet spot and think about what you love best. It'll stop you wanting to cry and hopefully, things will sort themselves out."

Gina was unimpressed with Lynn and Tracey's abandonment of her when they were supposedly holidaying together.

Her two friends probably weren't looking for her and she'd never find them but at least she wouldn't appear babyish among the sophisticated Parisians.

Gina did as her mother suggested.

I like speaking French, books, history and fashion, she thought, feeling calmer.

Eventually, she remembered what had initially brought her to Paris.

* * * *

"Come on, Gina, it'll be fun!" Lynn had said, glancing at Tracey, meaningfully.

They were lounging around her bedroom, trying clothes and experimenting with the latest beauty trends.

"Yeah, imagine. A week in Paris, the city of romance," Tracey chipped in.

Lynn nodded approvingly.

"I don't know," Gina demurred, subtly removing her best plum nail polish from Lynn. "Besides, what about my holiday job? I was lucky to get work at À La Française, that new delicatessen, on the high street.

"Hopefully, it'll look really good on my application to study French at university next year. Anyway, how would I pay for it?"

"You start work the Monday after we return! And you still have your eighteenth birthday money. It won't cost much," Lynn replied airily.

"Why not?" Gina frowned.

"Lynn's aunt Josie, who married a Frenchman, has a Paris apartment that she rents out during the summer," Tracey began, twisting a blonde curl idly.

"Only she's had a cancellation and the deposit's forfeit – so there's just the balance to pay," Lynn explained.

"Without your language skills, how will we chat up French boys?" Tracey asked.

As Lynn giggled, Tracey and Gina joined in.

"Go on then, count me in," she conceded "but if I regret anything, you'll hear about it – understood?"

Solemnly the girls nodded.

To Gina's relief, Josie's top floor apartment in the Butte Montmartre arrondissement was better than anticipated.

Dating from the fin de siècle, the beautiful old building stood in a delightfully bohemian quarter of the city.

It felt more like a small village, with winding cobbles, punctuated by quaint street lamps.

Having expected something less characterful and modern, Gina was thrilled – less so when the others took the only rooms with views.

"Well, it was my idea," Lynn argued at breakfast, dipping a croissant into a cup of chocolate.

"But I can only see a wall! Perhaps it's fairer to each move on one room over the week," Gina suggested tentatively.

"No – it'd be a drag!" Tracey replied, glancing at Lynn, who'd nodded in agreement.

"Anyway, with sightseeing, discos and eating out, we shan't be here much," Lynn reassured her. "Honestly, you won't even notice."

By way of consolation, they spent the day visiting museums, as suggested by Gina, including the Louvre, where they queued for hours to view the Mona Lisa.

"Well, I don't rate it, or understand the fuss," Tracey complained, to be shushed by other horrified tourists. "It's titchy.

"What's there to smile about, anyway? All that brown's miserable. Perhaps she should be renamed 'Moaner' rather than "Mona'," she added to more disapproving tuts.

"Shh!" Gina hissed, glancing round, blushing to the roots of her hair, before hastily ushering her friends away.

"What shall we do tomorrow?" she asked later, as they dined on steak frites and salad at a cheap and cheerful brasserie.

"I thought we might try a trip to Versailles, it's only forty-nine minutes from Paris and historically fascinating –"

"That's forty-nine minutes I'll never get back," Tracey muttered.

"Just imagine everything everyone who lived there, and all the things that happened," Gina continued dreamily. "Louis the XIV 'The Sun King', then Queen Marie Antoinette and her husband before they died so tragically . . ." she finished sadly.

"What of boredom?" Lynn asked sarcastically glancing at Tracey. "Personally, I fancy browsing the designer shops, then a trip to Galeries Lafayette in Boulevard Haussmann and buying stuff to take home."

"Agreed," Tracey said firmly.

They eyed Gina, who, nodding, reluctantly gave in.

"Right," Lynn said, "Tomorrow, we'll breakfast at Le Chat Noir, that café on the corner, then go shopping."

Only by the time she woke up, the other two had disappeared, leaving Gina a note saying: *We thought you needed some beauty sleep! Ha! Ha! See you at Le Chat Noir – L and T.*

Running to the window, she scanned the street but there was no sign of them.

Hastily, Gina washed and dressed in a white, layered skirt, pretty peasant blouse and laced espadrilles, before locking up and running down the wrought iron spiral staircase.

The apartment was at the apex of a crossroads, leading to four different almost identical streets, only Gina couldn't remember which led to the café.

Removing her guidebook, she tried to get her bearings without much luck, eventually turning into a nearby avenue.

After walking for some time, the café hadn't appeared. Realising she was lost, Gina began to panic.

• • • •

Back in the moment, Gina's thoughts were suddenly stirred by several successive clicks and shadows, in the otherwise sunny spot, shifting mercurially.

"No, don't move," a young, masculine voice breathed in French. "You're so beautiful.

"That faraway look is magical," he said, kissing his fingertips appreciatively.

"Hey! Who said you could take my photo?" Gina demanded in French.

The photographer was now walking around her, framing a shot and clicking again.

"You!" he smiled, lowering his camera, revealing, glittering green eyes over a strong Gallic nose and a tumble of long, black curls swept back off his tanned face.

"Your expression was begging to be photographed!" he explained, more seriously, fishing a business card from his jeans pocket and handing it to Gina.

Taking it, she read: *Fabrice Bastien, Photographe, "Paris Chic".*

"Oh, you're a photojournalist," Gina said.

She tried hard not to look impressed on learning that Fabrice worked for a revered French fashion magazine.

"Bien sûr." He nodded with a slight courtly bow. "My editor thinks great style is found on the streets of Paris, not in fashion salons or designer boutiques.

"When I saw you in that simple but elegant outfit with a faraway look – well . . . you epitomised what my editor wants," Fabrice explained.

"I was far away all right – I am lost," Gina said with a suitably Gallic shrug.

"How could anyone lose you?" he asked gallantly.

"I'm on holiday with friends –" she began

"A boyfriend?" Fabrice enquired.

"No, girls – Tracey and Lynn. I'm Georgina, although everyone calls me Gina. Lynn's aunt owns the apartment, but I think they only brought me along because I speak French.

"I hope to study that at university next year," Gina faltered, realising she'd probably told him far too much.

"So where are your friends?" he frowned, glancing around.

"In Le Chat Noir, having breakfast, but I couldn't find it – doubtless they've left by now, anyway," Gina said sadly.

"Then why not accompany me to Ma Maison?" Fabrice suggested.

"Go to your house?" Gina was aghast, backing away.

"No, my grandmother's café across the road!" He laughed. "She makes the best pain aux chocolat in Paris.

"Besides, I haven't had breakfast either," Fabrice added persuasively.

"OK." Gina smiled.

It would be nice to enjoy an adventure for a change, rather than always hearing about Lynn and Tracey's exploits.

"It's just down here," he indicated, further along the narrow alleyway they were facing, pointing towards a street sign, depicting a pretty townhouse, swinging slightly in the breeze.

"Fabrice!" an elderly lady cried as they approached.

Emerging from behind the counter, she greeted her grandson with la bise, kissing him on the right cheek then left before shaking Gina's hand.

"This is Liliane, my *grand-mère*. Grand-mère, may I introduce Gina?" Fabrice said.

"So, you've managed to part with that camera of yours and find a girlfriend at last?" The older lady nodded, her eyes twinkling.

"No, Gina is a . . . model and now my friend," he replied, raising his eyebrows at Gina meaningfully.

Smiling, Gina played along.

"Gina and I missed breakfast, so I suggested she join me to try the best pastries in Paris," Fabrice said, glancing at the mouthwatering baked goods displayed.

"In France, if you please," Liliane corrected with mock severity, seating them and providing coffee with a selection of pastries, butter and jam.

"Oh wow! This is amazing!" Gina exclaimed, swallowing a bite of rich, melting pastry.

"*Naturellement.*" Liliane preened, prior to attending some other customers.

"So, tell me more about yourself," Fabrice said as they ate.

"Well, I'm holidaying for a week before starting a job in a French delicatessen," Gina said, mentioning its name and the town where she lived. "I plan reading French at university, only . . ."

"Yes?" Fabrice prompted, his large, soulful eyes sympathetic.

"I feel like my friendship with Lynn and Tracey is slipping away – like today. They know I have a terrible sense of direction but still went off together, leaving me alone.

"Shopping's fun but I came to enjoy French culture, yet it seems they just wanted me here for convenience," Gina finished sadly.

"People change – you probably have, too." Fabrice shrugged. "Why not let me show you around Paris instead?"

"I'd love to but we've only just met. Besides, what about your assignment?" Gina asked, holding his gaze.

"We will combine them – I can take pictures while sightseeing, can't I?" he said.

"OK," Gina agreed, and they stood to leave.

"Everywhere in Paris there is history – from catacombs deep beneath the city, to five stones, marking where the guillotine once stood." Fabrice shuddered. "But today I'll show you some of its happier moments."

"*Oui.*" She smiled as they left café.

In the end, Fabrice proved to be an excellent companion and guide.

They visited the Arc de Triomphe then enjoyed the impressionist paintings in the Musee d'Orsay.

"Why do you think he adopted that style?" Gina asked, pausing before Monet's "The Artist's Garden At Giverny", depicting a haze of mauve flowers and indistinct trees.

"By seeing the world in his own way," Fabrice replied emphatically.

Later they explored Notre-Dame de Paris, marvelling at its Gothic splendour and breathtakingly beautiful stained-glass windows.

"Wait one moment," Fabrice said, as Gina was bathed in a kaleidoscopic shaft of sunlight, while he worked around her, snapping the spontaneous image.

"Is that for your article, too?" She smiled.

"No," Fabrice said, "just for me . . ."

Quickly, he turned away, asking some girls lingering by the entrance if he could snap some photographs of them.

"Won't it matter that they weren't posed?" Gina asked when they headed to their final destination, Jardin de Tuileries and a picnic Liliane had packed for them.

"They're intentionally natural." He shrugged, as they found a place on the grass and Fabrice removed his jacket for Gina to sit on. "I've taken enough photographs for today – besides, I got the best one to start with."

He smiled at her meaningfully.

"Where next?" Fabrice asked while they strolled towards the exit, disposing of their picnic remains on the way.

"Oh, I'd love to," Gina replied, glancing at her watch, "but the others will be wondering what's happened to me."

"You truly think so?" He shrugged again. "Well, I understand your concern, it's commendable. Let me see you safely back to the apartment."

"Thank you," Gina said gratefully.

When they arrived, she noticed Lynn and Tracey's curious faces peering from the top floor window.

Fabrice followed her gaze and winked.

"*Au revoir*," he said softly, kissing Gina on both cheeks, blowing her another as he began walking away. "Oh, and I'll let you have a set of prints," he called over his shoulder.

Gina waved as Fabrice disappeared into the pooling evening sunlight.

"What happened to you?" Lynn demanded as Gina made it into the apartment.

"Yes, we were worried," Tracey chided, joining her.

"What, when you sneaked out to enjoy breakfast at Le Chat Noir without me, or while wandering round Galeries Lafeyette, perhaps?" Gina asked casually, easing off her shoes.

"Don't be sarky!" Lynn remonstrated. "We couldn't wait all morning and we left a note! You still haven't said what happened!"

"Montmartre is like a warren. I tried finding the café but it was hopeless," Gina explained simply.

"So who was that boy, then?" Tracey asked. "Your knight in shining armour, I suppose?"

"Or 'chevalier', perhaps?" Lynn added.

"Oh, that was Fabrice," Gina responded coolly. "He took my photo for 'Tres Chic' magazine and when I mentioned being lost and missing breakfast, he invited me to join him."

"Gina! What were you thinking? He could've been anyone!" Lynn exclaimed.

"But he wasn't – besides, we went to his family's café. His gran owns it. She was lovely." Gina smiled wistfully.

"Then what? That doesn't explain where you've been until now!" Lynn remonstrated.

"Relax. You're beginning to sound like my mum!" Gina replied. "It's five in the afternoon – you're making it seem like I've been out all night. I'm not a child."

"Yes, but you're here with us and it's my aunt's apartment. If anything happened there'd be so much trouble," Lynn said.

"And we'd cop for it!" Tracey added.

"You're only annoyed because it wasn't you meeting a handsome Frenchman!

"Anyway, let's not spoil a lovely day or the rest of the week by arguing – but we do need to see more of Paris than the inside of shops!" Gina said, getting up. "Now, if you don't mind, I'm having a shower.

"Then perhaps we can try a nice place in Montmartre that Fabrice showed me, rather than having steak and chips again," Gina suggested before disappearing into her room.

• • • •

The next few days passed in a blur of doing all the usual tourist things.

Their final evening ended with a trip to the Eiffel Tower by night, when it was at its most spectacular.

"So, no more dates with that Fabrice then?" Lynn asked, as they gazed out on Paris under an indigo sky, lit by stars.

"No. And it wasn't a date, he was just being kind. Also, he's probably working," Gina replied.

She was still disappointed, especially as he'd promised to let her see the photographs.

On the morning of their departure, bags packed, Gina rose early and made her way to Ma Maison.

From the red Ferme sign, she could see that, unusually, given its breakfast trade, the café was shut.

She did consider calling Fabrice but had somehow lost his card.

Sadly, Gina walked back to the apartment before they bid Paris goodbye and returned home.

Contrary to the more temperate French weather, Britain was still enduring a stifling heatwave.

Gina was glad to be in the air-conditioned shop, learning about food and using her French.

Her French that had improved considerably, even in such a short time.

"How would you feel about working on Saturdays when you return to school, cherie?" Vianne, the owner, asked. "You're excellent with customers and speak French very well. It's almost as though you were born there!"

"I'd love that!" Gina said, her voice full of longing.

"In a funny sort of way, being here doesn't feel as if I'm working, but more like never having left Paris."

As summer eased into autumn, memories of the holiday eventually faded, too. Despite seeing Lynn and Tracey occasionally, with mock exams after Christmas, all three were too busy studying.

Going into À La Française – bustling with customers, Vianne's playful chivvying and music on the radio – was a relief.

Returning a quiche to the refrigerator, Gina stilled, as Bonnie Tyler began the first haunting words of her latest hit, "Lost In France".

"*C'est très romantique chéri, n'est-ce pas?*" Vianne said quietly.

"Yes, yes it is," Gina faltered.

"Which reminds me, this arrived earlier," she added, handing Gina a large envelope, "from Paris."

Vianne winked, melting into the recesses of the shop. When Gina opened it, she saw Fabrice's photographs and a letter.

Sorry these are late. Grand-mere was taken ill just before you left – she's fine now but needed me. By the time I got to the apartment, you'd left.

I remembered À La Française, and thought if I sent the photographs there, they'd reach you.

She glanced at his stunning images from Notre-Dame. She looked as though she was a butterfly or mystical goddess.

As you can see, the world is full of light and colour – all yours for the taking – don't let others dictate the terms. Shine, my beautiful Gina and who knows, one day, when you return to France, I hope we'll meet again.

It was signed with his name and contact details.

As the song on the radio faded away, Gina knew she would always remember Paris.

Not for being lost in France, but because she'd found herself.

Stargazing By The Sea

Stella helped me find a new way to look at this sleepy seaside town . . .

BY DAVID BALMER

Set in 1969

Illustration: Manon Gandiolle.

THE summer man placed a first foot on the Moon was the same summer I found my first love.

"Robbie, we need to get going or we'll never get to your grandparents," my mother said.

My dad gave me one of his knowing smiles.

"You don't want to go, do you?"

"I'm sixteen in a few weeks," I replied.

"And too grown up to spend the summer with your grandparents?" Dad asked.

"No, of course not," I said, giving Dad a reluctant nod.

I picked up my two bags, one full of clothes, the other full of books and magazines.

My little sister, Sandra, ran back upstairs to get her View-Master, an indispensable piece of equipment for any long journey.

"Where's she going now?" Mum asked.

"She forgot her View-Master," I replied.

Finally, at exactly 34 minutes past 10, we backed down the drive, waving to Mr Evans, who was mowing his lawn, and to Mrs Greenwood returning from the corner shop.

"Mummy, I forgot my chocolates," Sandra said.

"We'll get some on the way," Dad said.

"But –"

"'But' nothing," Mum said. "Besides, it's too early to start eating chocolates."

It was going to be a long summer.

I wished I were somewhere else – like on the Moon with Neil Armstrong.

I tried to unfasten my sports bag, but the zip got stuck on a loose thread.

Finally, I wrestled it open and took out the July edition of my favourite science fiction magazine and lost myself in a distant world.

The roads were busy and my father became more frustrated with the number of caravans in front of us.

"We'll soon be at that long straight, won't we?" I said.

"Yes, and then we'll leave this lot behind," he replied.

"Are we nearly there yet?" Sandra asked.

"No. Stop asking!" I said.

"Don't take it out on Sandra." Mum sniffed.

"Sorry, Sandra." I sighed.

"Ah, here we go," Dad said, as he slammed his foot on the accelerator and flew past the line of caravans.

We soon arrived in Llangollen, where we stopped for a quick lunch by the river.

Then we were off again, on our way to Fairhaven Sands, overtaking the caravans and tractors chugging along.

• • • •

There was a torrential downpour when we arrived at Fairhaven Sands in the late afternoon, which didn't help my mood.

"Sandra, you and Mummy make a dash for it," Dad said. "Robbie, help me with the cases."

"OK," I replied, opening the car door straight into the path of a girl running up the pavement.

A little dog was scurrying along behind her.

"Sorry!" I said, but she ignored me and kept going, keen to get out of the rain.

I dashed up the garden path and into my grandparent's bungalow.

Grandma put her hands on my shoulders.

"Robbie, just look how you've grown since we last saw you," she said.

I gave her an embarrassed grin and looked at the floor.

Grandad looked me up and down.

"Five foot six?" he asked.

"Seven," I replied.

"We're going through clothes like there's no tomorrow," Mum put in. "And he never stops eating."

"Well, it's the usual tonight," Grandma said. "I'll give Robbie an extra large portion."

Grandma always made a fish pie on our arrival. Then it was bread and butter pudding with jam.

It followed the same routine every year.

Mum and Dad stayed for the first week, and Sandra cried when they left.

I would tell her to stop being so soft and she would cry even more.

Grandma would give her a chocolate cupcake, and all would be well.

Our grandparents had retired to Fairhaven Sands on the Welsh coast a few years earlier, and Sandra and I had spent every summer holiday with them since.

It was a quirky place. Most of the dwellings were holiday bungalows.

They all fitted in neatly with the windswept surroundings, in a thrown-together sort of way, as if they'd sprouted up amongst the sand and pebbles and coastal grassland.

The beach was hidden beyond a grassy bank that my grandfather told me had been constructed to stop the farmland being flooded.

On top of the bank was a narrow path that ran parallel to the beach.

From there Fairhaven Sands was revealed in all its breath-taking beauty; golden sands that seemed to stretch on forever in both directions.

• • • •

I woke early the morning after Mum and Dad had gone back home and decided to take a walk along the beach before breakfast.

Sandra was fast asleep, still clutching her teddy.

I got dressed and went into the lounge.

"Morning, Robbie," Grandad said from the kitchen. "You're up early. I thought teenagers stayed in bed 'til lunchtime."

"Not me, Grandad. That's a waste of time. I'm going for a walk along the beach if that's OK?"

"Of course it is. Go and enjoy the sea air – but make sure you're back in time for breakfast or you'll incur the wrath of the management."

"The management?"

"Grandma," Grandad said with a wink. "Listen, you probably feel too grown up to be spending the summer with us, so don't be afraid to go off and do your own thing when you want to."

"Thanks, Grandad," I said, taking my coat off its hook.

The garden gate squawked at me like an angry seagull as I opened it.

A few strides up the grass slope and I was on the path that overlooked the sands.

The steep pebble bank that dropped down to the beach was wet from an angry tide the night before.

I made my way down, trying not to slip, the pebbles shifting precariously beneath my feet.

The soft sand glistened in the morning sunlight. I had the whole beach to myself.

I walked across to the breakwater, constructed from large rocks and boulders. It formed an enormous letter Y extending out into the sea.

I clambered up on to the rocks, found a flat slab to sit on, and listened to the water sloshing about below.

In the distance, the Welsh mountains lay dark and

brooding beneath a blanket of cloud, the occasional shaft of sunlight breaking through and illuminating a sharp ridge or deep valley.

My daydreaming was broken by the yapping of a little dog that came running across the sands towards me.

It tried to get up on to the rocks, but they were too steep and slippery for its little legs.

I looked up and down the beach for its owner, but couldn't see anyone.

Then I saw a girl clambering down the pebble bank with the ease of someone who had done it a thousand times before.

She came running across the sands, leaping across the puddles left by the receding tide.

"Parsnip, come here!" she called out and the little dog obediently ran back to her.

She picked the dog up and came over to the breakwater.

She looked about the same age as me, and the first thing I noticed about her was the mass of ginger hair being blown across her face by the sea breeze.

She was wearing brown, flared corduroy trousers and a green jumper that looked as if it should have been thrown out ages ago.

"Be careful on those rocks," she said. "I sprained my ankle on them once."

I climbed down from the breakwater and walked over to the girl.

"I suppose you're on holiday, like everyone else?" she said.

"Yes, I'm staying with my grandparents. We come every year."

"Who'd want to come here every year? I live here and I hate it. It's so boring."

"I don't think it's boring. It's nice," I said.

"Yeah, if you like building sandcastles in the rain. How old are you?" she asked.

"Fifteen," I replied, noticing her eyes were a startling green.

"But I'll be sixteen in a few weeks," I blurted out.

"I'm already sixteen," she said as she put her dog down on the sand and threw his ball. "I expect I'll see you around, then. What's your name?"

"Robbie. I'll look out for you. You haven't told me your name."

"Stella," she said, as she turned to leave. "My dad owns the amusement arcade at the end of the village. I'll give you some tokens if you come in."

"Yeah, OK. I like the arcade."

"It's a dump," Stella said.

I watched her as she ran back across the beach after her little dog, and when she reached the pebble bank she turned and gave me a little wave.

I waved back.

When she was out of sight I followed her footprints, counting every impression her feet had made in the soft sand.

Out of the blue came a weird feeling I'd never experienced before, and Fairhaven Sands suddenly seemed the ideal place to spend a summer holiday.

• • • •

"Fancy going to Caernarfon? We can go to the castle if you like," Grandad said, knocking the top off his boiled egg.

"We go every year," I replied, dipping a soldier in mine.

"I want to paddle in the sea," Sandra said.

"It was only a suggestion." Grandad huffed.

"Sorry, Grandad, I didn't mean to be ungrateful," I said. "I'd love to visit the castle another day when it's not so sunny."

"Quite right", Grandma said. "You should make the most of a sunny day like today.

"Now, Sandra, get your swimming costume. Robbie, you go and get the bucket and spade and blanket.

"We've got a new beach umbrella, so fetch that, too."

• • • •

Grandma and Sandra walked along the path to the slipway so that they wouldn't have to negotiate the pebble bank, and by the time they'd come back along the sands, I'd already laid out the blanket and set up the umbrella.

I looked to see if Stella was around, but there was no sign of her amongst the visitors preparing for a day on the beach.

I thought about what I had said to her by the breakwater.

Going to a boys' grammar school, girls might as well have been aliens from one of my magazines.

I wondered what Stella had made of me. Not much, probably, but then she had invited me to her father's amusement arcade, so I mustn't have seemed that uninteresting to her.

I found myself thinking about what I would say the next time we met, and I realised I couldn't wait to see her again.

"Here we are, Sandra. Robbie has got everything set up for us," Grandma said, putting the picnic basket down on the blanket.

"Let's play ball," Sandra said to me, but her voice seemed somewhere in the distance.

"Robbie?" Grandma said. "Are you going to play ball with your sister?"

"What? Oh, yes, sorry."

I picked up our inflatable beach ball and threw it as far as I could, just like Stella had thrown Parsnip's tennis ball across the sand.

"That's not fair," Sandra whined. "You've got to wait for me to be ready."

"Sorry," I said with a pang of guilt that I was thinking more about Stella than my little sister. "Come on, we'll play ball in the sea."

It was low tide and the sea was far out and warm and shallow. You could walk a hundred yards out in the water and it was still only up to your waist.

It was easier playing ball with Sandra this year.

She'd had a growth spurt over the winter and was throwing the ball like nobody's business.

"Come on, catch it!" she kept shouting at me.

I was trying my best to concentrate on our game, but I couldn't stop looking up and down the beach.

In the end, she threw the ball in my face and stormed off back up the beach to Grandma.

We had our picnic, and afterwards Sandra became preoccupied with digging a deep hole in the sand.

When she was satisfied with its depth, she ran down to the sea with her bucket intent on filling the hole with seawater.

"Reached Australia yet?" Grandad said, as he gingerly made his way down the steep pebbles.

"You should use the slipway, George," Grandma said.

"Oh, stop fussing," Grandad retorted, peering into the three-foot hole.

"She won't believe you can't fill it with water," I replied. "I tell her every year.

"Do you mind if I go for a walk and find somewhere quiet to read my mag?"

"Not at all. You go and I'll carry on digging," Grandad said. "I love digging holes in the sand."

Grandma shook her head and I set off along the beach, savouring the thought of a solitary afternoon, but at the same time hoping I might see Stella again.

Half a mile along the beach the pebble bank became a stretch of sand dunes, with endless hollows that made the perfect place to sit and read.

Behind the dunes was a disused airfield that Grandad said had been used during the war.

It was surrounded by a high wire fence and I'd already made my mind up that this year I would find a way in and explore the place. But that would be for another day, and there were plenty more to come.

I chose a hollow where I could sit and read and look out to sea.

A fine-looking sailing boat sailed past, and I wondered who it might belong to and where they might be going.

I opened my magazine and began to read, but it was no use.

I couldn't concentrate, so I stared out to sea with the summer sunshine on my face and the girl I had met that morning on my mind.

A smell of cigarette smoke came drifting over the top of the hollow, and I felt disappointed that my quiet little spot was about to be invaded.

The sand started to trickle down the slope on either side of me and with it came a little dog, his little legs at all angles.

"Parsnip?"

He gave me a friendly bark in reply.

Then the sand started to pour down even faster.

I leaped up, anxious that I was about to be buried beneath it, and with the sandy avalanche came Stella, one arm outstretched with a cigarette between her fingers.

She came to an abrupt halt in front of me and looked up and smiled.

"You again. Here, take this," she said, handing me her cigarette. "You're not following me, are you?"

"Of course not," I replied.

She stood up and brushed the sand off her shorts and sleeveless shirt that was tied up around her waist.

I looked her up and down and thought how pale she looked for someone who lived by a beach.

"Why are looking at my legs like that?" she said, taking back her cigarette.

"I'm not looking at your legs like anything," I replied, feeling myself blush.

"You are. I know what you're thinking. Pale and skinny? But you never know, the freckles might join up one day and then it'll be like a tan, not that I want a tan."

"You're not skinny, and you've got nice legs, like Twiggy," I blurted out. "And I couldn't care less if you have a tan or not."

"So, you were looking at my legs. What're you reading?" she asked, grabbing my magazine.

She flicked through the pages and handed it back.

"Did you see them land on the Moon?"

"Yeah, every bit of it, right from lift-off. I love anything to do with space."

"Me, too. I'm going to be an astronomer. I'll work at Jodrell Bank one day."

"The big radio telescope?"

"Yeah, I went there on a school trip, and I knew straight away I wanted to work there.

"I asked a woman and she said I'd have to get a degree in astronomy. So that's what I'm going to do."

Stella took a cigarette from her pocket and offered it to me. I shook my head.

"What's up? Don't you smoke?" she asked, pulling her hair from her face.

"No, I've never tried one," I said, thinking about how uncool I must seem.

Stella took out her lighter, put the cigarette between her lips and lit it.

"Here, try it," she said, handing me the cigarette.

I took the cigarette and did my best not to cough as I took my first draw on it.

Stella sat down and threw a piece of driftwood out on to the beach for Parsnip to go after.

"Aren't you going to sit with me?" she asked.

"You want me to?" I replied.

"I wouldn't have asked if I didn't. You don't have to. I really don't mind," she said.

"No, I want to," I replied, dropping on to the sand next to Stella, unsure as to what to say next.

Stella looked out to sea, smoking her cigarette.

I put mine to my lips and pretended to smoke it, hoping it would burn away by itself without Stella noticing.

"You'll never get used to it unless you draw on it properly," she said.

I reluctantly took Stella's advice and took a deep draw, and coughed my head off whilst Stella did her best not to laugh.

"You'll get used to it," she said, looking at her watch. "I've got to go.

"My dad will kill me if I'm late for work. I'm only doing it to save enough to escape this crumby place."

"It's not all that bad here, is it?"

"Yes, it is. You want to try being here in the winter."

"You must meet lots of people in the summer though," I asked.

"No, I avoid everyone like the plague." She shook her head.

"You don't mind me, do you?"

"No, you're OK." Stella gave me a look.

She threw Parsnip's stick out on to the beach again and off they went together.

She stopped for a moment and looked back at me, and the sea breeze caught her hair.

I wanted to get up and brush it from her face and tell that I really liked her, but I didn't have the pluck.

My cigarette had gone out.

I thought of Stella lighting it and how everything about her seemed so cool and different from any girl I'd encountered before.

• • • •

I stayed up late that night watching "The Sky At Night" with Grandad. When it had finished, he asked me an unexpected question.

"So, young man, while we're here alone, when did you start smoking?"

"I haven't," I replied, feeling a blush fill my face.

Grandad narrowed his eyes.

"I smelt it on you when you got back this afternoon.

"Don't worry – I'm not cross. I was just the same at your age. If Grandma finds out, though, there'll be trouble and I won't be able to come to your rescue."

"Fair enough," I said. "I didn't like it anyway."

"Where did you get it from? Old misery guts down the village shop didn't sell you some, did he?"

"No, it was . . . well, a girl."

Grandad let out a chuckle.

"A girl? You really are growing up, aren't you? On holiday, is she?"

"No, she lives here. She wants to be an astronomer and work at Jodrell Bank," I replied.

"Can't be all that bad, then, despite the cigarette," Grandad said. "Right, I'm off to bed."

"Me too," I said, feeling exhausted after a long and enjoyable day.

• • • •

You couldn't see beyond the garden gate the next morning for the drizzle.

I was up early again, intent on taking a walk along the beach and hopefully seeing Stella walking her dog.

But when I looked out from the front door, I knew I'd be wasting my time and only getting soaked.

So I went back to bed to read one of my magazines.

I realised after a paragraph or two that I had no idea what I was reading, and I threw the magazine to the floor and looked across at Sandra, still fast asleep.

I grabbed my t-shirt from the chair next to the bed and smelt it, hoping the cigarette smell had gone.

Sandra stirred and I pushed my t-shirt down the side of the bed.

"Are we playing on the beach again today?" Sandra asked, letting out a yawn.

"No, it's raining. We could go to the amusement arcade, if you want?"

"Yay!" Sandra said, jumping out of her bed and leaping on to mine.

She gave me a sisterly hug then sat up.

"You smell like Mr Evans next door at home when he smokes his pipe.

"You've been smoking, haven't you? I'm going to tell Grandma!"

"You do and we won't be going to the arcade!" I said, tickling her 'til she rolled off the bed in hysterics. "Not a word to Grandma, or else!"

"You'll have to give me some money for the arcade," she replied.

• • • •

The drizzle didn't ease off until gone eleven, and with

a warning from Grandma not to go wasting all of our pocket money, I took Sandra down to the amusement arcade.

It was packed with holidaymakers, and I looked for Stella amongst the people dropping coins one after another in the slot machines, but there was no sign of her.

Stella was right. The place was a dump.

You could feel your feet sticking to the worn red and blue swirled carpet that had obviously been on the receiving end of spilt drinks.

At the far end of the arcade, a bingo caller was calling out the numbers over a microphone, and I watched as a burly man repeatedly banged the side of a slot machine.

Sandra went straight over to the coin pushers, looking for the one most likely to dislodge its pile of coins teetering on the edge of the slider.

There was a clattering of coins and a boy greedily scooped up his winnings.

She stood by him in the hope he might move on to another machine, and he pushed her away.

"Hey, leave my sister alone or I'll give you more than a push," I said to him.

"She pushed me first," he replied.

"No, I didn't," Sandra snapped back.

"Come on, Sandra. Let's get some coins from the kiosk," I said.

One of the slot machines started sounding its tamper alarm and I turned to see Stella come out of the coin kiosk and go over to the burly man who was giving the machine a good kicking.

"Stop kicking that machine!" Stella shouted at him, above the noise of all the machines and people.

"You give me my money back or I'll kick it until I get it back," he shouted at her.

Stella grabbed the man's arm and he pushed her away, nearly sending her to the floor.

I told Sandra to stay by the coin pusher and went over.

"Leave her alone," I said to the burly man.

The man was a good six-foot plus. He looked down at me and grabbed my arm.

"Listen, kid – one more word from you and I'll kick your backside," he snarled.

"Go on then," I said, facing up to him. "Kick me and show everyone what a bully you are."

"Yeah, get out of here and don't come back!" Stella yelled at him.

"I'm not being ripped off in this dump again," he replied, storming off with all sorts of foul language emanating from him.

"See what I mean?" Stella said. "It's a dump."

Sandra appeared, pushing her way through the throng.

"Can we get some pennies, please?"

• • • •

From that day, Stella and met as often as we could, and it began to seem as if we'd been lifelong friends.

We never found ourselves short of something to talk about, mainly space and the Moon landing.

Then, we were equally happy sitting quietly amongst the dunes, with Stella reading one of her astronomy books whilst I read my sci-fi magazines.

Some days we would wander through the dunes; sliding down the sandy slopes, looking for the highest, steepest one we could find.

Parsnip never stopped yapping in all the excitement, running in circles around the two of us when we came to a stop at the bottom of the slopes, half-buried in the sand.

"Let's roll down this one," Stella said, at the top of a particularly steep slope.

She lay down, put her arms across her chest and let herself go.

I followed and rolled straight into her before she had chance to get out of the way, and we found ourselves in an embrace.

We looked into each other's eyes, not a word passing between us.

Parsnip barked like mad for our attention, but it seemed as if nothing could disturb the moment when we silently realised our affection for each other.

"You can kiss me if you want," Stella said, brushing her hair from her face.

I tried to give her a kiss on the cheek, but her hair had fallen back across her face and it was all a bit of an embarrassing failure.

"You've never kissed a girl before, have you?" she said.

"I have," I lied, giving Stella a quick, awkward kiss on the lips in a pathetic attempt to prove her wrong.

"No, you haven't," she said. "I've been thinking at lot about us, and I think I love you."

"Really?" I said, with a feeling of relief after my pitiful attempt at a first kiss.

"Well, yes. I mean, I never stop thinking about you.

"So I must love you," she replied.

"I never stop thinking about you," I said. "So I must be in love, too."

"That's OK then."

She stood up and looked down at me.

"Can you keep a secret?" I nodded.

"I want to show you something. But you can't tell anyone. Do you promise?"

"Yes, I promise."

Stella took my hand and we made our way through the dunes to the abandoned airfield and then along the fence, until we came to a section where the wire had been cut.

"Through here," Stella said, lifting the wire.

"What about that?" I asked, pointing at one of the signs along the fence warning of the presence of security patrols with dogs.

"It's fake. It's just to put people off," she said.

We climbed through and walked across grassland to what had once been the runway but was now no more than a fragmented strip of tarmac slowly being chocked by weeds.

A dilapidated control tower rose up in front of us, its lower half covered in graffiti.

A metal door at the base of the tower had DANGER – DO NOT ENTER spray-painted on it.

Stella pulled hard at the door, the sound of it grinding across the floor echoing up the tower.

It opened just enough to let us squeeze through.

Inside, a rickety metal staircase clung to the inner walls of the tower, looking as if it might give way if anyone tried to climb it.

"Is it safe?" I asked.

"Yes, come on," she said.

At the top of the stairs, she turned to look at me.

"Do you swear you won't say a word to anyone about this?" Stella said.

I nodded and Stella opened the door of what had once been the air-traffic control room.

I followed her in and found myself looking at an old sofa, a table and chairs, and a large rug that looked like it had come from India.

A Beatles poster had been taped to the front of a rusting filing cabinet, with Christmas lights hanging around it.

On the table was a camping lamp and a pile of astronomy books, and pens and notepads.

"What do you think?" Stella asked. "It's my den. I've been working on it for ages, but I think it's about right now."

"It's great, and no-one has ever found out about it?"

"No, they haven't. All those signs on the fence seem to work. Look at the view. You can see everywhere from here.

"And look, I found these old binoculars in one of the cabinets. They're great for stargazing. You can see the craters on the moon.

"I come here at night to study for university, where I won't be disturbed."

I looked out through the windows that occupied all four walls, first at the distant mountains and then the golden ribbon of sand below, and the choppy sea, full of white horse all the way to the horizon.

"It's so cool, Stella," I said.

"Yeah, I think so, too," Stella said, "but they reckon someone's bought the airfield and they're going to turn it into a holiday camp. I don't care though.

"I'll be gone by then, and I'll be listening to the sounds of the stars through that big dish at Jodrell."

I sat down on the sofa and looked down at the floor.

It was something I always did when I was struggling to put words to my thoughts.

"What's up?" Stella asked, flopping down on the sofa next to me.

"I've never met anyone like you before. You're so sure about everything. I wish I was more like you."

"There must be something you're sure about. Everyone's sure about something," Stella said.

"I'm sure I don't want to go home in two weeks. I mean, how will we see each other after that?"

"We won't. It's killing me, too, but it's the truth. We'll just have to live with it."

"So you can't love me that much then?"

"Oh, I do. I fall asleep thinking about you, and then I wake up wondering if you'll be on the breakwater waiting for me."

"Seriously?" I asked.

"Yeah," Stella said, taking a cigarette from her pocket and throwing one to me. "Do you like crabbing?"

"What? Crabbing?" I said, stopped in my thoughts by her change of topic. "Yeah, I love crabbing. Why?"

"I know a place where you can catch the biggest crabs ever," she said, lighting her cigarette. "I've got all day off tomorrow.

"We could walk along the coast path to the next village and go crabbing off the harbour wall. We can hold hands the whole way."

"How many boys have you kissed before?" I asked.

"I haven't, and that's the truth," she replied.

"You're the first girl I've ever kissed."

"I knew I was right," Stella said. "But that's nice to know."

"Stella, do you promise to do something for me?"

"Depends what it is."

"Stop smoking. It stinks."

• • • •

I met Stella the next morning at the end of the village where the road took a sharp left inland.

I'd told my grandparents I was going for a long walk and I wouldn't be back until teatime.

I'd said it in a manner that gave them little choice to refuse, and I wasn't pleased with myself.

"But Robbie, we're going into Caernarfon today," Grandma said.

"Leave him," Grandad said, as I walked off down the hallway, feeling guilty at showing such an attitude.

Stella now grabbed my hand and I took the bucket and crabbing nets from her.

We headed across the sandy grassland with Parsnip already well ahead.

A strong wind blew in from the sea, and the further we walked the more exhilarated and free I felt.

I never wanted to let go of Stella's hand, and I wanted to kiss her again, but she was intent on us getting to the next village.

I made Stella stop for a moment and gave her a hug. She must have sensed something was wrong.

"What's up?" she asked.

"I was rude to my grandparents when I left. I've never been rude to them, but I think my grandad understands."

"He knows about me, does he?"

"Yeah, he smelt the cigarette smoke when we first met, and I told him about you. He doesn't mind though. Grandma would go nuts if she found out."

"About me or the ciggies?" Stella asked.

"I don't know. Probably just the ciggies."

"Yeah, well, my mum wouldn't care. She smokes like a factory chimney.

"But I've decided to give up, like you asked, before it becomes a habit," Stella said, gripping my hand and dragging me onward.

After a mile or so, we approached an area where the ground began to rise.

At first the sloping fields rose gently, and then, as the gradient increased, the path became more rocky and suddenly veered steeply downward towards the sea.

There was no beach at that point – only rocky bluffs and coves.

The waves crashed against the rocks below, and in places the path was carved out of the rock itself.

A series of wooden walkways and steps had been constructed across the rock.

And as we made our way around the cliff face, we came to a set of steep, crumbling steps that led down to a small sandy cove.

A lone tree grew out of the rocks at the top of the steps.

Stella let go of my hand and grabbed Parsnip.

"You can't get down there," she said. "The steps have been washed away.

"I tried it once and nearly didn't get back up. Let's keep going."

We rounded a slippery outcrop, and the coast ahead was finally revealed.

In the distance I could see a small harbour with an assortment of brightly painted boats.

The path became less rocky. We crossed another stretch of dunes and came to a narrow lane into the village.

"I caught twenty-three crabs here once," Stella said, as we entered the village which was nothing more than a few fishermen's cottages and a snack bar.

We bought an ice cream from a van and found a spot along the harbour wall amongst the other enthusiasts hauling in the obliging crabs.

Parsnip ran off down the slipway to a small beach beyond the harbour, chasing after seagulls and other dogs.

We sat on the harbour wall and dropped our nets into the sea below.

Stella swung her legs, waiting to haul up her catch, and we were suddenly nothing more than children playing at the seaside.

The feeling of love I had for Stella seemed as if it had been left behind at Fairhaven Sands.

It was a strangely liberating sensation, as if the burden of knowing I might soon never see her again had been lifted.

Stella pulled on her line and up came the most enormous crab I had ever seen, trying its best to get out of the net in slow, awkward movements.

"Quick, get the bucket," she said, grabbing the crab without hesitation.

I leaned back as she swung it past me and dropped it in the bucket of seawater.

"You're not scared of them, are you?" she asked.

"No, of course not," I replied.

I pulled on my line and

didn't care for the weight of whatever I was about to pull up.

"Blimey, that's enormous," Stella said, as I lifted the net out of the water.

I looked at the crab, knowing I hadn't the courage to pick it up.

"Get it in the bucket!" Stella yelled in excitement.

I dropped the net on the quayside and the crab made its escape.

It headed straight for me and I nearly fell into the water trying to get out of its way.

Stella grabbed it and dropped it in the bucket.

"Two!" she said, with the grin of an adventurer.

We managed 18 crabs over the next couple of hours, but the competition from the children on either side of us began to annoy Stella.

"Come on. Let's get a hot dog and find somewhere to sit on the beach," she said.

"Shouldn't we be heading back? My grandma always puts tea on the table at five-thirty," I said.

"Still feeling guilty about coming here with me?"

"Of course not . . ." I said.

"You're nearly sixteen, Robbie, not six."

"I know, but I don't want to upset my grandparents."

"Go back on your own then, if you've got to have your tea," Stella replied. "I really don't mind."

"You don't mean that, do you?"

Stella shrugged.

"I'm staying here. It's up to you."

"All right. We'll stay a bit longer," I replied, shaken by Stella's bluntness.

I didn't have the worldliness to realise that she was testing my loyalty and that her change in attitude was no more than that of a feisty teenage girl.

"You find a spot on the beach and I'll go and get the hot dogs," Stella said.

As I made my way down the slipway, I asked a man if he had the time.

"Three-thirty," he said. "Watch the tide. It comes in fast here."

Stella took an age to return and when she finally showed up, she handed me a hot dog smothered with onions and tomato sauce.

"Sorry, there was a queue. Here – this will keep us going 'til we get back," she said, biting into her hot dog.

"It's gone three-thirty," was all I could say back.

"So?" she said, breaking off some of her hot dog and giving it to Parsnip.

"So I don't want my grandparents worrying about me, and we'll never be back for five-thirty now."

"All right. We'll eat whilst we're walking if you're that worried," Stella said, turning to leave.

I grabbed her hand and pulled her round to face me.

"Yes, I do worry what my grandparents think, as it happens. Don't you care what your parents think?"

Stella pulled free of me.

"Well, my mum doesn't care about me – that's for sure. She left home just before the season started.

"And as for my dad . . . All he cares about are his stupid slot machines."

Stella walked off without another word other than calling for Parsnip, and I realised I'd hit a sore spot.

I watched her walk up the slipway. She didn't look back and I didn't go after her.

I was stuck between a rock and a hard place.

I picked up a pebble and threw it across the sands in anger, and decided I wasn't going to move until I was ready, just to make a point.

Before long the water began to cover the beach, giving me no choice but to set off back to Fairhaven.

I'd catch up with her and apologise, and then say sorry to my grandparents for being late for tea.

I walked up the lane from the village and turned off on to the coast path, carrying the bucket and crabbing nets.

There was no sign of Stella, so I picked up my pace along the steep path and came to the first wooden walkway.

I stopped for a moment and looked down at the sea crashing on the rocks below.

Then I came to the next walkway and heard a dog barking in the distance.

It had to be Parsnip, so I ran along the path and soon came to the lone tree at the top of the ruined steps.

"Robbie, is that you up there? I need help!" I heard Stella call out from below, her cries sending my heart racing.

"Where are you?" I called back.

"Down here! Where do you think?" she snapped back.

I dropped the bucket and tentatively made my way down the steps.

I looked down and saw Stella standing on a large rock, the rising tide all around her.

"I climbed down to get Parsnip and I can't get back up. I'm going to drown. Get someone quick!"

"I'm coming down," I called back.

"No, don't, or we'll both be stuck. Go and fetch help."

"OK. Try and get higher up on the rocks. I'll be as fast as I can."

• • • •

"Grandad, we have to get help," I struggled to say with what little breath I had left in my lungs, as I sent the lounge door flying back against the bookcase.

"Where on earth have you been?" Grandma said.

"What's wrong, Robbie?" Grandad said, getting up from the dining table.

"Stella's stuck on the rocks along the coast path and she's going to drown!"

"Stella? Who's Stella?" Grandma asked.

"Now then, Robbie, calm down and tell me what's happened," Grandad said.

"She's where those broken steps go down to the cove – there's a tree growing amongst the rocks.

"She went down to get her dog and couldn't get back up, and she'll drown if we don't get help quickly – the tide's coming in!"

"Yes, I know the spot," Grandad said, going over to the phone. "I'll call the coastguard."

"I'm going back to her," I said.

"Wait here!" Grandad said. "Then again, you'd better had show the coastguard exactly where she is. For goodness' sake, be careful!"

"Can I come?" Sandra asked.

"No, you can't!"

• • • •

I felt sick to the stomach when I reached the cove.

I looked down but there was no sign of Stella, but then I heard Parsnip barking.

"Stella. Are you there?"

"Of course I am. Did you get help?" she called back.

"Yes, the coastguard are on their way."

I leaned over the edge as far as I dared and spotted Stella clinging to the twisted rusting handrail of what was left of the steps, with Parsnip tucked under her arm.

"I can't get any further up," she called out.

"Don't try. You might slip back down. The coastguard will be here soon."

"I had to get Parsnip, Robbie. I couldn't leave him, and I've hurt my leg."

"Don't worry, – they'll be hear soon, I promise. Just keep talking to me, OK?"

• • • •

The coastguard rescue team came with ropes and harnesses.

One of the team abseiled down and Stella was pulled to safety with Parsnip in her arms.

They wrapped a blanket around her and bandaged the gash on her leg.

I followed with Parsnip in my arms as Stella was taken back to Fairhaven on a stretcher.

Her father was waiting with Grandad by the ambulance.

"Stella, thank goodness you're all right," her father said, looking at her leg.

"It's nothing, Dad. I just slipped on some rocks."

"It's more than nothing! You had to be rescued!" he said. "I'm coming in the ambulance with you."

"No, don't. I'll be fine."

"I'll look after Parsnip," I put in.

"You don't need to. He isn't mine. He just follows me around everywhere," Stella said.

"Who does he belong to, then?" I asked.

Stella shrugged as the ambulance doors closed.

I put Parsnip down and he ran off up the lane following the ambulance.

"She'll be the death of me, that girl," Stella's father said.

"No, she's great," I said, as the lights of the ambulance faded in the distance.

"It's no use. I'm going to the hospital," her father said. "Her mother will go mad with both of us when she finds out.

"I'll have to tell her. She'll come back and all hell will break loose."

• • • •

Stella hardly said a word as we drove back from the hospital the following afternoon.

Her father had called round and asked if I wanted to go with him to get her.

She gripped my hand the whole way home, as if still clinging to the twisted rail above the cove.

Parsnip was snuggled up between us looking sleepy and disinterested.

"Robbie, Stella tells me it's your birthday next week?" Stella's father said.

"Yes. My parents are coming in a couple of days, and then after my birthday we'll stop a few more days and then go home," I said, feeling Stella's grip tighten.

She turned and looked at me with a strange, vacant expression on her face.

• • • •

Stella looked awkward and out-of-place as she watched me opening my birthday presents.

I smiled and said thank you for each of the presents as I opened them, but all I really wanted was to be alone with Stella.

Her being with me on my sixteenth birthday was the best present of all.

"Now, for your present from your grandparents . . ." Grandad said.

He left the room and came back a moment later with the biggest parcel of all, long and heavy and wrapped in silver paper.

I peeled back the paper and my eyes widened when I saw the picture on the box.

"It's a telescope. Stella, come and look," I said, as I removed the last of the wrapping paper.

"We know how much you like anything to do with outer space," Grandma said, before disappearing into the kitchen.

She returned with my birthday cake with 16 candles evenly placed around an iced rocket.

As everyone began to sing "Happy Birthday", I grabbed Stella's hand.

"Make a wish with me," I said.

We blew the candles out together.

Stella helped me put the telescope together and explained in great detail the function of each part of it.

"You seem to know a lot about telescopes," Grandad said to Stella.

"I'm going to be an astronomer," she replied, as she tightened the screws on the tripod.

"You'll have to take it on the beach tonight, when it gets dark," Grandad said.

"Can I?"

"Of course. I expect Stella would like to try it out, too."

• • • •

"What did you wish for?" Stella asked, as we carried the telescope down the slipway and on to the sands that night.

"I wished I could be with you forever," I replied.

"Bad wish," Stella said. "It's not going to happen.

"You're going home in two days and everything will be back the way it was.

"Even my mum is threatening to come home after what happened."

"I'll be back next year. We can write to each other in the meantime," I said.

"I suppose so," she said with little enthusiasm.

"What did you wish for?" I asked her.

"It doesn't matter," she replied.

We walked in silence across the beach.

The sea was far out, lazily lapping on the sand and catching the moonlight like a long jewelled necklace.

Stella stopped and looked up at the night sky.

"Look, Robbie! The whole universe, shining away above us. . . Trillions of stars in trillions of galaxies," she said. "Do you ever look up and wonder if anyone is looking back at us?"

"All the time. Why do you think I read all those sci-fi books?" I replied.

"I hope we're not alone. I'm sure people are out there, looking at their own night sky, asking the same questions as us.

"That's what I wished for when we blew the candles out on your cake. I make the same wish every year, that we'll find out."

I smiled at Stella's philosophising.

"You might be the one who does."

"You never know," she replied. "Put the telescope here, and I'll find Saturn."

I looked in awe through the telescope lens at the tiny white dot with its just visible rings.

The excitement of the night sky temporarily took my mind off everything, until Stella took my hand.

"I don't think we should see each other again after tonight," she told me.

"But I've still got two days left," I said, my heart sinking.

"Yeah, I know, but nothing can be better than this moment. This is what we should remember and not a sad goodbye with me waving you off."

She gave me a tender kiss, then let go of my hand and removed her sandals.

"Come on, I'll race you down to the sea!" she called, and she was off, just like the first time I saw her running across the sands.

I followed her footprints glistening in the moonlight.

• • • •

I went straight to my room the evening we arrived back home from our summer holiday and flopped down on my bed.

"Robbie," Dad called up from downstairs. "Where's your telescope?"

"In the car!" I shouted.

"No, it isn't. It's just the empty box," he called back up.

I closed my eyes and imagined the look on Stella's face when she discovered the telescope in her den.

I'd put it there the day before we left without her knowing.

I wanted her to have it in the hope she wouldn't forget about me.

Then I pictured Stella on the beach, brushing her hair from her face, revealing her beautiful eyes, and the moonlight illuminating the pale skin of her face.

My first love. My Stella by starlight.

According To Plan

Unexpected things kept happening on this holiday . . .

BY BETH WATSON

"FLY and flop." That was what he said when I asked Dan what kind of holiday he wanted.

Fly and flop? So we'd get there, to a sunshine paradise, and do . . . What exactly?

"Well, nothing," he said. "Lie on the beach. Catch some rays. Read. Snooze. Relax."

Now, if you knew Dan, you'd know how out of character that is.

Dan goes out for a run every morning, no matter how cold, wet or dark it might be.

Then he's out to work as a community nurse, which is pretty full-on from the moment his shift starts.

You'd think he'd want to take it easy the rest of the time. But no.

If we have a weekend off together, we'll throw our boots in the car and head out for a hillwalk or a seaside ramble.

His latest thing is finding lost villages he's read about.

That usually means a trek through dense woodland and tangled undergrowth.

"Just like the old explorers," he said last time, unsnagging my jacket from some savage bramble thorns.

So you get the picture. My husband likes to be on the go.

Holidays mean sightseeing and activities.

I was surprised he'd even heard of fly and flop.

"What do you think, Janey? Would you be bored?"

Honestly, I didn't know. But I've had a stressful time myself.

We've had a lot of redundancies at the packaging firm where I've been since I left school.

It's sad – the company's struggling, anyone can see that.

I've managed to hang on to my job so far, but the uncertainty is horrible, especially when you have a hefty mortgage.

And I know forty-one is no age, but still there's no certainty I'll find another job.

We've been saving hard, just in case. Cut down on trips and treats.

But a week of relaxation in the sunshine was so tempting, so fly and flop it was.

Dan tracked down bargain flights to Corfu, and I found an apartment which I got for a song due to a cancellation.

It even had a balcony.

"Perfect for lazy breakfasts," Dan agreed when I showed him.

The beach was nearby, shops a stroll away, restaurants around every corner. Ideal.

Day one got off to a leisurely start.

Dan popped out for some essentials – fresh bread and eggs, orange juice, coffee, milk.

Then we had that lazy breakfast on the balcony, feeling just a little smug that the apartment was even better than I'd hoped for.

It would be easy to relax here.

We had arrived the evening before, the taxi dropping us off at a gate that led into a small courtyard.

There were flowers everywhere, pink and scarlet geraniums overflowing from dozens of terracotta planters.

A vermilion bougainvillaea spilled down one wall.

The evening air was thick with perfume, the sky blue-black above us.

A flight of steps lined with more potted geraniums took us up to the first floor landing and our flat.

Our front door opened into a dining-kitchen, beyond which a squashy sofa, armchair and coffee table offered plenty of room to lounge.

Beyond that, French doors opened on to a balcony with a cane table and two chairs.

"Got any plans for the day?" I asked Dan after our scrambled egg and toast.

We were leaning on the balcony rail, looking out over a scrubby patch of land scattered with olive trees.

A warm breeze meandered through the branches. A donkey grazed in the shade, ignoring us.

"No plans – that's the point," he said. "Can you believe how peaceful it is here? Though I'm still worried you'll be bored."

I sighed with deep contentment.

"Not a chance. I'll make more coffee, shall I?"

It was waiting for the coffee to brew that I remembered the flowers in the courtyard.

I grabbed my phone. They'd make a beautiful photo to send Mum.

I just couldn't get the right angle on a selfie.

"Dan, come and take my photo, will you? I want to send it to Mum."

He joined me on the landing.

"Maybe go down a few steps?" he suggested.

I struck a pose.

"How's this?"

I heard the shutter-click – and a resounding bang.

Dan clapped a hand to his chest and laughed.

"Blimey, what a fright!" he

said. "It was just the door blowing shut."

I ran back up the steps and was at his shoulder as he grasped the doorknob.

It didn't turn and then the penny dropped.

Of course, we'd had to turn the key to open the door, not the handle – the key that we'd left indoors.

"No," I wailed.

"Yup," Dan said, rattling the handle uselessly. "We're locked out."

"So now what?" I asked.

I looked down at our bare feet, his shorts, my bikini bottoms. Thank heavens I had a vest on!

"Maybe . . ." I said. "Do you think all the apartments might have the same key?"

"I doubt it," Dan said, "but it's worth a shot."

So we went knocking at all our neighbours' doors.

No-one home, not a soul.

"But they all had lights on last night!" I protested illogically.

"They'll be at the beach, shopping, day trips." Dan shrugged. "Like we'd usually be."

We sank down on the steps, thinking.

"Could you climb up to our balcony, do you think?" I asked.

I heard his sharp intake of breath.

"I don't know, Janey. You know I'm not great with heights. The last thing we need is for me to fall and break something."

I couldn't argue with him there.

My palm was growing sweaty round my phone and I switched it to my other hand.

Dan's face lit up.

"Janey, your phone! Won't you have our landlady's number in there?"

"I never thought of that!"

Hope suddenly ignited. I trawled through my emails and eventually found it.

I dialled and Anna answered!

Anna's English wasn't great, my Greek hopeless, so it took a few minutes for her to catch my drift.

She was full of sympathy but . . .

"She's in Sidari, the other end of the island," I told Dan as I hung up. "She can't get back till this evening."

"This evening," he echoed, sounding as hopeless as I felt.

"There must be something we can do," I said, jumping up as if I had a plan – which I didn't.

Dan got to his feet.

"Maybe I could climb up to the balcony . . ."

"Don't do anything without me," I made him promise. "I'll be there in a minute."

I went snooping into every nook and corner. I didn't know what I was looking for. A magic key cupboard?

There was a door tucked away in a corner of the courtyard, almost hidden behind the curtain of bougainvillaea.

I tried it. It opened.

And inside, oh, the best sight ever.

"Dan!" I yelled.

"What? Are you OK?" He came running.

"Look what I found."

The anxiety in his face melted away.

"A ladder! Oh, you beauty!" He swept me up in a tight hug.

Together we man-handled the ladder awkwardly out of the cupboard and through the front gate and round to that scrubby patch of land.

Finally we managed to prop it up below our balcony.

It would be a stretch but –

"Careful." I squinted up as Dan climbed, his steps more uncertain with every rung.

But then first his body then his feet disappeared over the balcony rail.

"I'm in!" he hollered jubilantly.

We returned the ladder, making sure to take our door key with us, and then we collapsed in exhausted heaps on the sofa.

"I can't believe that just happened," Dan said faintly.

There was a knock at the door.

"Anna, maybe?" I guessed, though it was surely too early for her.

I trudged to the door.

"Housekeeping!" the woman announced brightly, clutching a mop and bucket.

Dan and I looked at each other. Housekeeping?

"And she'll have a key . . ." he said, rolling his eyes. How had we forgotten?

Laughing, we grabbed our beachbags and left her to it.

"Now to flop . . ." Dan said, grasping my hand.

• • • •

It was a lovely beach, so next morning we headed there again.

The temperature was rising and the beds and umbrellas were filling up fast.

But, at more than 20 euros a set, they would bust our budget.

Instead we spread out our towels on the sand in a patch of shade cast by a frothy tamarisk tree.

The water was only a few paces away for a cooling dip.

We had a blissfully peaceful day. This was fly and flop.

As we packed up to leave the beach later, I remembered we needed milk.

"I'll just pop round by the shop on the way back. Coming?"

Dan shook his head.

"I need the loo," he admitted. "I'll put the kettle on for you coming in."

I went on my way, got a flagon of milk and then set off for the apartment.

But as I turned a corner then another, I began to wonder.

This was the way, wasn't it? All the narrow streets looked the same.

Glistening white houses crowded together, doorways and windows picked out in yellow ochre, wrought iron balconies almost touching above my head.

That purple bougainvillaea – had I passed it already or was this a different one?

Finally, distant at the far end of an alley, I caught a glimpse of the sea.

Oh, thank goodness. If I could find the beach again, I could find my way back . . .

"There you are! I thought you'd got lost!" Dan opened the door wide to finally let me in.

"I did!"

Spluttering with laughter I told him my tale.

We were still laughing about it at dinner in the taverna later.

"I'll just pop to the loo," I said once we'd ordered.

"Watch you don't get lost!"

"Cheeky!"

The waiter was serving our food as I sat down again.

My mouth watered at the amazing aromas.

"So what'll we do tomorrow? Beach again or are you bored yet?" Dan asked, plunging his fork into the saganaki and watching the cheese ooze temptingly.

"Bored? It's been non-stop drama!" I protested.

However, we decided to explore the town a bit in the morning.

"Just don't expect me to guide us," I joked.

We went just after breakfast, already our favourite part of the day.

Our balcony was such a tranquil spot.

Hand in hand we wandered round the tourist shops.

Dan bought a leather belt for his jeans; I hesitated over a gorgeous pair of pumps, the leather soft as butter.

"You'll kick yourself if you leave them," Dan reasoned.

He was right. I wouldn't find a pair this quality for this price back home, so I gave in.

Fridge magnets for our two mums to add to their collections, a silly donkey keyring for me, and we'd done as much souvenir shopping as we wanted to.

"Coffee?"

We were passing a café with a free table right on the front, perfect for watching the world go by.

We plumped for milkshakes and kicked off our shoes.

The cafe was busy,

customers coming and going, and I realised it was because we were near a bus stop.

"Here comes another one." I pointed to where a streamlined white coach was approaching.

It stopped and the passengers spilled off – mostly tourists here for the afternoon.

The last of them was a young girl, her hand shielding her eyes from the sun's bright glare.

Other passengers milled around, waiting to board.

But there seemed to be a hubbub over something. Someone without a ticket, we speculated.

But no. I realised the girl had stumbled and was now being helped to her feet, her knee gashed and bleeding.

"Oh, that looks nasty," I said. "Should we . . .?"

But Dan was already on his feet.

"Hi, do you speak English? Can we help?" I asked, taking her elbow.

Glad to surrender responsibility to someone else, the crowd was already dispersing, the bus going on its way.

"I am English," the girl said. "My name's Ellie."

Her voice was muffled as she bent over examining her injuries.

"Come and sit down for a minute," I said. "Would you like my husband to take a look at that knee? Dan's a nurse."

One thing about being married to a nurse is that we never go anywhere without packing a little first aid kit.

I fished it out of my bag and within minutes Dan had cleaned Ellie's wound and closed the gash with paper stitches.

"Thank you," she said as he applied the final dressing. "I don't know what I would have done without you."

The colour had returned to her cheeks and we had no worries as she headed off to explore the town, while we set out for the beach.

The day was getting back to normal.

"Whatever this holiday's normal is," Dan said, rolling his eyes.

● ● ● ●

"Beach?" Dan asked over breakfast next day.

"Beach," I echoed.

At least a day tucked safely on the beach should be uneventful.

"Unless someone needs rescuing from the waves," Dan said.

"Don't even joke about it!"

We'd had quite enough drama, thank you.

I read seven chapters of my book while Dan alternated between snoozing and taking dips in the water.

The day remained blissfully peaceful and we were contentedly relaxed as we headed back to the apartment.

My eye was watering, though.

"I think I've got sun cream in it."

"Don't rub it," Dan warned. He stopped under the striped awning of a café.

"Go rinse your eyes in their washroom," he suggested. "I'll order us some coffee."

"Sorted?" He looked up from plunging the cafetière as I returned, and I nodded.

"It's still stinging a bit but better."

We sat watching a steady stream of passing holidaymakers as they returned to their hotels laden with lilos and beach bags and shopping.

A family took the table alongside ours.

I tried not to stare at the teenage daughter's beautifully manicured nails.

I spread my own fingers. They put mine to shame. Maybe I should . . .

"My rings!" I suddenly screamed.

Panic surged. There was a white, untanned line where my engagement and wedding rings should be.

Of course! I'd taken them off to wash my face and hands.

I could visualise them, on the side of the basin, the gold and diamonds twinkling in the overhead lights.

But the café had got very busy. Could they possibly still be there?

They weren't. I felt like crying as I wound my way between the tables back to Dan.

He could tell from my face.

"Oh, love . . ."

I felt a touch on my shoulder.

"'Scuse, *kyria*, but I think maybe I have . . . ?" The waiter pointed at my hand.

"My rings? Really?"

"Come," he said and led me inside.

He ducked behind the bar and when he reappeared, there in his hand were my precious rings, carefully wrapped in a napkin.

"I just find," he said. "Then I see you run in and out and I think, ah-ha!"

I felt like crying again.

● ● ● ●

We were tempted to stay at the apartment next day, out of trouble's way.

But we bravely ventured to the beach and it was all fine.

We swam, we read, we snoozed. I listened to music and Dan snorkelled.

"A perfect day," we agreed, wandering back to the apartment, though I did just touch a wooden bench for luck.

Dinner passed without incident, and as we sat on our balcony gazing up at the stars in the midnight sky, we let out a sigh of relief.

This was fly and flop. Thank goodness.

Could our luck stretch to two days?

● ● ● ●

Next morning, we took our towels down to the beach and spread out in our usual spot.

A squeal woke me from a snooze, but it was just kids larking about in the water.

A yell was a man waving to catch his friend's attention.

A crash-bang and an argument was the aftermath of a hire car reversing into a taxi on the road nearby.

Nothing to do with us. What a relief.

The evening and our final taverna supper went by just as peacefully, and I found I was sorry to be packing for our flight home next day.

I felt quite wistful as I clambered into the taxi.

"Goodbye, lovely balcony," I whispered, looking back as we set off.

● ● ● ●

The last passenger had boarded and all our carry-on bags were finally stowed.

The cabin crew were snapping the overhead lockers closed.

"They're taking the steps away," Dan said, peering out the window.

"Phew!" He flopped back into his seat. "Made it. We'll soon be home and d –"

Ping-ping! Someone was pressing repeatedly the button to call for assistance.

There was a stir some rows behind us.

The cabin crew bustled down the aisle with an air of purpose.

Dan and I eyed each other with dread.

Now what? Had someone been taken ill?

"I spoke too soon," Dan muttered with a groan.

One of the flight attendants returned to the front to pick up the intercom.

"If I could have everyone's attention, please," she began.

I clutched Dan's hand. She sounded awfully serious.

"To avoid confusion, the button for your reading light is the one above your seat with the lightbulb on it, not the outline of a person holding a tray."

Her smile was through gritted teeth.

Dan's hand tightened round my fingers. His shoulder nudged mine.

"So what did you think of fly and flop? Too boring?"

We were still laughing as the plane took off.

Paradise Found

Belize had provided a beautiful backdrop for Milla's new life . . .

BY JACQUI COOPER

THE Belize sun beat down on the island of Ambergris Caye. The fresh sea breeze beckoned Milla to the beach for her usual morning swim.

But today, having volunteered to cover the Hotel Xibalba's reception desk in order to allow one of her receptionists to attend her son's school assembly, she was stuck indoors.

She'd just finished arranging a spa visit for some new arrivals when a raised voice drew her attention.

Felisha, the other receptionist on duty today was extremely experienced, but the man she was dealing with was being difficult.

He was angled away from Milla, gesturing wildly so she couldn't get a proper look at him, but there was something familiar about him.

"You're not listening. I've told you that my friends will be here any minute and they will expect to go diving today," he stated in a tone that suggested he was used to getting his own way.

"Now you're saying we can't? Your coral diving excursions are the main reason we chose this hotel over the others. This just isn't good enough!"

"I'm sorry, sir," Felisha said patiently, "but as I've explained, we need twenty-four hours' notice to accommodate such a large group on the diving tours."

Ever the professional, Felisha didn't even glance at the prominent sign on the reception desk listing the tours which required such notice.

Nor did she remind him that he would have been told at check-in, or that the same information was clearly stated on the hotel's website during the booking process.

Instead, she offered a solution.

"However, I may be able to charter a private boat —"

"Then what are you waiting for? Snap to it, or you're going to have some very disgruntled paying customers."

Then perhaps you should have planned ahead, Milla thought.

But it was the petulance in the man's voice that did it. Now she recognised him.

Hugo Stone; a blast from the past.

He was still handsome, though his jawline had softened and a noticeable paunch had developed around his middle, despite him being, like her, only in his early thirties.

His signature charm appeared to have abandoned him, at least for today.

As the hotel manager, Milla considered stepping in before things escalated further but she had every confidence in Felisha, and, frankly, zero interest in reconnecting with Hugo.

But it was too late.

He had intercepted the look Felisha had shot her way and now he turned to face her.

"Are you in charge here —" He broke off abruptly, his eyebrows shooting up. "Camilla? No! It can't be! I don't believe it. Camilla! Wow! You look fantastic."

There was no avoiding him now.

"Hello, Hugo," she said quietly.

He engulfed her in a hug then held her at an admiring arm's length.

"I mean it. You look great. I always said it was just puppy fat, didn't I?"

Behind him, she saw Felisha's eyebrows shoot up but Milla kept her smile in place.

"You're staying here at the Xibalba?"

He nodded.

"Remember Jack Lawson? Good old Jack? He's finally getting hitched and I'm in charge of his stag party, so I flew out a day early to organise things."

Milla saw the very moment the penny dropped.

Hugo stumbled to a halt, talk of a wedding no doubt reminding him of exactly how and when things had ended between them.

"Of course I remember Jack," Milla said smoothly.

How could she ever forget Hugo's best friend and wing man?

"Mr Stone and his group are requesting to go diving this afternoon," Felisha told Milla. "I'm about to ring round and see if I can charter a boat."

"Why don't I do that?" Milla offered quickly.

She could make her escape and make the calls from her office.

"Hugo, why don't you wait in the bar, complimentary drinks, of course, and I'll let you know the moment I have some news."

But Hugo's bluster was already returning.

"Why not let her do it?" he said, indicating Felisha. "Then you can join me!

"It's been a long time, Camilla. We should catch up."

Milla had no interest in catching up.

"I'm sorry," she said with utterly false sincerity. "Unfortunately, we're rather shorthanded today —"

With perfect timing the absent receptionist rushed through the door.

"It went great," she told everyone. "He was a star. Thanks for covering, Milla, but I'm here now and ready to take over —"

She broke off, looking from Milla to Felisha to Hugo, aware that she had arrived in the middle of something.

Hugo pounced.

"So you are free, Camilla? Then I insist you join me. We really should talk."

He had the same, booming, public school voice he'd always had.

Once Milla had admired it as a sign of his supreme self-confidence. Now she cringed at the thought of that same voice broadcasting their history to all and sundry.

"I'm happy to make the calls," Felisha said helpfully. "Then you can go with your friend, Camilla."

She used air quotes behind Hugo's back.

Not very professional but Milla hid a smile.

"That's settled then," said Hugo as if he had never doubted the outcome. "This way, is it?" He turned and began to march in completely the wrong direction.

"Er, no. This way," Milla said, avoiding Felisha's eye.

He spun smoothly, never

acknowledging his mistake.

At this time of day the bar was empty, apart from a few people on the terrace drinking coffee, planning their day or awaiting pickup for excursions or transfers.

Milla cast a quick, professional eye over the neat and tidy area.

All was as expected, but the staff of the Xibalba needed little supervision.

She took a seat on the terrace overlooking the lush gardens and the pool, with a glorious view down to the sparkling turquoise sea.

Hugo sat back and steepled his fingers.

"Camilla Anderson. Well, well. What's it been? Ten years? Did I say you look great?"

"You did. I go by Milla now."

"Okay." He nodded. "Reinvented yourself. I get that."

She doubted it.

"You disappeared off the face of the earth after . . . I mean . . ." He broke off, his face flushing scarlet.

"After you left me at the altar?" Milla supplied helpfully.

Tony the barman, approaching to take their order, clearly heard that last bit.

Not that Milla's past was a secret to anyone at the hotel, but she would have preferred them not to know that Hugo was the other half of the story.

Hugo flashed an embarrassed look at Tony.

"Er, yes, quite," he mumbled. He cleared his throat. "So, what would you like, Camilla? Still addicted to those creamy coffees you loved so much?" He cast his eyes doubtfully over her slender figure.

"I'll just have my usual thanks, Tony," she said.

"And a beer for me," said Hugo.

The barman melted away, leaving them alone. Milla refused to be the one to break the silence.

Hugo squirmed.

"About that," he mumbled. "The whole wedding thing. That was a difficult time. A very difficult time. Still, water under the bridge, eh?"

Water under the bridge? That was all he had to say? He had broken her heart, crushed her self-esteem, humiliated her in front of everyone she knew and turned her out of the home they'd shared for three years.

Familiar indignation roiled through her at the memory but she was surprised to find that the pain wasn't as chest-crushing as once it had been.

"When you didn't turn up at the church, Jack said you'd had cold feet and gone to your parents' place in Edinburgh."

Of course, Jack hadn't mentioned that one of Milla's bridesmaids had accompanied him.

She'd had to find that little snippet out later.

"Er, yes. A very stressful time for all concerned," said Hugo.

That was it? And not an apology in sight.

Tony returned with the drinks, serving Milla's black coffee before slamming Hugo's beer down with a little too much force.

"Anything else I can do for you?" he asked.

Perfectly polite of course, but Tony from the glint in his eye, the bunch of his muscles, and the subtext was clear to Milla. Would you like me to throw this jerk off the terrace?

"We're fine, thanks Tony," she said.

With a last, lingering glower at Hugo, he left.

Hugo had used the interruption to regroup.

"This is the hotel we booked for our honeymoon, isn't it? I recognised it from the brochure. It's still got the same great reputation for diving."

Back then, diving had been his hobby, not hers. But she'd been so head over heels she'd have done anything to make him happy.

"It is. The honeymoon was paid for and non-refundable. And far enough away that I could escape the gossip and pity," she finished bluntly.

Hugo squirmed again; but then he had never liked being confronted with the consequences of his actions, which was why he'd had Jack do his dirty work for him.

He noticed her bare left hand. She never risked wearing jewellery at work.

"You never married?"

She saw no reason to answer his personal questions.

"Did you marry Elena?" she asked instead, naming the bridesmaid.

"Good grief, no. I mean, didn't she work in a coffee shop?" He took a deep slug of beer. "I did get married though. Twice, actually, but neither lasted. Foot loose and fancy free, that's me."

He leaned forward in his chair.

"But enough of the past. Tell me about you, Camilla. You've honestly been here all this time?"

"All this time," she confirmed.

She'd arrived broken.

By day she'd wandered the golden beaches. By night she had haunted the hotel bar, a lost soul amidst the happy, glowing holidaymakers.

The staff had known she was staying alone in the honeymoon suite.

They might have whispered amongst themselves, but they had taken her under their wing, always ready to offer a napkin for her tears, a kind word for her misery, or to deflect any unwanted attention from prowling men at the bar.

"I just fell in love with the place and the people," she explained. "At the end of the two weeks, someone asked me what I was going back to and I honestly had no answer.

"When I heard they were looking for room attendants here at the hotel, I applied for a position and got it."

The Xibalba had been a very different place back then, badly run and always short staffed.

Since Milla took over everything had improved.

"A room attendant?" His curled lip revealed his thoughts on that. "What a waste. You had a first-class business degree and a job lined up with a prestigious marketing firm, as I remember."

Yes, she had. But she had been in no fit state to pick up the pieces of her shattered life or take on a stressful new job.

The tranquillity and the slower pace here in Belize had been what she'd needed to heal.

"From a high-flying career, to a cleaner, to a –

sorry, what are you now? A receptionist?" She didn't correct him.

Hugo shifted uncomfortably under her steady gaze.

"I'm sorry," he mumbled. "This is all my fault, isn't it? I reduced you to this."

He gestured dolefully to the blazing sun, the turquoise sea, the lush green vegetation and the jewelled humming birds darting around the hotels overflowing flower tubs.

"You've buried yourself away here, all because of me."

He reached for her hands.

"I missed you terribly, you know," he murmured.

"When I got back from Scotland, I soon realised my mistake and looked for you. But you had disappeared off the face of the earth. No-one seemed to know where you were."

Milla had begged all their acquaintances not to tell him.

She deftly reclaimed her hands under the pretext of reaching for her coffee.

For years she had steamed and stewed, fantasising about what she would say and do if she ever saw Hugo again.

But now he was sitting right here in front of her, she realised it didn't matter anymore.

Hugo was right. It really was all just water under the bridge.

Out at sea she saw two boats approaching the hotel's private dock.

One was the launch which transferred guests to and from the mainland. The other was a sailing yacht, all clean lines and elegance as it cut through the water.

"Do you ever come home?" Hugo asked. "To England?"

This was her home.

"Not often," she told him.

His phone, which he had placed on the table, let out a shrill beep. Milla took the opportunity to make her excuses.

"I should let you get on."

Hugo stabbed a finger at the phone.

"It's just a reminder to take my blood pressure medication," he said dismissively. "I'm a partner in the family law firm now, you know. My father is close to retiring so I'll soon be taking over."

"Congratulations," Milla said, thinking that if he was already on blood pressure meds at his age, maybe he should be reassessing his career choice.

"It looks like your friends have arrived," she added, indicating the dock.

He followed her gaze to see the launch tying up.

"Excellent. Shall we go and meet them? I can't wait to show you off to Jack."

As if she was his to show off? But she was heading for the dock anyway, so she said nothing.

The half dozen men on the launch had clearly started their celebrations early.

Many slugged from beer bottles, and empty bottles littered the deck.

Milla suspected she would be rethinking today's diving trip even if Felisha had managed to arrange it.

"Listen," said Hugo urgently before his friends disembarked.

"Let's have dinner sometime. My treat, of course. I'm here for a few days and would enjoy the company.

"Besides, I feel I really should make things up to you."

"I'm sorry," Milla said, her attention now on the yacht. "I'm busy."

Unlike the launch, the deck of the yacht was immaculate.

A tow-haired toddler in a life vest was "helping" the crew tie up while a handsome blond man stood over him, making sure he didn't get in the way.

The man was bare chested, tanned and gorgeous and when he spotted Milla, a million-watt smile lit his face.

"My word," Hugo breathed. "Is that Duncan Hardy? I was at the premiere of his new film last week." He turned to Milla. "Don't tell me he's staying at the hotel?"

"No, he isn't." And then because she couldn't resist, "He has a villa up there on the hill."

Hugo turned to look at the impressive, sun-baked building.

Duncan was carrying the child down the gangplank. The toddler reached for Milla and she took him in her arms.

"Mummy! Daddy bought a lot of fish and I had a blue slushy and an ice cream and then I felt sick but I'm better now!"

"Is that so?" Milla hugged her son.

By now the men on the launch had also recognised Hollywood's biggest action star and were stumbling their way off the boat, staring in awe.

But the object of their admiration had eyes only for Milla. Duncan kissed her as though he had been at sea for days, and not just a quick hop over to the market on the mainland.

"Did you miss me?" he said.

"Always." She laughed.

Hugo was staring, mouth hanging open.

"Duncan, this is Hugo, a guest at the hotel. Hugo, this is my husband and our son, Jacob."

"You're married?" Hugo said, stupefied. "To Duncan Hardy? And you have a child?"

Yes, she was. And she had a fulfilling career, great friends.

A life that was little short of magical.

One that she would never have had if she'd stayed in England and married Hugo Stone.

> The object of their admiration had eyes only for Milla

But she didn't say that. She didn't need to. Hugo's expression was enough.

"Pleased to meet you, Hugo." Duncan was adept at dealing with speechless fans. "Maybe we'll see you around. Please excuse me, right now, I need to get this fish on ice."

"Of course. Um. Nice to see you, Cam – I mean, Milla."

"You too, Hugo. Look after yourself."

Without a backward glance she walked down the jetty carrying Jacob, with Duncan's arm around her shoulders.

Her husband drew her close and whispered.

"Am I right in assuming I have just met the dastardly Hugo Stone?"

"You have."

"Would you like me to push him into the water for you?"

"Thank you for the offer but that won't be necessary."

"Just think," Duncan mused. "If you'd married him, you'd be Milla Stone."

He was wrong. She could see that so clearly now. She'd never have been Milla Stone. She'd have been Camilla Stone, a very different person indeed.

Camilla had existed in the shadows, whereas Milla had blossomed in sunshine.

"Milla Stone. Sounds like millstone," Duncan deadpanned. "What do you think? Maybe we should change the name of the yacht. The *Millstone* has a bit of a ring to it."

Milla glanced over her shoulder.

Hugo, Jack and the others were still on the jetty, staring after them and talking excitedly.

Looking beyond them, she saw the graceful yacht bobbing on the sparkling water.

The *Paradise Found*. A wedding gift from Duncan.

"I think we'll keep the name exactly as it is," she said firmly.

After all, she couldn't think of anything more apt.

SHORT STORY

Without You

Edna was no longer here to spend the holidays with me . . .

BY EIRIN THOMPSON

It wasn't my first summer since Edna, my wife, passed away, but it was the first time I'd booked a summer holiday.

Edna and I had made excellent travelling companions, since we first went youth hostelling in Spain as teenagers.

We'd cycled round Ibiza and rested at scenic spots with a picnic. Edna always packed cream toffees from home, which we munched as we explored.

"They'll give us an energy boost," she used to say.

Then the children came along and I thought perhaps there would be a hiatus in our travels. But Edna wouldn't hear of it.

"I'm not knocking our everyday life," she explained, "but I absolutely need to get away at least once a year."

She persuaded me we could manage, even with a baby, and that it would be good for our children to sample other lifestyles.

Michaela's first word was "cat", when a little stray came and loitered under our table at a crêperie in Carnac.

Tim learned to swim in the sea in Rhodes.

No matter where we travelled, Edna always brought a stock of cream toffees from home, and the kids chewed them on aeroplanes or car journeys.

We were surprised but very pleased that, when our kids became teenagers, they still wanted to come on holidays with us.

And when Michaela and Timothy started their own families, they asked if we could all go away together.

Edna was delighted.

She had learned a few tricks, over the years, for keeping babies calm and happy on long trips, and with plenty of adults to go round, no-one got tired or cranky.

The grandkids should have had her for longer. We all should.

• • • •

I suspected that a driving holiday would be dreadful.

Alone behind the wheel in our car, I'd be horribly aware at every moment that I was missing my navigator. But the prospect of hanging about an airport on my own didn't fill me with gladness.

So I opted for an escorted coach holiday, hoping that there might be other solo travellers like myself, or even a guide I could chat to when they weren't too busy.

Tim dropped me at the pick-up spot.

"Have a great time, Dad," he said, as I unfastened my seatbelt. I gave him a grim little smile.

"You are allowed to enjoy this trip," he added. "Mum would want you to."

"Don't put words in your mother's mouth," I snapped, then instantly regretted it.

Timothy only wanted me to know that he and his sister didn't expect me to mope about for the rest of my days.

Michaela had more or less hinted at Christmas that the family would welcome me meeting someone new, but she didn't know what it was like to have spent over 40 years with one person.

I hadn't any inclination to start all over again with another woman. Not at my stage in life.

"Sorry," I said. "I think I'm just a bit nervous."

"It's OK, Dad," Tim replied.

• • • •

I was pleased to get a window seat, although there wasn't much interesting scenery to enjoy until we'd made all the pick-ups.

The coach was very comfortable, not like the so-called Magic Bus that Edna and I had taken from London to Athens when we were first married.

It had been basic and that was being generous.

At one stage, I thought no-one was going to sit beside me and felt a little disappointed.

I was just deciding to enjoy the peace and quiet when we stopped again and a slim woman in blue jeans and a Breton top boarded.

"Are you keeping this seat for anyone?" she asked me.

I moved my newspaper from the place beside me.

"No!" I answered. "Please, be my guest."

"I'm Angela," the woman said. "I used to be a teacher, but I'm retired.

"I have three daughters, two grandsons and no mortgage and I enjoy long walks and even longer cricket matches.

"I also have never been on one of these coach trips before, as you might have guessed. How am I doing?"

"Don't ask me!" I replied. "I'm new to this, too."

I couldn't have wished for a better person to sit with.

Angela was chatty and witty, even though she claimed to be nervous.

And she'd holidayed in lots of places we'd stayed in, too.

I was counting my lucky stars when I remembered something.

"My son gave me this bag of cream toffees for the journey," I said, showing her. "I couldn't bring myself to tell him that my dentist said my days of eating toffees are behind me. Would you like them?"

Angela laughed.

"We're in the same fix," she said. "I used to love those toffees, but I'll let you in on this little hack."

Here she fished in her bag and brought out a packet bearing the same branding, but these were cream fudge.

"Much easier on older gnashers," she murmured. "Fergus, I think you and I are going to understand each other."

I popped one in my mouth, returned Angela's sunny smile and turned to look out of the window.

Perhaps this trip was going to be OK, after all.

Surprise Me!

Trisha wished Chris could plan something special for her . . .

BY MARIE PENMAN

MOST people would consider Trisha to be a sensible and respectable member of society.

However, she had a side of herself that she kept hidden from others.

This secret version was carefree and spontaneous and loved surprises.

The only thing was, at the age of fifty-two, she had realised that this part of her personality was so well hidden nobody else seemed to know about it.

She had hoped her husband, Chris, might surprise her with a party for her fiftieth birthday, but nothing surprising happened.

Their silver wedding anniversary had also passed without a hint of a surprise party.

Trisha had occasionally given Chris the chance to do something unexpected for her.

On one occasion, he'd asked Trisha what she wanted for Christmas, and she said she'd really like a surprise to unwrap on Christmas day.

Which, to be fair, was what she got, as she ripped off the shiny gold paper and discovered a new set of kitchen pots.

Her face had fallen.

"What's wrong, Trish? Don't you like them?" Chris had said, looking genuinely concerned. "I heard you saying a few weeks ago that we could do with new pots so I made a note of it to remind myself."

Trish had smiled at her husband and accepted that surprises perhaps just weren't his thing.

And now, decades later, she knew that their marriage was founded on security and routine, rather than unexpected surprises. In many ways, that was a good thing.

Trish had recently taken early retirement from her job as a primary school teacher, and with 30 years of service behind her she'd built up a decent pension.

Best of all, no more being restricted to the school timetable in terms of holidays, she could take off whenever she wanted!

Unfortunately Chris was less keen on impulsive breaks.

"We need to plan these things carefully, Trish – do the research, source the best locations, check flight times . . ." he said when Trish announced that she'd like to go away in June.

Admittedly, this was only a couple of weeks away, but wasn't that the beauty of (her) retirement?

Being able to jet off at a moment's notice?

Not for Chris, who felt that holidays were best booked months in advance.

"That way we have something to look forward to all year!" he told Trish.

But she didn't really want something to look forward to.

After years of being locked into school schedules and timetable planning, she wanted a change – a holiday at the drop of a hat, to pretty much anywhere.

Then she spotted the advert, which popped up on her phone as she was scrolling one day.

Seeing it made her certain that her phone not only listened in to her conversations, but possibly also read her mind.

Book a mystery holiday, the advert announced. *Escape to Paradise with our mystery beach holiday!*

Leave next week – destination unknown!

It seemed too good to be true.

All her life, Trisha had craved surprises. Now here was one being offered to her on a plate.

She skimmed the small print of the advert.

Locations in Spain, Italy, Greece and Turkey were all listed as possible destinations, flying from her local airport.

She had made up her mind before she'd even finished reading.

After all, why wait for someone to surprise her when she could do it herself?

She decided to surprise Chris as well and waited till he got home from work that evening before pouring him a glass of wine.

"You look tired, love," she said as she stirred the pasta. "Working too hard, I expect."

He looked at her with a nervous expression, as though she were up to something.

He knew her so well.

"Not really any harder than normal," he replied, taking a sip of wine. "Maybe I'm just getting old."

Trisha smiled at him.

"What you need is a holiday! Why don't we go away next week?"

Chris frowned.

"Next week?" he asked. "Where to exactly?"

Trisha gave him her most excited and enticing smile.

"How would you feel if I told you it was a surprise?"

He frowned.

"Meaning you've chosen somewhere to go to but aren't going to tell me, or that it's a surprise for both of us?"

"The latter!" Trisha replied, clapping her hands in an attempt to maintain the spontaneity and anticipation.

But she quickly realised that Chris looked nervous and unsettled rather than happy and excited.

Not surprisingly, he was less than keen on the idea and cited work, lack of preparation and "doubts about the very idea of the trip" as reasons not to go.

It was this caution and lack of joy that forced Trisha to blurt out, "Fine! I'll go by myself then!"

And so the following week, on the first Tuesday in June, and having barely spoken to Chris since she'd booked the trip, Trisha headed off on holiday alone for the first time ever.

As she queued to get through security at the airport, she told herself that it was an adventure and a real novelty to be getting away in June.

Secretly she felt a bit nervous and unsure – what if something happened to her and nobody knew where she was?

Her destination had been loosely confirmed after she'd booked the mystery break, and she was heading for the Costa Brava in Spain for a week's half-board in a hotel near the sea.

Funnily enough, she and Chris had spent their honeymoon in this area of Spain, scraping together their meagre savings.

They had stayed in a cheap bed and breakfasts for a week, lying on the beach all day and wandering around bars and restaurants in the evenings.

Thinking back to that time, almost 30 years ago, Trisha could hardly believe that they'd got married at the age of twenty-three, fresh out of university and still acting like teenagers.

They had three children together, now all adults (in theory).

But how would Trish feel if one of her precious girls announced she was marrying her boyfriend after going out with him for less than a year?

She remembered Chris's marriage proposal, which although unexpected did not surprise her, so certain was she that they were meant to be together.

As she strapped herself into her seat on the plane, Trisha thought fondly of Chris, who had turned into such a strong and supportive man, and then worried that she'd been a bit hasty in booking this solo trip.

After all, he probably needed a holiday more than she did.

The flight took just over two hours and then Trisha got on a coach, full of boisterous fellow tourists, taking her to the hotel.

Although it was early evening and dusk was falling when they reached the resort, Trish recognised it immediately – the same beach town they'd spent their honeymoon in!

What were the odds?

After making every effort to go to a surprise destination, she had ended up back in a place she knew very well.

A lot had changed in the 30 years since they'd been here, of course.

But Trish was pleased to see that what had once been a fairly cheap and tacky resort had been noticeably spruced up.

The long promenade along the seafront had been completely renovated, with tasteful new paving stones, fancy street furniture and lovely artwork placed at regular intervals.

Trish checked in to her hotel then headed out for a bite to eat.

As she wandered through the cobbled streets, she gazed out over the sea and was just in time to see the sun setting over the horizon.

Trisha was entranced.

Although much of the resort had changed, the sunset was just as she remembered – breathtaking.

She remembered Chris taking umpteen photos of it on their cheap camera, hoping to catch the full burst of orange, red and pink colours that exploded across the evening sky.

He'd said it was the most perfect sunset he'd ever seen.

Thinking of this now, Trisha felt tears pricking her eyes, remembering how happy Chris had been, and how excited they had been at the start of their married life together.

As she wandered along the seafront, she spotted a small, wooden-fronted bar, El Pez Azul, which looked exactly as it had done back then.

Chris had used his trusty Spanish dictionary to translate and found that it meant "the blue fish" in English, and they'd made this place their local for the week, selecting a different cocktail to try every night.

Trisha decided to have a drink there for old time's sake, and took a photo on her phone of her piña colada with the sunset in the background.

Missing Chris more than she'd expected, she sent him the picture with the caption, S*till the most perfect sunset.*

Would he realise where she was?

Would he care?

Was he even talking to her after she'd taken off in such an impulsive fashion?

A few minutes later, he replied with a heart emoji and Trisha didn't know if this made her feel better or worse.

The next day, the sun shone non-stop and Trisha spent a couple of hours at the beach, ate some lunch, then lay by the hotel pool reading a book.

By four p.m, she was exhausted and decided to have a short siesta before heading out for a walk along the seafront.

She loved that particular time of day, when the full glare of the sun had moved on and the sky took on a rosy glow – the golden hour, Chris called it.

It really was a perfect location.

Over the years, when Trish had thought back to their honeymoon, she'd feared she was looking through rose-tinted spectacles and that it hadn't been anything special – but of course it was.

And now, as she wandered up towards El Pez Azul and a possible cocktail, she understood and appreciated her marriage, knowing that it had been built on the strongest of foundations.

The bar was busy as Trisha took a table on the terrace and turned to face the sunset.

As she did so, some trick of memory made her think she spotted Chris at the bar . . .

This is what happened when you spent the whole day living in the past!

Except this version of Chris was now walking across the floor towards her, carrying two cocktails.

"Surprise!" he said with a goofy smile on his face.

Trisha jumped up and threw her arms around her husband, laughing with sheer happiness but also crying with relief that he was back in her arms again.

They hugged and Chris said he'd booked a flight as soon as he'd realised where she was.

"How could I not?" he said. "Our honeymoon here remains one of my favourite memories."

Trish smiled at him, so glad that he'd finally surprised her.

"The funny thing is, though . . ." Chris continued, "I'd already planned a return trip here for our thirtieth anniversary.

"A room in a luxury hotel, an all-inclusive package, but apart from that, just like our honeymoon."

Trisha laughed, delighted that her husband had managed to surprise her not once, but twice in one day.

"That's such a great idea, love," she said. "And even better, we have a whole year to look forward to it!"

Sit Back And Relax

A week without technology was what Molly needed to recharge her batteries . . .

BY SHEELAGH MOONEY

"I COULD use a week off right now. So, yes, please," Molly replied to her line manager Ivy's unexpected enquiry on Friday lunchtime as to if she or any of her colleagues might be interested in taking annual leave at short notice.

The lull after a particularly busy period in the tech company where she worked had kicked in somewhat abruptly.

"That's great, Molly. I'd be really grateful to you. I know you've borne the brunt of the staff shortages over recent times, so it's time to relax a little.

"No doubt you'll find some exciting last-minute holiday as usual," Ivy replied, envy creeping into her voice.

Molly laughed.

"I hope so, Ivy."

She began to warm to the unexpected idea of a week away from the office.

That afternoon, she grabbed a sneaky few minutes to check out online holiday options. There were lots. A seasoned traveller, she loved exploring new places by herself.

Her colleagues were always envious of her ability to head off so effortlessly, without ties or commitments at home.

"Make the most of it, Molly. Enjoy your freedom while you can," they chorused as they rushed off to pick up kids or release childminders at home.

The disadvantage of being the youngest and only unattached person in the office was that she was constantly being called upon to fill in for people or take on awkward shifts. There was no winning.

Browsing online travel sites that evening, she spotted a week-long trip to the Greek island of Santorini at a knock-down rate.

That would be perfect, she thought, then ran to fetch her passport to confirm the booking.

"My passport expires this month. I meant to renew it after my last trip away," she lamented to her friend, Val, on the phone later that night. "It will take a whole week to get it renewed. It looks like I'm going to have to stay put after all."

Molly was annoyed with herself. Usually super organised, the frenetic tempo of her work life had resulted in her forgetting to renew the passport.

While she loved her job, sometimes it took over her whole life.

Was it any wonder she was free and single?

The following morning, instead of heading for the airport full of joy, she found herself eating a late breakfast at the kitchen table and wondering what she could do to entertain herself for the next seven days.

Then an idea loomed in her mind – something she had occasionally considered and then instantly dismissed as an impossibility in this day and age.

It was a scary proposition, really. The more she thought about it, the more she recognised that this would present a bigger challenge than travelling the globe solo.

Well, she had a whole week to try it, so after one last session of explanatory e-mails to friends and family, she pulled the plug and disconnected the broadband.

Putting away her laptop and smartphone, Molly knew this would be a break with a difference.

Outside, a pale watery sun brightened the garden as she donned a pair of gardening gloves and threw herself into the wilderness that she liked to claim was a biodiversity reserve.

She really loved gardening – on those rare opportunities that she managed to disconnect from technology and the busy world at large.

It took a little time for her to relax, but eventually she began to unwind and enjoy being in the moment.

She even wondered why she hadn't made more time for this detox available on her own doorstep.

As she weeded under the blue and pink columbines, with their little dove-like heads, and clipped back the grass, which had begun to scramble over the edge of the patio at the end of the garden, she vowed to spend more time in her little haven over the summer.

If it stayed fine today, she would cycle to the local garden centre for some new plants after lunch.

Dusting off her old bike and pumping up the wheels, Molly felt an unexpected sense of wellbeing.

Cycling down the street, she was just getting into the rhythm of it and enjoying the sensation of the breeze on her skin when she felt a rumbling.

She realised that she had a puncture in her rapidly deflating front wheel.

"Having bike trouble, Molly?" her elderly neighbour, Danny, enquired from the other side of the hedge.

An amiable sort, Molly and Danny had mostly spoken when she was either rushing for the morning bus or dashing to the supermarket before closing time.

"I'm afraid so, Danny," Molly replied. "I haven't used the bike for years, so I'd say it's in need of a good service and perhaps new tyres. I must take it to the cycle shop in town some day.

"Would you mind if I left it here while I walk to the garden centre?" she asked.

Danny nodded.

"Better still, leave it with me and I'll have it sorted in no time," he told her.

"My old repair kit is in the shed and iI was considered a bit of an expert on all things two-wheeled when my son, Seán, was a lad.

"Mind you, I haven't done it for a while, but I'm sure it's just like riding a bike." He laughed.

"I don't want to put you to any trouble, Danny," Molly replied with a frown.

"It's no trouble at all; I would be only too delighted to get stuck into it. Off you go now."

"Thanks, Danny I would be really grateful."

Danny smiled and was already unlatching the front gate and wheeling her bike inside.

When Molly returned a little later, clutching a bag

of scones along with a big bag of seeds and plants. Danny had the bike ready to go.

She handed over the scones with her thanks.

"Oh, lovely! They look just like the ones my Nancy used to bake. She was a great one for the sweet stuff." Danny smiled wistfully. "I don't suppose you have time for a cup of tea and one of these scones yourself now?"

Noticing her slight hesitation, Danny nodded.

"Ah, I'm sure you'll have more to be doing than sitting around drinking tea with an old man like me."

Molly, who had been looking forward to continuing her onslaught on the garden, heard the note of nostalgia in his voice and reminded herself that she was on a break from schedules this week and that she had plenty of time.

"Actually, that would be lovely, Danny." She smiled. "Do you mind if I have a look around your garden while I'm here? It always looks so beautiful when I'm passing."

Danny beamed with pleasure.

"Please do. Maybe we could have that cuppa in the garden. I have a nice pot of jam to go with those scones in here somewhere."

He sauntered up the steps towards the kitchen with renewed pep in his step.

In no time, the two of them were seated at the little garden table, sipping tea from china cups that Danny had hastily retrieved from the glass cabinet and feasting on scones with strawberry jam and fresh cream.

The day was unusually balmy with barely a cloud in the sky. Molly could barely remember the last time she had sat outside without her eyes being locked on her phone.

She was only beginning to recognise how much of her out of office life was also devoted to technology.

It was such a treat to sit outdoors, drinking tea and

chatting about the various plants packed into Danny's abundant cottage garden.

Admiring the sweetly scented honeysuckle and jasmine that scrambled up the wall near the doorway, Molly slowly inhaled its exotic perfume while Danny pointed to a collection of small plants nearby.

"I love taking cuttings to see if they will grow, but I've almost run out of space in the garden," he admitted. "So if you would like to take some of these off my hands you would be doing me a real favour."

The steps up to the doorway were covered with an array of plants in terracotta pots that Danny had successfully propagated.

"Are you sure? I'd love that!" Molly exclaimed in astonishment. "You've definitely got green fingers, Danny, if you managed to grow all of them from cuttings."

She was used to buying her plants fully grown from the garden centre to save time.

Danny laughed at her wonder and explained that, since his wife of over 50 years had passed away some years back, and his only son lived in Australia with his family, he had a lot of time on his hands and gardening was his greatest pleasure.

He explained that Seán, his wife and their sons came back to visit when they could, but that he still missed them.

"Well, I'm sure you Facetime them to keep in touch, though," Molly probed gently.

"I'm not great with technology," Danny confessed. "They telephone me every week, though, and while it's great to hear from them, it's just not the same as seeing them, is it?"

"I can help you with the technology side to set up video calls," Molly offered.

"Oh, I don't know. My mind goes blank when I see that laptop thing that they bought for me."

She smiled.

"Danny, anyone who can create what you have created here is definitely up for a challenge," she pointed out. "You just need some help to get you started."

"I'd be happy to help you in exchange for some plants, and maybe garden advice, too," Molly added with a smile, and she meant it.

Danny beamed.

"That would be marvellous. I warn you, though, that you will have your work cut out with me as your student."

"There is no rush. We will take it slowly. Why don't I come back this evening and we'll get you started then."

The following week, when Molly returned to work, people remarked on how refreshed and relaxed she was looking after her holiday.

"You look wonderful – positively glowing. Have you met a new man?" her friend Karen whispered. "I can't wait to hear all about it over lunch."

Molly laughed. She had had a wonderful relaxing time and, yes, she had met a new man – two of them, actually.

They were warm, generous people, one of whom had introduced her to the joys of gardening for the soul, and the other . . .

She smiled inwardly. She didn't intend to spill the beans to her colleagues just yet.

Molly had met Danny's grandson, Greg, while they were setting up his video calls. Greg with his twinkling brown eyes and kind eyes was a young version of Danny and they had clicked immediately.

Greg had told Molly privately that he was planning a big surprise for his grandfather.

Unbeknownst to Danny, Greg was moving to the UK next month to work and, if Danny agreed to it, to live with him, at least initially.

After they had convinced Danny to embrace technology as a way of keeping in touch with his Australian-based family, Greg and Molly had made excuses to continue their conversations, sometimes for hours at a time, and she was now really looking forward to meeting him in the flesh.

She had learned a few new things about herself this week.

Though she hadn't, in fact, managed a whole week without technology, she had rediscovered some of its merits and its limitations.

More importantly, she had discovered that she didn't need to travel very far from home at all to widen her horizons.

THE SEA

As I looked across the bay,
Lashing waters it portrayed,
Air scented by the salty sea,
Turquoise lights glittering free.

Fishing boats heaving in such a swell,
Rather them than me out there today,
Rocking and rolling fighting to control,
Shuddering and falling with the mighty waves.

Green at the gills but their hearts sing with pride,
Working for their catch taking it all in their stride,
While I struggle to stand in the wind on the land,
I just stand and stare at such a wondrous sight.

By Bridget Baldock

BODY BEAUTIFUL

From January first, it seems we've all been on a mission
To reinvent ourselves – the 2025 edition!
"Get Your Summer Body!" is the cry from all around,
And exercise and diets are the way it will be found.

I've read the plans with interest – I could lose a pound or two.
I've tried hard to keep track of all the things I'd have to do.
Bicep curls and crunches, many thousand steps a day,
Protein, fasting, cutting carbs to keep the weight at bay!

And now the summer's here, I stand before the looking-glass
Resplendent in my swimsuit – does my summer body pass?
It isn't lean, it isn't toned; it's soft and rather fat –
But I'm a girl who likes her grub, so I'm OK with that!

By Ros McKenna

Dreams of ROMANCE

Evocative and timeless, this collection of beautiful, beguiling tales of love will win your heart and nourish your soul.

In The Nick Of Time

Glenda needed Tom's help, if she wanted to make it for the wedding . . .

BY FIONA THOMSON

Tom looked at the hotel keycard in his hand – the receptionist must have made a mistake.

Yes, he was in Room 423, the number given to him by the woman when he checked in.

Everything around him was beautifully prepared with freshly made bed, folded towels and a welcome card on the table.

But from the noises filtering through the closed door on the right – probably the en-suite – someone was definitely in there.

Tom tapped the keycard against his chin.

He didn't want to frighten the person or make them think their room was being robbed. What should he do?

Yes, he'd go back into the lobby, closing the door quietly behind him, then ask the receptionist to double-check the number of his room.

Tom turned to go.

"Hello? Is anyone there?" a faint, tearful voice called out from the other side of the door.

Tom froze.

He could just tiptoe away, but the person, surely a woman, sounded upset.

He couldn't just leave her.

"Yes. Are you OK?"

"No!" This time the voice was louder. "I'm stuck in this bathroom and can't get the door to open.

"The flooring seems to have buckled up right by the bottom of the door and every time I try to pull it open, I seem to make it worse."

"I'll go down to reception, try to get someone to come and help."

"But that will take ages!" the voice wailed. "They're ever so friendly, but really short-staffed.

"When the man sent someone up yesterday to sort out the air conditioning, I waited for over half an hour.

"And I'm supposed to be at the wedding by now. Oh, please help!"

Tom slipped the overnight bag from his shoulder and propped it against the wall.

"Yes, of course I will. A wedding – goodness, you don't want to miss that."

He tried to picture the woman on the other side of the door.

"You're not the bride, I hope!"

A muffled chuckle of laughter filtered through.

"Goodness no! It's my only niece, Carrie, getting married and she's like a daughter to me. I'd hate to miss her big day."

Tom nodded, then grinned. No point in nodding his agreement when she couldn't see him!

"Don't worry. I'm Tom and I'll do everything I can to get you out."

"Thanks, Tom – I'm Glenda by the way."

Tom studied the room. What could he find to get Glenda out?

He opened drawers. Nothing. Even the wooden coat hangers were too big.

Got it! He unzipped his overnight bag and took out the shirt he'd packed for his meeting the next day.

The thin wire coat hanger might do the trick.

Tom explained his plan to Glenda.

"So when the wire comes through, pull it to where the flooring has become raised.

"Then if we both push down on the coat hanger and move it along, we might manage to ease everything back in place and get the door open."

"Ingenious!" Glenda said. "Let's hope it works."

Tom wiggled the coat hanger from side to side until half of it had disappeared under the door.

"I think I've – oh, no, it's bounced up again," Glenda wailed.

"Keep trying!" Tom urged.

"Yes! It's in place!"

Tom grabbed the thin wire and started to move it along under the door.

"I think this might be working!"

"Well, the flooring does seem to be flattening out," Glenda replied. "Hang on. I just need to – Ow! I don't believe it."

"What's happened?"

"I've just broken a nail. And I only got them done yesterday to match my dress and hat.

"Oh, well, when it comes to the photographs, I'll need to make sure –"

"Glenda!" Tom could hear the impatience in his voice, then tried to speak more calmly. "Our aim is to get you out of here and to the wedding – or you won't be in any of the photos."

"Oh, that would be terrible!" Glenda sighed. "The weather's so beautiful.

"They'll be taking them outside by the lake. Oh, I can't miss out."

"Let's see if we can get the door to open even a little way," Tom said as he pushed against the wood using all his weight.

Slowly the blockage at the base eased, then suddenly the door swung open and Tom rushed forward to grab Glenda before she toppled backwards into the bath.

"Oh!"

The feathered hat perched on Glenda's head slipped down so it was covering one eye.

Both her arms were pinned to her body in Tom's grasp and the two of them looked at each other for a moment before bursting into laughter.

Tom released his hold once he saw Glenda was steady on her feet again, only to be pulled back into a hug.

"You did it!" Glenda squealed, jumping up and down. "Oh, I can't thank you enough."

Tom stood back, smiling.

"I'm happy I could help. When I got here I thought I'd been given the key to the wrong room."

Glenda shook her head.

"No, it was all my fault. About twenty of us stayed overnight, ready for the wedding today.

"We'd all checked out, then I realised I'd left some tiny pearl earrings at the back of the bathroom shelf.

"They'd belonged to my mother and are a favourite pair. The cleaner had left the door open so I just nipped in and, well, you know the rest."

"Glad I was given the same room," Tom said, "or who knows how long you could have been stuck in there. But you need to be on your way to that wedding!"

Glenda frowned.

"I was supposed to be getting a lift from someone, but they'll have all gone by now. I'd better see if reception can sort me out with a taxi."

Tom took his phone from his pocket.

"Where's the wedding taking place?"

"The Four Pines. It's a big country estate."

Tom keyed in the name and watched as the map appeared on screen.

"It says it's a twenty minute drive, but how long will it take to get a taxi?" He bit his lip. "Look, my car is outside. Why don't I give you a lift?"

Glenda gasped.

"Really? Oh, that would be so kind of you."

Tom grabbed his car keys from his bag, then made sure the room keycard was safely in his pocket.

"Let's get you to this wedding!"

As they left the town behind and began driving through the sunny country lanes, Tom couldn't believe how chatty Glenda was, but put it down to the relief of finally escaping from the bathroom.

He soon knew that Carrie was a nurse and marrying Andrew, who was a teacher at a primary school.

Carrie's mum (Glenda's sister-in-law) had died four years ago so the aunt and niece had become even closer since then.

Glenda was to sit next to her brother Bill for the ceremony and the meal, so it was vital she got there in time.

"Goodness!" Glenda said, after finally pausing to take a breath. "I've prattled on and on about me and my family but never asked anything about you."

Tom smiled.

"Well, let me see. I'm an IT consultant – spent most of my childhood on computers so it was an obvious career choice – and because of that I do a lot of travelling."

"Not so good for anyone left behind at home," Glenda said.

Tom nodded.

"Very true, although I'm hoping for a promotion to department head, which will change that.

"At home it's only me and my cat, Trudi, who is very independent.

"Also I have a lovely neighbour who feeds her when I'm away."

Tom checked the rear view mirror, then indicated left.

"And if my sat nav is correct . . ."

Glenda pointed to the large sign.

"The Four Pines! Oh Tom, I can't believe you've got me here."

"And ten minutes before the wedding starts, too."

• • • •

"I insist – you've got to stay!"

The dark-haired woman in the long, blue satin dress stood in the doorway, blocking Tom's exit.

He had to laugh.

He'd just helped one woman escape from a room and now another was trying to stop him from leaving!

"Honestly, Claire. It's very kind of you, but what will the bride think when a complete stranger is sitting at her wedding?"

Claire shook her head.

"Not a stranger now after everything Glenda's told me.

"I've been friends with Carrie since primary school and know she'd be so disappointed if she couldn't thank you personally."

She looked at her watch. "

But with the wedding about to start, I don't think it's quite the right moment."

Glenda touched Tom's arm.

"As Claire said, one of the cousins had to call off at the last minute, so there is space. And it would be a shame to let a lovely three course meal go to waste."

Claire tried to stifle a laugh.

"It's actually a buffet," she whispered, leaning close in to Tom so he could smell her soft perfume. "But yes, please do stay."

"Claire's not only a teacher, but is head of her school," Glenda said, "so, Tom, as I know you've not got that promotion yet, I think she outranks you."

Both Tom and Claire burst out laughing.

"Well," Tom said, catching the mischievous glint in Glenda's eye. "In that case, I feel I've got no option but to stay."

• • • •

"Speech! Speech!"

Glenda drummed her hands on the table and nodded at Tom as the serving staff began removing empty plates from the long tables.

She raised her glass, took another sip and gave him a beaming smile.

Tom smiled back.

She certainly looked very different from the woman in distress that he'd saved from his hotel bathroom.

He looked round the room at all the happy faces, taking in Carrie and Andrew and then resting his gaze on Claire.

She really was the most beautiful woman he'd ever met.

"I think everyone is waiting for you to say something," Claire told him, "and Glenda looks ready to burst with excitement!"

Tom nodded then stood up and the room filled with applause.

"I'm sure most of you will have heard about my strange encounter with Glenda," he began, as he looked in her direction.

"And really, me fixing the hotel bathroom door to free her wasn't the only door that opened for me that day.

"Because when I arrived at Carrie and Andrew's wedding, I was greeted by the most wonderful person who urged me to stay for the celebrations.

"And we've been inseparable ever since." He squeezed Claire's hand.

"Eighteen months ago, when I watched Carrie and Andrew exchange their wedding vows, I never imagined that I would be doing the same thing with Claire.

"But you've all witnessed it today, so I'm not dreaming!"

Tom gazed round the room, taking in the radiant smiles of his and Claire's parents, their families and friends and finally Glenda, sitting at the end of the top table, dabbing her eyes with a handkerchief.

"So, on behalf of my wife and I, I invite you to raise your glasses in a toast to the woman whose predicament led to this happiest of days.

"To Glenda!"

Seas The Day

Just once, Caroline wanted the chance to enjoy some me time in her coastal town . . .

BY CHARMAINE FLETCHER

CAROLINE'S mother had never learned to ride a bike. "Just put your feet on the pedals and pump!" her father had instructed.

For her mother's lesson, he'd taken the family to a nice, straight, if slightly hilly, road, before holding the saddle, then letting go.

"Trust me, you'll have more independence under your own steam if you can cycle!" he'd added.

Instead, flummoxed, the poor woman had stuck her feet out and freewheeled, bowling down the road wherever the bike decided to go.

"Yes, but you can't get freer than this," her mother had called defiantly, before letting out a delighted whoop.

Her father and siblings had laughed, but Caroline wasn't convinced.

Throughout her childhood, Caroline had developed a sense of caution, planning and juggling.

At her former school, French skipping was all the rage.

Girls took turns to hook both ends of circular elastic around their legs while others skipped complicated patterns within the stretched middle.

In London, where they'd moved for her father's job, girls threw two balls against a wall, in perpetual motion, instead, chanting, "Keep the kettle boiling, keep the whistle rattling."

The really deft pupils added more balls and a turn with the chant before cleverly catching every third ball.

Caroline had mastered the game to its highest level so she could avoid the school bully's scorn.

Metaphorically speaking, it was a skill she'd never really forgotten, leading to her acquiring a reputation for reliability, at school, university and work.

"You're a model student," her headmistress had beamed at the Leavers' Assembly, after the A-Level examinations were over.

"It is marvellous the way you've managed revision, the school play, charity knitting and university interviews, together with your duties as Head Girl.

"Therefore, I am presenting you with the Best Allrounder Cup – and very well deserved it is, too!" she'd added, as everyone had clapped.

Eventually, Caroline had combined an administrative career with being a working mother.

Thanks again to juggling and list making, she was faultless at both – albeit undervalued.

"Micromanaging," her husband, Tony, grumbled before finally throwing in the marital towel.

Though saddened, Caroline had coped admirably when single again.

Applying her excellent organisational skills and resourcefulness, she'd even devised job and car sharing with another lone parent.

Her meticulousness later enabled Caroline to save enough for an early retirement.

Having downsized to a small property in a pretty, south coastal town, with plenty of amenities and a nice quiet beach, even that was well planned.

Caroline also managed to fit in paid part-time work, volunteering and leisure pursuits – not that there'd been room for them recently.

As an active grandma, Caroline's daughter also expected her to balance well-earned retirement commitments with looking after her grandchildren, Kiki and Joe.

Reluctantly, Caroline had relinquished her paper calendar, committing everything to the smartphone given to her by Milly, her daughter.

Not that she'd needed or wanted it, but Milly had insisted.

"It'll help you to become much more efficient with your childcare duties, Mum," Milly had smiled tightly.

Duties? Caroline remembered thinking bewilderedly – when had that happened?

How had spending time with her grandchildren, while helping out their parents occasionally, become an unpaid job?

Unsurprisingly, on sparkling days, when the sun was shining and the seaside called, Caroline often wondered what it would feel like to drop one of the balls she juggled.

Instead, she and Joe were trawling the local supermarket, completing a shop – or rather, two shops at once.

Typically, Caroline just wanted a handful of things, while Milly, unfortunately, was another matter.

Tutting, Caroline scrolled down her phone, swapping the sugary jelly Joe had put in the trolley for a fruity yoghurt that was actually on the list.

Protesting, Joe stood-up in the trolley seat.

"No, sweetie, that's dangerous," Caroline cautioned automatically, placing her smartphone on the shopping before easing a wriggling Joe to safety.

"Bored, Gramma!"

"Not long, now, darling," Caroline soothed, distractedly adding cheese to the trolley.

"Hey, no. You're not supposed to have that."

Noting his mutinous look, Caroline stroked Joe's peachy cheek, before gently removing her phone from him.

"All right, you can hold it but only if you help me finish the shopping." She held up the phone.

"Scroll like this," Caroline mimed, "and show it to me. Just don't press the buttons."

The fractious toddler looked up, his small hand reaching tentatively for the phone again.

"Remember: no buttons."

He nodded emphatically.

"No buttons, Gramma, see."

Caroline glanced at the phone, before doing a double take.

The list had vanished!

Feeling nauseous, she snatched it from Joe.

The screen was blank!

Frantically, she scrolled up and down, then went into other files: nothing.

"Joe, did you touch any buttons?" Caroline asked sternly while trying to sound calm.

He glanced at her sheepishly, his chocolate brown eyes wide beneath a long, floppy blond fringe.

"Only before you said," he mumbled, his tiny fingers spinning the special offer paper band on the trolly handle.

"Oh, Joe!" Caroline sighed, pushing her hand through her expertly styled, soft grey tresses.

• • • •

"Mum, where are you? You're supposed to be taking the children to their 'Music Makers' group – don't say you've forgotten!" Milly complained crossly, a few days later, having called Caroline's landline.

"I told you, Joe wiped my smartphone. They can't retrieve anything for a week! All my plans have gone awry. I'm at sixes and sevens!"

"Well, couldn't you have written it down, at least? Now I'm stuck with them!" Milly replied.

"Actually, it's probably too late anyway," Caroline said mildly, counting to ten before continuing. "Why not just drop them off here?"

"Perhaps. It's very inconvenient," Milly snapped sulkily.

"Surely you realise that it's my day off? I'm meeting a friend for coffee at that new place in town. How could you let me down?"

"Too bad, darling," Caroline responded, miffed at Milly's sense of entitlement. "As you're not working today, why not take the children, too? Bye!"

Caroline replaced the receiver before Milly could reply and unplugged the phone.

Perhaps not having a smartphone wasn't so bad.

Without those lists and nagging notifications bleeping constantly, the day was hers for once.

Gleefully, she selected a luxurious shower gel then opted for some leisurely pampering for the first time in months.

Afterwards, wearing a stylish sundress and sporting an elegant straw hat, with her bag packed, Caroline headed for the nearby beach.

She adored her grandchildren, but it was so much easier without a buggy and other paraphernalia for once.

Following a delicious paddle, Caroline settled down with the book and a cool drink.

As she became absorbed in a complex romance, Caroline couldn't help thinking how nice it was to read something grownup for a change.

Naturally, revisiting favourite children's books from when Milly was small and exploring new ones with Kiki and Joe was lovely, but she missed enjoying something for herself alone.

Soon, with the sun's warmth and soothed by the sound of the sea, gently lapping the nearby shore, letting her novel slip, Caroline relaxed, her eyes closing.

A little later, she was just waking from a snooze, when a dark shape covered the sun.

"Hello. It's Caroline isn't it? Caroline Bateson?" a familiar male voice asked.

She squinted up towards the attractive man smiling at down her, trying to place him.

Of course! Paul Neve. They'd met shortly after Caroline had moved there.

Rather than mope, she'd volunteered at the local charity shop. It had given her something to do and put everything into perspective.

Although she was at once single again and retired, she was, at least, solvent.

Paul was new in town, too, and she'd lent him a sympathetic ear as he'd deposited a box of CDs and books. Later, it emerged that he was in the same boat, too.

"I simply never saw it coming," he'd explained glumly, having filled her in on his story, when they'd sorted his donations.

"Yes, it's difficult but not necessarily the end, just another beginning," she'd said consolingly.

"The secret is to keep yourself busy.

"Focus on the future and what you really want, and don't think about the past unless you're learning from it," she'd advised wisely.

"It's a pity I didn't meet you years ago," Paul had joked.

"Ah but I was a different woman then." She'd laughed, watching Paul leave with more of a spring in his step than he had upon arriving.

"Paul! It's good to see you. How's everything going?" Caroline smiled, and placed down a towel so he could sit on the rock beside her.

"Great, thanks!" he replied, making himself comfortable. "Business is thriving; I joined some of the clubs you suggested and the gym, but I'm having a day off today.

"I'm freewheeling, you know? Just some sketching and a spot of lunch. Care to join me?"

Caroline eyed the seafront burger bar.

"A little farther afield maybe," Paul suggested. "There's a lovely Greek place nearby. Mezze goes beautifully with sea air."

"Why not?" Caroline smiled.

She gathered her things and they strolled towards the restaurant.

"This looks wonderful!" Caroline exclaimed.

"I've always wanted to share it with someone. Running into you must have been fate. Let me repay your kindness from when I first moved here."

"There's a courtyard at the back with a fabulous view. Shall we sit there?"

"Lovely idea!"

As they perused menus, Caroline paused, gazing out at the bay.

"Goodness," she said. "This is like being on holiday. Not that I've had one in a while."

"Really? Why's that?"

"I suppose it's my own fault," Caroline replied thoughtfully.

"I've always coped, but only through careful juggling. Everyone thinks it happens by magic.

"Unfortunately, my daughter takes it for granted. Like today . . ."

The waiter arrived with their food. Caroline began moving things around.

"No, allow me," Paul said. "You do this all the time. Let others take responsibility while you sit back for a change."

"I do believe you're right," Caroline replied, helping herself to olives.

Later, sipping glasssses of retsina, Paul said, "There's a jazz concert Saturday; I've a spare ticket if you'd like to come."

Caroline reached for her smartphone, then remembered she didn't have it.

Lists and schedules were useful, but maybe it was time for some "me" time.

Her mother's defiant glee all those years ago came to mind.

"Yes, please," Caroline said, her eyes sparkling. "I'd really like that." PF

Her Heart's Desire

Was accepting Dan's proposal the right choice for Jade?

BY SHARON HASTON

STANDING on the top deck of the cruise ship, Jade watched the deep pink and orange sunrise streak across the sky.

Had she done the right thing in accepting Dan's proposal last night?

They'd been sitting on their balcony, sipping champagne, when he'd taken her hand.

"Sorry I don't have a ring, Jade, but we get along so well. Would you like to spend the rest of our lives together?"

It had been lovely, even if it wasn't the most romantic proposal in the world.

But Dan wasn't that type of guy. He was practical to his core.

She'd been taken by surprise, squealed with delight, and said yes, but doubts had crept in later.

She kept thinking how her previous engagement with Steven hadn't made it to the altar.

He'd said their relationship "wasn't going anywhere", then started dating someone else a few weeks later.

She didn't think she'd ever fall in love again until she met Dan. But what if history repeated itself?

"Penny for them." Dan handed her a mug of coffee.

"I was just admiring the sunrise," she lied.

Dan put his arm around her.

"It's very pretty. What do you fancy doing today?"

It was a day at sea so there were loads of activities taking place.

"I'd like to go to the Zumba class, the photography talk, and try the quiz later," she said.

Dan watched the fiery orb of the sun cast its long reflection on the still water.

"Looks like it's going to be another glorious day. I'll go to the quiz but I'll give the others a miss. I'd love to catch some rays."

Jade nodded but felt doubts stirring again.

She was loving their first cruise but it seemed to emphasise differences between them that she hadn't really noticed before.

She loved getting dressed up in the evenings and dining in the posh restaurant, whereas Dan preferred wearing shorts and going to the buffet.

They compromised by alternating between the two.

He enjoyed relaxing by the pool, reading a book, whereas she wanted to take part in onboard activities and explore everything each port had to offer.

They returned to their cabin.

Dan grabbed his beach towel and Jade changed into her trainers for Zumba.

"Enjoy, sweetheart. See you in an hour or so." He pulled her in a hug.

She touched his cheek.

It felt slightly rough as he hadn't shaved that morning. The stubble made him look even more handsome.

With his chestnut hair, brown eyes and deep tan, he looked more like a Greek god than a Scottish accountant.

No man had ever made her catch her breath when she looked at them in the way Dan did. Not even Steven.

They'd only been together for a year and this was their first holiday abroad due to work commitments.

Would their differences be a barrier to a lifetime together or did opposites really attract?

• • • •

"I've booked us on that Tangiers trip you were talking about," Dan said whilst waiting for the quiz to start.

She flung her arms around him.

"Oh Dan, that's brilliant. I know you weren't keen but we've never been to Morocco and might never be back. I want to see as much as possible."

He laughed and pointed his phone at her.

"Sightseeing machine mode activated."

• • • •

It was searing hot when they reached the Place de la Kasbah viewpoint.

"Look, we can see our ship and the Straits of Gibraltar from here. Let's take a selfie," Jade said.

Once they'd posed, Dan looked longingly down at the sea and Jade knew he wished he was lying on a lounger.

"We've got some time before we need to get back on the coach. Let's explore," she said, suppressing her irritation at his lack of enthusiasm.

She started to walk away, but Dan pulled her back.

"Watch out! There's a guy over there with a snake!"

Jade screamed as the man approached with the small snake.

"It's not poisonous," the man said. "Do you wish to hold it for a photo?"

Dan took her hand and backed away. "Sorry. My fiancée has a phobia of snakes. Please take it somewhere else."

The snake man nodded. "No problem."

"Are you OK?" Dan asked as Jade shivered.

She took deep breaths. "I'm fine. Thank goodness you noticed him."

They strolled around the ancient medina's narrow alleyways. Many doorways were adorned with patterned tiles in blues, yellows and greens.

"They look like mosaics," Jade said, taking some snaps.

"Time to meet the tour group," Dan said. "I think the souk is up next."

• • • •

"Wow, I've seen it on TV but this is something else."

Jade stared in awe at the rows of spices which were piled high into multi coloured pyramids.

She breathed in.

"What a heavenly smell."

"Would you like to try some?"

She looked down at a smiling young man she hadn't noticed.

He was cooking lamb and couscous in a small terracotta tagine.

"Oh no, I couldn't take your lunch," she said, "but thanks for offering."

"Take some ras el hanout spice with you and you can have the taste of Morocco at home," the man suggested.

"Good idea," Jade said, buying a few packs.

"The guide said you're supposed to haggle," Dan reminded her.

She shook her head.

"It doesn't feel right to try to barter down the price."

Dan straightened her sun hat which had fallen slightly over her eyes.

"It's their culture. They expect you to haggle. It's all part of the fun. Watch."

He approached a stallholder selling Argan Oil and Jade smiled.

He may be loving and easy going but he was an accountant who liked a bargain.

"How much?" Dan asked.

"Three hundred dirhams," the man replied.

Jade had no idea how much that was in pounds or euros but knew that Dan would.

"No chance!" Dan said. "I need your best price."

They bartered good naturedly until eventually Dan handed over 200 dirhams.

"Present for you." Dan handed over the bottle containing golden coloured liquid. "I read in the guidebook it was good for frizzy hair."

Jade glared at him.

"Thanks very much for the compliment! Just what a girl needs to hear."

"What?" Dan asked, completely flummoxed. "You said yesterday that the sun and pool water were making your hair frizzy, so I thought the oil would help."

Jade sighed.

"I did say that. Maybe it will."

Why was Dan always so practical, Jade thought, doubts surfacing again.

But then again, Steven had been romantic, sending flowers and even writing a song for her. And look where that had ended up . . .

Deciding to enjoy the moment, she focussed on the buzz of the souk. It was jaw dropping.

A maze of market stalls with every product you could think of piled in mountains so high they nearly touched the roof.

It was crowded with people, wearing a mixture of North African and European clothes, weaving in and out of the myriad of stalls.

Jade loved the hubbub of chatter, the peeping horns from the traffic outside and the fragrant aroma from the spices.

She now understood what the term "an assault on the senses" meant.

Their next stop was for a camel ride which Jade had been looking forward to most.

Camels sat in rows with colourful blankets over their saddles. Some bellowed; others were placid.

"We have one-humped camels in Morocco," the guide said. "The herders will help you mount. Listen carefully."

"I'll take photos of you," Dan said. "I'm not bothered about riding one. Please be careful."

Jade nodded. She couldn't wait. Dan had said it wasn't for him – he didn't like heights.

Getting on was tricky. Once mounted, the herder told her to lean back.

"They stand using their back legs first."

Gripping the handle, Jade prayed she wouldn't tumble off.

Once up and moving in the caravan of camels, she understood why Dan had declined. She was very high up!

But exhilaration took over. She was riding a camel!

"It's fantastic!" she called, waving to Dan.

It was only a five-minute ride due to the tight schedule, but she loved every minute.

Dismounting wasn't easy either, but the herder helped.

Dan ran over and hugged her. "Well done. I'd have been terrified."

• • • •

"Welcome to Cap Spartel, where the Mediterranean and Atlantic meet," the guide said.

While others rushed to get photos by the sign, Jade and Dan stood at the viewpoint gazing at the water.

Huge cliffs tumbled into the cobalt sea. Waves crashed below.

"You can't see where they meet, can you?" Jade asked.

The guide, Sahid, joined them. "I've tried for years, but it's impossible. Yet they are different. The Mediterranean is warmer and saltier than the Atlantic."

Jade lifted her sunglasses. Two distinct bodies of water, but connected here. Mesmerising.

Sahid moved on, and Jade slipped her hand into Dan's.

He was still staring at the sea, as entranced as she was.

She felt a warm glow – nothing to do with the sun.

Of course she'd been right to accept his proposal.

The Mediterranean and the Atlantic were different but entwined, their waves dancing together.

She and Dan were different too, but they loved each other. That was what mattered.

He may not make big romantic gestures, but he looked out for her in quieter ways.

After some more photos, Dan dragged his gaze from the view and smiled.

"I got a couple of things for you at the souk when you went to the loo."

He handed her a jewellery box. Inside was a sparkling diamante ring.

"I felt bad I didn't have a ring when I proposed. Unusually for me, I hadn't planned it. But maybe this will do until you choose one back home."

He slipped it on her finger. She hugged him. "I love it. Thank you so much."

Reaching into his rucksack again, he handed her a small silver Aladdin's lamp ornament.

"I know I'm not the most romantic guy in the world, but I saw this and knew you'd like it."

He kissed the top of her head.

"I know you were hurt before, Jade, but I promise I'll do my best to make all your wishes come true."

"Dan, that's the most romantic thing I've ever heard," she said, blinking back tears.

How could she ever think he wasn't romantic?

Just like the Mediterranean and Atlantic, he had hidden depths – and she looked forward to exploring them.

She gently stroked the Aladdin's lamp, but knew she didn't need to make any wishes.

Her heart's desire was right here.

Throw In The Towel

Finding the owner of this eye-catching cloth on the busy beach is proving difficult . . .

BY STEFANIA HARTLEY

GREGORIO admits that there are kind women in the world, but his experience has convinced him that they must be a minority.

So he doesn't hold any hope to ever find a soulmate, and lives by the motto "better alone than in bad company".

Unfortunately, there are some practical difficulties with going through life on his own.

For example, there's no-one to look after his clothes when he goes for a swim at the beach.

But Gregorio loves Mondello beach too much to wait for his friends to organise a trip there.

So he wears his shabbiest clothes, takes his oldest beach towel – the one with the print of cartoon fish – and goes on his own.

• • • •

After months of arguing with her boyfriend over the domestic chores, Alessia is single again and intending to remain so.

The experience has convinced her that men are selfish, lazy slobs, and she's better off on her own.

Now that she's done all the crying and self-commiserating her mum and her friends could tolerate, they've sent her to the beach in the hope she will recover her zest for life.

Unfortunately, none of them can go with her, so Alessia packs her towel and water bottle and sets off on her own.

• • • •

When he finally reaches the beach, Gregorio is hot, sweaty and desperate for a swim. He stretches out his towel on the sand, drops his phone into a plastic bag and hides it under the towel, then piles his shoes and clothes neatly by his towel.

Finally, he puts his glasses on top of the pile and heads to the water.

• • • •

Alessia finds the beach crowded, hot and dazzling bright. She struggles to find a space to stretch out her towel and, when she finds it, it's littered.

Alessia picks up the ice-cream wrapper and the discarded magazine.

She will bin them on her way home.

She piles her clothes neatly by her towel, swaps sunglasses for goggles, and heads to the water.

Before diving in, she turns back to memorise the view from the sea, so she can find her spot on her return.

Thankfully, she thinks, her towel with the cartoon fish is easily recognisable.

Alessia returns from her swim tired and cold. She finds her towel and lies down to warm up in the sun.

She loves the feel of the sun on the skin of her back and soon she's thirsty.

She reaches out for her water bottle but her hand only clutches sand.

Strange. She remembers putting her bottle there. Never mind.

She closes her eyes and is gently dozing off when, suddenly, something vibrates under her tummy.

She jumps and scrambles off the towel. She watches with alarm as the eye of a cartoon fish vibrates. A snake? Or a crab?

She yanks the towel and stares. It's a phone, vibrating inside a see-through plastic bag.

She hasn't put it there and it's not her phone.

Neither are the clothes folded in a pile, nor the glasses on top of the clothes or the sneakers with the holes in the toes.

Which means that this towel is probably not hers either. She's been lying on someone else's towel!

She steps back and covers the phone with the towel again. Then, embarrassed, she scuttles away.

• • • •

Gregorio notices that something is wrong when he reaches for his glasses and finds a pair of sunglasses instead.

He's lying belly down on his towel so he's a little disorientated. He sits up and looks around.

Where are his shoes? What's this pile of flowery clothes?

The only thing he recognises is the towel.

But when he runs his hand over the place where he's buried the phone, he finds nothing hard underneath – just soft sand.

He leaps to his feet. This is not his place and this is not his towel, he realises with embarrassment.

He glances over his shoulder, looking for the owner of this towel.

Nobody is standing there, scowling at him. Gregorio leaves quickly and goes in search of his real towel.

He's owned it for almost 20 years and he had assumed there wasn't any other left in Palermo.

Curiosity grips him. Who is the owner of the other towel?

By the time Gregorio reaches his actual towel, he can't get this question out of his head. He puts on his glasses and sets off in search of his towel-twin.

• • • •

Alessia immediately notices that someone has been lying on her towel because he's left a man-shaped indent.

Around the towel, the sand has kept the shape of his steps as he arrived and then left again, hurriedly.

He, too, must have got a shock, Alessia reflects with compassion.

She's about to shake any trace of the man off her towel and lie down on it when curiosity assails her.

Who's this man who has kept his childhood towel for all these years like she has, and who isn't embarrassed of being seen at the beach with it?

Alessia would love to see him. She strolls nonchalantly back towards the other towel, glancing around casually.

The owner hasn't come back yet, so Alessia studies his things.

His sneakers have holes in the toes. He doesn't look after himself, she concludes.

His stained T-shirt and frayed shorts confirm that he's yet another lazy slob.

But she's still curious to see him. She waits a while, but he doesn't come.

Alessia worries about leaving her stuff unattended, so she decides to stroll back and forth along the shore between the two towels, keeping an eye on both.

• • • •

Gregorio has been swimming back and forward between the two towels, looking out for the owner of the other, but he still hasn't seen her.

He has strolled around the place and studied her clothes, her sandals and the magazine lying on her bag.

The title of the magazine's content splashed on the cover – *Treat Them Mean, Keep Them Keen* – makes him think that this woman is one of the unkind and selfish ones.

He really shouldn't give her any more of his time, but he's too curious to give up trying to see her.

He sits on the sand halfway between the two towels to keep an eye on both, pretending to sunbathe.

He remains there even when the sun dips towards the horizon and the other beach goers start packing up and going home.

• • • •

The sun is setting, the beach is emptying and Alessia is considering giving up and going home.

But just as she's about to return to her place and pack up, a thought comes to her.

What if her towel-twin has had an accident?

It's not normal to leave one's possessions unattended for so long!

Perhaps the man in is difficulty out at sea.

Alessia rushes to the lifeguards' post and tells them that a man might be missing at sea.

The lifeguards are packing up, too, but they stop and ask her questions.

Does she know where he's gone? How long ago? Can she describe him?

When it becomes clear Alessia has no idea where the man has gone, she has never seen him nor does she know that he actually exists, they reassure her and continue shutting down their station. Alessia feels silly. How ridiculous to wait all day for a stranger she knows nothing about!

Judging by the state of his clothes, he might well have abandoned them on purpose.

As for his phone, he could have just forgotten it. Men can be careless like that.

Her shoulders are sore with too much sunshine. She should go home.

• • • •

Common sense tells Gregorio that this is getting beyond ridiculous and he should go home at once.

The woman might well have gone home and forgotten her stuff behind.

Anyway, he shouldn't be wasting his time over someone who reads articles like "Treat Them Mean, Keep Them Keen".

Because of this stupid obsession with her, he's missed out on hours of swimming.

Gregorio decides to go for one last swim before heading home. The sea is warm and calm after a whole day of sunshine on the shallow waters.

Now that the crowds have gone, he can swim freely, without fear of bumping into other bathers.

Suddenly, a sharp pain shoots up Gregorio's foot.

He yelps, thrashes and another lash of pain strikes him in the arm this time.

Gregorio yelps again. It's got to be a jellyfish!

He leaps out of the water, hobbling on his stung foot.

A woman approaches him. "Are you OK?"

"Nothing serious. Just a jellyfish," Gregorio says.

"Ouch, that's very painful. I've got an ointment for it. I always take it with me when I go to the beach.

"Wait here," she says.

Gregorio watches her walk towards the towel with the fish and stop there.

She's his towel-twin!

As she returns with the ointment and applies it gently on his stings, Gregorio's chest fills with a warm feeling he hasn't felt for a long time.

"Maybe it's better not to swim when the sun goes down. Have you just arrived at the beach?" she asks.

"No. I've been here for a while," he replies vaguely, unwilling to admit that he's been waiting all day to meet her. "What about you?"

"I've been here for a while, too," she says shyly.

"I was just about to go for an ice-cream," Gregorio improvises, hopeful to spend more time with her. "Can I offer you one?"

"That would be very nice. I'm Alessia, by the way."

"I'm Gregorio. I'll just go and grab my stuff."

• • • •

Alessia watches Gregorio walk towards the fish towel and her heart makes a somersault.

So he's the one she's been waiting to meet all day! He hadn't abandoned his stuff and left the beach after all.

She watches him shake the sand off his towel then fold it neatly. This is not the behaviour of a lazy slob.

"We have the same towel," she tells him when he rejoins her.

"I know." He blushes.

"After my first swim of the day, I accidentally lay down on your towel instead of mine," he confesses.

Alessia chuckles.

"I did the same to yours! It was only when your phone started ringing underneath that I realised the mistake."

Gregorio laughs, then pauses.

"Do you always stay at the beach so long?"

"No," Alessia admits, touching her sun-sore shoulders. "How about you?"

"Me neither," he confesses. "I was too curious to see you to leave before that."

"Me too." She chuckles.

As they step on to the wooden decking, Alessia watches him dust the sand off his feet before putting on his shoes.

"Sand clogs up the vacuum," he explains.

Alessia is impressed that he's thought about that.

He can't be lazy slob, she reassures herself.

On the way to the ice-cream shop, they walk past a refuse bin and Alessia drops the litter she had found on the beach.

"Aren't you keeping your magazine?" Gregorio asks, surprised.

"It's not mine. I found it littering the beach and picked it up," she explains.

"Of course. I should have guessed," Gregorio says with a satisfied smile.

Turn Of The Tide

Could this beautiful treasure from the sea help Violet build a new life?

BY ANNE PACK

VIOLET braced herself against the unforgiving chill of the North Sea. Admittedly, the water only reached her ankles and would go no further and even though it was an almost daily ritual she was never quite prepared for that initial shock which snatched her breath.

As ever, after a minute or so she adjusted to the cold.

It was strangely purging, like a renewal and she wouldn't miss it for anything.

She fully understood the attraction in wild swimming, and the reported feeling of euphoria afterwards, but she certainly wasn't brave enough for that.

As she paddled the glow on the horizon grew in intensity until the first sliver of sun cast a golden ribbon on the choppy water and lit up the sandstone cliffs that sheltered the secluded cove.

It was time to start work.

She stepped out of the shallows, her feet gathering sand like sprinkles on icing and sat down on one of the boulders that protruded through the sand, as if placed there for her convenience.

She brushed off the sand and rubbed life back into her feet with the little towel she'd brought then put on her socks and trainers. Bliss!

From her vantage point, she scanned the beach for a starting point and decided on the wavy line of seaweed marking the highest point the sea had reached.

This was the second exciting part of the day. You never knew what the sea was going to throw up.

With her damp towel secured in its poly bag to be rinsed and dried at home, she repositioned the little basket on to her right hip and marched across the sand, seashells crunching beneath her shoes.

It wasn't long before a glint of blue caught her eye.

She bent down and prised out the first of today's treasures; a sizeable piece of sea glass. It was a promising start.

A short time later with her basket full to the brim she returned home, washed her haul under the outside tap and gravitated towards her sanctuary, the shed at the bottom of the garden, where she'd spend the rest of the day.

"There you go. I'm sure you're ready for this." June, Violet's mum, slipped a mug of coffee and sandwich on to the only vacant space on the work bench.

Violet removed her glasses and put down her pliers.

"Thanks, Mum. You're a star. I'm afraid I lose all track of time when I'm in here."

"I know you do. I expect you don't eat at all during the week when I'm at work." She looked into the tray of new finds. "Looks like it was a good morning's pickings."

Violet picked up a piece of turquoise glass and held it up to the light.

"It usually is after a rough sea. Big waves, big treasure. This'll do nicely as a necklace. I can bore a hole through here," she pointed, "and on the flat surface glue a little silver starfish. What do you think?"

June squeezed her daughter's shoulder.

"I'm sure it'll look stunning, like all your jewellery.

"Right, I'm off. I'm meeting the girls for coffee this afternoon. Your dad's at the golf club." She rolled her eyes. "Where else? So you won't see him for a while."

"I'll probably still be right here when you get home. I want to have plenty of stock for my stall at tomorrow's market.

"It's due to be a scorcher and we're bang in the middle of the school holidays so the town will be heaving."

"Have fun," June called over her shoulder as she gently closed the door.

That's what Violet liked about her parents.

They had welcomed her home after the break-up of her marriage, but weren't at all over-bearing.

It must have been painful for them witnessing her heartbreak and how she withdrew from everything, even giving up work because she couldn't bear to be in the same office as her ex. Yet they never asked any questions. They were simply there for her.

Violet bit into the sandwich. She hadn't realised just how hungry she was. She worked as she munched. There was no time to rest.

She twisted wire, glued pieces together, soldered and drilled her way through the afternoon completing several pieces of bespoke jewellery, after which she mounted them on card and popped them into cellophane pockets.

She didn't have much elbow room as she only had half of the shed for her use, but she was grateful for that.

Her dad had packed all his gardening tools to one side, when her habit of collecting sea litter had organically turned into a money-making venture.

• • • •

"Can you mind my stall for five minutes while I go and get a coffee, Alison?" Violet had been working for hours.

Business had been as brisk as she had expected, with holidaymakers, day trippers and faithful locals.

She was now in serious need of a caffeine fix.

"Off you go, love, and take as long as you like." Alison took the money belt from Violet and returned to knitting a pair of wrist warmers without dropping a stitch.

All the while, she paced up and down behind her stall and chatted to potential customers. It was quite unnerving to watch.

Violet had quickly learned the unwritten rules of the market.

One of which was that stallholders looked out for each other.

Alison, probably ages with her mum, had taken Violet under her wing from that first day when Violet nervously set up her stall.

Part of her had been terrified at her own foolhardy venture and she suffered terribly from imposter syndrome.

Who did she think she was to call herself a jewellery maker?

Yet as the weeks passed her confidence grew along with the transformation of her stall, influenced by what she saw around her.

After weaving her way through the crowds, she joined the queue at the coffee stall, a refurbished horse box.

Violet waited patiently in line, trying not to eye up the tempting muffins and tray bakes on display.

Instead, she determinedly looked the other way, beyond the esplanade which housed the weekly market, towards the beach.

It was still only late morning but there was lots of activity. Sandcastle building, kite flying, cricket, volleyball, and lots of people sunbathing.

A young couple strolling hand in hand caught her eye. She watched wistfully as the young woman held tightly to the top of her hat whilst giggling at something her boyfriend whispered in her ear, reminding her of happier times with Tom.

A tightness spread across her chest. Would the pain ever go away?

She was shaken out of her daydream by a tap on her shoulder and on looking ahead saw that the queue had moved forward but she hadn't moved with it.

"So sorry." Flustered, she turned to the person behind her. "I was daydreaming."

She couldn't see the eyes behind dark glasses but could tell from the little creases at the sides that the man was smiling.

"I don't blame you. I can't wait to get back on the beach myself. I didn't want you to miss your place in the queue, that's all. I'm sure you're desperate to get back to your stall."

Violet's heart missed a beat. She would surely have remembered such a good-looking guy strolling past her stall. She must have looked alarmed because he quickly added.

"It is you I sometimes see at the beach, isn't it, collecting things? Presumably to sell here."

"Yes. It's me, but I don't remember seeing you." The cove was set apart from the main beach and rarely did she see anyone else there.

"I'm usually out on the water on my sail board, so I have a good view of the beach and the cove. What is it you collect? Shells? Driftwood?"

"Sea glass, actually. I make jewellery out of it." She turned her head to the side and pointed out her dangly earrings.

He raised his eyebrows.

"Ah, mermaid tears."

Now at the front of the queue Violet ordered her hot drink before turning back to the man.

"I don't think I've heard that before."

He shrugged.

"Maybe I've got that wrong. I'm sure I heard a tale about it when I was a child. Anyway, nice earrings. I'll maybe drop by your stall later and have a look."

"Please do," Violet said, her insides doing a summersault.

"See you later, then," he said smiling, then turned to the vendor and ordered four coffees.

"Someone's very happy," Alison remarked as she handed back the money belt. Violet hadn't realised she was grinning from ear to ear.

"I've got my fix, that's why." She held up her cup.

All afternoon she couldn't get the man out of her head.

She kept watching for him to appear but eventually the crowds petered out and with no sign of him she had to accept it was probably a throwaway remark.

But there was something about the tall stranger that thawed her heart a little, which was a good sign.

During those awful months after she and Tom split, she swore she'd never get romantically involved ever again.

Over the following week the weather was gloomy, but she made her daily comb of the beach soon after high tide and occasionally found herself looking for him.

When she spotted some windsurfers in the water her heart leapt. It was a popular spot for windsurfers and paddle boarders and people came from all over.

She chided herself for overthinking the situation. Maybe he was just being polite in the queue.

On the other hand, he had noticed her on the beach.

• • • •

On Sunday morning Violet was up early, and her heart skipped a beat every time she thought about the windsurfer and whether she'd see him again.

If he had been sailing during the week he hadn't come ashore to see her, and she'd deliberately stayed longer on those days to give him that opportunity.

It wasn't quite so warm today and it was overcast but there was still lots of activity on the beach.

Footfall through the market was healthy, too, and she sold a few pieces of jewellery.

Between market days and online sales, she was making a living. She'd never be rich, but it was good enough to be doing something she enjoyed.

To think it had all started with long walks in the sand as she nursed her broken heart.

"Hello."

Violet swung round and came face to face with the man she couldn't put out of her mind.

He wasn't wearing sunglasses today, and she found herself looking into the most gorgeous brown eyes, like two swirls of delicious chocolate.

Her pulse raced and she knew her face had turned pink.

"Hello again," she said in a too-high voice.

"I had to leave rather quickly last week so I'm afraid I didn't get a chance to come and see your stall." He took in the entire display in a long, slow, sweep.

"You have been busy." He picked up a bracelet with different coloured pieces of glass hanging from it, like a charm bracelet, and turned it over in his hands. "This is very pretty."

"Thank you." It was one of her favourite designs.

"And you collect all this at the beach, you say?"

"That's right. It's funny to think some of this glass will have been tumbling around in the sea for decades."

He examined piece after piece as he spoke.

"What an amazing hobby. How long have you been doing it?"

"Nearly a year and it's not a hobby. It's my job."

He helped himself to a business card from the table.

"What a great job it must be – Violet." After a pause he added. "Even your name has an artistic ring to it."

"What about you?" she said, suddenly feeling bold. "Is windsurfing your hobby or do you run a school for sea sports?"

He put the card into the pocket of his fleece, looked directly into her face and feigned a frown.

"Alas, it's just a hobby. My friends and I come here as often as we can. It's hard to beat the waves we get here.

"But you're right about the teaching. I teach English at the local school."

Violet felt a warmth spread across her insides at the thought that he was local.

Suddenly his head shot to the side when someone shouted, "Rory!"

He waved his hand in acknowledgement and hastily scooped up the bracelet again.

"I'd like this, please."

"Of course," Violet said pleasantly.

She popped it into a paper bag and handed it over in exchange for payment, curious at the sudden hurry he seemed to be in, and even more curious at who the recipient of the bracelet would me.

"My friends are starting to get impatient," he said as if reading her mind. "They're desperate to get in the water."

He held up the bag before dashing off.

"Thanks for this. I'll . . . I'll see you again."

"I hope so," Violet said, but he didn't hear it.

Her eyes followed him as he caught up with a group of young men and a woman further along the prom.

The woman pointed to the bag and after an exchange of words he handed it over.

She removed the bracelet and held it up. Her face broke into a smile, and she gave him a big hug.

As the scene unfolded, the joy that Violet had experienced just a few minutes ago evaporated like morning mist.

Violet turned away.

She couldn't bear to watch any more. Of course he had a beautiful girlfriend.

Alison, who'd witnessed the whole thing, stretched out her hand.

"Give me your money belt, love. Why don't you take a break?"

Alison was well aware of the trauma Violet had been through, and – like Violet's parents – knew when not to say anything.

Violet ordered a double espresso and supped it whilst gazing out to sea from where she sat on a bench.

Inwardly she gave herself a good talking-to.

She was going to have to get used to the uncertainties that went along with finding a new boyfriend.

It was unfortunate that the first man to turn her head since her marriage break-up turned out to be already spoken for.

On a positive note, it was an indication that she was ready to move on. She had to hang on to that.

Lost in her daydream, she barely noticed someone had sat down at the other end of the bench.

She wasn't in a particularly talkative mood but didn't want to seem rude so to be polite she made up her mind she'd say hello, maybe comment on the weather then get up and return to her stall.

But when she turned to speak, she almost dropped her cup in shock.

"Hi." The man, whom she now knew was called Rory, looked sheepish.

"I thought you'd gone off with your friends."

"I had, but my sister made me come back."

Sister.

"You see I made the mistake of telling her I'd bumped into this amazing woman last week and she was like a dog with a bone."

"I see." Violet didn't see but she could tell he was anxious to blurt something out, so she kept schtum.

"She's very protective of me, her little brother, since my last long-term relationship ran to ground. I haven't dated for some time, and she says that's bad for me.

"I should warn you; she's probably watching us just now."

Violet was aware that his arm was now draped across the back of the seat and that he'd moved a little closer.

"I was a bit confused about the bracelet," Violet admitted.

"Oh, she gave me stick for that. I had told her I was going to ask you out, but instead I bought a bracelet."

"I can give you a refund," Violet offered, starting to see the funny side of it.

"Absolutely not. I really do like the bracelet, and I gave it to her as an early birthday present."

"When is her birthday?"

"Not 'til November."

Violet burst out laughing.

He nudged further closer and looked at her in earnest.

"Can we start again?" He took a deep breath.

"I'm Rory. The first time I saw you on the beach, picking things up, I was intrigued. But then each time I saw you after that I knew I wanted to get to know you.

"I didn't follow you to the coffee stall, for what it's worth. That was a happy coincidence." He fiddled with the hem of his shirt. "Are you doing anything this evening?"

The clouds suddenly parted and a shaft of sunlight filtered through.

Violet didn't need a sign to know this could be a life-changing moment.

"No, I'm completely free and I'd really like to go out with you."

"You would? Oh, that's great." He reached into his pocket. "Shall we exchange phone numbers so we can arrange a time?"

"Yes, let's do that."

Afterwards he stood up and gave her a beaming smile. "'Til this evening."

"I look forward to it." As she floated back to her stall Violet tried to ignore the whoops and cheers coming from the direction of Rory's friends.

The sun, now completely unfettered, glinted off some of her handiwork hanging from a rail and swaying in the breeze.

Out of curiosity she'd research that tale about sea glass being mermaid's tears later.

But for Violet these little bits of coloured glass thrown up by the sea would always represent healing when she needed it most.

She also dared to hope it would be responsible for bringing love back into her life. ■

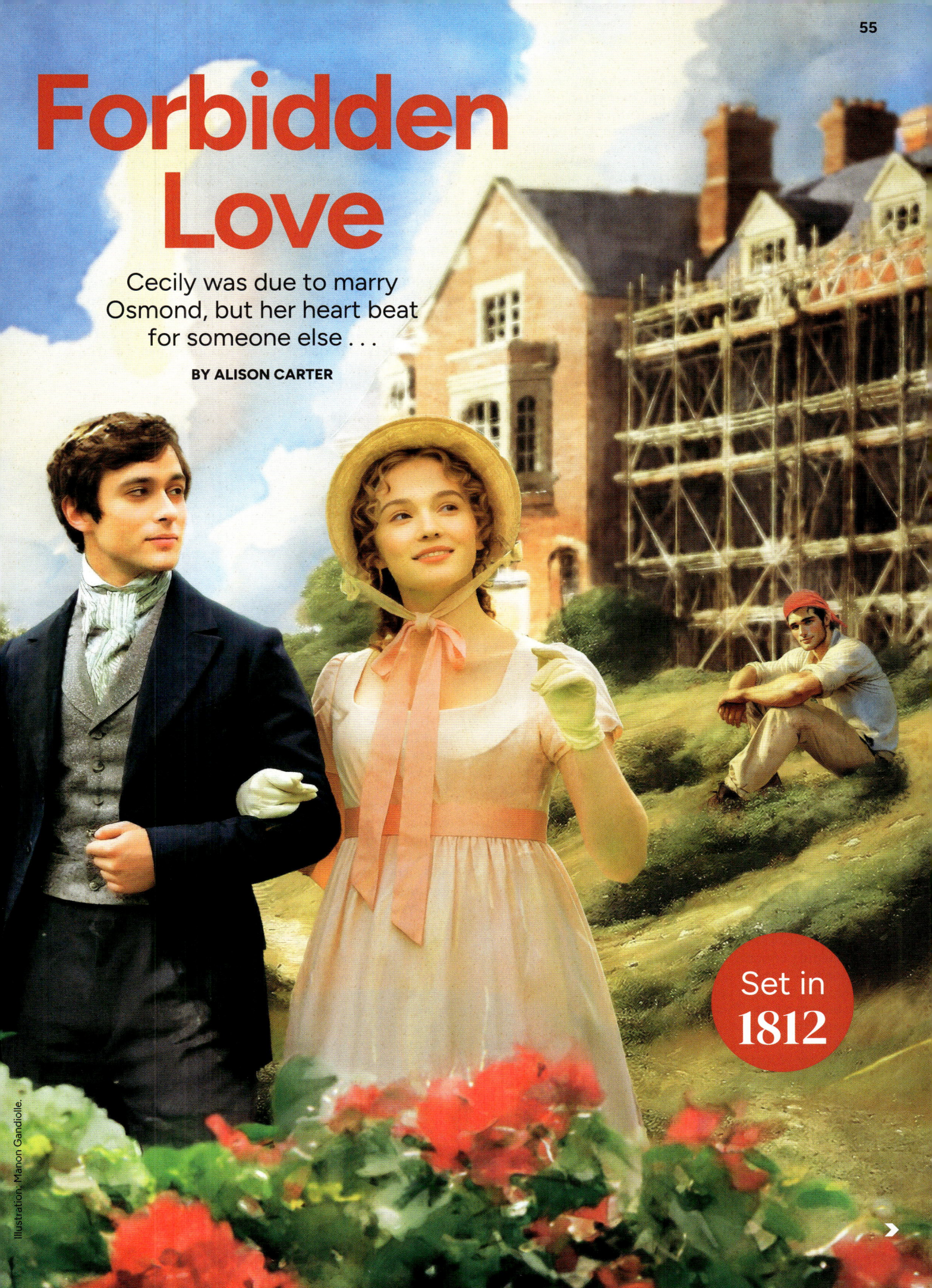

Forbidden Love

Cecily was due to marry Osmond, but her heart beat for someone else...

BY ALISON CARTER

Set in 1812

It was a hot day, hot even for Ryde, which enjoyed the frequent balmy weather and clear skies for which the Isle of Wight was famous.

Cecily Downe had wisely put on her lightest dress for the opening of the school, a double-layered pale pink day gown in lawn cotton.

It had a broad pink satin ribbon under the bust, which bunched up the cloth of the bodice and helped to keep her cool.

"It lets the air in," Cecily whispered to her mother. "Otherwise I'd faint."

"Cecily!" Mrs Downe said. "Must you be so indelicate? And in public!

"And put your bonnet back on! We've appearances to maintain."

Mrs Downe was an ambitious woman, and determined that her daughter would do well in island society.

The family was attending a sort of garden party in the half-planted-up and rather cramped grounds of Mr Playman's Academy for Boy Boarders.

The school was due to accept its first boys as boarders in the early autumn, or so Cecily had been told.

A site for the building project had been carved out of land owned by a friend of Cecily's father.

All the gentlemen of the town were friends of Henry Downe.

Ryde was a small place with a population of less than 1,700 persons, and the people of note knew all the other people of note.

These gentlemen – estate owners and businessmen – were eager to make Ryde larger and far more prosperous.

Her father would explain to Cecily that Ryde cried out for expansion.

As a land and property agent, he was intimately wrapped up in any moves to develop the town.

"We must attract the wealthy, the fashionable visitor," he said.

"All over England and beyond seaside resorts are the coming thing, and Ryde must take its share."

This school, he said, was a harbinger of great things.

It suggested to Henry Downe that money was already starting to flow in.

"There will be a wave of prosperity," he said.

"A veritable rising tide!"

Mr Downe enjoyed a seaside metaphor!

The Academy, like its garden, seemed half-made to Cecily.

She was sure that she could hear hammering from behind the new brick edifice, and a man's voice, shouting.

The school site was in

Upper Ryde.

The town was demarcated into Lower and Upper villages.

Nobody would ever build a school in Lower Ryde, which ran along the shoreline and was crammed with old, timbered houses.

Lower Ryde was inhabited by what Cecily's mother called "seafaring persons".

It was 1812 and the whole country was still basking in the success of Waterloo, and the hope of an end to the wars with France that had dragged on since Cecily could remember.

It was pleasant out in the sunshine, chatting to familiar people, but Cecily could not do that for a whole afternoon.

She wanted to know what lay behind the parts of the building that she could see.

Her mother noticed the direction of her gaze.

"No, you don't, Cecily," she said. "Stay right here beside me and be sociable.

"As soon as you could walk you were in and out of every corner, every part of the house from which you were barred!"

Mrs Downe tilted her parasol towards three approaching figures.

"My saving grace! Here is Osmond Cheverton and his father, too, with your father. Ho there, Henry dear!"

Osmond Cheverton was the son of an estate owner whose land skirted the higher parts of Ryde town, furthest from the shore.

He was a nattily-dressed young man of twenty-eight with accomplished conversation.

He had a certain charm, and Cecily had decided years ago that she liked him.

It was inevitable that Osmond would now become her escort at the garden party.

The older people would want to talk about the town and Osmond would guide her away for a walk.

She was correct in her surmise and five minutes later her arm was in his.

They were winding their way around flower beds and past a clean, white, new fountain with no water coming out of it.

"They need to get a move on, these builders," Osmond said, prodding a fledgling box hedge with his cane.

"A number of the men whom the site owners have engaged to do the donkey work here are lobster-basket fellows and skinners of fish, without the skills."

He chuckled.

"I've told my father we need men from the mainland, if we're really to get things moving."

Cecily suggested that they leave the chattering crowd of ladies and gentlemen and take a look at the rest of the building.

Osmond was reluctant, but Cecily talked about needing shade.

"My arms and shoulders are uncovered," she said. "The house faces south and so we are in full sun."

He gave in and led her round the gable end of the school.

• • • •

Osmond Cheverton was going to marry Cecily Downe.

The solidity of that fact that had crept up on Cecily before she had noticed.

All three parents wanted the match (Mr Cheverton was a widower).

She was a suitable twenty-three to his twenty-eight years.

He was healthy, he was rich (or at least, he would be in the future) and they knew each other well.

He was tall and slender with a good nose and could ride a horse, so why not?

This understanding meant that they naturally ended up together at functions and festivals, as they had today.

More recently, Osmond had begun to talk about their married life and Cecily had begun to get used to it.

The spring of 1813 seemed a good time to arrange the wedding, soon after her birthday but avoiding Easter.

It was a settled thing.

The back of Mr Playman's Academy for Boy Boarders looked quite different from the front. Cecily found it hard to imagine any little boys living here, in rooms that were open to the elements for now.

She could not think of them walking about with their slates and pencils in the brick and plaster dust that lay all around.

"Take the end!"

A big, raucous voice cut through the air.

Cecily recognised it as the voice she had heard faintly from the front of the building, shouting.

She looked up to see a big, tall man with a beam in his arms that was so large that she thought it might bring him down if he took a single step to right or left.

A smaller man was hurrying precariously along a naked joist to receive the other end of the beam.

"There you go," the voice said again. "Good man. Lower it down."

This dangerous-looking work was going on at height, two full storeys above her.

Even at ground level, Cecily could see the man's muscles, the shine of perspiration on his brow, the glint of his sharp blue eyes as he and his colleague brought the beam into position.

When it was set down, he turned and, sensing people below, sought out the figures of Cecily and Osmond in the half-shadow.

He removed a scarlet handkerchief that was tied around his head, just as though it was a cap being doffed, and nodded his head.

"Good afternoon," he said.

Cecily stepped forward without thinking – two, three, four steps.

Weeks after that July day, she came to understand that even then, even before she knew anything of the man, she had experienced an urge to get closer to him, and to see more of him.

Later, she also remembered how Osmond had followed her quickly, his arm stretched out as if to hold her back.

He was interrupted in his attempt to draw her away by a yell from the smaller man and the sight of him toppling.

"Whoa, there!" the big man called out. He reached out a hand, which was grabbed.

They hung there for a few seconds, the two labourers, in a balancing act, before straightening up and grinning at each other.

"Cecily, your shoes!"

She looked down. Osmond was pointing to her new silk shoes.

One of them was coated in red brick dust. The near-accident above her had dislodged it in a shower.

"It's a disgrace!" Osmond called up to the men. "Look what you have done."

Cecily tried to say that it was unimportant.

She had been silly to wear cream-coloured silk to a garden party, she said, and they could be cleaned.

"These men have no idea what they're doing." Osmond was scowling.

Cecily saw a look pass between the men.

The face of the labourer above was neutral, but she was sure she saw the slightest hint of challenge.

The face of Osmond, the man below, was angry, his cheeks flushed.

"Come," Osmond said, and at last they moved away. "I know that fellow.

"He's one of the beach porters. They're low sort of men, all of them."

"Do you know that porter in particular?" she asked.

"He's called Luke Attrill. They say he's one of the good ones, and I suppose that's down to his size.

"He seems thoroughly insolent to me."

• • • •

Ryde had a special and inconvenient geography.

Its unusually shallow coastal waters stretched a mile out to sea, making it impossible for a vessel of any size to approach the shore, except at the highest tide.

Anyone coming to the town from the sea had an uncomfortable experience, coming ashore.

There were horse-drawn carts for hire that went out and trundled travellers through the shallows, but they often got stuck in the sand.

There were also mud flats that were dangerously slippery with their patches of blue slipper clay.

Cecily had seen a hundred strandings.

The other method – less dignified but more likely to succeed – was to be borne ashore, piggyback-style, by one of the beach porters.

Once a passenger got to the tide's edge, whether in a vehicle or on a man's sturdy back, he (or she) could continue on foot.

They would still have to walk as much as half a mile across wet sand, depending on the state of the tide, even after their ride on a cart or porter's back.

Cecily walked back to the party with Osmond, shaking dust from her shoe.

"I know that the porters are ranked according to how well they do their job," she said. "It's not written down, but it's known by everyone.

"I think my cousin Mary, who comes across from the mainland often to visit us, has her favourites."

"Let's talk no more of the porters," Osmond said.

"Let's talk of which house we shall live in, next year when we are married.

"I have my eye on a newly built one on the Fishbourne road."

Cecily knew more than she was saying about the porters.

She knew that a man called Attrill often carried Osmond's sister, or his mother, ashore.

She was fairly sure that he must have carried Osmond, too, several times – though Osmond would never admit to that.

Like most men, even sailors, he could not swim, but he would want to appear manly.

Cecily herself had only been carried once or twice – she had little reason to go out in the bay.

• • • •

Osmond's sister Lucinda found them as soon they got back to the party.

Lucinda was less than a year younger than Cecily, and they had been friends since their toddling days.

Sometimes Cecily forgot how close they were in age, because Lucinda was much younger in her ways.

She liked to stay close to her brother as much as she could, like a pretty little shadow.

She was an unusually adoring sister.

Their mother had died when Lucinda was seven and their father was always taken up with business, so Osmond was her world.

Cecily had observed her friend as the years had passed.

Lucinda was fragile, her motherless state more problematic for her than she would admit to.

It seemed to Cecily that her marriage to Osmond would provide Lucinda with certain guarantees – a safe place among people she knew, and the tying of many familial knots.

"Sister Cecily!" Lucinda cried, taking Osmond's other arm and addressing Cecily by leaning forward as they walked, so as to see her friend as she spoke.

"My brother is naughty, taking you away like that.

"We will be sharing him in time, as well you know, and you are not to steal him!"

She was laughing as she said it, but to Cecily it was a reminder of the girl's reliance on her brother.

Osmond loved Lucy and he liked to be adored, but sometimes Lucinda seemed like a lap dog to him.

He would lay her down in her basket, as it were, when he had more pressing or interesting matters to hand.

• • • •

Cecily returned to the school a few days later in the early morning.

She was carrying a package of books tied with string, a donation from her mother.

Cecily struggled to see how the boys would benefit much from the volumes of sermons.

They'd be walking down to St Thomas's Church almost daily anyway, to be talked at by the minister.

However, the Downe family had an interest in

supporting the school, because Cecily's young cousins from Portsmouth would be attending as boarders, once it opened.

She walked towards the grand oaken front door, but then changed her mind.

There was no need to bother the school's new headmaster, or any of the academic staff.

She could simply go around the side, or possibly round the back, and leave the books with a member of domestic staff.

If Cecily had been entirely honest with herself, she would have acknowledged that hardly any domestic staff had been engaged.

As yet they had no finished kitchens, nowhere to ply their trade, with those parts of the school still under construction.

She pushed those facts from her mind as she came in sight of the little team of labourers, working away.

The big man was nowhere to be seen.

Cecily stopped another man in shirt sleeves, and asked where she could leave the books.

"I haven't a clue, miss," the man answered.

She was about to go back round to the front, when Luke Attrill appeared from behind her, wiping his hands on a rag.

Cecily swallowed.

He shut out the sun that was about to dip behind the building, and his presence made her feel a little dizzy.

"I believe you are Mr Attrill," she said.

"Are you foreman here? Could you take charge of a donation for the school? These are books."

Lamely, she held out the parcel to him.

He nodded. His blue eyes matched the sky.

"I can see they're books, miss," he said.

"I am sorry," she said. "I did not mean to suggest you don't recognise a book."

A second passed, then his face broke into a grin.

"No need for sorry," he said. "I can read, but I'm no foreman.

"Come with me. I'll see if we can find Mrs Parsons.

"She's by way of a housekeeper, and the only domestic staff so far."

He had an easy way about him that was new to Cecily.

It was captivating – the swing of his leg, the roll of his shoulders.

Without her making any enquiry, he told her things about the project, the number of its rooms.

"But this only is what I hear," he said. "I only do piece work, in the time I can spare from my main job.

"Usually I'm here in bad weather, when I can't work my usual craft, but today they needed extra labour so I came."

"You are usually a porter down on the beach?" she enquired casually.

He paused, and the books swung in his hand from the bow that Cecily had tied an hour before.

Suddenly, she wanted to be that bow in his grasp, and she raised her hand to her throat at the shock of entertaining the thought.

"I am. It's good that there's plenty of building underway in Ryde, for I have brothers and sisters to keep now my father's dead.

"The porterage hasn't been enough, even in summer," he said.

• • • •

It took some time to find Mrs Parsons.

As they went along, putting their heads around doors, making enquiries, Cecily felt that she would like to stay here for ever, on a dirty building site.

Most of the men seemed to be taking a rest; the whole place was quiet.

Birds sang loudly in the beech trees and she was sure she could hear the wash of the sea, far below.

"That lady has run away to America, I think," Luke Attrill remarked.

"Or she's a-hiding from us." He looked down at her. "Do you think she is a-hiding, Miss Downe?"

He had an eccentric way of speaking, a lively way, full of odd twists and turns.

He had made her laugh many times in the 20 minutes of their acquaintance.

"I would like to believe she has gone to America to seek her fortune," she said.

He laughed. When he stopped, he looked at her again.

The skin at Cecily's throat prickled under his gaze.

"Perhaps she likes to see a maid and a man in good conversation," he said.

"And so she has tucked herself behind a laundry basket to watch us, and will come out when we stop."

Cecily wanted to say, "perhaps".

She wanted to smile her sweetest smile and say, "Then we shan't stop".

She wanted to touch him, if only to put her hand on the hand that held her package.

But it hit her forcibly that this man was not for her, and that she was promised to another man in her own station in life.

"I will come back another day," she said.

She held out a hand for the books, and he gave them to her.

Yet when she left, Cecily knew her life had changed, and so had her heart.

• • • •

There was far more planned for Ryde in the way of construction.

There was something other than schools, houses and hotels and shops – something remarkable.

But it was only weeks later that Cecily Downe found out about it.

Her mother had gone to Newport to buy notions, and the task fell on her daughter to serve coffee and cakes to a group of the important men of the town, who had met for a discussion.

Mr Cheverton was there, lounging in a carver chair with his jacket off.

He gave Cecily a wave when she entered with a tray, and made her blush by calling out that Osmond had not seen her for days and missed her.

The other men smiled or laughed, and she wished that Mr Cheverton had not singled her out.

The coffee served, she waited on the other side of the half-closed door and listened.

They talked of a new corporation they had formed, and of its purpose.

"We did it in timely fashion," her father said.

"The Ryde Pier Company is set up and ready, and now we have an Act of Parliament to allow it to do its great work!"

Cecily stayed where she was for half an hour, and in that time learned about the thing which Ryde needed most for its success as a destination for holiday-makers and other visitors.

It needed a pier.

She had heard of piers, but felt sure as she listened that there were none yet made in Britain.

One of the gentlemen confirmed this.

"Our pier will be the first in the land!" he said.

The excitement was evident in his voice.

"We need a pier more than

any other coastal town in Britain, and now we may have one. And the funds are being raised!"

The men agreed, slapping each other on the back.

Cecily understood their meaning.

Ryde's unique geography meant that, if a way could be found to take people, vehicles and goods out to where the water was deep enough for normal vessels, the town and its fortunes would be transformed.

"An Act of Parliament, just for us and passed days ago," her father declared.

"Gentlemen, we are at the start of a great work!

"A timber pier of 1,600 feet is permitted in the act."

They fell silent, absorbing for a moment the enormity of it. Then there was uproar, the stamping of feet and the clinking of coffee cups.

"To the pier!" Mr Cheverton called out.

"To the pier!"

Cecily retreated to the kitchen and watched the cook work on luncheon.

Of course a pier was the answer, and she was proud that these men had made all the progress that they had worked for.

Their motivation was powerful, she knew.

All of them would be enriched by the changes in Ryde, whether by selling land, profiting from the sale or expanding their various businesses.

However another thought struck her.

This great structure, sticking out into the sea and serving so many purposes, would alter the look of the coast for ever.

It would change all the industries of the town.

More shellfish would be sold, more young men and women hired in hotels and shops and leisure destinations.

But one group of men would lose their livelihood – one important, unique, valued group.

It was the porters who carried folk to the beach.

Cecily reminded herself sternly that she was not to be concerned with those men. She was the daughter of an important gentleman in the town.

With the help of these friends, her father was driving forward the future of Ryde and its people.

Cecily thought of the pier and tried to forget the blue, blue eyes of Luke Attrill.

• • • •

Cecily's head told her to keep away from Luke, but her heart – and her feet – disobeyed.

She found reasons to go to Lower Ryde – offers to fetch shellfish for Cook or pay a bill for firewood.

A retired maid of the household now lived with her son down on Castle Street, and she was unwell.

Cecily said she would take a basket of food.

"You will wear out your new shoes," Mrs Downe remarked.

Cecily looked at the shoes and saw the faint cast of red across the silk.

She felt a rising anxiety that she might never see Luke again. Not if she acted as she ought and kept herself away from him.

Yet she did see him.

One day she told her mother she would fetch eggs for Cook, who had several extra guests for luncheon.

Luke Attrill was returning from his shift in the water, stomping up the cobbles, drips falling from him.

There was spray that day, the result of a sharp summer wind, and his dark brown hair was frosted with salt crystals.

"Miss Downe," he said. "I'm not fit to be seen."

He reached for the red kerchief and found it was not on his head.

His breeches were plastered to him, dark and slick, and the odd bespoke galoshes worn by all the porters were blue-black with mud.

The words flowed out of her like spilled milk before the jug can be righted.

"You look very fine to me," she said.

The sentence might have meant nothing, had it been framed as a simple politeness.

But Cecily was looking at Luke as she said it, and on her face was expression of longing.

It was as though she could see her own face in a mirror, her eyes shining, the cheeks flushed, her heart beating visibly through the wall of her chest.

"Miss Downe," he said again.

There was distress in his voice, or perhaps it was the same longing she felt.

They were standing near the entrance to an alley, an ancient, narrow passageway that ran up from the shore. It was a way for crates to go to carts on the higher road.

Instinctively, she took the three steps necessary to be hidden by its high walls and obscured from view by its shade.

After a moment staring down the alley towards her, he did the same.

There was hardly an inch between them now, and the mud, the salt and the fear could not stop them.

He knew she had invited him. He kissed her and told her he could think only of her, every minute of his day.

She gave him the same in return, just as earnestly and just as honestly.

Finally a figure appeared at the far, upper end of the alley and they both hurried out into the sunshine, popping out of the passageway like two corks.

Cecily's dress was smeared, and her head was reeling with excitement.

• • • •

Osmond called at the Downe home the following afternoon.

Mrs Downe ordered tea and was about to make some excuse to leave the lovers alone.

"But Mrs Downe, we hardly have a moment to converse," Osmond said. "Do stay – there are three cups, after all."

Osmond was not usually a man who sought the company of forty-five-year-old ladies, and Cecily's mother was clearly surprised.

Still, she sat and he talked about the heat and the pier.

The date when a foundation stone might be laid was uncertain.

"I think you were by the shore yourself yesterday, Cecily?" he said.

"Cecily went on an errand, yes," Mrs Downe said.

She paused, the sugar tongs suspended over Cecily's cup.

"But now I think of it, did I not see Cook walking down to the lower village later?"

She turned to Cecily, the silk of her gown rustling.

"Did you fetch the eggs, after all, Cecily?"

"I don't know about the eggs," Osmond said. "But my sister saw Cecily on the cobbles, in the spray."

Mrs Downe dropped in the sugar cube and smiled.

"And how is darling Lucy? I declare we must think of finding a young man for her. I was only with Mrs –"

"Lucinda is well, thank you." Osmond interrupted.

He was angled towards Cecily now, his legs crossed in her direction.

"My sister came home, worried. She believes – no, she is sure – that one of the beach porters took liberties with Cecily."

Mrs Downe's mouth fell open. She turned sharply to face her daughter.

"Liberties? Is this true, my dear?"

Cecily tried to respond, but Osmond kept going.

"One of those big fellows always thick with the mud and sand.

"Lucinda was passing and saw the man follow Cecily down an alley."

Cecily could see that he was weighing up his next words, deciding whether or not to say them.

"Lucinda was certain the blackguard must have acted badly, because Miss Downe had stains of sand and mud on her gown and she appeared upset.

"I understand that you would not want to speak of

such an incident.

"I hope it is in fact untrue, because I would have the fellow horsewhipped and —"

"I was not upset by Mr Attrill," Cecily said clearly.

She would not lie, yet she could not be entirely honest either.

"I was perfectly all right. The alley was too narrow for both him and I, that is all."

That was true. It was too, too narrow!

He leaned towards her.

"I will protect you, Cecily," he said. "Know that I will."

Mrs Downe was flustered, not really understanding what was happening.

Cecily knew.

Lucinda loved her, but she loved her brother more, hung on his every word and obeyed him in everything.

Lucinda had most probably seen what had happened on the cobbles, or at least had seen her before and after the alley, and she had reported all to Osmond.

• • • •

Cecily and Luke contrived to meet.

It was a difficult thing to achieve, but nothing would keep them apart now.

Between their kisses they talked, but skated carefully around the central subject, which was how they could ever be together.

They walked inland on quiet paths cracked by the July sun. They spoke of the pier project, and how it threatened to wipe out all the porters' jobs in one fell swoop.

"Yet we cannot stop it. And we should not," Luke said philosophically.

She nodded sadly.

"I know. Progress will come, and it must. The town needs this change."

"The rich men want it and the poor need it," he said. "Think of what can be sold to visitors, think of the new jobs that will be the result."

"But not for you, Luke," she said mournfully.

"Not for a porter, no. But I have a reputation, of sorts. The wealthy men will give me other work, I'm sure.

"The school up there is nearly done, but I have high hopes that my name will be passed on for other projects."

"Your name passed on. Luke Attrill," she said. "It is the sweetest name."

She took a breath and dared to murmur, "Mrs Cecily Attrill."

He pulled her close.

"That's far sweeter," he answered.

• • • •

A fortnight later Lucinda Cheverton returned from a visit to her aunt and uncle in Gosport, over on the mainland.

It was a dull, humid afternoon.

The girl rarely travelled, preferring the safety of life at home.

Cecily was surprised Lucinda had gone.

Osmond had told Cecily that he would be accompanying her.

"It's a jaunt," he said. "Brother and sister."

Cecily was not present when Lucinda fell into the sea on the way back into Ryde.

She heard the sorry tale in all its detail from Lucinda herself, soon afterwards.

News was brought to the Downes' house that poor Lucy Cheverton had nearly been drowned in more than three feet of water.

Cecily ran the half mile to the Cheverton mansion, further up the hill.

"It was the biggest of those porters!" Lucinda said.

She was sitting in a large chair, swathed in blankets despite the heat, a pair of her brother's leather slippers dwarfing her feet.

"It was that dark-haired one with the eyes!"

It seemed that this porter had dropped Lucinda, with appalling clumsiness, into the water.

"I was tipped in like so many pounds of potatoes!" she said. "I should have hired one of the carts, and not entrusted my person to such a fellow. Never again!"

"This was Mr Attrill?" Cecily asked, her face turning pale.

"I don't know why you should call him 'mister', Cecily," Lucinda said. "He's a brute. I don't think he took any care of me at all!"

It seemed unlikely to Cecily that Luke had been so clumsy, especially in calm waters.

She could not remember any slips or accidents among the porters for years, at least not when the weather was fine.

Luke was the strongest of them and had the most experience.

Lucy Cheverton was light as a feather.

"Luke Attrill?" Cecily repeated, laying a hand on her friend's knee.

Lucinda looked away, her face flushed, and in the movement Cecily saw the evasion in her.

Lucinda's story was not all it purported to be.

• • • •

Luke told her the facts of the incident.

He was distressed, pacing back and forth.

They had stopped in front of an iron bench that they had passed on their walk.

"I never lose my grip!" he declared.

There were tears coming and his voice was cracked with emotion and frustration.

"I know my job, though it's a lowly one, and I have earned my reputation.

"The young lady cast herself down! She lurched and wriggled.

"I held on — I know how to be delicate, Cecily, but still keeping my passenger secure.

"She made sure that she got out of my arms and she cast herself into the sea.

"And if I'd not taken her up again right away and borne her high on my shoulders, she might have got into trouble, with all the thrashing she did!"

Cecily asked if anyone had witnessed the accident.

Luke pressed his lips together and hesitated.

"Tell me," she said.

"Only Master Cheverton, her brother," he said in a quieter voice.

• • • •

Luke was banished from his porterage job.

Mr Cheverton made sure that there was no dissention among the influential men of Ryde.

The safety of a lady, they said, was paramount, and a man who had shown this disregard could not possibly continue in the work.

"This gives us even more reason for the pier," Mr Downe said. "It can come at no better time."

Luke found doors closed to him all over the island.

Downe, Cheverton and the rest had fingers in many pies, and the news of his failure went ahead of Luke.

One day he dared to call at Cecily's house.

He stood at the side door, his clean handkerchief twisting in his hands.

"I saw your mother and father leave a quarter hour ago," he said, "in the carriage, and so I came.

"I don't care that your servants may see me. I had to come to you and say goodbye.

"A man I know on Hayling Island has offered me work, and it's a good position."

Hayling Island was only seven miles away by sea, but to Cecily it was as though it was a distant place, as inaccessible as the Indies.

"No," she said. "Please."

"But I have to earn for my family. I have to. I can send money home with this job."

"But you cannot come yourself. You cannot send yourself back to me."

"One day?" he said, a question in his tone.

But she could not see how it could be. The island was closed to him.

"When do you leave?" she asked.

"Michael Lawson, a friend among the porters, has a brother who lives west of Ryde. He says he can leave off fishing for a day.

"I'll pay him to carry me across the Solent. He says we can go Sunday next."

"That's five days away," she said eagerly. "In five days, we can —"

"We cannot," he said. "We part here."

He kissed the palm of her hand and gently let it go, so that her arm slowly fell into the space between them.

"I could not bear to stretch this pain out longer than another minute."

He was crying, the tears falling to the step, and she cried, too.

Their marriage had never been a possibility, not really. But now it was a fantasy.

• • • •

Cecily carried on living. She got herself through the rest of that day, and the next.

Her mother complained that she ate nothing. Cecily tried to eat and to talk, but the light had gone out of the landscape.

The birds in the garden seemed to have stopped singing and the air was hot and thick as soup.

As the next few days passed, July turned into August, and on the Friday, Lucinda was shown into the drawing-room.

Cecily was sitting by a window, not looking at the book in her lap.

"We are to go on an adventure!" Lucinda said. "Osmond has bought a boat and we are to have an expedition in it!"

"A boat?" Cecily repeated.

It seemed an odd thing for a young man to purchase, especially a man who was hoping to marry.

Boats for leisure use were rare – Cowes was only just showing signs of becoming a place where the yachts of gentleman were moored.

Any boat cost a great deal of money.

However it seemed that Osmond had indeed bought a brand-new boat with a single lug sail, and a small ring sail at the stern.

It had comfortable benches for ladies, and a wooden store on deck for stowing a picnic.

The weather was set fair and a party of six including Cecily would set off in the Chevertons' carriage, along the coast to Cowes, where they would set sail for a half day of boating.

"You will come, of course," Lucinda said.

She was pleading.

Cecily looked into her small, vulnerable face and was certain that she saw guilt there.

Cecily did not know who had thought up the scheme to discredit Luke out in the bay.

It was easy to believe that this girl, who would give her right arm for her brother, had acted alone.

Lucinda simply wanted Cecily to marry her brother.

Cecily decided to be charitable towards Osmond.

She only knew that Lucinda had thrown herself into the sea; Osmond might well have had nothing to do with it.

Lucinda was so much her brother's acolyte that she could feasibly have contrived to disgrace the man who might stand in the way.

And would Cecily marry Osmond now?

In her low mood, she did not see that there was anything else to do.

• • • •

Osmond was in fine fettle that Sunday morning.

In the carriage, tucked between Cecily and a third young lady, he talked about his boat.

"It's only a Jolly Boat," he said happily. "But I've had it fashioned exactly to my liking in Cowes harbour."

Cecily knew what a Jolly Boat was – a one-sailed vessel with oars, usually for ferrying sailors on and off a large ship.

"I am in exalted company!" he said. "You ladies will know that the first boat built at Cowes was made for Elizabeth I in 1589. The *Rat O'Wight* was its name."

"What a funny name," Lucinda said, and the other girl laughed with her.

"That's only because you don't know history," Osmond said. "Mark my words — yachting will be fashionable at Cowes, and I am in the vanguard."

Osmond was fractious with his sister, interrupting her and saying she talked too much.

When he handed Lucinda out of the carriage, Cecily heard him say that Lucinda should have stayed at home.

"You put limits on me," he said softly. "I want to enjoy myself."

Lucinda scuttled away, her head bowed, dabbing at her eyes with a handkerchief.

Later, as they walked to the quay, and Lucinda offered to serve the picnic for her brother, he batted her away and made a remark that Cecily half-heard.

It was something about Lucinda "suffocating" him.

• • • •

Cowes harbour was not large, and on a Sunday it was quiet.

Cecily could see only a dozen or so men who were removing barnacles from an upturned boat.

Beyond that, on a short jetty 25 yards distant, a group of men were loading up a small fishing lugger.

One of the men stood to his full height and Cecily saw that it was Luke.

Her stomach turned over and, with an involuntary movement, she put out a hand to steady herself.

Osmond, standing beside her, took it.

"That's the porter, isn't it?" he said softly.

"The fellow who nearly drowned my sister."

Cecily wasn't listening.

Her eyes had locked on Luke's, even with so many yards between them, and even with swaying masts criss-crossing the space between them.

They stayed staring for what seemed an hour but was probably seconds.

Then Luke got back to getting his things on board, ready for the crossing.

"That oaf," Osmond said, "off to pastures new.

"Do you know, in the disaster of Lucinda's accident, I near forgot that you suffered at his hands."

The third young woman on the trip, Emma, the good-natured daughter of a local landowner, saw where they were looking and came to stand beside them.

"Oh, wicked Mr Attrill," she said. "I confess that he'll be missed for his handsome face and his strong arms.

"Half the ladies on the island have sighed for Luke."

Cecily saw Osmond's fist close, the knuckles turn white, and his chin stiffen.

He wanted rid of his rival.

Once they were on board, Osmond showed Cecily and Emma the boat.

He said he had plans for a larger one, in time.

Cecily wondered again about the expenditure.

The Chevertons were well off, certainly, but did Osmond's father approve?

He noticed her puzzled look and laughed.

"Oh, once we are married, my own Cecily, I will be a veritable angel of a spouse!"

• • • •

The flat calm in the Solent that day should have warned the three young gentlemen aboard that a change in the weather was coming.

Even four minutes out from the quay, with the two other men rowing and laughing and arguing about which was port and which was starboard, the water had begun to rise and fall in a long, bilious swell.

Cecily wanted nothing more than to go home.

Seeing Luke and hearing Osmond insult him, she was beginning to understand that Osmond the husband might be a different man from Osmond the beau.

Her spirits had plummeted.

"Cheer up, ship mate!" Osmond said to her.

Cecily could no longer see Luke. The lugger was hidden behind a larger boat.

She took deep breaths and told herself to be dutiful, to take the good things offered to her, to be realistic.

She had her eyes half closed and her mind on her own thoughts, and did not see Osmond stand up in the middle of the boat.

No attempt had yet been made to use the sails, and Cecily had already sent up a little prayer that they would never get far enough out of the harbour for Osmond to think of it.

"Ship the oars!" he cried, and Cecily opened her eyes.

He was swaying, laughing, pointing at his friends.

"Put them away!"

She saw the main boom before she heard it swing slowly across and come into contact with the back of Osmond's head.

It wasn't a dangerous impact; in fact there was something comical about it.

Osmond teetered, tall and slender like a willow sapling in a high wind, before losing his balance and tipping over the side and into the sea.

The loud laughter of the other men and the third girl carried on for seconds before it stopped abruptly, interrupted by the cries of Osmond as he flailed in the water.

"But he can swim, surely?" Emma asked.

"No." Lucinda's voice was high and thin.

"Neither of us can."

In fact there was nobody on the boat who knew how to swim.

It took them three seconds to realise it and another two to be all staring down at Osmond.

The swell lifted him up and down. He managed to seize the rudder for a little while, but a bigger wave dragged him away after a quarter of a minute.

Cecily felt powerless.

Lucinda was letting out short screams, waving her arms in the air.

Emma, bolder, had flung herself beside the men, over on Osmond's side of the boat and all of them were reaching out uselessly.

Osmond was ten feet away, between the boat and the quay, his head in and out of the waves, his face ashen, shouting at intervals for help.

The boat itself was tipping perilously in his direction, with so much of the weight of passengers displaced.

Then Cecily saw a dark head and two arms, cutting rhythmically through the water towards them.

She knew instantly that it was Luke and she almost laughed in relief.

Naturally he would come; of course he would have heard the commotion.

He was the best swimmer on the Isle of Wight.

Emma and the men fell back, landing on their rears in the bottom of the boat and watching events unfold.

Cecily did laugh, but to herself. It was a little piece of theatre.

Lucinda was watching, too, enthralled, as if she were waiting for a scene to begin in an opera.

It took Luke only minutes to pull Osmond to shore, his strong arm tucked under Osmond's chin.

The men rowed the boat back in chaotic fashion. Everyone disembarked and went home.

Osmond was not a bad man; he was just a rather trivial one.

He was suitably grateful for being saved.

"I would have drowned," he said soberly.

• • • •

They were all together the following morning, the Cheverton and Downe families.

Lucinda was plying Osmond with hot toddies. He was pushing her away.

"The fellow had no thought for himself," Mr Cheverton said.

Next, Osmond confessed that it had been his idea to destroy Luke Attrill's reputation, and that his sister had merely cooperated in the scheme.

"I'd do anything for you," Lucinda said, her eyes wild.

There were further conversations, Cecily knew, in the Cheverton house.

Osmond, she was informed, would be going away for a year.

"On the Grand Tour, to Italy, France, Switzerland," Lucinda said.

"Father will send him a fixed allowance. Father did not know about the purchase of the boat."

Lucinda looked miserable. She was thinner than she had been even days before.

"How will I go on without my brother?" she asked Cecily plaintively when they were alone.

"Can you forgive me?"

"I can, dear," Cecily said.

Lucinda was a child and a sorry sight, and had been so much led on.

"Osmond may write to me now and then," Lucinda said with a sob.

"Perhaps the time has come to think of yourself. You have your own life and your own future, Lucy," Cecily said.

The girl looked up at her, confused, as though she did not believe such a thing.

"Osmond should not make your choices for you."

"He has before," Lucinda said with a frown.

"But you have your own brain. I know you can find your own way."

"It feels frightening," Lucinda confessed.

"Since before I can remember, he made my choices. Perhaps not all of them perfect."

"Perhaps," Cecily said. "He will come home a better man, and a man with experience."

"He will."

• • • •

Mr Cheverton asked Luke to take on a new role, overseeing five or six construction projects in Ryde and elsewhere.

There was no point in reinstating him in his porterage job, because in less than a year the building of the Ryde Pier would begin.

All the porters would be found other work.

Cecily was present when the gentlemen of Ryde put their proposals to Luke.

None of them begrudged his status because they had seen that he was an unselfish hero.

They had all learned about the wrong done to Luke.

"Perhaps you will give an opinion of the pier project as the work goes on," Mr Downe said. "As a man who knows the beach, the sand, the mud."

"I'd be honoured," Luke answered.

The foundation stone of pier, designed by John Kent of Southampton, was laid on Tuesday, June 29, 1813.

Cecily and Luke were not yet married.

They had delayed their wedding day until the Friday of that week.

"So as not to steal glory from the pier," Cecily said.

"So as not to steal glory from my beautiful wife," Luke replied.

They were man and wife by the time the pier opened a year later, in the summer of 1814.

There was a baby on the way, and that prospect had finally reconciled Mrs Downe to having a porter for a son-in-law.

"The best of the porters, Mother," Cecily said.

"The strongest and best. Never forget that."

SHORT STORY 63

Set in 1976

The Last Scoop

Could ice-cream girl Carol keep her crush under wraps?

BY BECCA ROBIN

It was only nine-thirty a.m. and so hot already. Although not long since breakfast, a queue had formed at Carol's ice-cream cart.

The holiday park was expecting a delivery of ice-cream and lollies today, which was just as well as stocks were running low.

It was the hottest summer on record and everyone was trying to cool down.

This morning, Carol's supervisor had agreed she could move her cart into the shade of some bushes, but the air was so heavy it didn't seem to make much difference.

It had moved her nearer the kiddies' paddling pool, but Carol didn't mind the noise of yelling and splashing as she liked seeing children having fun.

Unfortunately, it looked like the paddling pool would soon go the same way as the adult pool and close, as new drought restrictions made topping up the water impossible.

"One tutti frutti and one mint choc chip, please."

"Cones or tubs?"

"Cones."

Even though she was busy serving, from the corner of her eye she noticed Mike approach along the path leading from the West Chalet block.

It wasn't hard to spot him or any of the other orangecoats dressed in bright citrus-coloured blazers, which marked them out as the holiday park's entertainers.

The difference was how handsome Mike looked in his. With his fashionable shoulder length hair, he looked a lot like David Essex.

Carol's heart rate doubled as Mike veered off the path and headed her way.

He waited until she'd finished serving a customer before speaking.

Unfortunately, what he said burst her bubble of joy.

"I thought Rosie was serving here this morning?"

Of course, who else would he enquire about? Why else would he even be speaking to Carol?

Although he flashed his gorgeous smile, she could tell that in his mind's eye he was somewhere else.

"We swapped carts, for a change," Carol said, flustered. "She's over by the tennis courts."

With a quick "thanks", Mike headed back across the blanched lawn. Carol watched him go.

"I said, a choc-ice and two rocket lollies."

The customer, a mother holding the hands of two little girls in swimsuits, was clearly giving her order for the second or third time and it jolted Carol back to the present. "Oh sorry. Coming right up."

It was like torture, feeling so tongue-tied and silly whenever Mike was around.

Her recent awareness that he'd taken a shine to her best friend made her heart ache.

So far Rosie hadn't succumbed to his charms, but surely it was only a matter of time.

At least Carol had managed to keep her crush to herself and no-one else suspected – at least she hoped not.

The thought of Mike himself finding out was mortifying.

Carol and Rosie had worked as ice-cream girls at the park every summer since their schooldays.

Now they were both living away from their hometown – Carol at teacher training college and Rosie at secretarial school.

Still, Carol had been delighted when her old friend had written to suggest they return home for the summer and take up their old holiday jobs, maybe for the last time.

If she'd known how hopelessly she would fall for one of the orangecoats, would she have agreed?

Of course she would.

Carol spent her days hoping to catch glimpses of Mike while he organised competitions for the holidaymakers and appeared as a singer in the evening floorshows.

Although she and Rosie knocked off work at five, they were allowed to take part in the evening entertainments.

When it was time to head home, she would count the hours until she could see him again.

The hands of Carol's watch crawled their way to her mid-morning break.

She found Rosie in the staffroom, loading her orange squash with ice cubes from the freezer.

"It's so hot, I'm wilting," Rosie said.

For a moment, Carol stood with her face upturned to

the small, inadequate fan on top of the filing cabinet.

Then she fetched her own glass of squash and joined Rosie on the brown PVC sofa which seemed at risk of melting.

"Mike was looking for you earlier," Carol said casually.

"He found me," Rosie said with a giggle. "He asked if I was going to Party Night on Friday."

"Did you say yes?"

"We always go, don't we?" Rosie raised her eyebrows, but Carol didn't respond.

"You will come, won't you?"

"They say three's a crowd."

"Oh please, Carol. I don't want to go on my own and it's not like me and him have a date exactly.

"He just asked if we could have a dance after the floorshow. Party Night's always fun, isn't it?"

The prospect of watching Mike and Rosie flirting was anything but fun, and the pleading look in her eyes was starting to grate.

Did she appreciate how lucky she was to be receiving so much attention from Mr Wonderful?

Carol would have given anything to swap places with her. Yet if Mike was about to become her best friend's boyfriend, Carol would have to start getting used to the idea.

"OK, I'll tag along," she said.

Mrs Aimes the catering manager put her head around the door.

"Sorry to bother you on your break," she said. "But I need to tell you something.

"We're starting an ice-cream delivery service each afternoon between one and three p.m."

Carol and Rosie looked at each other blankly, then back at Mrs Aimes.

"Fewer people are venturing out in the middle of the day. Who can blame them? A lot seem to be staying in their chalets, having a siesta.

"We're offering this service to make them more comfortable. We've had lots of orders: here are the lists.

"I'll draft in a couple of orangecoats to help you. All right, girls?"

She handed them a piece of paper each, on which a column of chalet numbers corresponded with ice-cream orders. The girls agreed to the plan.

There was a strong sense of the staff all pulling together these days to ensure the park stayed open and ice-cream deliveries seemed a good idea.

Carol would deliver to the north and west blocks, Rosie to the south and east.

They'd just have to be ready for all the climbing up and down stairs, since each block of chalets was arranged on three floors, with balconies.

When their break was over, the girls peeled themselves off the hot PVC sofa and returned to their carts.

• • • •

Carol and Rosie met for lunch in the main canteen, queuing up for their food alongside the holidaymakers.

They took their trays to one of the red formica-topped tables near the open windows, which seemed to tease them into imagining what it would be like if a cool breeze blew in.

They were finishing their ham salads when they were joined unexpectedly by Mike and another orangecoat.

"Mind if we sit with you?" Mike directed this at Rosie.

"We don't mind, do we?" Rosie giggled at Carol, who shook her head. She was so shocked by the arrival of Mike she could barely look at him, which was awkward since he took a seat opposite, next to Rosie.

"Hi there," a voice at her side greeted.

She drummed up a quick smile for the orangecoat who'd sat next to her.

This lad always seemed rather shy but he hadn't worked long at the park, so he was probably still finding his feet.

Mike reached for the red plastic tomato and squeezed sauce on to his chips.

"It's no coincidence we've come to sit with you," he said, raising a handsome eyebrow which sent Carol all a-quiver, although she tried desperately not to show it.

"Oh?" Rosie said airily.

"We've been sent to ask if you want help delivering ice-creams this afternoon. If Dave goes with Carol, I'll come with you."

"I suppose I could do with some help." Rosie gave him a sidelong smile.

Before he could reply, Carol cut in.

"I don't need any help thanks. My list isn't very long."

"Are you sure?" Dave's face fell. "I don't mind at all."

"No, and I just remembered I left something in the staffroom. See you all later."

Carol hurried from the canteen, only pausing to place her tray with her empty plate in the rack by the door.

She hadn't left anything in the staffroom. She just couldn't bear to watch Mike and Rosie together.

How an earth was she going to cope on Friday night? Yet, if she didn't go to Party Night, wouldn't it look odd?

Wouldn't it be awful if Rosie or any of her friends started taking more notice of her behaviour and it led them to guess how she felt about Mike?

Perhaps it was best to go as usual and try to act natural.

At any rate, if it all got too much, there was always the option of making some excuse and leaving early.

• • • •

It soon became clear Carol had cut her nose off to spite her face.

It was exhausting work, delivering ice-creams to the 29 cabins on her list.

She couldn't take too many at a time or they'd melt, so she had to keep returning to the cart.

Not only that. A couple of orders on the list were mixed up and it took a while to get the problem sorted.

It was ten past three when she climbed to the third floor of the West Chalet block for the umpteenth time, to take the final order to chalet number 60, at the farthest end.

The chalet's occupant was sitting in a chair on the balcony with her feet up and a fan on the small table next to her.

The older woman appeared to be on her own.

"Sorry, I'm running late," Carol said. "A tub of raspberry ripple. Is that right?"

She handed over the ice-cream.

"Lovely, thank you," the woman said. "I've been watching you buzzing about down there, backwards and forwards to your cart in this heat, you poor thing.

"You deserve a rest. I've a flask of iced lemon tea here, if you'd like some?"

"I'm not really supposed to," Carol said.

"Five minutes won't hurt, will it? Grab a stool from inside and come and sit by the fan."

Well, part of Carol's remit was to spend time chatting with holidaymakers and she'd never tried iced lemon tea before, but it did sound good.

She thanked the woman, who poured some out while Carol fetched the stool.

"I'm Marjory," the woman said. "I'm here with my niece and nephew and their little girl. Their cabin's next door.

"They've gone to the beach today, but I decided to stay here."

Carol could see why.

Marjory had succeeded in making a little oasis for herself at the end of the balcony.

It was a relief to sit in a breeze, and the ice-cold tea was wonderfully refreshing.

"You have a lovely view," Carol said.

The balcony overlooked the main concourse, which in normal times, when there wasn't a hosepipe ban, would have been lush with colourful flower beds amongst which there were seating areas and a kiddies' playpark.

"That's why I always ask for this chalet," Marjory said. "People watching's my favourite hobby."

"People watching?"

"Yes. That's why I have to tell you something, Carol."

Marjory had read the name badge pinned to Carol's work blouse.

"What?" Carol asked.

"You need to forget about that dishy orangecoat with the floppy hair.

"Even if he did ask you out, he'd only break your heart. He'll break your friend's heart, if she's not careful."

Carol's jaw dropped. Marjory smiled sympathetically.

"I was young once," she said. "I know how these things hurt but trust me — you're better off not getting any attention from that fellow."

There didn't seem any point in denying what the woman said, but Carol's worst fears had been realised.

"Is it that obvious?" she said in a small voice.

"Not to anyone down there," Marjory said. "Everyone's so busy, they don't notice. But up here you spot all the little looks and interactions.

"You probably think I'm terribly nosy, but I like you ice-cream girls and I don't want to see you fall out with one another or make a horrible mistake over this chap."

Somehow, her kindness overcame any issue Carol had about being watched.

She also felt Marjory had more to tell.

"Mr Floppy Hair has several female members of staff on the go. I see it all from up here."

"Does he?" Carol asked.

"Oh yes, but none of them can love him as much as he loves himself, judging by how often he admires his reflection in his pocket mirror."

Carol didn't know what to say. In the heat of her longing, Marjory's words were like a sudden, cold shower of common sense.

"You must tell your friend," Marjory said. "I don't want to see her get hurt."

"Not only that. There's someone who likes you very much Carol, someone you've never noticed.

"Several times I've seen him try to approach while you're at work, but he always backs off at the last minute."

Here was something else Carol hadn't expected.

"Who do you mean?" she asked.

"He's one of the orangecoats. I don't know his name but he seems a decent lad."

Carol strained to think who on earth she could be referring to.

"If you can just take your mind off Mr Floppy Hair and look around, you might notice him."

Carol didn't stay much longer. Still bowled over by what she'd heard, she said goodbye to Marjory, who said she'd place another ice-cream order the next day.

Was it true or was Marjory just a busybody who'd got hold of the wrong end of lots of sticks?

Carol's main issue now was whether to tell Rosie about Mike.

The trouble was, might Rosie assume she was telling her because she was jealous? How much could she trust what Marjory said?

Carol remained in a quandary for the next couple of days.

It was so on her mind, she forgot to look around for her supposed admirer.

Rosie seemed very excited when she called for Carol on Friday night and they walked over to the holiday park. Both girls wore fashionable cheesecloth blouses, flared trousers and platform shoes.

Party Night began with a floorshow and as usual, Mike was taking centre stage singing the latest hits.

He wasn't in his orange jacket and looked gorgeous in a big-collared paisley shirt and white flared trousers.

Nevertheless, Carol's feelings towards him had started to cool.

She was more concerned for Rosie and wished she had given her some kind of warning, to take care. Would Rosie have listened, though? Probably not.

As soon as the show was over and the dancing began, Mike made a bee-line for the girls' table and flashed his hundred watt smile at her friend.

"How about that dance?"

When he held out his hand, Rosie flew from her seat and he led her on to the dancefloor.

Carol sipped her bitter lemon. At least they'd disappeared into the crowd, so she wouldn't be treated to a grandstand view.

"Hi again."

She turned but didn't recognise the boy who'd spoken immediately.

What was his name? Ah yes: Dave.

"Anyone sitting here?" he asked.

"No. Help yourself."

Realising she'd sounded a bit offhand, she smiled and he smiled back.

"Do you mind if I ask you something?" she said.

"Ask away."

"It might not be very fair, since he's your friend, but has Mike really got a reputation as a bit of a ladies' man?"

Dave winced and took a sip of his pint. It told Carol everything she needed to know.

"I'm sorry. Forget I asked."

They sat quietly a moment, Carol lost in thought. So it was true! How was she going to break the news to Rosie?

"I'm glad to have the chance to speak to you," Dave interrupted her thoughts. "I've been trying to summon up the nerve to do it for ages."

"Pardon?"

Marjory's words returned to her.

Was Dave the lad who'd been attempting to approach Carol? Was this her admirer?

Dave repeated what he'd just said and she found herself smiling at him with genuine warmth.

All at once there came a shriek from the dancefloor.

First, a stranger who looked furious pushed her way through the dancers and raced past Carol and Dave's table, heading for the exit.

She was pursued by none other than Mike, looking guilty and flustered. Finally Rosie appeared at the table. She seemed close to tears.

"Carol, can we go please?" she begged.

• • • •

"So Mike had no idea his girlfriend from Manchester would be arriving?" Carol said the next day.

"You mean his ex-girlfriend," Dave said. "Hopefully he'll learn from the experience."

Rosie was still upset about the scene on the dancefloor but relieved she hadn't been going out properly with the two-timer.

Carol had apologised, but Rosie said she understood her friend hadn't felt comfortable passing on hearsay.

Meanwhile, Mrs Aimes had promised to send a different orangecoat to help Rosie deliver ice-creams that afternoon.

On the other hand, Carol was more than happy that Dave had turned up to help with her deliveries.

"How shall we do this?" He studied the list. "You take one half and I take the other?"

"Except the last on the list. Let's do that one together."

Carol pointed at chalet number 60, where Marjory had ordered another raspberry ripple.

She was looking forward to introducing her new love interest to Marjory and vice versa.

They could join her in her little balcony oasis and maybe cool off with some iced lemon tea — the perfect combination.

THIRTEEN-YEAR-OLD Chloe lived a life that her grandmother, Isabel, found hard to recognise.

Unlike any teenager Isabel knew of, Chloe rose from bed early.

She stretched out on the decking, then took Boodle, the goldendoodle, for a walk along the shore.

Isabel's dog wasn't about to look a gift-horse in the mouth and willingly went on explorations with Chloe everywhere.

"You should exercise more, Gran!" Chloe said on her return.

What was she, some kind of teenage guru?

"I've had plenty exercise all my life, thanks. I'll stick to dancing."

"Oh! I have an idea! Do a dance with me, and we'll send it to Liam. He'll love that!"

Chloe instantly looked crestfallen.

"But he's probably too busy to look at it, now he's working in London."

Isabel hugged her granddaughter to her side.

"You miss your brother."

"I do not!" Chloe protested, "Well, maybe just a bit."

The sigh that followed was long. Something in it alerted Isabel.

"It must be strange being at home without him, especially since Oliver and your mum got married?" she tried.

"Liam was away at uni for years, so, not really, but I guess it does feel different knowing he's away down there. London. Doing the most exciting job."

Chloe looked forlornly out of the caravan window, over the golf course, sand dunes and out to the Dornoch Firth.

They'd been coming on holiday to the north-east coast of Scotland since Chloe was little, when the whole family would gather on the beach with a windbreak, tartan rug, colourful spades and pails, and kites that entertained for hours in this windy spot

Let's Dance

Howie had found the perfect way to help Isabel put a spring in her granddaughter's step . . .

BY JACKIE MORRISON

beyond the golf course. Now it was just the two of them.

Chloe's mum, Nadia, had recently qualified as a nurse, having gone to university herself when her children were at school.

Now Liam was working in creative marketing down in London and living a young person's dream.

At least that's what Chloe seemed to think.

"She spends all day on her phone. I'm worried about her." Nadia had said just the other week. "You should take her up to Scotland with you for some fresh air.

"I've got so many shifts to cover this summer, I just can't make time."

Isabel had thought it a grand idea to spend some time with her youngest grandchild.

Chloe reminded her so much of her father, Isabel's son, David.

Since retiring early from teaching art, Isabel had kept herself busy helping Nadia with the children through their school year activities and managed to volunteer at an after-school art club, too.

Isabel was pulled out of her reverie by cheerful music coming from the veranda.

"Come on, Gran! I've set it all up."

Out there on the wooden decking, Chloe was all legs and arms, her hair flying around her as she spun and laughed.

Isabel clapped but Chloe beckoned her on.

"Come on! I'm going to teach you the moves, gran!"

Isabel was always up for a challenge, and she enjoyed Zumba classes at the local community centre, so she soon got the hang of the moves Chloe was performing to a modern take on a western tune.

Over and over, they did it, side by side, chuckling each time Isabel mucked up a turn.

"Wait a minute, Gran. I know what'll help."

Chloe ran barefoot through the caravan and came back out with a cowboy hat each for them.

"My Taylor Swift souvenirs! I've got my cowboy boots too, but only one pair!"

Isabel remembered the concert Chloe had attended along with a couple of friends.

When Isabel was taking a break in the patio chair fanning her face, she noticed the man on the decking of the caravan next door watching them.

He tapped his hand to his head and called over.

"Howdy, young lady!"

Isabel bowed to him, stifling a laugh at his attempt at an American cowboy accent.

"I'm Isabel and this is my granddaughter, Chloe!" she called back.

Isabel recognised him as a member of the family who'd used the caravan next door over the years.

Like Isabel, he'd had three generations enjoying holidays here. She seemed to recall, like her, he'd been a teacher.

"I'm Howie. Howard, but that's a bit . . . well, just Howie is what everyone calls me.

"I used to come here with the whole family when the grandkids were young."

"We used to come here as a family, too. There's just me and Chloe now. Everyone else is doing their own thing," Isabel said, noticing that Chloe had disappeared inside with her phone and tripod.

"You know, if you and your granddaughter like dancing, there's a special line-dancing thing that happens in the car park next to the beach.

"It has a lovely view nearer to sunset when the dancing finishes."

"Really?" Isabel couldn't think of anything stranger than a load of people doing line dancing in a car park.

"No obligation to dance with me, if you come. I do watch a bit of 'Strictly' and am light on my feet!" he said, twirling around on his decking, coming back around to face her again and holding out an arm. "What do you think?"

"An eight. Room for improvement." Isabel chuckled.

"There's a pipe band in the town tonight, too, and Highland dancers on the stage," Howie added.

Isabel watched him carefully as he turned to look out towards the sea.

He'd a head of salt and pepper hair and a well-trimmed beard.

In his checked short sleeved shirt and fine cotton trousers, he was in fine shape.

It had been a long time since a man had turned her head as she'd been committed to helping with Liam and Chloe, and she'd gotten used to life on her own.

• • • •

Chloe was deep in her laptop and mobile phone.

"How can you use that all at one time?" Isabel asked, flabbergasted by Chloe's concentration.

"I'm putting together a video. I don't have the editing programmes that Liam has, but I can still put together a little film on Instagram."

"Oh, don't you be putting me on social media!" Isabel warned.

She'd heard about how things went viral, especially the embarrassing things.

"I'm just playing about with it, Gran."

"I can do without social media!" Isabel answered, although she did have her own accounts these days, as a way of staying in touch with Liam and Chloe although she rarely commented on their posts, preferring to direct message them.

She'd been told how embarrassing the "olds" could be and she didn't want to get banned by her grandchildren.

"Do you fancy going to see the pipe band march through the town tonight? There's line dancing afterwards at the beach car park," Isabel said nonchalantly as she made a cup of tea.

Chloe sat to attention.

"Line-dancing? That's a great idea, Gran. The sunset from up there in the evening is amazing! I've seen it online!"

Isabel shook her head.

"There's more to life than social media you know! It's not real!"

"Gran, it is real. If I'm not on social media, well, I . . . cease to exist."

"Oh, Chloe! You can't mean that! That's awful."

"I'm making it work for me, Gran." Chloe said sagely, "Don't worry about it! It's how I stay in touch with Liam, too.

"Yes, to the line-dancing thing. Let's do it! I'll take my Swiftie hats with us, and wear something colourful, Gran!"

Isabel smiled. She liked it when Chloe was animated like this.

It reminded her of when her granddaughter was small and they'd painted together or splashed through puddles making up adventures.

Chloe was arty like her gran, and Isabel was ever so grateful Chloe had held on to that part of herself as she'd reached her teenage years.

If social media, her phone and laptop kept her connected to art, then it couldn't be so bad, could it?

• • • •

"How do I look?" Chloe asked later, standing in a pink fringed top, denim shorts and cowboy boots.

She popped a pink cowboy hat on to her head.

"You look the part!" Isabel beamed.

The sunshine of the last few days on the beach had given Chloe a glow and it seemed that her melancholy had left her for now.

"What about me?" Isabel twirled in her cropped jeans and red checkered top.

"For you!" Chloe chimed as she placed a white cowboy hat on top of Isabel's silver hair.

She had trouble fitting it on as Isabel's hair was pinned loosely on top of her head.

"Let your hair down, Gran. You have lovely waves."

When Isabel looked in the mirror, she thought her hair did look good against her red top.

"I don't think we can take Boodle. The pipe band might be a bit loud for him and we don't want him tripping people up at the dancing. He can have a nice sleep instead, can't you Boodle?"

The dog sighed contentedly as Isabel scratched behind his ears.

"Let's go dancing!" Chloe said, placing a friendship bracelet on her gran's wrist. "From the Taylor Swift concert, Gran. You're my best friend, so you should have this one."

Isabel felt she might cry as she felt Chloe's arms around her waist.

Her grandchildren were both growing into independent young adults, but it was lovely to know Chloe still appreciated her.

"Thanks, darling. Let's go and have some fun."

• • • •

Although they'd seen the pipe band perform in previous years, tonight felt special.

The drums and bagpipes made Isabel's heartbeat skip along and they smiled as they watched two young girls demonstrate their Highland dancing.

Chloe took photos and videos of their kilted skirts whirling.

Dornoch might be where Madonna chose to get married, and where shops sold goods by royal appointment, but this, the whirl and the noise of the Scottish bagpipes, the energetic dancing, this was the true heart of it all.

It was where the community and visitors came together.

Afterwards, they walked towards the long sandy beach.

The car park was empty of cars because it was full of lines of dancers.

There was a string of multi coloured lights between two large vehicles and speakers up on stands.

Already people were moving to and fro, hands tapping hats, then heels, turning around, rows all moving as one to jaunty country and western music.

Chloe brought out her mobile which she always seemed to be using.

"Oh, be careful, love. People may not want to be on camera!"

"That's OK, Gran. I'll time it for when they turn. I know what I'm doing!"

Howie was standing tall in front of them, taking in a deep breath.

"Think we should join them?"

He looked the part in an open necked checked shirt and cream chinos.

He proffered his arm to Isabel, and with a nod from Chloe who was moving around photographing people's feet, off they went to join the fun.

Between musical numbers, they had a good chat about Howie's recent retirement from teaching English, his screen-writing successes and his interest in design.

Hearing about his volunteering with a local

theatre assisting with set design left Isabel appreciative of all the unnoticed work that went into theatre shows.

Like herself, he'd lived alone for years, and he'd found himself a good community in the volunteer theatre group.

The evening went by quickly as one musical number merged into another. Isabel danced alongside Howie, and even Chloe at one point.

It was then that Isabel noticed how golden Chloe looked in the evening light.

"Do you mind if I sit this one out, darling?" Isabel said over the music as Chloe and Howie stomped their feet to a energetic, more modern tune.

Isabel held Chloe's phone for her and took the opportunity to take some snaps of Chloe twirling as golden hour reached them.

The multi-coloured lights reflected onto the dancing crowd in the car park, but the colours could never compete with the sunset reds, pinks and purples that were streaking over the waters of the Dornoch Firth.

"Told you it would be spectacular!" Howie said into Isabel's ear, his beard tickling her.

"It really is." Isabel replied but she was looking into the soft blue eyes of this gentleman who had somehow recognised just the right opportunity to bring them all together to make the most memorable moment of their holiday.

"What do you think?" he bowed and twirled.

"A ten!" She replied as if she was a judge from "Strictly Come Dancing".

• • • •

It was no surprise to Isabel to hear Chloe up and about in the morning, the doors to the patio opening.

Howie waved from his veranda.

"Still recovering from last night?" he raised his coffee cup.

"I was just telling Howie. We're an overnight sensation." Chloe clapped her hands together and twirled.

What on earth was Chloe on about?

"Look, Gran! It's you and Howie!"

Chloe held her phone aloft and there was a most magical sight.

In the darkening twilight, warmed by the sun-streaked purple shades, were dancers twirling, touching their hats, Isabel and Howie twirling arm in arm, broad smiles lit by nature, and perhaps from within, too.

The next shots were people's feet adorned by all sorts: sandals, trainers, cowboy boots of many colours.

Then came some stills: the snaps Isabel had taken of Chloe dancing in her Taylor Swift outfit, the sun illuminating her cheeks, her hair shining with natural sun-streaked highlights.

It was all playing to a lovely tune.

"But we didn't dance to that tune, did we?" Isabel asked, slightly baffled.

"No, Gran! When you do an Instagram reel, you can put it to any music you want. That's the best bit!" She jumped up and down.

"It's one of Liam's tunes, Gran. One of his very own compositions. You remember it?"

She turned the sound up and Isabel recognised the song Liam had played on his guitar for his mum's marriage to Oliver the year before.

Liam had played it solo as his mum walked down the aisle at the historic castle just down the road from here.

This version though was more jazzy. A studio sound, or perhaps even a proper recording.

"It's very good!" Isabel smiled.

Her grandson's talent always had been in music.

She was very grateful that he was still connected to music via the creative videoing he did in his marketing job.

"Good?" Chloe screeched, "It's gone viral, Gran! And I linked it to Liam's account. His DMs have gone bonkers!"

By this, Isabel took it to mean he'd had a lot of enquiries on direct messaging which was surely a good thing.

The video was paused on the part where Howie was holding Isabel out at arm's length, ready to twirl her back towards him again and they were both in rapt eye contact.

Isabel smiled warmly and beckoned Howie over to join them for toast and coffee on the veranda.

"I told you social media was life, Gran!" Chloe said.

"Are you sure it is Liam who is the creative director?" Isabel joked.

"He says I can go into his office to see how things all work if I can go down to London before the end of the holidays. Would you take me, Gran?"

Isabel felt relieved that Chloe was doing better than they all might've imagined.

The children had lost their dad to illness when they were very young.

Isabel still missed her son, David, every day. When Oliver came on the scene years later, they'd all taken to him and his kind nature, welcoming the wedding.

Still, Chloe's mum had worried when her eldest moved away from home changing the dynamic at home.

"London, eh?" Howie winked, sitting down. "Can't beat a show and some sightseeing. I have some friends down in London. Theatre types. We haven't seen each other for an age."

"Sounds doable." Isabel said, deep in thought. "I'll check with Liam to see if he can fit us in."

Howie's eyes sparkled as he talked about the friends he'd worked with in theatre design.

Although it had been screen writing that introduced him to the theatre group, it seemed Howie had a real talent for stage design and was willing to turn his hand to any job that needed doing.

Isabel was thankful for the way he'd recognised how the Car Park Line Dancing would put a sparkle in her eye. Now she might put a sparkle in his.

"You're welcome to join us, Howie. We haven't seen Liam since Christmas. I'm sure we can work something out if Chloe's mum agrees."

"Oh, Mum will be happy enough. She's got work. And Oliver," Chloe said.

Chloe had been so grown-up about all the changes over the last year.

"You are OK, love?" Isabel said into Chloe's ear.

"Oh yes, Gran. I'm just, you know, working things out. I've got choices ahead of me at school. I'm thinking about what I might like to go and study afterwards."

Chloe popped her headphones on, no doubt to listen to Taylor Swift again.

She pointed to the crashing sea, her voice rather loud due to the headphones.

"I'm off to film the waves. I've got an idea." She popped a headphone off to the side and smiled. "You're right you know.

"Social media isn't life – life is highlighted on social media!" She stuck her thumb up.

"She's something, isn't she?" Isabel smiled contently as Chloe jumped down the steps to the sand dunes. "Very talented."

"She's not the only one!" Howie said as he twirled Isabel at arm's length, pulling her closer. "Now, about this trip . . . I've heard that one of the judges from 'Strictly' is doing a show in London this summer. What do you think? My treat."

"That sounds great. Maybe we can see something at the theatre, too?" Isabel smiled.

"That sounds like a ten out of ten to me." Howie laughed.

And, Isabel thought, Howie might turn out to be a perfect ten, too.

Picture This

Leanne didn't expect to find such a photo in her book . . .

BY CHRIS SUTTON

With one chapter to go, Leanne reluctantly closed the book.

A romance set during World War II, it had been engrossing, filled with trials and tribulations threaded through with bravery and unswerving love.

Although fictional, the struggles of the two main characters – Hester, a nurse, and Joe, a wounded soldier – had touched her heart.

She was eking out the pages, delaying the moment she'd have to say farewell to a couple who'd come to feel like friends.

"Oh, Meg, why can't I find someone kind and sensitive like Joe?" she asked her retriever, curled at her feet.

At twenty-eight, and still bruised from the break-up with Rick, Leanne was starting to think she'd never find that special someone meant just for her.

Deciding to save the rest for bedtime, she reached to set the book on the table.

As she did, something slid from inside the dust jacket on to the grass.

She picked it up.

It was an old black-and-white photo of a smiling couple standing in clouds of confetti outside a church.

The groom was ruggedly handsome in uniform, the bride young and pretty in a tailored two-piece with a neat, veiled hat.

Leanne flipped it over.

Rene and George. August 17, 1955.

Seventy years – their anniversary was on Sunday!

The picture had likely been used as a bookmark by a former borrower – but who, and when?

The novel was so old it could've sat on the library shelf for decades.

Intrigued, Leanne knew she had to finish it and take it back. She lay back and read on.

• • • •

Leanne felt oddly flustered entering the library, fearing she might be wasting time but too curious not to try.

It was warm, so she'd pulled on denim shorts and a cotton top over her bikini.

Her ponytail swished across her shoulders as she approached the counter.

"Excuse me – could you help?"

The assistant smiled.

"I'll do my best."

Leanne opened the book and took out the photograph.

"I found this tucked inside. Any chance of tracing who it belongs to?"

The woman looked doubtful.

"Unlikely. Books get borrowed dozens of times. But I'll check."

She scanned the barcode, then raised her brows.

"Oh! Only borrowed twice since our system updated five years ago. Most recently by you. Before that – October 2020."

"Well, that narrows it down," Leanne said. "Do either names on the photo – Rene and George – match the earlier borrower?"

The woman typed.

"Hmm, the name's Irene, so it's possible."

Leanne glanced around. The library was nearly empty.

"Is there a phone number for her? I'd love to return this. Their anniversary's coming up – it's platinum."

The woman nodded.

"There is. Let's try."

She dialled. After a pause, she gave Leanne a nod.

"Mrs Wilson's grandson's on the line. He'd like a word."

Leanne took the receiver.

"Hello?"

"Hi, I'm Jack Wilson. I hear you found a photo that might belong to my gran?"

He had a calm, velvety voice that soothed her nerves.

"I think so. A wedding photo. I'd love to return it – if she's . . ."

She paused, unsure how old the picture was.

He chuckled. Her stomach fluttered.

"Still around, you mean? Very much so.

"She's ninety and preparing to celebrate her seventieth with Grandad George on Sunday."

"How wonderful!" Leanne said. "And what timing. May I bring it to her?"

"No need – I'll come to you. I'm nearby helping with party prep."

"Great. I'll be here a while – choosing new books."

As she handed back the phone, the assistant's eyes sparkled.

"Now, doesn't he sound lovely?"

Leanne blushed. It was exactly what she'd been thinking.

Ten minutes later, the doors swished open and a man entered.

Dark wavy hair, hint of stubble. White shirt and jeans. Gorgeous.

He crossed to the counter.

"Hi, I'm Jack Wilson. You called about a photo?"

Leanne caught a whiff of zingy aftershave.

"Hello, Jack. I'm Leanne Keen. I think this is your gran's."

As she handed him the photo, emotion flickered across his face.

"Oh, this will mean so much. They lost all their wedding photos when a pipe burst and flooded their bedroom last year."

"I bought them a platinum frame for the anniversary. This is perfect."

He looked up, eyes meeting hers.

He smiled – and her pulse quickened.

"Please, may I buy you a drink to say thanks?"

Grinning, Leanne held up the book.

"The answer's in the title, Jack: 'A Heartfelt Yes'."

A Sight To Behold

Without her glasses, would Lindy be able to enjoy this voyage?

BY FIONA THOMSON

LINDY sat down at her table for one in the cruise ship dining-room and thanked the waiter for the menu.

She scanned the printed card, but apart from the word "Breakfast" in bold letters, the rest was a blur.

How on earth would she manage two days at sea without her glasses?

The young woman groaned as she remembered the awful sound of her flip-flop crushing the frame and lenses into the cabin floor when she'd got up that morning.

Since starting work at the travel agency, she'd written plenty of articles for the website blog.

Just a shame she hadn't followed her own advice.

If you wear glasses and have a spare pair, remember to pack them.

Lindy gave a wry smile, remembering the exact location of her second pair, safe in the bedside drawer at home.

What could she do?

Maybe, if she used the camera on her phone to zoom in on the menu, she could at least order some breakfast.

Yes! The menu appeared on-screen, but when she tried to enlarge it, only part of a word could be seen.

Oh, this would take ages and Lindy could hear her stomach rumbling already!

"I'm sure there's no need to photograph it – they'll let you take it home as a souvenir."

Hearing the voice, Lindy turned to see the man at the next table – who had managed not to mangle his large, dark-framed glasses – smiling at her.

She returned a puzzled smile.

He held up his menu.

"It's got today's date on it, so they won't be using it again.

"In fact, I might keep mine, too – make all my mates jealous at the incredible selection.

"Bit better than the coffee and banana I usually grab on a work morning."

He held out his hand.

"I'm Adrian."

"Lindy. Nice to meet you."

"Have you decided what you're having to eat?" Adrian pointed at one of the items on the card. "It'll be Eggs Benedict for me."

"My favourite, too!" Lindy said, sighing with relief as she placed her order with the waiter who'd just poured them each some coffee.

One problem solved, but there would be many more challenges ahead.

Until now, she'd not realised how much she relied on her varifocals.

Everything was blurred, and at the worst time, too.

The new, two-night mini cruise, All at Sea, was designed to encourage people to try cruising and was also the first free trip she'd had since starting work at the travel agency.

Her manager would be relying on her to produce plenty of articles and photos for the website blog and had also asked Lindy to give a presentation at the special cruise evening for their customers.

How could any of that happen when she couldn't see things properly or even write down any notes?

"Are you OK?" Adrian put down his coffee. "Just that you don't look great. Feeling seasick?"

Lindy shook her head and then, to her horror, felt a tear trickle down her cheek. She wiped it away.

"Oh, I'm fine really. It's just –"

And as Adrian moved to the chair next to her, she blurted out the whole sorry situation.

"So, here I am, with today and tomorrow at sea, supposed to be capturing every detail of this trip – all without my glasses!" She gave a tearful smile.

Just at that moment the waiter appeared and placed one Eggs Benedict in front of Lindy and the other at Adrian's empty place.

He stood up to move.

"Oh please," Lindy said, pointing to her table. "Let's have breakfast together. I could do with some company while I work out what to do."

The two of them began eating and there was silence while they enjoyed the food.

"Well, at least my taste buds are still working," Lindy said, after a few mouthfuls. "This is delicious."

Adrian nodded.

"There's an amazing spread on the buffet table, too. If you like, we can go together when we've finished this."

As she swallowed the last of the delicious pastry she'd chosen from the laden trays, Lindy had to admit it was great having some company.

The free place was for a single traveller only, but that suited her, having broken up with her boyfriend a few months before.

She looked at Adrian and wondered why he was holidaying on his own.

"Hey!" He grinned. "Just had an idea. Why don't you try on my glasses? Here."

He held them out and Lindy put them on. Suddenly she could see again!

Smiling, she looked up at her breakfast companion, taking in his quizzical look, dark brown eyes and soft smile.

"Wow! They're almost the same strength as mine."

Lindy gazed round the room, seeing the dining-room in focus for the first time, then rummaged in her bag for notebook and pen.

"If you don't mind I'm going to write down a description of this place while I can."

Adrian picked up his coffee cup.

"Fancy a refill?"

"Oh, yes please!"

When Adrian returned, he had two sheets of paper tucked under his arm.

"Grabbed one for each of us. It's a list of all the onboard activities over the next two days."

"Well, there's certainly plenty to do," Lindy said, scanning the programme. "I was worried that being at sea for the whole time would be boring.

"Films, yoga and tai chi, entertainment this evening – even a quiz in the bar this morning."

"I love a good quiz," Adrian said. "In fact, I think I might go – if I can have my glasses back!"

Lindy gasped. Of course! The only reason she

could read the programme was because she was still wearing Adrian's glasses.

Quickly she took them off and returned them as the world around her went out of focus again.

"Maybe," Adrian said, as he put on the glasses, "we could be a team of two at the quiz and share them?"

• • • •

"I'll display this ship on my fridge door, as a reminder of actually winning something!"

Adrian held up the souvenir magnet they'd just won for second place.

"This is very cute, too," Lindy said, looking at her keyring, which showed the ship with its teddy bear mascot waving from the deck. "I can't believe we did so well – oh, and thank you."

She handed Adrian the glasses, which they'd been taking turns to wear while they studied the clues and wrote down the answers.

"I'm booked in for a massage and facial this afternoon, so no need to see clearly for that." Lindy sipped her sparkling water. "What are your plans, Adrian?"

"I'd say a swim, but six strokes and I'll be at the other end, so let's just call it a dip before I get into the jacuzzi.

"I think it will be quite a unique experience to be relaxing in warm water while looking out at the sea – wouldn't fancy swimming in those waves."

Lindy looked thoughtful.

"Would you mind if I interviewed you for my feature? Just it's always good to have another opinion for potential travellers to read."

Adrian nodded.

"This sounds fun!"

• • • •

Yes, Lindy thought, as she used the borrowed glasses to read over her notes after dinner.

Adrian's quotes would really make her blog come alive. And it had allowed her to find out more about him.

During dinner, conversation had been so easy, with the two of them chatting like old friends.

She'd learned Adrian shared a flat with two other friends and was unattached.

After a few years working in restaurants, he was in the process of taking over a small business that provided lunches for local companies, which would open the following week.

When he saw the special offer for the first cruise, he'd decided to take a break, knowing he'd have little time for a holiday over the rest of the summer.

Lindy thought back on the evening.

Before the cruise began she'd been worried the time at sea might drag, but now she was disappointed that tomorrow afternoon it would come to an end.

Adrian was such great company, good looking and so kind, even letting her borrow his glasses overnight.

All she needed to do was keep them safe so she could return them at breakfast time!

As Lindy switched off the bedside light, she remembered her car, sitting in the terminal car park.

No way could she drive home without her specs.

She'd have to ring her parents, see if one of them could pick up her spare pair from the flat and bring them to the port.

Walking to the dining-room for breakfast the next morning, Lindy caught a glimpse of herself in the reflected glass.

The bold, dark blue frames were not something she'd have chosen for herself, but they did look good.

As soon as she walked in, she spotted Adrian at the table they'd shared the previous morning.

Both of them chose smoked salmon and scrambled eggs for breakfast and once their plates were empty, spent so long chatting that they were last to leave.

It was Adrian's turn to try a massage, so Lindy kept the glasses and headed off to check out the ship's library.

They'd arranged to meet up in the bar before lunch after which the ship would return to the cruise terminal, ready for disembarkation.

What a great time I've had, Lindy thought, as she left the library and headed for the bar, noting all the people who were sitting, relaxing and enjoying looking out to sea.

This mini-break seemed to appeal to all ages, something she'd include in the presentation she was preparing.

Entering the bar, Lindy looked round. There was Adrian at the corner table, with his back to her.

She recognised his dark hair and striped sweatshirt.

But walking over, Lindy hesitated, because this man, who was busy studying his phone, was wearing glasses.

"Sorry I'm a bit early," Lindy said.

Adrian glanced up, looking shocked, then embarrassed.

"Lindy, I can explain."

"I don't understand." She frowned.

Adrian held up the glasses. "I should have told you I'd another pair with me right at the start.

"But when I suggested we team up for the pub quiz and you said yes, I'd such a great time and realised it was an easy way for us to spend time together.

"Before I decided to change jobs, I was so busy working late nights in a restaurant kitchen that I'd no social life at all." Adrian sighed. "In fact, I'd pretty much forgotten how to ask someone out.

"Once I saw how well we got on together, I couldn't find the courage to tell you the truth."

"So were you ever going to tell me?"

Adrian shook his head.

"Because I'm getting a bus home, I thought I could lend you my glasses, so you could drive home.

"Then I could suggest meeting up again as a way of returning them.

"But honestly, I'm happy for you to keep the glasses and just post them back. Don't want you to be stuck with no transport."

Lindy looked thoughtful.

"Well, I've had a great time with you on the cruise and would have happily agreed to your little plan.

"But," she said, smiling, "I was actually working out my own scheme to see you again, inviting you out for dinner as a thank you.

"Why don't we get some drinks and then look at our diaries to fix up a date – both of us wearing glasses this time!"

Coming Back To The Cove

This hotel held many precious memories for Cathy . . .

BY SALLY WATERBURY

CATHY slammed the taxi door and looked up at the façade of the Cove Hotel.

It sparkled white in the bright light of the afternoon.

Apart from a lick of paint and new pots either side of the front door, it was much as she remembered.

Ten years – was it really that long since she had been here?

The summer after her exams.

It was going to be yet another boring holiday with her parents, or at least that was what she had thought.

How wrong she had been.

Cathy lifted her suitcase and pushed through the glass doors.

The reception area was just as she pictured it, with wooden panelling to the walls and impressive floral arrangements.

The ceiling was high and the chandelier sparkled.

A rush ran through her heart.

She was sixteen again, standing here while Dad checked the family in for a two week stay.

She remembered how much she hadn't been looking forward to being dragged around country houses and taken on long walks.

Cathy pulled herself back to the here and now. She put down her suitcase.

"Hi," she said to the girl on reception – a label on her lapel said her name was Sasha. "I'm Catherine Tyler. I think you're expecting me."

Sasha turned to the computer. She frowned.

"Checking in today? I don't seem to have anyone by that name."

"No," Cathy said. "I'm the new deputy front of house manager."

Sasha flushed.

"Yes, of course, Miss Tyler. Sorry, I'll get someone to show you to your accommodation and let Mr Parkin know you've arrived."

She reached under the counter and rang a distant bell.

• • • •

Cathy followed the porter through the corridors.

The carpet was new, beige and modern, quite unlike the swirls of old.

The cream walls were freshly painted for the season.

She tried to remember where exactly her parents' room had been located.

It had been clear in her head during the train journey, but now it was all a muddle.

Left turn then right, or was it the other way around? Up a short flight of stairs, or possibly down?

She couldn't remember, but the details didn't matter.

It was the feeling she was here for, and that was the same. The flutter of her heart, the excitement of possibility.

She felt herself beginning to smile for the first time in months.

"Here it is, miss," the porter said. "I hope you'll be happy here."

He opened the door for her and gave her the key.

Cathy thanked him and went in.

The flat was tiny and dark, tucked under the eaves.

There was a bedroom with a hanging rail, a sitting-room just big enough for a small sofa, the kitchenette at one end and beyond that a shower room.

It was small but it was hers.

She crossed to the window and raised the blind letting the sunshine stream in.

Cathy looked out across the village rooftops.

There were some new houses to one side, a small caravan park to the other, but beyond them in the distance she could see the white spume of the waves.

Her head began to spin.

The beach. That was where she had first seen James.

He had been walking from the sea, his wetsuit peeled back from his torso, his surfboard under his arm.

She had looked up from where she was sunbathing, as far away from her parents as was possible without them realising what she was doing.

He had caught her eye.

When he smiled at her, she had blushed, buried her face in her book.

When she glanced back, he was nothing but a speck on the far side of the beach.

Cathy sat down heavily on the bed.

It was madness, to think that she could recreate the headiness of those two weeks by coming back here.

She was a professional young woman now.

She was independent, with a life of her own and a pot of money saved in the bank.

She would no longer think of it as her wedding fund, or their wedding fund.

There was no going back. Ben was with someone else now and she just had to get over it.

It didn't really matter if the people who said that she was running away by coming here were correct.

She needed a change, a fresh start. It was the only way she was ever going to move on.

• • • •

Mr Parkin, the hotel manager, was older than he had appeared during her online interview.

He seemed a little surprised at her appearance, too – perhaps she was younger than he expected.

It was a family hotel, he told her. Traditional. They didn't go in for late nights and loud noises.

A good deal of the clientele were visitors who returned year after year, who knew exactly what they were getting here and liked it.

Many of the permanent staff had been here a long while, too, but of course they had casuals for the season.

He was expecting her to keep a close eye on them. If there was going to be any trouble, that was where it would be.

Cathy nodded. She reassured him she would take a firm line.

She had been assistant office manager in her previous job, and before that, she had a good deal of experience in hospitality.

Mr Parkin rolled his lips together. He tapped his pen on the desktop.

She should settle in. It was too late now to do anything useful today.

She could start in the morning. She should expect hard work and long hours.

Cathy told him she expected nothing less.

She didn't tell him that she needed an all-consuming job to take her mind off her troubles.

Back upstairs, Cathy took another look at the view.

It was so beautiful, so much better than the grey of the office buildings she had left behind.

She changed into her comfortable sandals and picked up her cardigan.

It didn't sound as if there was going to be much time for the beach in the days to come.

She should make the most of this brief opportunity.

By the time Cathy got down to the seafront the wind was a little stronger, the sun had dipped behind a cloud and the holidaymakers had started to pack up.

Tired parents dusted sand from their toddlers' feet. They rolled up towels and repacked beach bags.

It was busier than Cathy remembered – smaller, too.

That was how it was as a grown up. wasn't it? Everything one went back to looked smaller.

The feel of it was the same though. The thrill of it.

She slipped her feet from her sandals and walked down to the sea.

The wet sand oozed between her toes. If she shut her eyes, she could still see James, standing here in the shallows.

He had seen her on the beach the following day, said hello.

He had asked if she like him to teach her to surf.

She could still feel the horror when her dad came across, interrupted, and asked him who he was. But James had charmed her father.

He was on holiday, too, with his parents.

He pointed them out to her dad. They waved back from across the beach.

He'd learnt to surf last year; it really wasn't as hard as it looked.

It was certainly more fun than lying on the beach.

Cathy let the waves wash over her feet, the cool water lapping at her ankles.

The pale blue of the clear sky turning to pink in the early evening light.

She should be getting back; a decent night's sleep was needed.

She would begin by getting someone to show her around, not just the public areas but the workings of the hotel behind the scenes. There was a lot for her to learn.

The following morning Sasha led Cathy upstairs to view the bedrooms, the family suites, the smallest economy rooms.

She showed Cathy the main restaurant and the conservatory where breakfast was served from seven until half past ten.

They passed through an ornate ballroom, used mainly these days for weddings.

The passed through a heavy door to the ramble of offices and storerooms and finally to the kitchen.

"This is the real hub of the business," Sasha said. 'We have quite a reputation for our food. People come from all over now we are open to non-residents.'

"Gosh," Cathy said, thinking of the ample pies and thick bowls of porridge of her summer holiday. "Well, that's one thing here that has certainly changed."

"You've been here before?" Sasha asked.

"Yes, just once. A holiday years ago."

"And you came back. How lovely."

"It was a special time for me."

She tried to disguise the dreamy look which came to her eyes. It had been special because of James. She had spent every moment with him, surfing, chatting, laughing.

They had escaped their parents, held hands on the beach. He had kissed her under the stars on that last night.

Cathy raised her fingers to her face, that first brush of his lips against hers, her first proper kiss.

She could still feel it.

They had promised to write, to meet again, but the letters had fizzled out.

James had gone off to college. Her own life took a new direction.

Then she had met the disaster that was Ben.

The hotel kitchen was

small. Steam was rising and everyone was busy.

Even though it was still early, the air was filled with the crackle of cooking, the slap of chopping and peeling.

"You must come and meet the chef," Sasha said. "He'll be out the back."

Cathy followed Sasha to an office behind the kitchen. Sasha knocked on the door and pushed it open.

"Hi," Sasha said. "I'm just showing Miss Tyler around. She's the new deputy front of house."

"Thanks." A young man looked up from where he was leaning over the computer on the desk.

A look of puzzlement spread across his face.

"Miss Tyler?" he said.

Cathy's heart lurched.

Surely not – it couldn't be. Ten years on. Here in this same hotel.

He hadn't recognised her. He didn't remember.

"Cathy," she said, her voice trembling.

"Cathy." Slowly the recognition dawned and a smile spread across his face.

That lovely smile she remembered so well. He was just the same.

"What are you doing here?" he said. "I mean, I can't believe it's really you."

Cathy held her breath as he stood up and came around to greet her properly.

"James," she said. "I didn't know you worked here. I . . ." Her voice trailed off. "Really, I had no idea.

"I was just looking for a job and I remembered how happy I'd been . . ."

She shut her mouth hard.

She couldn't tell him how her sixteen-year-old self had felt about him or how often she had thought about him since.

"How long have you been here?" she asked then.

"I started as a sous chef five years ago," he said. "I came back, too. I didn't mean to stay.

"I was looking for something, but I've just realised it wasn't something – it was someone."

SALAD DAYS AND STRAWBERRY NIGHTS

Venturing into my garden patch,
Where fruit and vegetables thrive,
I listen to the buzzing bees,
Visiting flowering mint and chive.

With trusty secateurs in hand
I welcome the cooling breeze,
Picking only what I need to make
A meal that is sure to please.

Fresh lettuce leaves, washed and chopped,
Cucumber with peppers so sweet,
Tossing in cherry tomatoes, too,
Makes this refreshing meal complete.

Then later, by the garden pond,
Warmed still by the setting sun's light,
We feast on homegrown strawberries,
And welcome this short summer's night.

By Angie Keeler

Illustration : Shutterstock.

MAGIC!

It can't be a coincidence
That all throughout the years
The greatest wizards of all time
Were blessed with flowing beards.

Dumbledore and Merlin,
Even Gandalf in his place.
The proper magic users
Had to have a hairy face!

There's not a day goes by
When I don't prove this theory true.
No matter how upset I am,
How angry, sad or blue

A happy smiling Staffie,
A wriggly newborn pup,
A calm and regal lurcher
Never fails to cheer me up.

It's a special kind of magic
And they do it with such style;
They wave their tails like magic wands
And conjure up a smile!

By Ros McKenna

Cosy CRIME

Enjoy these exciting stories of acts most wicked, and the intrepid investigators keen to stop the criminals in their tracks. Will our heroes save the day?

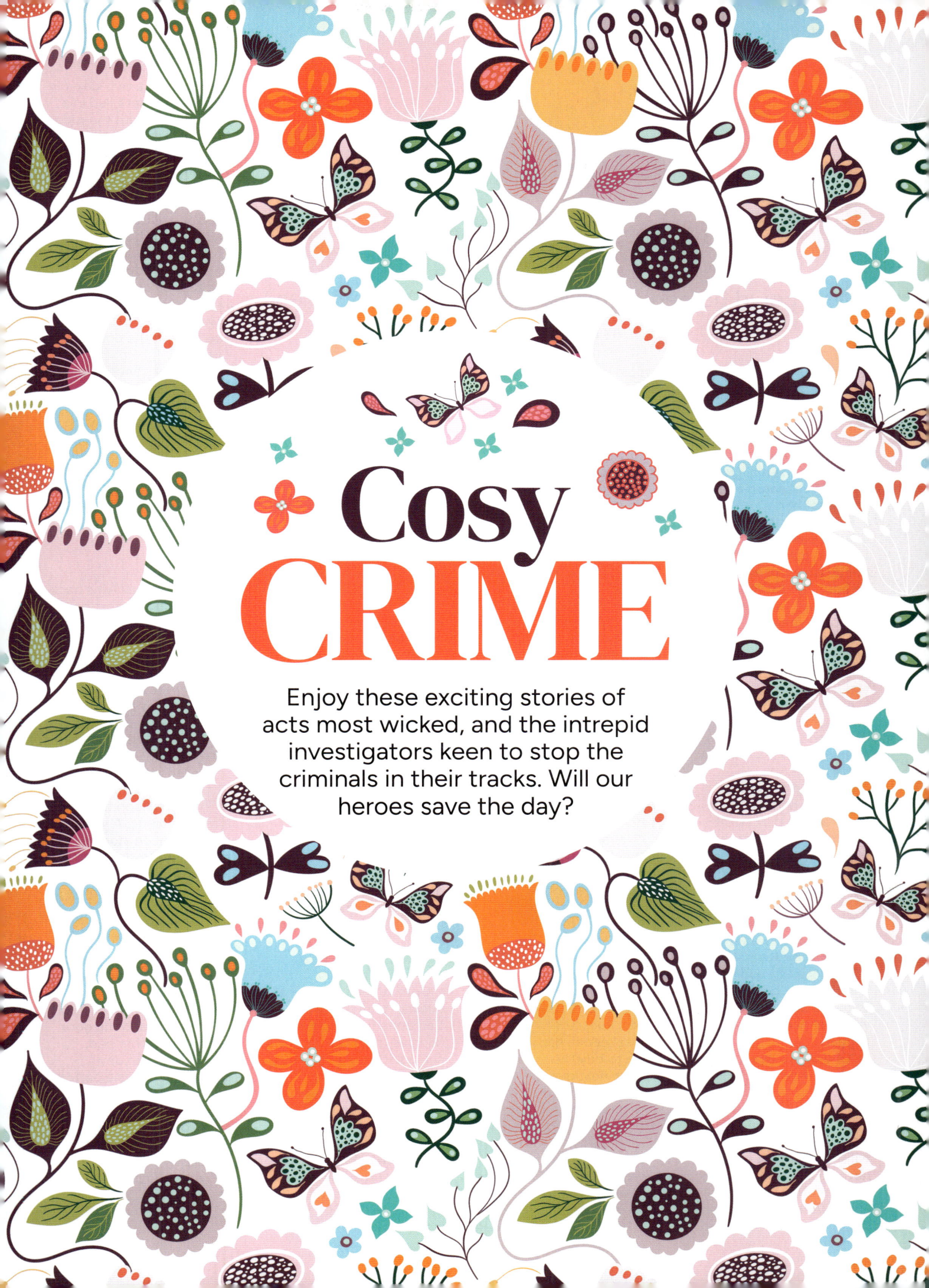

Elsie Investigates

Who could be behind the murder of Mr Henry Voles?

BY BECCA ROBIN

A SINGLE gunshot rang out, followed by a piercing scream.

It brought the gentle chatter and tinkle of teacups in the main lounge of the Winstanton Hotel to an abrupt halt.

Elsie Roberts, the maid who'd been about to serve Lady Drydale, abandoned her dessert trolley and ran through the foyer, where the woman who'd screamed was being helped to a chair.

A dreadful scene awaited on the front steps of the hotel this summer afternoon.

A man lay sprawled on the steps while Mr Dukes the doorman was holding what looked like the man's scarf to his chest.

Everyone else was panicking, and two male hotel guests barged into Elsie as they raced up the steps.

"He's been shot!" Mr Dukes cried. "Fetch a doctor!"

Elsie heard a police whistle, which was shortly answered by several more.

Word was spreading fast, and the local bobbies were trying to apprehend whoever had just pulled the trigger.

"One of our guests is a doctor; I'll get him!" Elsie cried.

She ran inside to fetch retired Dr Evans, who'd been taking tea with his wife. Sadly, there was nothing Dr Evans could do.

The murdered man was Henry Voles, a high-class commercial traveller who would stay at the hotel to impress his wealthy London clients, to whom he sold soft furnishings.

Inspector Bush of Scotland Yard arrived to interview the witnesses.

Jones, the boot boy, said he'd caught a glimpse of a man standing in the alleyway, holding a revolver.

"What was Mr Voles like, Elsie?" Inspector Bush asked her.

With his long overcoat, bristling moustache and smell of pipe tobacco, Bush looked out of place perched on the dainty blue settee in the small lounge.

"He seemed a nice, quiet man," Elsie replied.

"Did you overhear any conversations suggesting he might have enemies?"

"No," Elsie said. "He didn't seem the type of man who'd have enemies."

"Never mind. It was worth a try." Bush sighed. "Do me a favour, Elsie. Keep your eyes and ears open."

Elsie bobbed a curtsey and left the room.

Poor Henry Voles's bedroom on the third floor had already been searched by the police and his personal effects removed.

Mrs Rees, the housekeeper, had instructed Elsie to tidy the room ready for the next guest.

It did seem brutal to straighten the room so soon after the man's death, but Elsie did as she was told.

As the staff lift was awaiting repairs, staff were allowed to use the guest lift.

Elsie pressed the brass call button. When the doors opened, she was pushed aside by two men who got out – the same men who'd barged into her earlier.

Elsie felt like telling them good manners cost nothing!

An argument was clearly going on between the two.

Elsie entered the lift, but held the doors open long enough to overhear their conversation as they headed through the foyer.

"Walter, I've told you what will happen if you don't give me those shares," the younger one said.

"Shh, Sidney!" The other man looked around warily.

"There's nobody about." Sidney laughed.

"What about her?" Walter pointed at Elsie, who was pretending to have difficulty making the lift buttons work.

"She doesn't count," Sidney scoffed. "She's hardly going to ring up my dear sister Adeline and inform her she's been married to a two-timing rat for the past nine years!"

"For heaven's sake, keep it down."

Elsie could see how shaken Walter was.

Unfortunately, it was all she had time to take in. Someone on an upper floor had called for the lift and she couldn't prevent the doors from closing.

So many grand people passed through the doors of the Winstanton Hotel, but Elsie had learned that their lives were not always as blissful as they seemed.

As she was clearing the last bits of rubbish from Henry Voles's room, she came across a two-day-old newspaper that filled in a few details about the rude pair and cemented her suspicion that blackmail was afoot.

In the financial section, there were photographs of Mr Walter Cramton, who had recently become the chairman of a large investment company upon the sudden death of his father, and his brother-in-law Mr Sidney Drope, who was also on the board of directors.

The story concerned an upcoming shareholder meeting.

Putting two and two together, Sidney Drope was threatening to expose Walter Cramton to his wife as a serial adulterer unless he was given more shares and more power in the company.

• • • •

Inspector Bush was back at the hotel the next day.

The murderer hadn't been caught and Bush admitted to Elsie that he was still stumped for a motive.

"You were right," he told her. "It seems Mr Voles didn't have an enemy in the world. Who would want to kill a man like that?"

Elsie shook her head. It just didn't add up.

That afternoon there was a terrible to-do. A valuable item had been stolen from Mr Sidney Drope's room.

He stood at reception, ranting and raving and accusing the maid Doris of being light-fingered.

Although Doris's little bedroom was searched by Mrs Rees, the item was not discovered.

When Elsie went to find Doris, she found the poor girl crying on her bed.

"He's a rotten devil, blaming you." Elsie patted her friend's arm.

"I feel so ashamed." Doris sobbed. "Even though I haven't done anything wrong."

"What's gone missing?" Elsie asked.

"I'm not supposed to say."

"Why on earth not?"

Set in the 1920s

Doris sat up and dried her eyes.

"I don't know," she admitted. "Mr Drope made such a fuss, but the other one, Mr Cramton, came up afterwards and tried to play it down, saying we didn't want the police involved, and Mrs Rees agreed.

"That's when he told us – me and Mrs Rees – not to say what had gone missing."

"You can tell me." Elsie was suddenly interested.

"Well, all right. I don't see why it's so important not to say. The item was a yellow cashmere scarf. It's his lucky scarf apparently, and he wears it all the time."

"Oh, yes." Elsie nodded.

In her mind's eye, she could see Sidney wearing the scarf when he'd nearly sent her flying on the front steps.

"What would I want with his yellow scarf?" Doris's eyes filled with tears again.

"No-one who knows you would think you'd taken it," Elsie reassured her.

Mrs Rees had decided to swap Elsie and Doris around, so now Elsie was servicing the bedrooms on the first floor and Doris those on the third.

Elsie's suspicions were on fire.

Why would Cramton not want everyone talking about the yellow scarf? Why didn't he want the police involved?

Could the scarf be a clue to the much bigger crime under investigation?

That evening, Cramton and Drope were dining in the Cairo Room with its sumptuous gold palm tree decor.

They were sitting at separate tables and talking animatedly with other members of the board who had joined them for dinner.

No-one seeing Cramton would have guessed there was anything wrong.

Elsie spotted her chance and slipped upstairs. She used her pass key to let herself into Cramton's room.

She gave it a thorough search and found what she was looking for hiding in the bottom of a wardrobe.

The yellow scarf had been rolled up tightly and squeezed into a sock.

Elsie left it where she'd found it. There was one further check she had to make before ringing Scotland Yard.

She went to see Mr Dukes, who was standing in his usual place, in the portico of the hotel entrance.

"I know you held a scarf to Mr Voles's chest when he was shot," she said. "Was it Mr Voles's own scarf?"

"That's right," Mr Dukes confirmed. "It's all there was available."

"A yellow scarf, if I remember rightly?"

"Yes, definitely yellow."

If Elsie was right, the shooting had been a case of mistaken identity.

Poor Henry Voles had been wearing the same bright scarf as the intended victim: Sidney Drope.

Cramton had hidden the one belonging to Sidney to stop the police noticing the coincidence.

Elsie kept calm as she crossed the foyer on her way to use the telephone in the small lounge.

Her hand was resting on the door handle when she heard a voice within.

It was Cramton, talking on the phone.

When Elsie put her ear to the door, she could hear what he was saying.

"Tomorrow morning at ten o'clock sharp we'll leave by the front entrance. That's right. A black briefcase patterned with white diamonds, and I know there's only one in existence. I'll make sure Drope is carrying it."

• • • •

At ten the next morning, a carriage was waiting in the sunshine at the front steps of the Winstanton Hotel.

It had been booked to convey Mr Cramton and Mr Drope to their shareholder's meeting.

"I don't believe it!" Sidney Drope slammed his fist on the reception counter. "The briefcase was here just two minutes ago and now it's gone. It's been stolen! What kind of hotel is this?"

"I'm sorry, sir." Mrs Rees was flustered. "We'll look everywhere until we find it."

Elsie could see Walter Cramton turning pale.

"This is ridiculous." Drope was furious. "I'll just have to manage without it; we can't wait here any longer.

"But this time, I will be contacting the police."

He stormed out through the doors and into the carriage.

"Here's the briefcase. It must have fallen over and got kicked across the floor," Elsie said, pulling the black briefcase with distinctive white diamonds from beneath the coat stand where she'd hidden it.

"Here you are, Mr Cramton." She attempted to pass it to him.

"Oh, er – no, I won't take it," he said hastily.

"Whyever not, sir?" Elsie pressed.

"Go and get Mr Drope. He'll take the briefcase."

"But you're going to be late for your meeting, sir. You'd better take it."

"Just do as I say!," Walter Cramton snarled.

"No, sir." Elsie scowled back. "I will not."

"Quite right, Elsie." Inspector Bush's voice rang out and he emerged from the office. "Of course he won't take the briefcase, and I don't blame him.

"The hitman waiting outside has never actually met you, has he, sir?" he said to Cramton. "He might shoot the wrong man – again. Except my officers have overpowered him and he is about to be taken into custody.

"As are you, Mr Walter Cramton."

• • • •

Elsie descended the stairs into the kitchen to a round of applause from her fellow members of staff. Doris had made her a cup of tea.

"I'm glad Drope wasn't murdered," the boot boy, Jones, said. "Even though he's such a horror. Poor old Mr Voles, though, was a real gentleman. Murdered for wearing the wrong colour of scarf. It's a shame."

"Sidney Drope owes our Doris an apology," Elsie replied. "Although I wouldn't go holding your breath."

"And what about me?" Mrs Rees demanded. "My nerves are all of a dither.

"All these murders and accusations. I've never known the like, and I've worked at the Winstanton Hotel for thirty years!"

Elsie winked at Doris, who suppressed a smile as she fanned Mrs Rees with a tea cloth. ■

The Guest List

Someone at the wedding must be responsible for the missing statue . . .

BY ALISON CARTER

"It will be fine," Patricia said. "I trust you, Lisa. And this castle is perfect for us. How many brides can be married in such a venue?"

Patricia was right, but that didn't stop Lisa from worrying. This was her first job as a wedding planner.

Patricia's father, a family friend, had given her the chance, and another local connection had given her access to the Castello Grassiano.

The castle, perched atop a Tuscan hillside village, was undergoing massive renovation.

Parts of it were shored up with planks and string, but it had immense charm.

Creating a perfect wedding, however, was about more than just the setting. Patricia and Luigi's families had requested simple elegance and taste for their 40 guests, but there had already been some setbacks.

Lisa's original caterer had pulled out, and the replacement seemed disorganised.

What Lisa had really wanted to make this event perfect was a wedding artist. It was a new trend, and Patricia and Luigi loved the idea of having a set of professional paintings to capture their joyful summer wedding.

Lisa had dreamed of hiring Cinzia Iacomo, one of the most famous wedding artists in the field. But Cinzia was already booked.

"It's just one element," Lisa told her sister, Sara, her assistant in the business.

"Yeah," Sara agreed. "I'd be more worried about those friends of Luigi's coming from Rome."

"Me, too. We'll keep an eye on them."

They had already met these two ex-colleagues of Luigi. He had once worked for a multinational gambling corporation but now ran a holiday villa business with Patricia. He had privately told Lisa that he'd rather not have invited them.

"They knew about our engagement and basically invited themselves," he explained.

Lisa had even been warned to watch the silverware.

• • • •

Lisa was tense on the morning of the wedding, waking before five. She spent an hour pacing her hotel room, trying to calm her nerves. At seven, her phone rang.

"Lisa Vaschi?" a female voice asked.

It was Cinzia. She had a cancellation and could take the job!

"I can only give an hour and a half," Cinzia said, "but I'll sketch, take photos, and produce three to four watercolours of the ceremony and reception.

"A limited number of prints will follow."

The price was steep, but Lisa knew that Patricia's parents would want Cinzia Iacomo. She couldn't believe her luck.

"Thank you," Lisa gushed. "You're doing me a huge favour."

Cinzia was well-known for her talent and organisational skills. She arrived promptly at ten, accompanied by a strikingly handsome man.

"My brother, Vitaliano," Cinzia explained. "He helps me with my stuff."

"Of course," Lisa said.

Vitaliano had never seen the Castello Grassiano before, and he was fascinated by it.

He was an archaeologist, back in Tuscany to visit family and help Cinzia during the busy wedding season.

"I usually only assess things I've dug up," he said, "but I know that's extraordinary."

He pointed to a statue of the Madonna in a wall niche, traces of blue paint still visible on her robes.

"It's fifteenth century, maybe earlier. I'm sure I know the sculptor from Montepulciano," he continued. "It's worth a fortune, and I'm surprised the new owner hasn't protected it."

Lisa noticed that the men from Rome, dressed in shiny suits and slicked-back hair, had moved closer. She saw Vitaliano glance at them and step away, clearly regretting his earlier comments.

The Roman men seemed harmless enough, but they were already tipsy hours before the wedding even began.

• • • •

The ceremony in the front courtyard was magical. Cinzia sat just in the guests' eyeline, sketching, while the family looked on in delight.

Cinzia took dozens of photos in between swift strokes of her brush and pencil.

At half-past noon, the guests were directed to the larger piazza further back in the castle. More than half of them, as Lisa had anticipated, nipped off to explore the gardens with their giant flowerpots and fragrant lemon trees.

About 12 guests were milling around the lunch tables when Cinzia approached Lisa.

"I'm sorry," she said, "but did you not read my email? I cannot have guests snapping photos until the paintings are finished. My work is the only record."

Lisa hesitated. She wasn't keen on bossing the guests around, but the family was so delighted to have Cinzia there that she agreed to politely ask them to tuck away their phones.

Lisa checked her watch – it was now 12.50 p.m.

The meal would be served at 1.15 p.m., and she needed to gather the stray guests. Suddenly, her eye was drawn upwards, and she saw, five feet up on the wall, that the niche was empty.

The statue had gone!

Her heart skipped a beat. The new owner would be furious at her lack of security. If she raised the alarm now, the beautiful day would be ruined. But she had to do something.

Vitaliano was suddenly at her side, and her panic began to subside.

"I just noticed," he said, horrified. "Goodness knows how or who. I have my motorbike, and I'm going to go right now. The thief can't have gone far."

"No," Lisa replied. "It was there just minutes ago."

"The village only has one road in and out," Vitaliano told her. "I'll call you. Cinzia's given me your number."

Five minutes later, Lisa received a breathless call from him.

"I crossed paths with the police just now."

"Yes, I summoned them," she replied.

"Good. I identified myself, and they were fine with me giving chase."

The next hour was difficult. The police could not avoid disrupting the wedding, and the guests stood around confused as they shut down the entrances to the castle.

Their chief explained that they were already aware of the statue's existence and had planned to ask the new owner about security measures.

Cinzia approached, folders under her arm, just as the officer was asking Lisa to gather the guests' phones for examination.

"We'll need times, and we need to know who was here," he said.

"I don't want to interfere," Cinzia began, "and I am sorry that it's my fault no photographs were taken.

"But I did record every person present. Brides and grooms want absolute accuracy."

The officer nodded. "I've seen your work, *Signorina* Iacomo. I know the level of detail." He shook his head.

"Even as we arrived, guests were dispersing. It's almost impossible to lock down a place like this."

Lisa looked about for the Roman men. They were nowhere to be seen. She told the police she was sure it had to be a guest.

"We did have a single security guard at each exit," she explained, "and they had guest lists with photos.

"This village swarms with tourists in the summer, so we had to."

She sighed.

"I wish we'd been faster in appraising them of the situation," she added.

Cinzia surrendered all her work to the police, and they went away to list all the figures present during the minutes before the theft.

The Roman men showed up later that evening, in a bar in the next village. Luigi said he wouldn't put it past them to do something so awful – he barely knew them these days – but they were apparently astonished when questioned, and nothing was found on them or at their hotel.

They did say they'd slipped out as the police arrived. "Not fans of cops," one of them said, "but what do I want with a Madonna?"

• • • •

As the days passed, each guest in Cinzia's painting was questioned.

A few were asked to stay in the village, and they found the delay disruptive. Lisa saw the disappointment and embarrassment on Patricia and Luigi's faces and squirmed.

The statue was not insured, and the whole affair had become a fiasco with Lisa's name on it.

Vitaliano hung around for a while. He asked Lisa out to dinner and was kind and supportive. She liked him, but everything about the event had gone sour.

• • • •

Vitaliano went back to work, and their fledgling relationship fizzled out.

Lisa dropped her ambition of being a wedding planner and moved to Perugia, where she worked in admin at the university.

Two years passed, and the mental scars faded. Patricia messaged her from time to time, insisting that nothing had been Lisa's fault.

Luigi and I are really happy, she wrote. *You arranged our wedding in a beautiful place and did your very best. Come visit us.*

For more than a year, Lisa avoided the village, but eventually, she began to feel that she was being overdramatic.

The following August, on a blazing hot day, she drove back to stay with her sister.

She stopped off in Montepulciano for water and a sandwich.

A few new shops had opened, and down an alley, a wonderfully messy junk shop had bric-a-brac stacked around its doors.

Lisa's eye was drawn to a painting, half-hidden behind another. Its colours immediately reminded her of Cinzia Iacomo's work.

She moved aside the dreadful oil painting of a puppy that obscured it.

Surely this was one of the records of Patricia's wedding? The castle was unique. The picture was barely begun, with the tables and cypress trees only pencilled in, but the faces, and some colourful pieces of clothing, were already detailed.

It made Lisa smile but also feel sad. That moment had held such promise.

It was interesting to see Cinzia's methods at play.

The guests smiled out at Lisa, holding glasses, searching for name cards at a table. There was even the statue in its niche – a sight that made Lisa wince.

Then she thought of

Vitaliano, how charming he had been. He had been another loss. She bent and scanned the painting for his face, his sweep of dark hair and narrow eyes, but he was nowhere to be seen.

The guests who'd been in the piazza as one o'clock approached had been mostly older relatives.

But Vitaliano had been there. He had come up beside her just as she realised the statue had gone.

A noisy group of schoolchildren passed behind Lisa, jostling her, but she didn't notice.

Maybe Cinzia had not painted her brother into the image because he wasn't an official guest, but if he had been included, he would have been questioned by the police.

Lisa drove towards her home village and stopped at the police station on the way. It seemed mean to Vitaliano, but she asked the desk sergeant if she could get confirmation that officers on the day had received a call from Vitaliano as he left to chase the thief on his bike.

As luck would have it, the sergeant had been there that day, and he agreed to look at the file.

He remembered him – a friendly man who had calmed her on that horrible afternoon with kind words.

"No such name in the file," he said. "Why do you ask?"

Lisa felt her stomach drop. Vitaliano had lied.

• • • •

The police discovered that Vitaliano wasn't Cinzia's brother. He wasn't even an archaeologist. His real name was linked to several art thefts, including the Madonna statue.

"Neither of them needed money," Lisa told Sara. "It was just greed."

"It's a good thing you stopped dating him," Sara commented. "How's it going with that lovely desk sergeant?"

"Well!" Lisa smiled. "Really well."

Isabella's On The Case

Set in 1933

Though the sightings seemed genuine, she knew there was no such thing as ghosts . . .

BY SHARON HASTON

DID you hear the latest? That cinema ghost has caused the cleaner to die of fright!"

Mrs Brown's eyebrows shot up as she imparted this juicy news.

The purple hat she was wearing seemed almost to quiver with the force of her words.

Reaching for the room key from the hook, Isabella frowned, unsure how to respond.

"Are you talking about Lizzie Taylor?" she asked. "I'd have thought she'd be more likely to chase the ghost with her mop and give it a piece of her mind."

Mrs Brown snatched the key from Isabella's hand. "I'm only repeating what I've been told."

"Spreading gossip, more like," Isabella muttered under her breath as Mrs Brown stomped up the stairs to her room, her face flushed with indignation.

Aunt Clara, who had been tidying up behind the reception desk, emerged and immediately wagged her finger at Isabella.

"Isabella, I've told you a hundred times. The customer is always right in my guest-house."

"I'm not surprised you lost your last job at the dressmaker's. You were far too cheeky."

Isabella sighed, shaking her head.

"I wasn't cheeky, Aunt Clara. I was honest. Women wanted Greta Garbo-style evening dresses when they had Oliver Hardy figures."

"Isabella!" Aunt Clara scolded, but then, unable to resist, she turned away to hide her smile.

"Anyway, you don't believe in ghosts, do you, Aunt Clara?" Isabella asked as she wrote out the bills for the departing guests.

Aunt Clara shrugged. "I don't know. There's been a lot of strange things happening at that new cinema. I heard Mystic Mary-Anne is going to try to speak to the ghost and persuade it to leave."

Isabella snorted. "That woman's a charlatan."

"Isabella, that's an unladylike noise! You must stop making it in front of our guests, or you'll ruin their appetites."

Isabella sighed deeply. Being employed at Aunt Clara's guest-house was better than working at the dressmaker's, but the guests were so stiff and imperious. She longed for some excitement.

• • • •

"How did you do that?" Isabella marvelled at Freddie's latest card trick.

Freddie, a magician, tapped his nose and gave a sly grin. "Fascinating Freddie never reveals his secrets."

Isabella laughed, enjoying the show.

At least Freddie was an interesting guest.

She'd miss him when he moved on.

She loved trying to figure out how he performed the tricks he practiced on her.

"What do you think about this ghost business at the cinema?" he asked, his hands shuffling the cards.

"Total mumbo jumbo!" Isabella declared, flicking the Queen of Hearts from the deck.

"It's 1933, for goodness' sake. I can't believe people still fall for that nonsense."

Freddie shrugged. "Apparently, Mystic Mary-Anne spoke to the ghost and discovered he died in a fire. The cinema's built on the site of his old, burned-down house."

Isabella snorted just as Aunt Clara appeared on the staircase. "Isabella! What have I told you about making that undignified noise?"

"But the cinema's been open for two years now," Isabella reminded Freddie. "Why has the ghost waited until the last six months to start haunting it?"

"Not everything can be explained," Freddie reasoned, pulling the Queen of Hearts out from behind Isabella's ear.

• • • •

On her day off, Isabella decided she would visit the cinema to investigate what this ridiculous ghost business was all about.

The whole town was abuzz with the story.

Plus, they were showing "Little Women", her favourite book. She couldn't wait to see Katharine Hepburn play Jo, her favourite March sister.

"This ghost is really hurting business," Tim, the ticket booth attendant, told her as she handed him her money.

"What does this ghost do exactly?" Isabella asked, curious.

"He's an elderly man who wears a top hat and wanders around, then vanishes into thin air," Tim explained.

"He's also damaged some films – like 'King Kong' – and last week, the auditorium filled with smoke for no reason, making people panic, thinking there was a fire."

"He sounds like a very bad-tempered ghost," Isabella said, raising her eyebrows. "He'd better not destroy 'Little Women' tonight, or I won't be happy."

"I like this job," Tim confided, his voice low. "I don't want to lose it. I really hope Mystic Mary-Anne manages to get rid of him."

"Does the cinema owner have any enemies?" Isabella asked, a thought striking her.

Tim looked taken aback. "What a strange question. I don't think so."

After the film ended, Isabella decided to stay behind and investigate further. She was convinced the "ghost" was merely a clever attempt to harm the cinema's business.

As she wandered through the dimly lit aisles, she caught a glimpse of something – or someone – out of the corner of her eye.

A gentleman, dressed in a black cloak and top hat, was wandering around, just as Tim had described.

Curious, Isabella followed him. He walked quickly and opened the door to the gentleman's toilet. So much for ghosts being able to float through doors, she thought wryly.

Knowing Aunt Clara would faint if she saw her entering a gentleman's toilet, Isabella hoped no one else was inside.

She tiptoed in after him. The toilet was empty, but the window was wide open.

"Ghosts don't need windows to help them disappear," Isabella muttered to herself, noticing a magician's wand lying on the floor. She picked it up, intrigued.

• • • •

Freddie examined the wand carefully when Isabella showed it to him. "Mine has my initials on it, but this one doesn't. We could ask Mr Desmond if any of his magicians have reported losing one."

"That's a great idea," Isabella said, excited by the prospect of solving this mystery. It was far more entertaining than setting the breakfast table for her guests.

Mr Desmond, the theatre manager, shook his head when they showed him the wand. "Nobody's mentioned a missing wand," he said, his expression unreadable. "Let's focus on your act, Freddie. I wish I'd thought of that sword trick myself."

Isabella raised an eyebrow, noting how quickly Mr Desmond had changed the subject. She was beginning to suspect he was hiding something.

Just then, a comedian entered the room and sat on Freddie's top hat by mistake, making it look more like a flat cap. Mr Desmond offered to lend him his own hat. Isabella excused herself, saying she needed to return to the guest-house.

But as they left for the dressing rooms, Isabella quietly hid inside one of the magician's boxes on stage. From there, she overheard Mr Desmond and the comedian.

"How many tickets have we sold tonight?" the comedian asked.

"We're about half full," Mr Desmond replied with a sigh. "People would rather watch 'King Kong' than see live dancing. Honestly, I wish films had never been invented."

Isabella felt a sneeze coming on, but she held it in. The last thing she needed was to be caught. But suddenly, a tickle in her nose was too much, and she sneezed loudly.

Mr Desmond opened the box door, and Isabella, following Freddie's advice about the trap door, slipped underneath the stage before anyone could spot her.

• • • •

"So, you think Mr Desmond is pretending to be a ghost to drive people back to the theatre?" Freddie asked, wide-eyed when Isabella told him about her discovery.

Isabella nodded. "But we'll need proof before we go to the police."

A few days later, Freddie shared new developments with her. "The stage curtain's been opening and closing by itself, and the clock in the foyer keeps stopping at ten o'clock."

"If Mr Desmond wanted people to leave the cinema, why would he cause ghostly activity in the theatre?" Freddie wondered aloud.

"I don't know," Isabella confessed, though she was still convinced Mr Desmond was involved in the scheme somehow.

That evening, Aunt Clara told Isabella, "Mary-Anne's been asked to investigate the theatre ghost after she helped banish the one at the cinema. I'm going to watch."

Isabella raised an eyebrow. "You mean she really convinced the ghost to leave?"

Aunt Clara nodded. "Apparently, she spoke to the ghost and appealed to his better nature. I doubt her powers, but she might actually have the gift."

• • • •

At the theatre, the crowd sat in rapt silence as Mystic Mary-Anne, deep in a trance, claimed to be speaking to the ghost of a trapeze artist who had died in an accident. The audience was mesmerised by the haunting voice.

But Isabella's instincts told her something wasn't right. She slipped out of the stalls and, following her hunch, crept up to the box. Sure enough, a young girl was crouched there, pretending to be the trapeze artist, answering Mary-Anne's questions.

When the girl saw Isabella, she screamed.

"No!" Isabella shouted, holding the girl's arm. "She's alive and well!"

Chaos broke out as people started shouting and pointing.

Sergeant Henderson, who had been keeping an eye on the event, blew his whistle and ordered everyone to leave.

On stage, he gathered the key players: Isabella, Mr Desmond, Mary-Anne, Aunt Clara, Freddie, and the young girl.

"What's going on here?" Sergeant Henderson demanded.

Mary-Anne began to sob.

"I just wanted to drum up business. I thought if I got people talking about ghosts, they'd come to me for readings."

"The cinema manager paid me to exorcise the ghost. Then I came up with the idea of charging people to hear me communicate with the theatre ghost."

Isabella pointed at Mr Desmond. "You were the cinema ghost I saw."

Mr Desmond, gazing at Mary-Anne with affection, sighed. "She was my first love. I helped her because I hate the cinema. It steals my customers."

Sergeant Henderson nodded. "Good work, young lady," he said, shaking Isabella's hand. "If you ever want to join the police force, come and see me."

Aunt Clara gasped. "A policewoman! How unladylike!"

Freddie smiled and placed a hand on Isabella's shoulder. "She'd make a great policewoman."

Isabella winked at Sergeant Henderson as Aunt Clara led her away, though a smile tugged at her lips.

• • • •

"Isabella, you're on the front page!" The newspaper delivery boy pointed to her photo as he handed her the local paper.

Smiling, Isabella put on her cloche hat.

Soon she would be replacing it with a policewoman's smart cap.

With a bounce in her step, she made her way to the police station to see Sergeant Henderson.

She had a feeling there would be many more newspaper articles in the years ahead starting with the headline *Isabella Investigates*.

She had finally found her calling.

Set in 1970s

All That Glitters

Everyone at Silver Moon disco was waiting in anticipation . . .

BY SALLY WATERBURY

THE queue outside the Silver Moon discotheque snaked around the corner.

The revellers were lined up near the door, warm in the summer air.

It would be a few hours until the sun set over the town, but the club would be open soon and no-one wanted to miss this special Saturday night.

It was going to be tough night for the other local disco, Rays Of Gold, which was usually the busier venue on a Saturday night.

Lauren was hanging on to the arm of her best friend Sandra.

They both had on their new flares, bought that afternoon in Chelsea Girl in the high street.

They both looked great. It was going to be a fantastic evening.

"Hiya," Lauren said to a passing group of youths.

Sandra blushed as Geoff turned her way.

She remembered him from school. He worked in the solicitors in town now.

She'd always had a soft spot for him. He was quieter than the other boys. A bit of a thinker.

She wasn't sure he even knew that she existed.

"It's going to be a great do tonight," one of the lads called. "I'll catch you later, Lauren. You're going to be unmissable under the new glitter ball."

"That's the idea!" Lauren laughed.

It was exactly the plan.

The Silver Moon disco was ten years old this week.

To celebrate, rumour had it that they had bought a new glitter ball. An enormous one, just like in "Saturday Night Fever".

Every single person in the queue was ready for it, ready to dance the night away underneath it.

"You're looking pretty funky yourself," Lauren said as the boys went by in their flares and collars.

Slowly the queue began to inch forward past the bouncer and into the club.

The music was already blaring and the lights flashing.

Lauren and Sandra dropped their jackets at the coat check and made their way to the bar.

"I thought I saw you out there, Sandra." It was Geoff. "Want a drink?"

Sandra felt herself blush again. It was a good job it was so dark in here.

"OK," she agreed.

So he did know who she was!

The club started to fill up and it got hotter and noisier.

It was difficult to hear Geoff over the hubub.

Finally, Sandra realised he was asking her to dance.

She looked around for Lauren, but she had disappeared.

In fact, the atmosphere had changed completely.

"What's going on?" Sandra asked.

"I think they're about to unveil this new glitter ball," Geoff replied.

They pushed their way through the throng towards the big room where the DJ was spinning his records.

The floor shook with the beat under Sandra's feet and the flashing lights throbbed overhead.

In they went and found Lauren just inside, too.

The room was packed, but no-one was dancing, not even the girls who always got up on to the podiums.

The red and orange lights of the dance floor spun through their colours, but there was no-one strutting their stuff. Not even Bobby Bradshaw, or Boogie, as he was generally known – the town's answer to Tony from the film.

He was standing in the middle of the dance floor, his white suit glowing.

His neck was bent back, eyes up as he stared at the ceiling.

Everyone was looking up at the curtain, which was about to be pulled down to reveal the new glitter ball.

The DJ ground to a halt, moved into a drum roll and started a countdown. 10, 9, 8 . . .

Anita, the manager, grasped the ribbon and at the right moment gave a massive tug to whisk the curtain away.

The crowd gasped. Hanging from the ceiling was a silver chain that swung with the breeze from the curtain.

There was no glitter ball to be seen!

"Gosh," Sandra said. "I wasn't expecting that."

A wave of disappointment ran through her.

The crowd started to boo, so the DJ turned up the volume of the music.

No-one moved.

"What's happened?" Sandra asked, but she doubted anyone could hear her over the pounding of the record.

The music quietened and then stopped.

Anita climbed on to the podium.

"I'm so sorry," she said, her voice cracking. "I don't know what's gone wrong. I was assured the new glitter ball had been fitted this afternoon.

"It only arrived yesterday and, it's all been a bit of a rush." She tried to smile. "Let's make the best of it."

The crowd were not so happy.

Next to Sandra someone was saying they were going to ask for their money back.

Everyone began to drift out on to the street. Most people seemed to be heading for Rays Of Gold or home.

The evening was ruined. Lauren and Sandra stood

outside and Geoff joined them.

"I've just been chatting with Anita," he told them. "The glitter ball has vanished. She can't imagine what has happened to it. She definitely took delivery of it yesterday."

"That's dreadful," Lauren replied. "Someone must know where it is. It'll ruin her business, letting everyone down so badly."

"We should help her find it," Sandra suggested. "Come on, let's go back in."

They went back through the doors. The bouncer was leaning on the wall, his services no longer needed.

Inside, the main lights were on and all the punters had left in disgust.

Behind the bar they were washing the last of the glasses and the DJ was packing up his records.

Anita was sitting on one of the banquettes near the dance floor. Her mascara had run from crying.

Lauren put an arm around her.

"We've come to help you find the missing glitter ball," Lauren told her. "There must be some explanation."

"It'll be Ray," Anita replied.

Ray Francis was the owner of Rays Of Gold.

"He doesn't think there's room for two discos in a town this size," she said. "It feels like he's been trying to ruin me ever since I opened.

"I should talk to him about it, but I don't want to admit I need help. The glitterball was going to solve all that."

Sandra was shocked to hear that. Ray was well known in the town as he had an interest in a lot of local businesses.

"It could just be a misunderstanding," she said.

"What about Fred, your handyman?" Lauren asked. "Wasn't it he who was supposed to put it up?"

Anita nodded.

"He's disappeared, too."

"Maybe he stole it," Geoff replied. "They're popular at the moment, glitter balls. It would be easy to sell on."

"Do you have any security footage?" Sandra asked.

Anita shook her head.

"I've looked. It's been wiped." She threw her hands in the air. "It's a disaster!"

"Let's track down this glitter ball," Geoff declared. "It's got to be somewhere. I'll go down to Rays Of Gold and have a word with Ray. My dad's a mate of his."

"I'll go round to Fred's house," Lauren put in. "If he's got it, I'll find it easily."

"Anita and I can have a good look here," Sandra added. "It's a big building. It could be anywhere."

Anita sprang to her feet.

"We'll start at the top of the building and work down. It could even be on the roof – there's a big hatch to get out there."

"Let's meet back here in an hour," Geoff suggested.

Sandra and Anita climbed the stairs and then the ladder out on to the roof.

It was a glorious evening. The sun was just beginning to set and the view across the town was magnificent.

There were crowds on the pavement outside the pubs, teenagers hanging about in the park and, in the distance, they could see people being turned away from Rays Of Gold. It must be completely full.

Sandra tried to distract Anita, pointing out the church tower in the opposite direction and commenting on how beautiful it looked with the sun going down behind it.

They went back inside, looked through the attics and the offices on the upper floor.

In a dusty corner, Sandra found a box of records a decade old, and Anita found four dozen cocktail glasses still in their boxes.

"I did wonder what had happened to them," she said.

Time flew by and soon they had to hurry back downstairs as the hour was up.

"I don't think Ray had anything to do with it," Geoff admitted. "He seemed genuinely surprised that his disco is full to bursting tonight. He was quite upset when I told him what had happened.

"I don't think he's a bad man; just a man worried about his business. How did you get on, Lauren?"

Lauren kicked her new platform shoes off. They weren't as easy to wear as she'd hoped and she'd walked all the way to Fred's house and back.

"Fred wasn't at home," she told them. "His wife knew nothing of any glitter ball. She said he didn't come back from work last night. She was quite worried."

"Oh no," Anita replied. "We've got a missing person and a missing glitter ball."

"Whatever are we going to do?" Sandra asked.

She glanced around the disco. It looked so different with the house lights on. So much more ordinary.

A glint in the middle of the dance floor caught her eye.

"Look," she said.

Sandra walked across the dance floor and bent down.

She found a small shard of mirror, then another one.

They led to the edge of the dance floor and across the carpet, out of the door.

"I reckon our glitter ball has been taken across here, and it's damaged."

Together they followed the trail of tiny slivers of mirror.

"Mind your feet on this," Geoff warned Lauren.

Reluctantly she put her shoes back on.

The trail led them to the door of the storeroom, where it stopped.

Sandra tried the handle and gave the door a push.

It was dark inside, but in the corner there was a silvery glint. The glitter ball.

Slumped next to it was a body – it was Fred, the maintenance man, fast asleep.

Fred woke with a start and staggered to his feet.

Anita's body was stiff with anger.

"You'd better have a good explanation, Fred."

Frowning, Fred explained how he'd struggled with the glitter ball and how he'd spent most of last night and most of today trying to secure the fixing.

He told them how he'd assured everyone that he would be able to do it on his own, but that he should have asked for help, but was too proud.

Then it was too late, so he'd strung up the curtain and rolled the ball in here.

He'd wiped the tape so that no-one would laugh at his efforts, and by then he was so exhausted that he'd fallen asleep.

He was so sorry that Anita forgave him on the spot.

"It's late now," Geoff said. "Let's go home. Tomorrow I'll get some of the lads together and we can come over and give you a hand.

"There's a bit of glueing to be done on those pieces that have fallen off, but I'm sure we can get it up and working."

Anita breathed a sigh of relief.

"And when it's up," she began, "I'll do a free evening, to apologise to everyone. I'll even invite Ray.

"In fact, I'm going to call him tomorrow so we can talk business," she went on. "Sometimes it's better to swallow your pride and ask for help."

As they all walked out to go home, Geoff hung back.

"You were great in there," he said to Sandra. "I never realised you were a detective."

Sandra felt herself blush again. She wished he didn't have this effect on her.

"Maybe when Anita opens up again you might like to go there with me," Geoff suggested.

Sandra was sure he was a little bit pink, too, just across his cheeks.

"And in the meantime, perhaps I could have your phone number?" he added. "I had a dreadful crush on you at school. It was so bad that I couldn't bring myself to look at you, let alone speak to you."

"That would be lovely." Sandra smiled.

She wasn't going to tell him that she'd had a crush on him, too. Well, not yet.

Double Exposure

Set in 1965

Somehow, June had found herself caught up in a dangerous plot . . .

BY JOANNE DUNCAN

As the waiter removed her pudding dish, June sat back with a contented sigh and smiled at Philip across the table.

"Coffee?"

This fortnight's stay at a hotel on the Yorkshire coast – her twenty-first birthday present from his parents – was their first proper holiday together.

She couldn't help marvelling at how posh the other guests were – even posher than her in-laws, if that were possible.

Even in 1965, it seemed, class distinctions hadn't been done away with completely.

It was only Monday, a mere two days after their arrival, but already they'd got into the habit of having their coffee served in the lounge after lunch.

The hotel provided a selection of the more respectable daily newspapers, and Philip would scan the headlines in "The Times" or "The Telegraph" as he sipped.

June herself preferred leafing through "Punch" or "Country Life". The property pages alone were a revelation.

They'd just settled into their favourite armchairs when a couple she'd seen earlier, checking into reception, made a beeline for them.

"Hello, Phil." The husband was in his late thirties or thereabouts, boyish but confident looking.

"Good lord, Dickie and Betty!" Philip cried, getting to his feet. "Where did you spring from?"

"And you must be the new Mrs Clarke," the man went on pleasantly, turning to June. "Sorry we couldn't make it to the wedding, but please accept our belated congratulations.

"I'm Richard Aysgarth," he explained, "and this is my wife, Elizabeth. I was a very humble Third Secretary when Philip's father took up his posting at the British Embassy in Bonn ten years ago."

"I was just a teenager at the time, of course," Philip added with a grin.

"No need to rub it in," Richard said and they all laughed. "We hear you're at the Home Office these days."

"Don't you work there, too, June?" Betty was rather intimidatingly elegant but had a humorous curve to her mouth.

"Yes," June replied shyly, "but we're in different sections."

Richard preened a little.

"I was talking to the Home Secretary only the other day, as it happens."

"Before you ask," his wife said dryly, "he means at a palace garden party. We were lucky enough to be among the chosen few this year, and he hasn't shut up about it since."

"Nonsense. Are you interested in fishing, Phil?" Richard asked. "I've arranged for a local to take me out on his boat tomorrow and I'm sure he wouldn't object to your joining us. It'll mean an early start."

"Would you mind, June?" Philip asked.

"Of course not." She smiled. "I'll do some shopping."

"Perfect!" Richard replied. "Let's meet up for drinks in the evening, if you've nothing else planned. We're off to Scotland first thing on Wednesday."

"You do mind, don't you?" Philip asked June when they were alone again. "I can tell by your face."

"No, not at all," June assured him. "It's the drinks I'm dreading. You know I'm no good at making small talk with people I've just met."

For once, he wasn't very sympathetic.

"I expect both my mother and Betty felt exactly the same at your age, but they'd married diplomats and had to learn as they went along. If it helps, Betty won't let the conversation flag. She's known for being charming, even when forced to talk to the most crashing bore."

"Honestly, Phil," June retorted, "if that's your idea of being helpful, it's just as well you didn't try for the diplomatic service yourself."

"Good shot!" a voice called, and there was a ripple of applause.

Philip's eyes widened, then he burst out laughing.

"It's the old lady," he whispered, nodding in the direction of a half-open door. "The one who spends most of her time in the TV room. She must be watching Wimbledon.

"Sorry," he added. "What I said came out wrong. All I meant was that there's no need to worry. Putting people at their ease is the Aysgarths' bread and butter."

• • • •

Philip left before six on Tuesday morning, and June, unable to doze off again, went downstairs far too early.

The dining-room wasn't open, so she sat forlornly in the lobby, trying not to listen to the scolding one of the desk clerks was receiving from an elderly lady, presumably the tennis fan of the previous day.

The lady was hard of hearing, which only made matters worse.

"If you'd let me explain, Miss Gillespie," the clerk kept saying, but she simply talked over him, insisting that something or other was simply not good enough.

After breakfast, June washed a few items in the

hand basin in their room before walking down to the harbour. She bought some picture postcards and, finding a café with tables outside, sat in the sunshine to write them.

This took her more than an hour and she had to order a second pot of tea.

Finally, having posted the cards, she noticed a chemist halfway along the high street and decided to treat herself to a new lipstick.

She very nearly hung back when she saw Betty entering the same shop, but pulled herself together and followed her new acquaintance inside.

There were two counters facing each other. One was for prescriptions and proprietary medicines with a dispensary behind (June glimpsed the chemist through the hatch).

At the smaller one, Betty was spelling out Aysgarth to an assistant.

"The gentleman who looks after the photographic side of the business only comes in on Thursdays," the young woman told her, "so I'm afraid your film won't be collected until then and the prints will take a week."

"That's fine," Betty replied and, turning away.

She gave a little start on seeing June.

"Hello! This is a nice surprise!"

"I'm after a new lipstick," June explained.

"If you'd like a second opinion, I'm at your service. I love make-up."

"I thought Richard said you were only here till tomorrow," June remarked as they stood side by side in front of the cosmetics display. "Won't you have left by the time your snaps are ready?"

"Yes, but we're stopping off here again on our way back," Betty explained. "Not that I'm keen to see them. They were taken at a wedding and the hat I bought for it was not a success."

"That shade would suit you."

"You think so?" June tried the tester on the back of her hand. Unsurprisingly, Betty had very good taste.

While she was paying for the lipstick, the chemist emerged, minus his white coat.

"I'll be back by one o'clock, Rosemary," he called.

"Right-oh, Mr Draper," his assistant replied, but he'd already departed, leaving the doorbell jangling.

Betty raised her eyebrows.

"He's in a hurry. Meeting a lady friend, perhaps?"

The girl giggled.

"No, his wife. She always has his lunch on the table by ten past twelve, and woe betide him if he's late."

"Is it gone twelve already?" June asked, then turned to Betty. "Phil and Richard will be back by now, won't they?"

"I expect so," Betty replied with a grin. "Come on, love's young dream. Don't forget your lipstick."

• • • •

Drinks with the Aysgarths went much better than June had expected, Richard and Betty both making them laugh with tales of embassy life.

Betty, it transpired, played a part in her husband's day-to-day work.

"Only odd bits of typing and filing," she told them. "Diplomats' wives aren't allowed to have proper jobs."

"Don't you mind?" June was surprised.

According to Philip, Betty had a degree from Cambridge.

"Not really. I'm kept pretty busy on the whole. And there are compensations," she added with a half smile. "Would you like to see the outfit I wore to the palace the other day?"

"Yes, please."

The Aysgarths' room was even nicer than their own. It had a private bathroom and more cushions than June had ever seen on one bed.

Instead of heading straight for the wardrobe, however, Betty hesitated.

"I'm afraid I invited you up here on false pretences," she admitted. "The thing is, I've taken a certain step and I'd like to explain the reasons behind it to at least one other person.

"When you hear what it is, you'll understand why that person can't be Dicky."

"Oh." June had never before been confided in by someone older than herself and she felt terribly embarrassed.

What if Betty were having an affair or instigating divorce proceedings?

"A few months ago, a woman bumped into me on the Friedrichstrasse. She apologised, but I later discovered a note in my coat pocket with a telephone number written on it."

This was the last thing June had expected to hear.

"What's the Friedrichstrasse?"

"A busy shopping street in Bonn," Betty explained. "I made contact out of curiosity and, before I knew it, I was being offered money in return for photographing classified documents.

"They knew everything about me – my political affiliations at university, names of friends, even our holiday arrangements. The instructions were very precise.

"On our way to Scotland, I was to book a two-night stay at this hotel and drop the film off at the local chemist's," she finished.

June felt dizzy. Everything had suddenly become unreal. She'd seen stories about spies and defections on the news, of course, and she loved the James Bond films, but this was a far cry from Sean Connery on a tropical beach.

"After being developed, the prints would pass to a third party," Betty continued. "My guess is an officer on an East German cargo ship docked at Hull or Whitby.

"Meanwhile, a bogus set of ruined negatives would be returned to the chemist's with an 'overexposed' sticker on the packet. They think of everything, you see.

"Don't look so horrified, June." Betty laughed. "I haven't done what they asked."

"But I saw you hand the film over," June pointed out. "Does this mean somebody's wedding photos are going to end up in enemy hands?"

"That was a cover story. The photographs are of documents, but they're fakes, based on the kind of stuff I type for Richard."

"Let me get this straight," June said slowly.

"Foreign agents have given you money, which you've kept . . ."

"And an expensive camera."

". . . but instead of keeping your side of the bargain, you're double-crossing them?" June went on. "Isn't that quite dangerous?"

Betty nodded.

"June, I love Richard dearly, but I've been so bored these last few years. You can't imagine how much I envy you girls who have jobs of your own. I wanted an adventure . . ."

Just then, someone knocked on the door and she broke off.

To June's astonishment, the gatecrasher was a tearful Miss Gillespie, who had apparently lost her room key.

The timing was so bad that it was almost funny.

"Don't worry," Betty was saying. "I'll phone reception and ask them to send up a duplicate."

"No, don't do that."

Closing the door behind her, the old lady turned to face them.

She was now perfectly calm and there no longer seemed to be anything wrong with her hearing.

"I'll come straight to the point, Mrs Aysgarth," she said. "I need to substitute another film for the one you left at the chemist's."

"Have you been eavesdropping on our conversation?"

"I was already in possession of the bare facts. It shouldn't surprise you to learn that not much goes unobserved nowadays, not even a chance encounter on the Friedrichstrasse."

Betty was silenced.

"At least I'm now sure you acted in good faith," Miss Gillespie went on, "but it was foolish of you. You're not a professional and your deception would have been seen through at once.

"The replacement film will not only fool the enemy, it'll steer them in the wrong direction entirely."

"Aren't you taking a risk, talking to us like this?" Betty asked. "If you can listen in, so can they."

"It's my job to make sure they don't. What I need from you is a full account of everything that happened this morning."

"Very well," Betty agreed, as though accepting defeat. "The young woman dropped the film in its canister into an envelope on which she wrote my name and address.

"My real name, that is," she explained. "I was told that giving a false one might create complications. The envelope was similar to those used by Boots – the kind that comes back with a wallet inside for the prints and negatives."

"What did she do with it?" Miss Gillespie asked.

"I'm not sure."

"She put it in a cardboard tray with some other envelopes," June piped up. "The tray's on a shelf behind the counter and all the films are collected on a Thursday. Is the chap who does their processing the spy?"

"Mrs Clarke, isn't it?"

June blushed.

"Yes."

"I shall have to ask you to sign the Official Secrets Act, Mrs Clarke," Miss Gillespie told June.

"Thursday," she went on. "That doesn't give me much time to familiarise myself with the shop's routines. It might be best to arrange a simple break-in, even at the risk of attracting unwanted attention."

June and Betty looked at one another.

"If by familiarising yourself with the shop's routines," June began, "you mean finding out who works there and what time they go to lunch and so on . . ."

"Yes?"

"The chemist's assistant told us all that. She's called Rosemary and his name's Mr Draper," she explained. "And he sits down to his dinner, which his wife cooks for him, at ten past twelve every day."

• • • •

Next morning, among all the things that were bothering June, two stood out. The first was that she'd forgotten about early closing day.

Despite her assurances to Miss Gillespie, might not Mr Draper's wife delay the midday meal until one o'clock on Wednesdays?

The second was what she was going to say to Philip. In the event, she improvised, glancing at her watch with an exclamation just as they were finishing lunch.

"Oh, no! I must pop to the shops before they close. You order your coffee, Phil. I'll be back by the time you've drunk it."

He looked a bit put out, but it couldn't be helped.

The high street was deserted, as they'd hoped, except for Miss Gillespie, who was making her way slowly along it.

Right on cue, she staggered slightly and June quickened her steps.

"Are you all right?"

"Faint. I feel faint."

"There's a chemist further along, if you can manage it," June said.

"Here we are. You'll be right as ninepence in a minute," she added as she pushed open the door.

This was pre-arranged code, meaning there were no other customers inside and Mr Draper was absent.

She could see his white coat hanging up against the glass panel in the door of the dispensary. Having helped Miss Gillespie to one of the chairs for customers, she turned to face a terrified-looking Rosemary.

"I'm afraid this lady's not well."

"The pharmacist is at lunch."

"Is there a telephone?"

"Well, yes. In the dispensary . . ." Rosemary replied.

"I'm staying at the same hotel as Miss Gillespie," June told her. "Could you ring for a taxi? If I can just get her back there . . ."

"I'm not supposed to leave the shop unattended."

"Why don't you change the sign to closed and lock the door? I'll stay with her in case she takes a turn for the worse."

"All right."

As soon as Rosemary could be heard speaking to the operator, June darted behind the small counter.

The cardboard tray was still on the same shelf, and she rummaged through the envelopes with shaking fingers until she located the one with Betty's name on it.

Removing the canister, she set it down on the floor to avoid any possibility of a mistake, then reached into her shoulder bag for the replacement.

"Excuse me!"

June nearly jumped out of her skin, then realised that Rosemary had called to her from the dispensary.

"Yes?"

"Sorry, which hotel is it?"

"The Royal."

June couldn't help reflecting that if Rosemary had put her head round the door to ask her question, the game would have been well and truly up. Moments later, the substitution was complete and they were on their way back to the hotel.

• • • •

The Aysgarths left straight after breakfast the next morning. Later, at around nine-thirty p.m., June wandered into the TV room where Miss Gillespie sat alone, as usual.

To her great surprise, she was greeted with a smile.

"I was hoping I'd get a chance to thank you for your kindness earlier. I return to London tomorrow."

"That's a shame," June replied. "I wish we could have talked more. I expect you did war work, like my nan? The WVS or something like that?"

"Something like that, yes," Miss Gillespie told her. "Would you mind turning over to BBC2 for me, dear? The Wimbledon highlights are just about to come on."

Despite all the excitement being over, it was still hard to relax. More than once, June woke up in the night, convinced she'd accidentally put the wrong film back in the tray.

"You'll never guess who I saw getting into a cab with all his luggage just before you came down," Philip whispered on the Saturday while they were waiting to order lunch. "That desk clerk – the one you saw having the argument with Miss What'shername."

"Perhaps he was only temporary," June suggested, startled by a new idea.

Had Miss Gillespie and the so-called clerk been working together? Had he helped her set up her listening equipment, for example?

If so, they must have staged the argument in response to June's unexpectedly early arrival for breakfast. She glanced up and found Philip watching her, as if trying to decipher her expression.

"You've been very quiet since we had those drinks with the Aysgarths," he commented. "Sorry if I upset you the other day by making stupid comparisons.

"To be honest," he went on, "I used to have a crush on Betty when I was a teenager. She seemed so perfect – beautiful, capable and clever. The sort of woman who'd never put a foot wrong."

"Nothing like me, then."

"There's such a thing as being too perfect, you know." Philip took her hand and she wondered if she'd ever be able to tell him the truth. One day, perhaps. When she was an old lady herself.

School For Murder

The death of a teacher here wasn't an accident, and Evelyn was going to prove it!

BY LIZ FILLEUL

Set during WWII

EVELYN didn't like admitting it, but when her father – a chief inspector in London – had advised her not to join the police force, she should have listened.

She'd listened to him at first – a few years ago, when she was about to leave school and told him she wanted to follow in his footsteps.

"Join the police force!" He'd almost spilled his tea in consternation. "You put that thought out of your head immediately, you hear me?

"All they'll have you doing is making cups of tea and typing up their case notes.

"The police won't think you even have a brain, let alone give you the chance to use it."

"You're not like that!" she'd argued.

"No, but too many of the policemen I work with are. You're a clever girl, Evie.

"Don't waste your life in a job where there's no chance of being able to prove your worth. Go into teaching."

Evelyn had acquiesced, done her teacher training then taught in a primary school for two years.

But she'd been frustrated with being in a classroom all day and longed for something more exciting.

Then the war had broken out, and at the end of 1940 she'd decided to join the Women's Auxiliary Police Corps.

"Teaching's an important job," her father had said.

"So is war work," she'd returned. "You said yourself that the best policemen of fighting age have gone into the armed forces. I'll get a chance to prove what I'm capable of in the WAPC."

But now, as she dismounted her bicycle outside South Newhampton Police Station, Evelyn felt glum at the prospect of a long shift spent relaying telephone messages and typing up case notes.

Even though the war had seen an increase in crime, thanks to the blackout and the black market, Evelyn was always consigned to clerical duties rather than helping to catch looters or trace black marketeers.

When she entered the smoke-fogged police station, Sergeant Weaver called out to her.

"Over here, WAPC Masefield. I've got a little job for you."

Sergeant Weaver was a burly man in his late forties. Evelyn suspected he held his rank only because so many talented policemen were away at war.

"Do you know where Padham is?" he asked her.

"Yes, sir."

Evelyn had been for a picnic with friends at Padham. It was a riverside village about three miles from South Newhampton.

"There's a posh girls' school currently evacuated to Coningsby Hall, just outside the village," the sergeant informed her.

"One of the teachers was found drowned in the swimming pool this morning.

"PC Horton, the Padham village policeman, reported it to us a few minutes ago.

"It seems to have been an accident – the teacher was cycling back to the school during the blackout – and the teachers and pupils are likely to be upset, so I think it's better to have a policewoman take statements," he explained. "I'll give you the details."

Evelyn scribbled down the address of Coningsby Hall, the name of the teacher who had drowned – Miss Irene Griffiths – and the name of the headmistress, Miss Ellen Sutcliffe.

"The name of the school is Greenwoods School for Girls. It was evacuated to Padham when war broke out. It's open to day pupils, so some local girls attend."

He tapped his cigarette on his ash tray and nodded at Evelyn to signify that the conversation was at an end.

• • • •

Evelyn leaned her bicycle against the iron railings, smoothed down her police uniform skirt and made sure her peaked cap, bearing the Newhampton constabulary badge, was straight.

It was a warm day and she'd enjoyed the ride along quiet country roads.

She hoisted her bag on her shoulder and opened the wrought-iron gate.

The sprawling, three-storey Victorian-era house loomed ahead, at the end of a driveway flanked by what must once have been lawns but were now garden beds.

A tall man wearing overalls was plucking fruit from one of the bushes and placing it in a cardboard box.

When he spotted Evelyn he waved, then indicated that he wanted to talk to her.

As he approached, she guessed him to be in his thirties.

"You must have come about poor Miss Griffiths," he began.

"Yes. I need to speak to the headmistress, Miss Sutcliffe," Evelyn replied.

"I'll take you along to her study. I'm Larry Coningsby," he said. "I own Coningsby Hall, so you could say I know my way around a bit."

"I'm Woman Auxiliary Police Constable Masefield. Has the hall always belonged to your family?" Evelyn asked, falling into step beside him.

"The present hall has." Mr Coningsby nodded. "My great-grandfather had it built after the previous one burned down in the 1880s.

"It had belonged to the Coningsbys since the early 1800s, when they married into a previous family that owned it.

"The original hall dated back to the sixteenth century. I inherited it in 1938 after my father died, but when war broke out I decided we should move into the old coach-house.

"It had been converted into a house before the war, meaning we could offer the hall to Greenwoods when the school needed to be evacuated from London.

"It helped me feel I'm doing my bit for the war effort. I got turned down for the services because of having flat feet." He grimaced. "I help our old gardener, and the Greenwoods girls help to dig for victory, too.

"Here we are." He pushed open the front door and Evelyn inhaled the smell of beeswax polish.

Mr Coningsby led Evelyn past the grand staircase and along a passageway.

A slightly ajar door gave her a glimpse of what – judging by the high ceiling and wooden panelling – had once been a drawing-room and was now a classroom.

Rows of wooden desks and a blackboard took the place of pre-war sofas and side tables.

Mr Coningsby tapped on a door at the end of the passageway before opening it.

"Sorry to disturb, Miss Sutcliffe, but Woman Auxiliary Police Constable Masefield is here to talk to you about Miss Griffiths," he explained.

Miss Sutcliffe looked to be in her fifties, with hair styled in a victory roll. She sat behind a desk in a small, panelled study.

The window behind her had a view over the victory garden.

"I'll take these strawberries down to the kitchen," Mr Coningsby said. "I'll leave you two to it."

He closed the door behind him as the two women shook hands.

"I'm sorry to hear about Miss Griffiths." Evelyn settled down in a chair and flicked to a fresh page of her notebook. "Had she taught here for very long?"

"She came to us in September 1939," Miss Sutcliffe replied. "The term we evacuated.

"To be honest, I expected to lose her at the end of that term as I thought she'd join one of the auxiliary services like some of our other younger teachers."

"I used to be a teacher," Evelyn admitted. "I taught in a primary school for a couple of years before joining the WAPC."

"Irene and the other younger teachers who've stayed with us take the view that the young women they're currently teaching will have to rebuild this country after the war, so teaching is important," Miss Sutcliffe replied.

Evelyn, sensing Miss Sutcliffe's disapproval, changed the subject.

"What did Miss Griffiths teach?"

"She was our games mistress," Miss Sutcliffe said. "She was determined to make the girls' lives as normal as they could possibly be, despite the war.

"She organised sports matches against other schools in the county. She was organising an end-of-term swimming gala for the second year running."

"And she lived here at the school?" Evelyn asked.

"Yes. Several mistresses live on site, as I do. Others share flats or have bedsits in Padham.

"Irene was visiting two of our other mistresses there last night. They told me this morning that she'd stayed later than usual. She usually cycled home before the blackout."

Evelyn, who sometimes had to cycle back to her bedsit after a late shift, could understand that.

The lack of visibility made it all too easy to go off course and collide with a prickly bush or a wall.

"Where is the pool she fell in?" she asked. "I didn't notice it on my way in."

"It's behind the hall, on the edge of the grounds," Miss Sutcliffe replied. "There's a side gate by the pool that leads to a short lane that takes you down to the riverbank.

"It's quicker to get here from Padham village along the riverbank."

She rubbed her temples.

"I wish Irene had accepted her friends' offer of sleeping on the couch. We're going to miss her a great deal.

"In addition to her work here, she used to teach some of the local children and evacuees to swim," she went on. "And she worked as a volunteer telephonist with the National Fire Service in Newhampton once a week.

"She wouldn't finish till six in the morning, then she'd cycle back here and do a day's teaching.

"She never once complained that she felt tired, though she must have been exhausted.

"I must say that, while I'm not surprised she cycled off course and into the pool in the blackout, I am surprised that she drowned," Miss Sutcliffe admitted. "Before the war, Irene was a top-ranked British swimmer.

"Had the 1940 Olympics taken place, she might well have made the British team."

That did seem odd, Evelyn thought, but if she'd fallen from her bike, Miss Griffiths

could have hit her head on the bottom of the pool and knocked herself out.

"Could I take a look at the pool?" she asked. "And I'd like to talk to the friends she visited, plus whoever found her this morning."

• • • •

The swimming pool was in a walled-off area on the edge of the grounds, past the tennis courts and behind a shady stand of trees.

The pool itself looked far from tempting – the water was murky and full of leaves.

"Mr Coningsby or the gardener Mr Walker usually rake the leaves out of the pool in the morning," Miss Sutcliffe explained.

"But I've told them to leave it for today. There'll be no swimming here today."

The pool was accessible via two gates – one that opened on to the lane that led to the riverbank, and the other that separated the pool from the rest of the Coningsby Hall grounds.

A brick structure with a door at each end and high, glassless windows stood next to the pool.

"These were built as changing-rooms, but Mr Coningsby says they haven't been used since the 1920s," Miss Sutcliffe said. "The girls change into their swimming costumes before coming down to the pool."

"The family don't use the pool at all?" Evelyn asked.

"Not during term-time anyway. They might during the holidays when we're not here." Miss Sutcliffe glanced at her watch. "It's almost break and I have a lesson straight after.

"I'll introduce you to our gardener, Mr Walker, as he discovered poor Irene."

Evelyn followed the headmistress through the grounds to the victory garden, where an elderly man with white hair was picking strawberries alongside Larry Coningsby.

"It's hard to get gardeners, handymen and maids today with all the young people joining up," Miss Sutcliffe commented. "Ernest Walker was retired but came back to help out and do his bit for the war effort."

Mr Walker tipped his hat as the two women approached.

"WAPC Masefield would like to ask you a few questions, Mr Walker," Miss Sutcliffe said.

"I can't tell you anything that I didn't tell Mr Horton, the village policeman, this morning," Mr Walker replied. "I got here at seven-thirty.

"I live in a cottage near the river, so I use that side entrance.

"The first thing I saw was Miss Griffiths in the pool, and her bicycle as well. I went straight up to the school for Miss Sutcliffe.

"We were all in the dining hall having breakfast," Miss Sutcliffe put in. "I had noticed Miss Griffiths' absence, but assumed she was simply running late."

"A terrible thing to happen," Mr Walker commented. "Miss Griffiths was a lovely young lady."

A bell rang, rapidly followed by the sound of girls' excited voices.

"It's break," Miss Sutcliffe said. "I need to go back to my study for some books.

"Did you want to talk to Miss Kane and Miss Homer now, WAPC Masefield, or wait until lunchtime?"

"I'll speak to them now, if I could."

"Very well, but you'll need to see yourself off the grounds when you've finished."

They ran into Miss Kane and Miss Homer before they reached the hall.

Like the schoolgirls spilling out into the grounds, the two young teachers wanted to spend their short break in the sunshine.

Miss Kane and Miss Homer confirmed that Miss Griffiths had spent the evening with them.

They'd sat out in the small communal garden at their flat, talking about their plans for the upcoming holidays.

The three teachers had lost track of time until suddenly it was nightfall.

"We asked Irene to stay the night, but there was a full moon, so she said she could get back to school easily," Miss Kane told Evelyn tearfully. "I wish we'd talked her into staying now."

Clusters of girls dressed in green-and-white-checked summer uniform dresses were now helping to pluck strawberries and raspberries from the bushes.

As Evelyn approached the front gate, she overheard a group of girls aged around twelve having a heated conversation.

"I don't believe you," one girl said. "You're always telling stories, Ginny."

"It's true!" Ginny rebutted. "Shirley will tell you – I asked you if you wanted to come with me, didn't I, Shirley?"

"She did," Shirley agreed. "I didn't want to in case we got into trouble."

"You should have woken me," another girl said. "I'd have enjoyed a midnight swim."

"Well, I didn't get to swim, did I?" Ginny replied. "When I got to the gate, I heard the door to one of the old changing-rooms opening.

"Then I heard footsteps coming towards the gate, so I hid behind one of the trees.

"I heard the gate open and someone walked back through the grounds towards the school."

"Who was it?" a girl asked.

"I was scared to look in case it was one of the mistresses or a prefect.

"When I couldn't hear the footsteps any more, I went to the pool and saw Miss Griffiths – but I didn't know it was her," Ginny admitted.

"I just knew there was a dead body in the pool, so I ran back to the dormitory."

One of the girls snorted.

"What rubbish! You're telling lies as usual."

"No, she woke me up when she got back. She was upset," Shirley insisted.

The bell rang and the girls picked up their boxes of fruit and scurried back to the hall.

Evelyn considered cornering Ginny for a formal statement, but decided against it.

If necessary, she could get one later, after she'd spoken to Sergeant Weaver and told him she suspected Miss Griffiths's death had been no accident.

If it had been, why hadn't the person Ginny heard reported it straight away? Unless it was a second girl out on an illicit midnight jaunt and afraid of getting into trouble.

Either way, it was worth taking a look inside the old changing-rooms.

Evelyn pushed open the door to what had been the ladies' changing-room first.

The room had fallen into disrepair all right, with peeling paint, an old curtain around the shower, heavy layers of dust coating the benches and a musty smell.

The gentlemen's changing-room smelled worse, and the mouldy shower curtain had been pulled from its rails and left on the grubby floor.

Next to it, though, lay a clean-looking handkerchief.

Evelyn picked it up. It was a large handkerchief, like the ones her father used, with the initial *H* embroidered in one corner.

Of course, it could have been here for a while, but she needed to find out who it belonged to.

Most likely, its owner was the person Ginny had overheard the previous night.

• • • •

"Ah, you're finally back, WAPC Masefield. Bicycle get a puncture, did it?" Sergeant Weaver smirked.

The policemen in earshot chortled and Evelyn flushed.

"I spent longer at the school than I expected," she replied.

"But it was all straightforward, I take it? Clearly an accident?"

"I'm not so sure."

Evelyn told him about Irene Griffiths being a champion swimmer.

PC Collins whistled.

"I thought I'd heard the name Irene Griffiths before! She was England's top-ranked woman backstroker before the war."

"Falling into the pool while riding a bike is a bit different to swimming laps, though," Sergeant Weaver pointed out. "She could have injured herself falling in."

Evelyn told him about Ginny's story, but Weaver dismissed that with a wave of his hand.

"A schoolgirl's overactive imagination!"

He was equally dismissive about the handkerchief she'd found.

"At least one of those teachers is bound to have a boyfriend she meets up with sometimes. Or one of the older girls might have a boyfriend she meets in secret. A moonlight tryst."

"I'd like to investigate a little more, if I could, sir," Evelyn told him. "Set my mind at rest."

"Go ahead," the sergeant surprised her by saying. "There's no reason why you shouldn't ask a few more questions.

"Before you go, though, type up your statements from this morning, and PC Collins has some statements for you to type up as well."

It was frustrating having to type up statements when she was anxious to get back to the school and start asking more questions.

It was late afternoon when she finally cycled back to Coningsby Hall.

The sun was high in the sky and she felt hot in her uniform when she rested her bicycle against the railings.

Lessons had finished for the day and several girls were working in the victory gardens, accompanied by some of the teachers.

Evelyn made her way to Miss Sutcliffe's office.

Miss Sutcliffe looked up in surprise when she entered.

"I thought we'd seen the last of you."

"I just have a couple more questions," Evelyn replied. "I know you said that Miss Griffiths was a popular member of staff, but did she have any enemies?"

"Enemies?" Miss Sutcliffe's eyes widened. "You surely don't suspect foul play?"

"We're just investigating Miss Griffiths's death thoroughly," Evelyn replied.

"Well, I'm sure some of the less sporty girls disliked Irene, but I can't imagine that any of them drowned her. Besides, how would they have known she'd be returning to school so late?"

Miss Sutcliffe frowned.

"Actually, there's a couple in Padham village with reason to dislike Irene, but it's hard to believe either of them killed her . . ."

"Tell me about the couple," Evelyn pressed.

Miss Sutcliffe nodded.

"We have some evacuees who attend Greenwoods as day girls. Among them are two sisters who were initially billeted to a couple called Mr and Mrs Day – she works in a munitions factory in Newhampton and he's an ARP warden.

"Irene noticed they were tired and also saw bruises on the older girl's arms," she explained. "She spoke to the girls about it and they opened up to her.

"It turned out that they were being made to get up at five to complete all the housework before coming to school.

"Irene complained to the authorities and had them moved to another family, where they're much happier.

"Families are paid to take care of the evacuees, as you know, so the Days would have lost that payment."

"Do you know where they live?"

"Yes. Hold on for one moment. It'll still be in the girls' files."

Miss Sutcliffe looked through a filing cabinet drawer until she found the information Evelyn wanted.

Evelyn didn't want to get Ginny into trouble, but needed to know a little more about her.

"There's a girl in the school – about twelve – called Ginny," she began.

"Virginia Martin? What about her?"

"I overheard her saying something earlier."

"You shouldn't pay much attention to anything Virginia says. When she tells a story, it's exaggerated, if it's actually true at all."

Evelyn decided to let this go. Instead, she asked if there were any men on staff with the initial "H".

"Goodness, no. There's Ernest Walker, who you've met, and his grandson,

Raymond, who's fourteen and helps out at the weekend. Then there's Bob Sykes, who comes over from Newhampton to teach music."

"Would any of the teachers have a husband, fiancé or boyfriend whose name begins with 'H'?" Evelyn persisted.

"Most husbands, fiancés and boyfriends are away fighting the war, and I don't recall all their names.

"But Miss Kane's fiancé is named Harold. He's at the Haweshill airbase." Miss Sutcliffe named a small town four miles away.

Evelyn asked for Miss Kane's address so she could ask her about Harold later.

"Did Miss Griffiths have a boyfriend?" she added.

"Not that I'm aware of. She never mentioned one."

"Thank you, Miss Sutcliffe. Do you think I could have a look at Miss Griffiths's room before I leave?"

• • • •

Miss Griffiths's bedroom on the top floor of the hall was sparsely furnished, with just a narrow bed, a wooden wardrobe and chest of drawers, a small dressing table with a mirror and a desk in the window.

Miss Griffiths had done little to personalise it.

A photo on the dressing-table showed a pretty, dark-haired girl in her twenties alongside an older couple, standing beside a five-barred gate.

This must be Miss Griffiths and her parents, Evelyn thought.

She flipped through a diary that she found in a desk drawer – it included details of upcoming school sports fixtures and various appointments for tea with friends, including with Miss Kane and Miss Homer the previous night.

But Evelyn could find nothing in the drawers or among her clothes to confirm her suspicions that the teacher's death had not been accidental.

She sighed. She was starting to feel tired and hungry, but she wanted another word with Miss Kane and Miss Homer, and to visit Mr and Mrs Day before she retired to her own bedsit.

Miss Kane and Miss Homer were surprised to see Evelyn again, but invited her into the small living-room in their flat and offered her a cup of tea.

As she sipped gratefully, they confirmed that Irene had not had a boyfriend.

"There was a fellow she was sweet on in her home town, but he threw her over at the start of the war," Miss Kane explained.

"She's come to Saturday evening dances at Haweshill and danced with a few airmen, but she hasn't been on any dates."

"I suppose it would be

difficult dating when you live at a girls' school," Evelyn commented.

Miss Kane chuckled.

"It's not easy," she said. "Miss Sutcliffe discourages live-in teachers from having boyfriends. I've been dating a vet from Haweshill, but I'd never take him anywhere near the school."

So it hadn't been Harold's hanky in the changing-room, Evelyn noted.

Evelyn's next visit was to the Days' house. They lived in a terraced house just off the high street.

Evelyn climbed the two sparkling clean steps and knocked on the door.

Mrs Day looked to be around Miss Sutcliffe's age, but her hair was mostly hidden under a scarf, knotted at the forehead.

She eyed Evelyn suspiciously.

"Alfred's not home. He's out somewhere with his ARP work."

"Do you know what time he'll be back?" Evelyn asked.

Mrs Day eyed the insignia on Evelyn's cap.

"It's like your work, love. Could be anytime. There's a war on, isn't there?"

"Perhaps you can help me, Mrs Day. May I come in?"

Mrs Day stood aside.

Evelyn stepped into a dark passageway and Mrs Day pointed her towards an open door on the left.

The Days' living-room furniture was arranged around an empty fireplace, with a table beneath the window and a wireless in the corner.

Mrs Day motioned Evelyn to sit in one of the two armchairs.

She picked up a packet of cigarettes and held it out to Evelyn.

When Evelyn shook her head, she shrugged, lit a cigarette and leaned against the mantelpiece.

"What can I help you with, then?"

"Have you heard what happened up at the girls' school at Coningsby Hall?" Evelyn asked her.

"You mean about that teacher getting drowned?" Mrs Day blew out smoke. "It's all over the village."

"Apparently Miss Griffiths was responsible for having two evacuees removed from your care?"

"Yes, and she could have cost me and Alfred our jobs, too, with her lies. It was lucky Mrs Coningsby didn't take it any further, though she said we couldn't have any more evacuees."

"Mrs Coningsby?"

"Yes." Mrs Day nodded. "Mr Coningsby's wife up at the hall. She was one of the volunteers matching evacuees with families.

"Me and Alfred both told her that the girls were lying, but that teacher was out to cause trouble.

"I suppose the Coningsbys didn't want to lose the rent from the school for the hall any more than we wanted to lose the money for looking after those girls."

"So what was the problem with the girls exactly?" Evelyn queried.

"Me and Alfred both work hard, so we expected the girls to do a few chores, like our own girls did growing up. We expected them to make their own beds, help me dust and sweep the house out, things like that.

"But no! Spoilt rotten they were. Had maids at home," Mrs Day went on. "They did everything they could to get out of helping me.

"Then one day I'd had enough and I slapped one of them. I was tired, worried about the air raids and I lost my rag. I shouldn't have done it, I know. But that teacher made mountains out of molehills."

"Where were you and Mr Day last night?" Evelyn asked her.

"Oh! You're trying to make out she was murdered now, are you, and trying to pin the blame on us?

"Well, we were nowhere near Coningsby Hall! I was here knitting and Alfred was out with the ARP."

"Can anyone vouch for you being here?"

"Mrs Bartlett next door called round at about nine o'clock," Mrs Day replied.

"She was returning a magazine I'd given her and she wanted a chat. It's miserable having to draw the blackout curtains these beautiful evenings."

That was a sentiment on which Evelyn and Mrs Day could agree.

Evelyn took her leave of Mrs Day and called on Mrs Barlett next door, who confirmed she'd spent a couple of hours with her.

Alfred would have alibis, Evelyn thought, but there was no need to check them out yet, if she needed to check them out at all.

She still had nothing to confirm that someone had murdered Irene – just the words of a notoriously untrustworthy schoolgirl and her own suspicions.

• • • •

Evelyn felt gloomy again as she set off for work the next morning.

She was certain that, given she'd got no further with her investigations, Sergeant Weaver would want her back on clerical duties today. But as she walked in, Sergeant Weaver turned to her.

"There's another job for you up at that snooty school, WAPC Masefield," he told her. "One of the girls has run away.

"I've got men looking for her, but I need you to talk to her headmistress and friends to see if you can find out where she might have gone."

"Yes, sir. What's the girl's name, sir?"

Sergeant Weaver checked his notebook.

"Virginia Martin."

"Virginia Martin?" Evelyn's pulse quickened. "That's the girl I mentioned – the one who claimed to have heard someone in the school grounds around the time Irene Griffiths drowned."

"Maybe one of her teachers heard her talking about it as well and she found herself in trouble, so she's run away," the sergeant suggested.

"Or maybe she thinks Miss Griffiths was murdered and the murderer might target her now," Evelyn replied.

"That all sounds very fanciful, WAPC Masefield." Sergeant Weaver smiled. "Go up to the school and establish some facts."

• • • •

Miss Sutcliffe raked a hand through her hair as she ran through the morning's events.

"When the rising bell went this morning, Virginia was missing. At first the other girls thought she'd gone to the bathroom, and her friends became suspicious when she didn't return.

"We've looked all around the grounds for her but she's nowhere to be seen."

When Evelyn told her what she'd overheard the previous day, Miss Sutcliffe shook her head.

"I didn't know anything about that. Which isn't to say one of the mistresses or prefects didn't know about it. They could have given her a warning about being outside after lights out. I shall check with them."

"I'd like to see the other girls from her dormitory," Evelyn said.

"I'll have them sent here now."

The five girls looked apprehensive as they entered the study.

The girl who had yesterday been addressed as Shirley had been crying.

"I'm WAPC Masefield," Evelyn told them. "I'm hoping you'll be able to tell me where you think Virginia might be, so that we can find her and bring her safely back to school."

A tear trickled down Shirley's cheek and she scrubbed it away.

"I think she's dead!" she cried. "And it's all my fault!"

"Of course she's not dead," another girl sneered. "She'll just have run away."

"Why didn't she take some other clothes with her then, or her pocket money?" Shirley retorted.

That was a good point, Evelyn thought. How could a girl make her way home by train with no money?

"What makes you think she's dead, Shirley?" she asked gently. "And why is it your fault?"

"Ginny told us she'd gone for a midnight swim and seen Miss Griffiths's body in the pool," Shirley began.

"Yes, and she thought she'd heard someone using one of the changing-rooms and going back towards the hall," Evelyn replied. "I overheard her talking."

"Oh." Shirley looked surprised. "Well, she and I talked about it, and I told her I didn't think she'd overheard a murderer, but that one of the mistresses or prefects had slipped out to meet her boyfriend.

"Ginny agreed that was probably what had happened, and she thought it would be a lark to slip out again around the same time and see if they were there again. She was going to climb one of the trees near the pool and watch."

"She wanted me to go with her," Shirley added.

"But you didn't want to go?" Evelyn guessed.

"At first I did. Ginny set her alarm for eleven o'clock, but when she woke me up, I chickened out.

"I'm not good at climbing trees and I didn't want to get caught. I hoped Ginny wouldn't go, either, but she went off on her own.

"I was going to stay awake until she got back, but I fell asleep. When I woke this morning, I went straight to her cubicle to see if she'd seen anything, but she wasn't there."

Evelyn's heart sank. Part of her had hoped that Ginny had run away, because it wouldn't have been difficult for the police to find her.

But if she'd hidden near the pool and disappeared, it sounded like Evelyn's theory that Miss Griffiths had been murdered had been right.

In which case, the police might now be looking for someone who'd taken two people's lives.

• • • •

Evelyn sent the girls back to lessons and made her way back to the pool area.

Mr Walker was poolside, using a long rake to get rid of the leaves.

When he saw Evelyn, he called her to him.

"I was going to take this to Miss Sutcliffe when I'd finished," he told her, resting the rake against the wall and reaching into the pocket of his overalls. "But you'll do instead.

"I found it on the side of the pool. Lucky it didn't fall in and get wet."

He handed Evelyn a beige ration book.

Evelyn flipped through it. None of the coupons in the book had been used.

"Thank you, Mr Walker," she said. "I'll find out who it belongs to. Would you mind not mentioning it to anyone for the time being?"

"Fair enough. I wouldn't want it to end up with anyone other than the right person," Mr Walker replied, picking up his rake again.

Beige ration books were for adults, so this ration book didn't belong to any of the Greenwoods girls – and Evelyn assumed that the girls' coupons would have gone to the headmistress at the start of term anyway.

Perhaps one of the teachers who lived on site had dropped it, but Evelyn thought it unlikely that someone would carry it around while strolling through the grounds.

The other possibility was that it belonged to the Coningsbys, who shared the grounds with the school.

She decided to call on the Coningsbys, find out if they had seen anything of Ginny or heard any suspicious noises the past two nights.

The coach-house was adjacent to Coningsby Hall and, judging by the sloping roof and casement windows, had been built at the same time.

Evelyn knocked on the door. A tall woman in her late fifties, wearing an elegant wraparound dress, answered the door.

Evelyn introduced herself.

"You must have come about the child who's run away. I'm Hilary's mother, by the way." The woman held out her hand.

"I'm afraid there's only me at home at the moment."

This must be Mrs Coningsby's mother, Evelyn thought.

She grabbed the ration book from her bag.

"Someone from the school came upon this in the grounds. I just wanted to check if one of you had mislaid it."

The woman chuckled.

"It's not ours. I'd have known all about it if we'd lost it! Hilary and Sylvia have driven into the village to do some shopping."

"Who's Sylvia?" Evelyn queried.

"Hilary's wife, of course."

Hilary? Evelyn's heart thumped.

Larry was short for Hilary! It had been his hanky she'd found in the changing-room.

There was no reason why he shouldn't use his own pool, but Miss Sutcliffe had said the family didn't swim there in term-time.

Even if he'd fancied a midnight dip on a warm summer's night, why wouldn't he have reported Miss Griffiths's drowning?

It made no sense.

Evelyn tucked the ration book back in her bag.

"Thank you, Mrs Coningsby," she said. "It must belong to one of the teachers. I'll ask Miss Sutcliffe about it."

• • • •

Miss Sutcliffe confirmed that none of the staff or prefects had heard Ginny Martin's story about being in the grounds the night that Miss Griffiths drowned.

She said she would ask the teachers who lived on-site if the ration book belonged to them.

Evelyn was confident that the ration book didn't belong to a teacher, though.

There had been no air raids for several weeks now, but criminals were still taking advantage of the blackout to rob warehouses.

The ration book she'd found could be from a supply stolen from a warehouse in London or Newhampton. Or it might be a forgery.

She decided to poke around the pool area a little more before heading back to the police station to alert Sergeant Weaver.

Mr Walker had gone now, but the swimming pool water didn't look any more inviting minus its leaves.

She pushed open the door of the former gentlemen's changing-room again, screwing up her nose against the smell.

The shower curtain had shifted on the ground, and she lifted it gingerly to see if she could find any further clues beneath it.

She hadn't expected to see a trapdoor.

Heart thumping, Evelyn pulled on the ring and grabbed her torch from her bag.

Judging by its shape, this had been an old well.

A rope ladder hung down one side, and it looked like there was an opening at the bottom of the well.

Leading to what, Evelyn

wondered. A room? A passage?

Might Ginny have discovered this trapdoor and climbed down the rope ladder? Could she be trapped in a room down there?

Evelyn was tempted to climb down and check, but realised it wasn't wise to do so on her own. Someone could come along and close the trapdoor.

Or, if she had stumbled on a secret tunnel being used by black marketeers, she might well end up murdered like Miss Griffiths.

She needed to return to the station and return later with some policemen.

How irritated Sergeant Weaver would be that a woman's auxiliary police constable had tracked down a black market operation before the regular police did!

Evelyn closed the trapdoor and covered it with the shower curtain.

It was no wonder Larry Coningsby had let the changing-rooms deteriorate – just the smell was a sure-fire way of ensuring that any schoolgirls didn't go snooping around in them.

• • • •

Sergeant Weaver looked dubious as Evelyn told him her suspicions, but his expression changed when she produced the book.

"A pound to a penny these are forgeries.

"Either that or they're part of a consignment that went missing from London that we've been told to keep an eye out for," he told her. "PC Collins will drive us up to the school so you can show us where this trapdoor is."

Evelyn had to hold on to her cap as PC Collins sped along the winding country roads.

Sergeant Weaver wanted Evelyn to show them the trapdoor without alerting the headmistress.

"We have no idea exactly who is involved in this," he explained. "We don't want to give them any forewarning."

Several girls spending break working in the victory garden eyed the police officers curiously as they marched through the grounds.

A couple of teachers approached as they passed the hall, but Sergeant Weaver waved them away.

"You stay here," Sergeant Weaver told Evelyn after he'd flashed his torch down the old well.

"Hold on, sir," PC Collins piped up as Evelyn tried to swallow her disappointment.

"If the missing girl is down there, then it would be better if WAPC Masefield accompanies you, so she can comfort her.

"Also, it's better if one of us is here should a member of the gang turn up."

"Good points," Weaver conceded.

He glanced at Evelyn.

"Can you manage the rope ladder?"

"Of course," Evelyn replied, hoping she sounded more confident than she felt.

She'd climbed rope ladders at school, but descending one down a dark well was a bit different to using the equipment in the school hall.

She proved more comfortable on it than Sergeant Weaver, however, who descended slowly with a good deal of huffing and puffing.

PC Collins grinned and winked at Evelyn.

"Uncovering all this was your work," he told her as she started down the ladder. "I didn't want you to miss out at the end."

Weaver led the way along a narrow stone passage.

As they walked carefully over the uneven ground, Evelyn recalled Larry Coningsby telling her about the history of the hall and how the original had burned down in Victorian times.

This passage must have been built centuries ago, perhaps for hiding priests during the Tudor era.

"We seem to be going in the direction of the hall," she told Sergeant Weaver.

Weaver stopped abruptly, causing Evelyn to barge into him. They'd reached an old door with an iron latch.

They both breathed a sigh of relief when the door opened and they stepped into a windowless room, containing several sacks.

Weaver headed straight for the goods, while Evelyn made a beeline for the terrified girl in the corner.

"It's all right, Ginny," she soothed the girl. "You're safe now. You'll soon be out of here."

"Take her back to the school and get her statement," Weaver ordered. "And tell PC Collins to call for back-up.

"There are ration books in these sacks, as well as sugar and tea. We're going to have to get all of this out of here."

• • • •

"I didn't really want to go out there on my own," Ginny admitted. "But I'd said Shirley was chicken for not coming, so I couldn't very well not go."

They were seated in Miss Sutcliffe's study.

The headmistress sat behind her desk, while Evelyn and Ginny occupied the visitors' chairs.

Ginny was tired, grimy and in need of a bath and sleep, but Evelyn figured those comforts could wait until she'd given her statement.

"I used my torch to get to the front door, then turned it off because of the blackout," Ginny expained.

"It was a moonlit night again, so I climbed up one of the trees and waited.

"I'd been there for a while and I was about to climb down and come back to bed when two men came out of the old changing-rooms.

"I recognised Mr Coningsby and there was an ARP warden with him.

"They were talking, but I couldn't hear what they were saying," she went on.

"Then I sneezed and they came round and found me. I wasn't really worried, other than thinking I'd get into trouble.

"I thought the warden was here because a light had been left on somewhere, or that Mr Coningsby had seen something suspicious and called him.

"I didn't expect them to grab me and force me down here. I couldn't believe it when I saw all the goods.

"They told me they were going to get rid of all the goods then let me go.

"Mr Coningsby said he knew I had a reputation at school for being a liar and that no-one would believe my word against his once I was released."

Once she'd finished taking Ginny's statement, Evelyn went in search of Sergeant Weaver and the police officers.

They were ferrying some of the goods to the police cars.

Inside one of the police cars, with a grim-looking PC Collins, was Larry Coningsby.

When Evelyn quickly relayed Ginny's information to Sergeant Weaver, he went over to the car to have a word with Larry.

"Alfred Day's our man," she heard him tell one of the other policemen. "Go and arrest him now."

• • • •

"And so Alfred Day and Larry Coningsby were charged," Evelyn explained.

It was midday a few days later, and she was sitting on a bench along the riverbank with her father.

He'd been sent to South Newhampton to verify that the black market goods were the same ones that had been stolen from London.

"It turns out that Larry Coningsby drove the stolen and forged items from London and stored them in the cellars at the hall so they could be sold on the black market here," she explained. "He used to stay in his London flat on occasion, ostensibly for work.

"He was the boss of a criminal gang who would raid warehouses during air raids, wearing counterfeit ARP uniforms so no-one suspected them.

"He had people working for him here in Padham, including Alfred Day.

"There is a second tunnel to the cellars from the coach-house, so they didn't have to carry heavy goods up and down while using a rope ladder."

"I'd been wondering about that." Her father nodded.

"But they also used the changing-room entrance regularly, because it would have looked suspicious having Alfred Day and other men always turning up at the coach-house," Evelyn continued.

"Neither Mrs Coningsby's wife nor his mother knew anything about his activities."

"What about Alfred Day's wife?" her father asked.

"She hadn't a clue," Evelyn said. "The other thing we discovered was that Larry Coningsby didn't have flat feet at all.

"He had a doctor sign a note to get him out of fighting. He blackmailed the doctor into it."

When the Newhampton chief inspector had turned up to praise the officers for uncovering so much, she'd been surprised when Weaver had grudgingly admitted that it had mostly been the work of WAPC Masefield.

"So how come they murdered the teacher?" Mr Masefield asked. "Did she stumble on them when she was making her way home?"

"She did," Evelyn confirmed. "They were carrying some of the goods when she came through the gate on her bicycle.

"She saw what they had and they realised that they weren't going to be able to talk themselves out of it.

"Alfred Day disliked her because she'd had two evacuees removed from his home, stopped them having more evacuees, and he thought she was going to take away his black market living as well.

"So he pushed her into the pool, thinking she mightn't be able to swim, but she started swimming towards the poolside, so he got in and held her under until she drowned.

"Then he chucked the bicycle in to try to make it look like an accident.

"Larry Coningsby said he was shocked by Day's actions, that he would have done with Miss Griffiths what they ended up doing with Ginny – keeping her in the cellar until they'd cleared it of the goods," Evelyn continued.

"Though we can't be sure of that, as Miss Griffiths was more likely to have been believed than Ginny."

"That's fine work, Evie. I'm proud of you."

Evelyn blushed.

"Thanks. So are you beginning to change your mind about me being in the police force now?"

Her father smiled.

"Tell me something, Evelyn," he replied.

"Now that you've solved a murder case and thwarted a black market gang, has your sergeant given you more to do at the station than answering the phone, typing up notes and occasionally going on the beat?"

"Well, no," Evelyn admitted.

"There you are, then!" he said. "You've proved you're more than capable, but you're still no further ahead than you were before.

"I know this is important war work, but you should think seriously about going back to teaching when the war is over. With your brains, you'd be a headmistress in no time."

"No," Evelyn retorted.

She'd thought a lot about Miss Sutcliffe's words about preparing the younger generation to rebuild the country in the future, but nothing in her previous career had compared to the thrill of excitement at catching criminals.

"I know you mean well, Dad, but nothing's ever going to change for women in the police if women like me don't fight for better cases and promotion," she told him firmly.

"I'm going to stay on after the war, and I plan on climbing the ranks."

"Somehow I had a feeling that I wouldn't be able to change your mind," her father replied, grinning.

"Come on," Evelyn said, standing up. "There's a British Restaurant in the high street.

"Let's celebrate my success with a meal. We'll have to eat quickly, though – my shift starts at two o'clock."

SHORT STORY

Set in 1900

Seaside Sleuths

Would Cordelia's beau turn out to be a thief?

BY KATE FINNEMORE

THE blast of the train's whistle jolted Augustine Brown out of her thoughts. The regular chug-chug of the engine was slowing. The train would soon be entering the station.

Augustine looked at the letter she held in her hand, the letter that had brought her down from London.

Dearest Gussie, her sister Cordelia had written. *I've fallen in love again. Come and save me from myself! Aunt E is in two minds. Kiss kiss, C.*

The train drew to a halt. Moments later Augustine was in a gleamingly clean open-top carriage, her two suitcases stowed in the rack behind her.

"Where to, miss?"

"The Royal."

The breeze was gentle and it carried with it the tang of salt from the sea.

Augustine smiled. Opening her parasol, she sat back against the leather-covered upholstery.

Yes, she was going to enjoy her short holiday at the seaside.

But first, with Aunt Ermyntrude's help, she would assess the suitability or otherwise of Cordelia's latest beau.

Both she and Cordelia had inherited a sum from their grandfather, the founder of Brown's Emporium just off Regent Street.

It meant they were fortunate to have no money worries, but it also made them the targets of impoverished bachelors in the marriage market.

So far, Augustine, twenty-four and sensible, had resisted all attempts to capture her heart.

But Cordelia – only twenty-one and always falling in love – was rather more vulnerable.

The Royal was an imposing four-storey building on the seafront, its stucco walls almost too white in the bright sunshine.

Cordelia must have been waiting just inside the foyer, because she came running down the steps towards Augustine the moment the carriage pulled to a stop.

"Gussie! How lovely to see you!" she cried. "And you made such good time. I've got so much to tell you."

Laughing, Augustine embraced her sister.

"Let's go in first, shall we?"

Looking round to check one of the hotel staff had taken her cases, Augustine linked arms with Cordelia and the two of them made their way into the hotel.

"I'm looking forward to meeting this man you've fallen in love with," Augustine told her sister.

"You will meet him after lunch," Cordelia said. "He's invited me to walk with him this afternoon. Aunt E says you can be my chaperone.

"He had some important business this morning. His name's Reggie Carter. Reginald. The handsomest man I ever set eyes on."

Augustine's eyebrow went up.

"Indeed."

She loved her sister's enthusiasm. She just hoped it was justified.

"He's clever, too," Cordelia insisted. "His room's on the first floor. We've a suite on the second. He's here with a friend of his brother's, Sydney Winterton."

Cordelia stopped and pointed.

"Stairs or lift?"

• • • •

An hour later, Augustine, Cordelia and their aunt entered the hotel's dining-room for lunch.

One of the staff ushered them past the other diners to their table by the window.

"The colonel's in his cups again," Ermyntrude said as she sat down, her tone thick with disapproval.

Smiling and nodding to acquaintances in the room, she gestured with a look at the man who sat at a corner table, contemplating the two-thirds-empty bottle of wine and the empty glass before him.

"Disgraceful."

Mouth curving into a smile, Augustine exchanged a look with her sister.

Their aunt, never one to keep her opinions to herself, was clearly on top form.

"Cordelia has told me all the good things, Aunt, about Reggie," Augustine said. "You have reservations, though, it appears."

Pursing her lips, Ermyntrude shook out her serviette and smoothed it across her lap.

"Nothing I can put my finger on, my dear," she admitted. "He comes from a good family. His father runs Carter's Comestibles."

"And Reggie's following in his father's footsteps?"

"Supposedly. He's rather vague as to what he does exactly."

"Only because he doesn't want to bore you, Aunt," Cordelia put in.

"Possibly. But there's something mysterious about him." Ermyntrude frowned. "Where has he been this morning, for example? It's a lovely day. He should have been out and about with –"

"With me," Cordelia breathed.

"Perhaps," Ermyntrude allowed. "Instead, he had important business . . ."

She broke off as voices from the foyer, a man's and a woman's, intruded, followed by the hotel manager's soothing tones.

The voices died away. Augustine imagined the manager ushering the speakers into another room.

Moments later, a young woman came running into the dining-room.

"You'll never guess," she burst out, addressing the whole room. "It's Lady

Dalrymple-Jones. Her necklace has been stolen!"

There were gasps of shock and hands flew to mouths.

"It was such a beautiful thing," Cordelia said to Augustine. "Lady D wore it last night at dinner. Diamonds and rubies. Earrings to match."

"Foolish woman," Ermyntrude muttered. "She should have put it back in the hotel safe. The earrings, too."

They had just finished dessert when Cordelia looked over towards the doorway.

All at once a beaming smile lit up her face.

"Reggie!"

Doffing the boater he wore, a broad-shouldered man made his way towards their table, his gaze never leaving Cordelia's, his face wreathed in smiles.

The three women stood up to greet him.

If it were only looks that mattered, Augustine couldn't help thinking, then Reggie Carter was perfect husband material.

Smartly dressed in a lightweight summer suit, he had thick dark hair and a strong-boned face. He was a devilishly handsome man.

She was introduced and Reggie shook her hand, his grip firm but not too firm.

He asked her about her journey and listened politely to what she had to say.

Cordelia then told him about her morning.

"What about you, Reggie?" Ermyntrude asked. "Have you had a good morning?"

There was the briefest of hesitations.

"Uh, yes. I have."

"Your business successfully concluded?"

"Uh, yes."

Ermyntrude said nothing else, inviting him, by her silence, to continue.

But he didn't speak and Augustine frowned.

Her aunt was right: there was something off about Reggie Carter.

As though seeking an escape route, he looked towards the dining-room door.

A man now stood there.

"Ah, here's Sydney." Reggie's relief was evident. "Let me introduce you, Miss Brown. Your sister and aunt have already made his acquaintance."

As she drew nearer, Augustine could see that Sydney's face and hands were tanned and his hair bleached by the sun to the colour of straw.

He must have come from one of the colonies. South Africa, perhaps, or India.

"Delighted to meet you, Miss Brown," Sydney said, shaking Augustine's hand.

Like his friend, Sydney Winterton was devilishly handsome. His eyes were a remarkable sapphire blue, while his accent evoked adventure and excitement.

"I walked to the Olympia and had my lunch there, on the terrace," Sydney told them. "But the sea air can be so tiring. I'll be up in my room for a while."

He swivelled on his heels, and Augustine was aware of an odd tightness in her chest as she watched him stride across the foyer to the lift.

There was something rather exciting about Sydney Winterton.

• • • •

"I could spend all afternoon out here," Cordelia said dreamily.

The two sisters were strolling along the prom, one on either side of Reggie, their arms linked through his, each holding a parasol in her free hand.

The afternoon sun was beautifully warm and the sky a sparkling jewel blue.

Overhead, seagulls called and wheeled in slow, graceful curves.

The tide was out, revealing expanses of sand between the breakwaters.

Children were building sandcastles while men with buckets dug for bait.

"Did you hear about the theft, Reggie?" Cordelia asked.

"Theft?" Reggie broke his step for an instant, but picked it up again straight away.

"This morning, while you were out," Cordelia explained, going on to give him all the details.

Augustine said nothing. She was watching him closely.

That little break in his stride – did it mean anything?

Reggie paid a few pennies at the kiosk and the three of them joined the throngs of people already on the pier.

"A marvel of modern engineering," Reggie said.

Sturdy wooden boards on a cast-iron framework stretched a third of a mile out to sea.

Anglers leant with their elbows on the rails. Others sat on folding chairs or strolled along, arm in arm.

A line of stalls backed against a central partition.

The canvas on some of them had been folded back to form temporary shops selling all manner of things.

The three of them walked to the very end of the pier, and Augustine loved every minute of it: the bustle all around, the scent of the sea several yards below – and Reggie's company.

He was attentive to her sister, could hold an interesting conversation, had a sense of humour and was good to look at.

Cordelia was obviously deeply in love with him.

It was all very positive and Augustine's misgivings were beginning to look foolish.

"I hope you won't find me impertinent, Reggie," she said much later as they slowly made their way back to the hotel. "But how do you know Sydney? He has a colonial accent, but you don't. Is he a relation?"

Reggie shook his head.

"He's a friend of my brother's. They both live in Johannesburg, in South Africa. We met when I went to stay with my brother and kept in touch."

"Ah." Augustine was silent, digesting the information.

She had that odd tight feeling in her chest again.

She was looking forward, she realised, to making Sydney Winterton's further acquaintance at dinner.

• • • •

Alas, neither Sydney nor Reggie was at dinner that evening.

It was while Augustine was half-thinking about the two men, half-listening to her sister and aunt discuss that morning's theft, that a devastating thought slipped into her head.

What if Reggie were the thief? What if his business that morning involved the theft of Lady Dalrymple-Jones's necklace?

Augustine dismissed the idea with an angry shake of her head.

It was ludicrous. It didn't fit with the Reggie Carter she had come to know.

Yet once the idea had popped into her mind, Augustine found it hard to dislodge it, and when she and Cordelia retired to their room later that evening, she felt compelled to voice her suspicions.

"No!" Cordelia's eyes were bright with sudden tears. "I won't believe it."

"Keep your voice down." Aunt Ermyntrude had gone to bed. Augustine could hear her snores from the adjoining room.

"Reggie's a good man," Cordelia protested. "An honourable man. He'd never steal anything."

All at once Augustine had a lump in her throat.

"You're right." Drawing her sister to her, she pressed a kiss to the top of her head. "I'm sorry. Let's forget it."

But she found it impossible to put her suspicions out of her mind.

"I've got a plan," she said the following morning, shaking Cordelia awake. "Something that'll prove –"

"No, Gussie. Don't be so hateful." Cordelia pulled the blankets up over her head.

"Have you two had a spat?" Aunt Ermyntrude asked at breakfast, breaking into the taut, angry silence between the sisters.

Tight-lipped, Augustine looked away. She felt wretched.

"Maybe," she managed.

Cordelia said nothing.

Leaving Ermyntrude in the dining-room reading the newspaper, Augustine took the lift up to their suite.

Cordelia took the stairs, bursting into the room a few seconds after Augustine.

"All right. Go ahead with your plan. Whatever it is." Cordelia's chin tilted defiantly. "You'll see that Reggie isn't a thief."

"Cordelia . . ." Augustine wrapped her sister in her arms. "It's best we know for sure. Let me tell you what I have in mind."

• • • •

"The tea leaves tell me you will cross water," Augustine pronounced, speaking in a portentous monotone. "And you will live a very happy life."

"Ooh, I know exactly which water you mean. Thank you, Madam Fortuna."

Another happy customer, Augustine thought, watching as the woman left the booth, letting the curtain of canvas that served as a door drop back into place.

"Consult Madam Fortuna," the youngster Augustine had hired for the morning, along with the booth, called out. "Madam Fortuna, reader of tea leaves."

"This is the one, Reggie."

It was Cordelia's voice.

Augustine's heartbeat quickened. This was it. This was why she'd set the whole charade in motion.

"It's a waste of money if you ask me, Cordelia." Aunt Ermyntrude, on top form as always, put in. "I'm going on to the end of the pier. There's a steamer coming in to the landing stage."

"Reggie." Augustine could hear the faint tremble in Cordelia's voice. "You go in first."

"Cordelia, dear heart, you're very pale. Are you all right? Would you –"

"I'm fine. Please go in."

With canvas on all sides including the roof, it was gloomy inside the booth.

Augustine saw Reggie pause, letting his eyes adjust before coming all the way inside.

"Good morning, madam."

The scarves and shawls that covered her from head to toe would ensure, she hoped, that she was unrecognisable.

Gesturing to the chair on the other side of the table, she pushed a tea caddy and cup towards him.

"Take a handful of leaves," she intoned in a breathy, rasping voice. "Put them in the cup, shake it and spread the leaves over the cloth."

Having no access to hot water, she'd been forced to improvise.

The three (unexpected) customers she'd had in the half hour since she'd set up the stall hadn't complained, though.

The moment Reggie had done as asked, she drew in a sudden sharp breath.

"Can it be true? The leaves are saying 'Flee at once. All is discovered'."

"What?" The word was an explosion of disbelief. "Is this a joke? What are you talking about, woman?"

"The leaves are telling me you've stolen something. A necklace. A diamond and ruby necklace –"

"They're saying no such thing. And I'll tell you why." He scraped back his chair and jumped up. "Because I haven't stolen anything. Ever."

He turned to leave, looking back as he pulled the curtain aside.

"You, madam, are a charlatan. A fraud."

His anger should perhaps have frightened her, yet Augustine wanted to laugh out loud.

She felt relief.

Reggie's sincerity was clear. He wasn't the thief.

Tugging off the scarf that covered her hair and much of her face, she followed him out.

"Mr Carter. Reggie –"

About to take Cordelia's hands in his, he glanced back with a look of utter incredulity crossed his face.

"Miss Brown?" He frowned and there was renewed anger in his voice. "What is going on?"

"It was an idea I had." Nervousness was making Augustine twist the scarf between her hands. "Before I continue, I must emphasise that Cordelia only agreed to prove I was wrong."

"And you were." Cordelia's voice cracked.

With a murmur of concern, Reggie put his arm round her, drawing her close.

His actions were gentle, but the look he shot Augustine blazed with anger.

"You'd better explain."

"It was something I read in 'The Strand'. It told how the author of the Sherlock Holmes stories sent a telegram to five famous people that said 'Flee at once. All is discovered'.

"All five must have had a guilty secret of some kind because they all promptly fled."

"I see." Reggie nodded. "So you accused me of robbing Lady Dalrymple-Jones. But I didn't react as a guilty man would, thus proving my innocence."

Augustine nodded and for a moment Reggie said nothing.

"Would you be prepared to go through the whole farce a second time?" he then asked.

Cordelia turned to face him, a question in her eyes.

Augustine started wrapping the scarf round her hair again.

"Yes, of course. Who do you have in mind?"

• • • •

"Can it be true? The tea leaves are saying 'Flee at once. All is discovered'."

"What!"

Was there an edge of fear in Sydney Winterton's voice?

Her heart beating quickly, Augustine rushed on, glad Reggie was just outside.

"They are telling me you've stolen something. A necklace. A diamond –"

"No." Sydney pushed his chair back, toppling it. "How is this possible? How can tea leaves know the truth?"

With sudden decision he turned, pushing his way past the canvas curtain and straight into Reggie's arms.

"Run and fetch a policeman," he called to the youngster staring at him goggle-eyed.

• • • •

"The police tell me Sydney's confessed," Reggie declared.

It was the afternoon, and the sisters were strolling along the promenade, arms linked through his.

"What made you think he might be involved?" Cordelia kept twisting round, gazing at Reggie with adoration in her eyes.

"I'd begun to suspect something a while back," he replied. "There's been a spate of robberies in London and along the south coast. I'd read an account of them in the newspaper.

"They'd started two days after Sydney arrived in the country, and took place wherever he happened to be at the time."

"So it's all over," Augustine murmured.

She felt a warm glow inside her. Her doubts about Reggie had vanished. He'd make a wonderful husband, she knew it.

It was just a shame that Sydney Winterton had turned out to be a thief.

"Over? No." Reggie pulled to a halt, forcing the sisters to stop, too. He looked at Augustine. "I'd like to know why you thought I was the thief."

"Because you act in such a mysterious way when one of us asks you about your business."

To her surprise, he laughed.

"It's quite simple, really. I import fine wines from the continent – and your Aunt Ermyntrude has strong views on the subject of wine."

"Oh, I'm sure you'll be able to win her round." Augustine smiled.

Out For A Duck

Someone at the cricket club had wanted rid of Ryan Overton . . .

BY ALYSON HILBOURNE

A CHEER went up, and Agatha opened her eyes in time to see her husband swing his bat under his arm and walk away from the wicket, peeling off his gloves as he went.

A little frisson of guilt ran through her as she realised she'd slept through her husband's first innings with the Stoneleigh village cricket club.

Oh, well, she thought, closing her eyes again and feeling the warmth of the sun on her face, he would undoubtedly tell her later about either his triumph or the unfairness of his dismissal.

Meanwhile she was going to enjoy this rare afternoon off, appreciating the lingering smell of cut grass.

Agatha could almost imagine it was idyllic if she hadn't been involved with a murder at the club during the last week.

• • • •

She and Jack had been having a quiet weekend.

Jack had the cricket commentary on the radio – England versus India. He'd planned to get tickets for one of the matches but then hadn't got around to it, so now he was glued to "Test Match Special".

Agatha didn't mind. She found the commentary soporific, and she was drifting off to sleep on the sofa when her phone rang from the kitchen, making her jump up.

"Sorry to bother you at the weekend, ma'am, but a suspicious death has been reported. SOCO are on their way. I thought you'd want to know." It was her new, young detective constable talking: DC Alison Price.

"Where is it, Alison?" Agatha asked.

"Stoneleigh village cricket club, ma'am."

Agatha thought of the beautiful village with a single standing stone on the village green, several half-timbered houses and the cricket pitch surrounded by horse chestnut trees.

Houses cost more than a detective inspector could afford, but it was where Jack dreamed of retiring.

"I'll meet you there," she said, grabbing her bag and changing her shoes.

Then, waving to Jack, she drove out of town, taking a leafy country lane to Stoneleigh.

When she arrived, Alison handed her some shoe protectors and led her across the grass to the back of the pavilion.

"A storage area?" Agatha asked.

"The groundsman's shed," Alison replied. "Although I'm told everyone takes turns with cutting grass before matches. They can't afford full-time staff."

In front of a dilapidated shed was a huge roller and a white site screen.

Lying between them was a young man in chinos and a T-shirt, flat on his back with congealed blood crusted on his forehead.

Crouching down beside him was a man in white plastic overalls with a hood and mask.

"Hello, Agatha." He turned and touched his forehead to acknowledge her.

"Steve. What have we got."

"Well, it's not a natural death," Steve told her. "A nasty blow to the head so death was probably fairly swift."

"Time of death?"

"I'd hazard a guess at last night, but I'll need to confirm that at the lab."

"Any ID?" Agatha asked.

"Ma'am," Alison interrupted. "The gentleman who found him identified him as Ryan Overton."

"And there was a wallet and a phone in his pockets," Steve added, handing over two evidence bags."

"Not a robbery, then," Agatha mused. "Right, Alison, let's talk to this gentleman who found him. Steve, let me know if there's anything more, please."

Agatha and Alison went round to the front of the pavilion where a portly older man was waiting on a bench.

"Good morning," Agatha greeted him. "I'm DI Agatha Lewis and this is DC Alison Price. And you are?"

"Nigel Pemberton," the man replied. "Club chairman and this morning's groundsman. We've a match later, so I came to roll the wicket."

Agatha sucked in her breath.

"It might be better if you cancel the match," she advised him. "In the circumstances."

The man winced and nodded.

"Fair enough."

"You said you knew the victim?"

"Yes. It's Ryan. He's a very keen player. He's been organising a tour for us. Wants to take the club to Cornwall to play some matches."

"When did you last see him?" Agatha asked.

Nigel thought for a moment.

"Last night. At nets. Just about the whole team were practising. We went to the pub afterwards." He pointed at the Shoulder Of Lamb public house that stood across the road.

"Although," Nigel added with a frown, "come to think of it, I don't think Ryan came for a drink."

"Right." Agatha nodded. "We'll need a full list of all the members of the club and another list of those who were here last night."

Nigel nodded, and as he walked away, Agatha turned to Alison.

"See what you can dig up on Ryan Overton," she said. "Wife, girlfriend, employment etc. We need to know who to notify of his death and any background as to motive."

• • • •

Two hours later, Agatha was back at the station about to bite into a tuna sandwich she'd picked up from the garage.

Before she could take a bite, another constable came over to her desk.

"Ma'am, I have information on Ryan Overton. It seems he was in a bit of trouble in the past. Warned for shoplifting and a pub brawl. He came up before magistrates but never served any time."

"Oh." Agatha raised an eyebrow. "Recent?"

The constable shook his head. "No. Last was five years ago now."

"Thank you."

Alison came over to Agatha's desk.

"Ryan was living with a girlfriend," she told the DI. "Faye Wilson. According to several members of the cricket team, he wasn't that faithful and was seen about with other women."

"Well, we'd better go and see the girlfriend," Agatha reasoned. "Break the news to her and see where she was last night."

The small house where Ryan and Faye lived wasn't in Stoneleigh but on a newish estate on the edge of town.

The house was compact and had a paved front garden where a battered Fiat was parked.

"Faye Wilson?" Agatha asked as willowy blonde woman in a spaghetti top and shorts answered the door.

"That's me," the woman said brightly.

"Can we come in?" Agatha asked, showing her warrant card.

"What is it?" Faye asked when they were seated in the small living-room. "Has Ryan been up to his old tricks?"

"What old tricks would that be?" Agatha asked.

Faye rubbed her nose.

"Well, he was in a bit of bother when he was younger," she admitted. "But he said he was putting all that behind him and we're buying this place together."

"Did he come home last night?" Agatha asked.

"No, he didn't."

"Any idea where he might have been?"

"He went to the cricket club." Faye sniffed. "It's all he talks about at the moment. He's organising a tour for them. Sometimes he has a bit too much to drink after a game and crashes at someone's place."

"Well, that's not what happened last night, I'm afraid," Agatha said, and as she explained to the woman about finding Ryan's body, she watched the blood drain from her face and her body slump.

"Do you know of anyone who might have wished him harm?" Agatha asked.

Faye shook her head.

"No. Ryan was a laugh. Life and soul of a party."

"Can I ask where you were last night?" Agatha asked.

Faye's head shot up.

"Me? Why? You don't . . . I wouldn't . . . I mean –"

"We have to ask," Agatha assured her gently.

"I was in all evening," Faye said quietly. "I must have got in from work around six and then I watched telly until I went to bed."

When they left Faye, Agatha and Alison went to where Ryan had worked at a garage on the edge of town.

The repairs section was closed, but the sales room was still open.

"Ryan? No," the man said when they explained what had happened. "David Crease was his boss. I'll give you his number. He'll be missed."

Agatha drove to David Crease's home.

Sounds of laughter came from the back garden where his children had a paddling pool and were playing with water guns.

David gave a rueful smile as he shook water from his hair and pulled a wet T-shirt from his skin.

Agatha explained what had happened.

"No! That's terrible." David seemed shocked. "He loved cricket and was so excited about the tour."

"Was he in any kind of trouble? Can you think of anyone who might have wished him harm?" Agatha asked.

David frowned. "He could wind people up," he said. "He was never serious about anything, but he was a good worker. We never had a problem with his work."

"We heard he might have been cheating on his girlfriend?"

"Faye? Nice lass. But yeah, he might have been. Like I say, he wasn't that serious about anything."

For their final visit of the day, Agatha and Alison went back to the cricket club to collect the lists of members from Nigel. The man appeared truly shocked now the death had sunk in.

"I can't believe it," he said as he handed over the names. "I'm sure it wouldn't be anyone from the team. Most of the members have been around for years. Some of them man and boy."

He gave Agatha and Alison a brief run-down on all the players.

"Lastly is Josh Hartley. He's only been playing for us this season, but he's a star and very unusual in that he can bat left-handed to a left-handed bowler and right-handed to a right-handed bowler."

Agatha quirked an eyebrow at Alison.

"How unusual?" she asked Nigel.

"Oh, very," he replied. "Josh should have been playing for a county team. He might have been good enough to make an England eleven, but he says he likes the feel of the Stoneleigh club, and he's bought a house in the village."

• • • •

"So what have we got?" Agatha asked Alison when they were back at the station.

"It sounds as if he could have annoyed any number of people, but everyone seemed to like him," Alison replied.

"Exactly." Agatha nodded. "It's not much to go on, is it? Let's sleep on it and I'll see you in the morning."

When Agatha got home, Jack was still listening to the radio and making spaghetti for dinner.

"I don't deserve you," Agatha said, kissing him.

"I'm glad you realise." Jack grinned, waving a wooden spoon in the air.

"I've a question for you," Agatha began. "How unusual is a cricketer who can bat left and right-handed?"

Jacked sucked in his breath. "Unusual, but not unknown," he told her. "There have been a few ambidextrous batters and bowlers over the years, but it's not common."

"So someone like that would stand out?"

Jack nodded.

Agatha didn't sleep well that night and was up early and in the office soon after eight.

Alison was already there.

"Didn't you sleep, either," Agatha asked, putting her bag down.

"I wanted to check these members," Alison admitted. "They are all well-heeled. Solicitors, teachers, a doctor, retired businessmen. All squeaky clean as far as I can see. Barely half a dozen points on driving licences between them."

Agatha wrinkled her nose.

"So Ryan was a bit of an outlier, being a mechanic and living in town rather than Stoneleigh."

Alison nodded.

"Any information on their star player, Josh Hartley?"

"No," Alison replied. "I have an address and telephone number from the members list but nothing else. He doesn't appear on any systems I can find. It's as if he has no online presence at all."

Agatha rubbed her chin.

"Interesting," she said. "I wonder why? What is he hiding? Let's go and talk to Mr Hartley, shall we?"

They drove out to Stoneleigh and followed the satnav to Elm Road, a short street lined with tall trees that rustled in the breeze and provided a green canopy over the road.

Alison pulled up at number 14.

There was a metal gate with an entry phone and a thick beech hedge along the front of the property.

"He doesn't welcome visitors," Agatha muttered, pushing a button on the keypad.

After she had explained who they were, the gate slid open quietly and they drove in. Agatha nodded towards the cameras and security lights that covered the front of the house.

"Is he cautious or worried?" she asked Alison.

Josh opened the door to them, wearing a white T-shirt that emphasised his tanned skin and jogging pants. He was barefoot.

He led them through to a deck at the back of the house, and they sat in the sunshine with glasses of lemonade as they talked.

"I expect you know that Ryan Overton was found dead yesterday morning," Agatha began.

Josh nodded.

"Nigel rang round everyone cancelling yesterday's game and telling us," he replied. "Shame. He was a nice fella."

"Did you know him well?" Agatha asked.

"Not well. Socially for the games and for a drink in the pub after. We could have a conversation, but I didn't see him apart from at the club."

"On the surface," Agatha began slowly, "he doesn't seem a good fit for the club."

Josh looked at her for a moment. "Oh, you mean he didn't have money or live in Stoneleigh?"

"Exactly."

Josh pushed back against his chair and regarded Agatha. "I don't think there are any restrictions on membership," he said. "I believe any application goes to a committee and is either approved or not."

"Are many people refused?" she asked.

"I don't know. You'd have to ask Nigel or one of the other committee members," Josh replied. "I'm not involved."

"How long have you been a member?" Agatha asked.

"Only this year," Josh told her. "I only moved here recently."

"And where were you before?"

Josh shrugged.

"I moved around a lot."

"If I had to pin you down?"

"Scotland, Newcastle, Cornwall."

"And what do you do for a living, Mr Hartley?"

"Is that relevant to Ryan's death?" he asked.

"You tell me."

"I don't do anything any more. So, no, it's not relevant."

• • • •

"He was cagey," Agatha stated when they got back to the station.

A constable came over with a sheet of paper.

"Here are details from Ryan's phone, ma'am."

"Oh, good work," Agatha replied. "Is there any news from the autopsy."

"He was killed by a blow to the head, causing a subdural hematoma. Doc thinks between nine and eleven p.m. He suggested from the shape of the impact and location of the body that it might have been a cricket bat."

Agatha raised her eyebrows.

"Well, that's not cricket," she muttered as she turned to the board where the team had put all their findings. "Right, Alison, what have we got?"

"We know Ryan was a lively chap, but everyone seems to have liked him," the constable began. "There are some suggestions he was playing away from home, so his girlfriend has to be a suspect."

Agatha nodded.

"And Josh Hartley is an odd character," she reminded her. "Very cagey about his job and where he's lived. He did mention Cornwall, though, and that's where Ryan was organising the cricket tour.

"Can someone check with Devon and Cornwall police to see if they have anything on him?"

"The body was discovered by Nigel Pemberton, the club chairman," Alison continued. "It seems he might be one of those who decides who is a member or not.

"Ryan's work gave us nothing, did it?" She appealed to the team. "No, so the death is probably linked to the cricket in some way, given where the body was found."

Agatha stared at the board.

"What are we missing?" she asked, tapping a pencil against her teeth.

• • • •

That evening, Jack had made a chicken curry and a dahl for dinner.

"How is the case going?" he asked.

"Nothing," Agatha said with a yawn. "We're a bit stuck."

Despite being tired, she didn't sleep. She couldn't help feeling they were missing something. Something she should have spotted. She was up early and arrived at the police station as a harried-looking woman was practically dragging a teenager in school uniform through the door behind her.

"The murder in Stoneleigh." The woman's voice was strident and directed at the desk officer.

Agatha paused as she was going through the secure door to CID. She turned and went back to the woman.

"Can I help you?" she asked. "I'm DI Agatha Lewis, in charge of the case."

"Zac saw something," the woman stated. "He's good at cricket and the PE teacher said he should join that club, but them stuck up lot won't have him because he doesn't live in Stoneleigh."

She pushed the boy forwards towards Agatha.

"What did you see, Zac?" Agatha asked gently.

Zac shuffled from foot to foot. "Two men fighting near the groundsman's hut," he muttered.

"Do you think you could identify them again?" Agatha asked.

• • • •

Agatha was dozing in the deck chair when she heard Jack's voice.

She looked up drowsily.

"Look!" Jack pointed at the wicket. "Just watch him. He's amazing."

Agatha shielded her eyes with a hand and followed Jack's direction.

"Oh, it's Zac," she said.

"Yes, and he's a fantastic bowler. Alternates arms. The opposition don't know what's hit them."

"So now the team has an ambidextrous batter and bowler?" Agatha asked.

"They do," Jack replied. "And they have me!"

"What more could they want?" Agatha asked.

"Well, a few more runs probably," Jack said with a smile. "It's just as well you worked out that it was Nigel Pemberton that did for Ryan. Apparently, he's been putting a block on all sorts of new members. Zac and me, for starters. Now we get our day in the sun."

"Well, it wasn't so hard once we had Zac's information," Agatha admitted.

"And when it became clear he was embezzling funds so there was no money left for the tour, we had him. He confessed he'd struck Ryan when he refused to cancel the trip."

"Tsk, tsk," Jack said, shaking his head. "That's just not cricket."

Agatha rolled her eyes at his joke, but she was pleased to see him enjoying the match.

Hopefully playing for Stoneleigh would be enough for him, but if he still wanted to move to the village, she'd be working for a few more years yet.

A Small Fortune

Size doesn't matter when it comes to expensive things...

BY ALISON CARTER

Tracey opened her front door, peeling off her jacket as she headed for the washing machine.

She was drenched. A lovely summer evening had given way to a brief but violent summer storm.

Her mobile rang as she ran upstairs for dry clothes.

"Ma'am, there's been a theft in the area. Are you nearby? Some kind of statue has been nicked."

Tracey was still on duty and closest to the address.

She looked at her blouse, plastered to her skin. She'd have to leave that on and get to the scene.

The apartment in question was gorgeous, in the posh area of Dean Village.

"This statue?" Tracey asked a well-groomed man who introduced himself as the owner, Mr Gunn. She looked at an empty corner. "Did it sit over there?"

He looked puzzled and handed her a photo. On it a china dog lay curled up.

Someone's finger had been photographed beside the dog, indicating that the statue was only inches long.

"A netsuke," Mr Gunn told her. "Worth about £45,000."

"I see. Well, we'll get to work, Mr Gunn."

Her DC took a statement while Tracey knocked on the door of the next-door flat, which seemed a fraction of the size of Mr Gunn's.

A young man in a faded T-shirt blinked at Tracey.

"You did get wet, didn't you? Don't worry; the rest of the night will be clear, and tomorrow's rain free."

Tracey asked what he had heard that afternoon.

"Zilch," he replied, "except the assistant going home."

"Assistant?"

"The fashion-obsessed kid who works for Mr Gunn. Goes home at half five."

The DC had the name of the assistant, so they visited him next.

As they drove, they worked out that the theft occurred between 5.30 p.m. and 5.50 p.m.

Tracey read the notes.

"Thomas Sanderson, the PA, leaves at five thirty and Mr Gunn was back by ten to five, held up in traffic."

Thomas Sanderson was a nervy young man, in clothes that the DC later said were "designer, and a bit fey".

Mr Sanderson was shocked at the theft and confirmed his movements.

Next morning, Tracey spoke to the building manager.

"It's funny," the manager said. "My electrician was in that corridor from half past five, for twenty-five minutes or so. It was a socket repair."

She assured Tracey that entry via the windows was impossible, and that every door had to be opened with an electronic card.

It wasn't impossible, she admitted, to clone a flat's entry card.

The electrician said that he had begun work in the corridor at half past five.

"This is weird," Tracey told her DC. "An apartment constantly observed or occupied is broken into by an invisible person. We have to widen the net."

Back at the station, they focused on technological aspects of the case.

When he got a look, the police IT expert whistled his appreciation.

"If they didn't have access to a card, this is expert hacking," he remarked.

Tracey asked to meet Thomas Sanderson again, in a café to put him at ease.

She had a hunch that he knew more.

On her way back to the table she splashed tea on Thomas's suit – the same suit he'd been wearing on the day of the crime.

He leapt out of his chair.

"This fabric can't tolerate liquids!" he yelled.

It wasn't a great interview and Tracey left frustrated.

In George Street, she stopped in front of a travel agent.

A display of paper suns made her think of the weather, and specifically the unusual weather on the day of the theft.

She called her DC.

"Look into the next-door neighbour," she told him.

She remembered the T-shirt man's greeting. His detailed weather forecast had seemed odd.

His name was Ted McNeish and his girlfriend was a programmer at a commercial meteorology firm.

Tracey asked her IT guy to check it out and talked her boss into a warrant, allowing access to tech logs.

Half a day later, the IT guy came into Tracey's office.

"The company supplies a phone app," he informed her. "Thomas Sanderson uses that app. The forecast supplied for one area of the city was tampered with."

Tracey nodded.

"The thieves brought the timing of the storm forward, knowing that Sanderson could not abide water on his suit. He left before his usual time to avoid the storm!"

"And that's when they got in, having hacked the entry system! Two brilliant hacks!"

The netsuke was still in McNeish's flat.

He knew Sanderson's fussy ways with his suits. He had even stolen his brolly the previous week.

Thomas also admitted to leaving the apartment at five, when his mobile alerted him to the coming downpour.

"I had to get home before the rain." He shuddered. "I don't wear mackintoshes. I didn't want Mr Gunn to know I didn't do my hours, so I didn't tell you."

McNeish had had time to take the netsuke once Thomas had left.

Tracey herself returned the netsuke, marvelling that something so tiny could cause such trouble.

Sting Like A Bee

Marcia had to be sure of her suspicions before she accused anyone of murder . . .

BY CHARMAINE FLETCHER

"KNEE to elbow, step right and turn!" a blonde in scarlet Lycra shouted, bouncing energeically to Latin rhythms reverberating around the gym.

Opposite, several women puffed through her new Zumba class.

Meanwhile, watching from the sidelines, were Marcia Porter and Tansy Leighton, manager of Starfields Retirement Village.

"Look at her," Marcia observed scathingly. "It's like bees to honey!

"Ever since Bambi arrived, she's had everyone buzzing around her. Worse, she's practically running the place, despite only being here a few months!"

"Do you think so?" Tansy replied, studying Bambi.

"Yes," Marcia, a retired personnel officer, said firmly. "Residents presenting recreational classes might be cheaper, but she's controlling and changing everything.

"Somebody should tell her that, if roused, bees sting quite nastily – often when the victim's least expecting it," she finished.

The next day, while enjoying a morning stroll, Marcia's words returned to haunt her.

She saw police tape surrounding Begonia Cottage, Bambi's home.

"What's happened?" she asked as villagers milled about outside. "Has Bambi finally been arrested for crimes against retirees?"

"Marcia, really!" Lucinda Capelton, a retired teacher living in Hellebore Cottage, said. "Poor Bambi's dead!

"Her door was ajar and I found her. It was a heart attack, probably."

"A heart attack? Don't make me laugh; Bambi didn't have a heart. She was a bully," Marcia replied.

"Yes," Doug Everette from Hyacinth Cottage said. "She did rather dominate things."

"Finally someone who agrees!" Marcia cried. "I mean, doubtless she read the brochures and had the tour, so why come here only to alter Starfields so much?"

"Because it's inexpensive with lots of wealthy widowers," Annie Farmer, a retired store detective and Marcia's friend, drawled, approaching them. "And now the plot thickens."

"How?" Marcia asked.

"Well, I was wandering past the admin office – close to an open window –"

"Isn't that where the police are?" Lucinda interrupted suspiciously.

"Exactly. There's more to Bambi's demise than meets the eye.

"Apparently it wasn't a straightforward heart attack. She'd no history of illness, the police said.

"A cup, found nearby, was removed for examination," Annie finished enigmatically.

"Poison?" Lucinda said.

"Why doesn't that surprise me?" Marcia asked. "Plenty of people disliked her: wives, rejected suitors, even riled club members."

"Come on," Chris chided her. "She wasn't that bad.

"I asked her out once, but Bambi was younger than most of us, so we had little in common. She mentioned moving to London and modelling in the Nineties."

"Did Bambi have a chap there?" Annie asked idly.

"She never said," Chris replied.

"Still, she chased the men here – even married ones!" Marcia snapped. "Some irate wife probably gave Bambi a taste of her own medicine."

"Stop it, Marcia!" Annie hissed, drawing her away from the others. "If foul play is suspected, fingers will point in your direction!"

"All right," Marcia conceded grudgingly as they returned to the group.

"I didn't cross paths much with Bambi yesterday, either," Annie admitted, "but after returning from lunch, raised voices were coming from her garden.

"I don't know what it was about, but someone said: 'No, you don't. Not again'."

"I m-must dash," Lucinda stuttered suddenly, stooping to collect her shopping bag, its wilting flowers peeping out.

As she did so, something fell from her jacket pocket.

"You've dropped . . ." Marcia began, picking it up, but Lucinda had hurried off without a second glance.

"What's got into her?" she asked, watching Lucinda disappear.

"She's upset probably," Annie suggested.

"Or perhaps it relates to this," Marcia suggested, revealing a USB memory stick in her hand.

Gasping silently, Annie pulled her aside again.

"Was it Lucinda's or Bambi's? Does it relate to Lucinda discovering Bambi's body?" Marcia whispered.

"It's hard to tell without reading it. Although finding Bambi does place a question mark over Lucinda, as they weren't that friendly," Annie mused.

"So what do you suggest?" Marcia asked as a police officer approached, moving everyone on.

"Simple." Annie smiled. "We investigate."

"OK." Marcia nodded, scanning the scene one final time as she and Annie headed to her cottage.

"So," Marcia began, handing Annie a coffee,

"where do we start?"

They were sitting at a table in Chrysanthemum Cottage, which, like all of Starfields' properties, was identical to Annie's.

"With Bambi's recent movements, apart from the Zumba class and that altercation I mentioned, I doubt if there's more we can add. Although the police seemed to think she died late yesterday evening. I heard them telling Tansy."

"My, you've got big ears!" Marcia laughed.

"Absolutely," Annie said, "but not sufficiently so to determine who was arguing with Bambi.

"What if she annoyed a resident and they slipped her something to inconvenience her? You know, to give her the collywobbles?"

"Only, maybe accidentally, went too far," Marcia joined in. "Like whatever Bambi did, according to that row you overheard."

"Yes, but who and why?"

"There are many battered hearts and bruised egos," Marcia reminded her friend.

"Possible, but too simplistic," Annie replied, sipping her coffee. "Everyone's so long in the tooth here, surely they've had to cope with flirtations or rejections without resorting to murder?"

"But there's always a first time," Marcia reasoned. "Or a last one."

"Let's set aside reasons and consider possible culprits," Annie suggested.

"They're lining up. Bambi got herself on to lots of committees and was, it seems, angling to chair them, putting numerous noses out of joint. Finally we have Chris, and especially Lucinda," Marcia replied.

"No, Chris is too laidback and sporty for passion, if you ask me. He's a nice chap, though. That leaves Lucinda and the mysterious USB," Annie replied.

"Yes but everyone has USBs now — especially somewhere like this, where residents have downsized," Marcia pointed out. "It's a convenient way of retaining photographs and projects.

"Besides, Lucinda seemed genuinely upset about Bambi."

"Maybe she was just deflecting attention away from herself," Annie replied sceptically. "Anyway, we'll find out when you return that USB and discover why she was carrying it around."

"Meanwhile, let's keep our eyes and ears open," she added, getting up. "But right now I have a yoga session.

When she'd gone, Marcia eyed the USB stick.

Normally she wouldn't have considered prying into someone's private business — besides, USBs sometimes contained malware, including viruses.

Reading it on her laptop might be risky, but there was always her old one . . .

A few minutes later, Marcia inserted the USB and opened a file.

Southwood Grammar School, it said.

Perhaps this would shed some light on things, Marcia thought, settling back to view it.

By the end she had enough information to suggest a motive and possible murderer — perhaps even two.

"Well?" Annie asked the next day, after Marcia arrived at Rudbeckia, her cottage. "What did you discover?"

"You go first," Marcia said.

"I know who Bambi was arguing with — Ted Allerdice from the gardening club told me. It was Tansy!

"Audrey objected to Bambi's interference with the art club and asked her to intervene," Annie explained.

"Bambi also campaigned to modify the landscaping here, prohibiting plants that attract bees and insects."

"Why? Starfields is garden-themed and insects are environmentally beneficial."

"True," Annie replied. "But she was allergic to them — and rumour now has it that a sting killed Bambi, so it wasn't murder."

"Not necessarily," Marcia muttered enigmatically.

"You read the USB, didn't you?" Annie said sternly.

Shamefaced, Marcia nodded.

"I had to. Lucinda's finding Bambi, her furtiveness, then the USB stick all pointed in one direction."

"Go on," Annie pressed.

"Bambi, or Beryl Barclay, Lucinda and Tansy are connected by Southwood Grammar School."

"But Lucinda's about ten years older." Annie frowned.

"Yes — in the 1980s she was their teacher, a young graduate. They were O-level pupils and Tansy's mother was an administrator. Apparently, there was some scandal concerning money.

"It was usual to take a party of leavers on a school journey after their exams, so Lucinda suggested Paris," Marcia continued. "Those involved paid weekly, then a large final balance.

"Evidently, as payment monitor, Bambi was controlling even then. Come the final instalment, Lucinda checked the cashbox contents were correct, but Bambi made Tansy deliver it to the administrative office.

"What nobody knew was that, in the interim, the money had disappeared. Bambi provided an alibi, so Lucinda, Tansy and her mother were blamed.

"Tansy was allowed to finish her exams on condition that her mother repaid the money and resigned.

"Lucinda kept her job but any career prospects were curtailed. Yet all three denied taking the money.

"Meanwhile, Beryl became 'Bambi', skedaddling to London and a successful modelling career — later retiring to Starfields."

"So that's why Tansy warned her off — fear!" Annie exclaimed.

"Or retribution, explaining Lucinda's evasiveness — but did you notice something else?" Marcia asked.

"What?"

"The flowers in her bag were dead. She was probably removing them and evidence of her involvement on the USB — that's really how she found Bambi's body.

"It's time to visit Tansy!" Marcia exclaimed. "But I've something to do first . . ."

• • • •

"I wondered when you'd show up," Tansy said drily.

"We know about the Southwood scandal," Marcia said. "Was this a revenge?"

"Bambi died of natural causes. Who could have known she was allergic to bee stings?" Tansy smiled.

"Someone whose mother was a school administrator with access to information about such matters.

"Gardening cub members were aware, too, including Lucinda," Annie replied.

"Oh, a blame game, is it? Well, I'm not playing this time. Anyway, how could I persuade a bee to target Bambi?" Tansy sneered.

"By sending Lucinda, along with flowers — supposedly making amends for your earlier row — concealing or encouraging a bee," Marcia said. "Flowers Lucinda later conveniently removed from the scene."

"Then perhaps you shouldn't cross me, either. Bees have a nasty sting if roused, don't they, Marcia?" Tansy snarled.

"I think that's my cue . . ." a voice came from behind them.

"Chief Inspector Coltsfoot!" Tansy cried.

"The ladies have shared their theory and the potential evidence on Miss Capelton's USB stick," the chief inspector told Tansy. "She's being questioned.

"Meanwhile, we found a dead bee in the victim's cup — probably being shooed out when it attacked her.

"Whether that's murder or not is for the authorities to decide. Officers." He nodded as two constables stepped forward to caution and handcuff Tansy.

"I think we're good at this detection lark," Marcia said as they headed home.

"The bees knees, you might say." Annie smiled.

Pick A Pocket Or Two

Someone in this seaside town had itchy fingers . . .

BY ALYSON HILBOURNE

"SHOULDN'T we be doing something?" Detective Constable Kay Grant leaned over the desk towards her partner, Detective Sergeant Connor O'Neill.

Connor stared at her for a moment, before folding his arms across his chest and rocking back in his chair, which squeaked wearily.

"What?" he asked. "Wander around looking for the pickpocket? It would be like looking for a needle in a haystack."

Kay sat back, her shoulders slumped.

"But we're not getting anywhere with these reports," she pointed out. "I've been through them several times and can't find any connections."

The team had been tasked by the chief constable with catching the criminals behind a wave of pickpocketing of mobile phones and wallets over the last month.

"It's beginning to affect tourism," the chief had told them. "Holidaymakers are staying away from town because of the thefts."

"But it's only petty crime," Connor had scoffed.

"It would be if it was occasional," the chief had snapped. "But we're getting a dozen reports a day. We need action!"

And with that final word he'd stamped out of the office.

Kay, being the newest member of the team, had been tasked with trawling through the individual crime reports, trying to spot any similarities.

After three days she'd noticed nothing: not time of day, not brand of phone, not even locations.

Nothing except that everyone had been in town, in the sunshine, enjoying themselves until they'd found their phone or their wallet was missing.

"Where do you suggest we go?" Connor asked now.

Kay shrugged.

"The seafront? The pier?"

Connor stretched, exposing a roll of stomach between his shirt and trousers, then stood up.

"I suppose we could go out. It's almost lunchtime."

Outside, Kay took a deep breath, but the air was still and sultry.

As they walked towards the seafront she could smell cooking oil, onions, vinegar and popcorn, and music sounded from the arcade.

The promenade was crowded, despite the chief's warning of visitor numbers dropping.

Kay had only moved to the town a few weeks ago, but it seemed to her that the place got busier by the day.

They walked along.

A small crowd had stopped to watch a juggler, while an accordion player had placed a hat on the ground hopefully, but it was woefully empty.

It must be difficult to make a living as a busker these days, Kay thought. Not many people carry cash any more.

"I'm going to see a source," Connor said, pointing to a takeaway shop across the road.

"Shall I come with you?" Kay offered.

"Best not," Connor replied, tapping the side of his nose. "I'll meet you back here in ten minutes."

Kay clamped her lips together, saying nothing.

The only thing she could imagine getting from the takeaway was a nasty stomach bug.

She wandered further along and stopped to watch a street artist.

The man – she thought it was a man, but the figure was huddled in a cloak with a hood pulled low over its face – held a staff like a Jedi and appeared motionless, despite the fact he appeared to be levitating, sitting at least a foot off the ground.

She frowned, wondering how it was done, as people jostled around trying to get a good photograph.

A boy bent down to peer under the Jedi's robes, but he didn't appear to find anything untoward.

Kay was still there when Connor joined her.

"It's Jedi magic," he told her, wiping ketchup from the corner of his mouth.

"Find anything?" Kay asked.

Connor shook his head.

"They've not seen anyone behaving suspiciously."

"No," Kay echoed. "Where next?"

"You can buy me an ice-cream. As a thank-you for offering you the benefit of my experience in the town," Connor said.

"And what experience would that be?" Kay asked.

"I know where the best ice-cream is." Connor grinned. "This way."

They walked on to the pier, where the worn wooden boards were warm in the sun.

Connor directed her to an

Italian-style gelato stall run by a girl with arms covered in tattoos.

"Connor!" she cried with obvious delight.

"Miri, this is my partner, Kay. She's buying the ices." He leaned over the glass counter. "Have you noticed anyone hanging around, Miri? Anything suspicious?"

The girl shook her head.

"I'm rushed off my feet with this weather, Con. Hardly have time to put my head up during the day."

• • • •

"You're so lucky to live here, Auntie Kay!"

Kay was back on the promenade the next morning with her sister and two nieces, who were visiting for the day.

It was her first day off since she'd arrived, and she could have done with sorting out her flat, but she didn't begrudge her family a visit.

"I want to come and live here," her younger niece, Ellie, announced.

Kay laughed.

"Well, when I get my flat organised, maybe you can stay," she replied.

As they walked along, she kept her eyes peeled for unusual activity.

Yesterday's outing with Connor had been a complete waste of time. She was determined to do better on her own.

"Can we go on the beach?" Clare, her elder niece, asked.

"The pier?" Ellie added.

Kay looked at her sister, who shrugged.

"I don't mind," she replied. "It's nice to be out in the fresh air and see the sea. I might take a photo."

She pulled out her phone and angled it to the sea.

"That reminds me," Kay said. "Put that away in an inside pocket. There's been a swathe of phone thefts here lately."

Her sister snapped the picture and carefully put her phone back in her bag, which she held tight.

"I don't want to ruin the day," Kay said, putting a hand on her sister's arm, "but it would be ruined if your phone went missing."

They continued along the prom towards the pier, the girls stopping to watch the juggler and the musicians.

When they came to the levitating Jedi, they were fascinated.

"Can I take a photo?" Ellie demanded, putting out her hand for her mother's phone.

Kay watched as the nine-year-old expertly held the phone up, adjusted the setting and took a picture.

She showed the photo to Kay and her mother.

"Good one," Kay said, turning to the Jedi, who raised a hand apparently in acknowledgement.

Kay felt obliged then to put some money in the box that was on the ground, but the Jedi didn't acknowledge that.

She went back to her sister and the girls, then looked around as other people took photos.

Sometimes the Jedi seemed to see them and raised a hand.

Other times he ignored the photographers.

Something niggled at the back of Kay's thoughts, but Ellie and Clare were clamouring to get on the pier and she thought no more about it.

The girls rolled pennies in the coin-pushing machines and struggled with grappling hooks to win a pink teddy bear.

They bought candy floss and Kay took them to Miri's ice-cream stall.

"Nice to see you again," Miri said as Kay ordered. "After you'd gone yesterday, I had a customer find their wallet had vanished."

"Did they report it?" Kay asked.

"I told them to," Miri replied. "What we need are more police walking around to act as a deterrent."

• • • •

When Kay had dropped her sister and the girls off at the station, she'd gone home and climbed into bed early, exhausted from the fresh air and the sun.

She dreamed of the Jedi, floating effortlessly above the promenade.

For some reason, in her dream, he waved to her and pointed at her directly.

She half woke, aware of something she should have thought of, then turned and went back to sleep.

The next morning, Kay was groggy from a disturbed night.

She made a salad and took it into the office.

"Six more phones and two wallets," Connor declared as she sat down in her chair. "Can you see if you can find any connections?"

Kay shifted through the new reports, then she phoned a few people.

"You did? OK, thanks," she said.

"What's that?" Connor asked, returning just as she finished a phone conversation.

He put his mug down on the desk and liquid slopped over the top. He mopped it up with his hand.

Kay winced.

"I've had a thought, Connor. What sort of phone do you have?"

Connor frowned and held up the latest iPhone.

"Top of the range?" Kay asked.

"Yeah."

"So were all the ones nicked," she told him. "That's the connection. Our thief knows their phones."

Connor's eyes widened.

"Good spot," he told her.

"And," Kay went on, "I think I might know how they are doing it."

• • • •

They walked along the prom. When they got to the Jedi, Kay pulled out her phone and took a photo.

"Now you take one," she whispered to Connor.

"Why?" he asked with a frown. "I don't —"

"Connor."

"Oh, all right. But I don't see why," Connor grumbled as he pulled out his phone and snapped a photo of the Jedi.

"Did you see that?" Kay asked.

"What?"

"The Jedi raised his hand at you."

"So?"

"Do you know him?"

"No, of course not."

"OK, put your phone in your back pocket and walk away," Kay told him. "I'm going to follow at a distance."

Connor frowned, but did as she asked and ambled along the prom.

He'd barely gone 500 yards when she observed a teenage girl moving towards him.

Kay waited until the last minute, when the girl's hand was on his pocket.

"What the —"

Connor spun round as Kay gripped the girl.

"Check her pockets, Connor."

• • • •

The chief constable clasped his hands behind his back and rocked on his feet.

"Exemplary work by our two newest officers," he stated. "A very neat trick where one girl would identify high-end phones and indicate to her partner which ones to lift.

"We've recovered a fair number of those that were stolen, as well as bank cards and some cash. There are many relieved businesses today, happy that a couple of criminals have been apprehended."

He turned and left.

"Who'd have thought of two young girls?" Connor remarked.

"It was a clever ruse," Kay replied. "I only spotted it because my sister has a new phone."

"Well, it was good work," Connor said. "But don't let it go to your head. Keep your feet on the ground."

Kay snorted with laughter.

"That was awful!" she teased him.

"I know." Connor grinned. "I specialise in awful.

"Come on, it's almost lunchtime. I'll buy you a burger to celebrate your success . . ." ■

WISH YOU WERE HERE?

In a shoebox tucked away
Lie images of distant lands,
Ancient ruins, cityscapes,
Snowy peaks and golden sands.

Sketched out briefly on the back,
Details of vacation fun,
Tours, museums, woodland walks,
Romantic meals, games in the sun.

Neighbours, colleagues, penpals dear,
A child's first trip with the school,
So kind they took the time to write,
Especially those on their honeymoon!

Through the years they've all survived,
Crossed the oceans, travelled miles,
Though many were delivered late,
Now, as then, they raise a smile.

By Laura Tapper

¡Y VIVA ESPANA!

Our first trip abroad was to Lloret in Spain,
It was the first time I'd ever been on a plane.
The glamorous air hostesses with beautiful smiles,
Served little trays of food as we flew hundreds of miles.

The hotel swimming pool was inviting and blue,
The tiles so hot, I needed my new flip flop shoes!
The food was unfamiliar so we ate egg and chips,
And enjoyed seeing the sights on organised trips.

Our skin turned red so we rubbed on "After Sun"
We swam in the warm sea and had so much fun,
We went to a nightclub to watch a flamenco show,
Castanets were clicked by a dancer called Angelo.

My Spanish souvenir doll gave me so much pleasure
Memories from that trip I always will treasure.
Most of all, it gave me a lifelong love of travel,
And showed me our world is full of wonder and marvel.

By Sharon Haston

Sunshine DAYS

The long days of summer are full of delights and possibilities. These heartwarming stories are sure to put a smile on your face and a glow in your heart.

All At Sea

The coastal village of Little Fletcher was beautiful but it just wasn't home . . .

BY TESS NILAND KIMBER

"ARGH, get off!" Rach screamed, dropping her ice-cream with a splat on to the promenade as a shrieking seagull pecked the caramel mess.

A man laughed.

"Happened to me, yesterday, love. Seagulls love their ice-creams. Or rather our ice-creams!"

"That's it!" she said, storming away from a flummoxed Jeff and their two-year-old daughter Alana. "I've had enough!"

"Rach! Come back!" Jeff called.

But she was too quick, anger powering her pace.

"I don't want to move. I love London. And I love our life here," she'd told her husband when he'd first said his company were relocating to Devon.

"I do, too, but it's a great opportunity. Your mum and dad live nearby and think, how much better, healthier, quieter life will be for Alana," he'd added.

It had taken weeks of persuasion, she thought, rushing past the busy arcade, before she'd even look at Devonshire property with him.

It had been the house that had sold the coastal village of Little Fletcher to her.

Although they'd had a great flat in Greenwich, their space had rapidly decreased since Alana's birth.

Houses in Devon were twice the size and half the price. Here, they'd have a spare bedroom, a garden, driveway – a dream come true.

There were downsides.

"London's so vibrant. We can go to shows, the cinema, museums, catch a train, go anywhere."

"Well, Little Fletcher has a theatre and restaurants, too, you know." He'd grinned. "And the sea, beaches, tourist attractions, parks."

Eventually she'd agreed to put the flat up for sale.

It went from being their home to someone else's dream within four days.

The thought of having more disposable income and savings for the first time in years did also appeal to Rach and they put an offer on the Grange.

"The central heating's gone on the blink again, Jeff," she said with a frown on the first week they moved in.

It was May but the evenings were still chilly.

"And the bulb's blown in Alana's bedroom."

"It's an older property, love." He'd smiled. "It's bound to have a few foibles."

"You call the boiler breaking down twice over the weekend and the roof leaking 'a few foibles'?"

"The builders are coming Monday, it'll get sorted. But think, we have space! A garden for Alana.

"Next year she'll be big enough for a swing and we'll have our own apples in autumn . . ." Jeff said, wrapping his arms around Rach's waist.

"I know. And when you do go into the office, you've only a twenty-minute commute rather than an hour and a half," she'd said, quietly.

Of course, Jeff was right. There were lots of pluses for him living in Little Fletcher, she thought now as she strode past the kiosk hiring deckchairs.

But for her, the cons outweighed the pros.

"We've run out of milk," she'd said, just that morning. "I'll pop and get some. There's bound to be a little shop nearby."

But she couldn't find one.

"Excuse me," she asked a woman walking an elderly whippet. "Do you know where the nearest shop is, please?"

"Oh, now they've closed the sub post office, nearest is the supermarket."

"What, out of town?"

"Yep." The woman nodded, waiting while her dog sniffed the long grass.

She then told Rach the history of the sub post office. "Mrs Lucas, she sold up and bought a bungalow by her son and the owner before that, re-trained as a teacher. He's working at the secondary . . ."

It was interesting and sweet of her to chat, but Rach still needed milk.

She thanked her and returned to the Grange.

Now she'd have a drive, just to buy milk.

In Greenwich, she'd had a choice of shops on her doorstep. And takeaways. And restaurants.

Little Fletcher had shops, but most were along the seafront and geared towards tourists.

As it was still spring, some wouldn't open for several weeks. She sighed.

Coastal and urban were opposite worlds.

• • • •

After she'd cooled off, Rach walked back to the seafront.

"Ah, there you are!" Jeff said, concern shining in his eyes.

For a split second, she regretted walking off. It wasn't fair to worry him.

He was sat on the beach, watching Alana build a sandcastle.

That was the beauty of him working from home; he could pick his hours, giving them extra family time.

"I'll buy a bucket and spade," he said. "We might have a future construction engineer on our hands here."

She nodded, watching their daughter, absorbed in her task.

"You know, I do understand, love," he whispered. "Little Fletcher's so different to London."

A tear slid down her cheek.

"I'm sorry. I'm just finding it hard to settle. I loved Greenwich."

He pulled her to him, kissing her forehead.

"I did, too. Give it time. Try to notice what's right about the move as well as what isn't so great."

• • • •

Rach tried to do as he'd suggested but it was too quiet, the pace of life too slow, the roads too empty. It all felt dull, dull, dull.

With the builders repairing the roof and installing the new kitchen, she took Alana to the park. They'd just reached the bench when her phone rang. It was her old friend, Sally, who was pregnant with her first child.

"Rach, I'm having a baby shower. Wanna come?"

"I'd love to! When? Where?"

"Sebastien's. Next Thursday. All the gang will be there."

"Great – you know we've moved? To Devon."

"I had heard, but I imagine they've trains, even in the back of beyond," she laughed.

Rach smiled. It would be great to see the girls again. And go back to London, feel the buzz. Jeff was working from home most days lately and even if he was busy, her parents always relished extra Alana time if she asked.

"I'll have to sort something for Alana, but if I can, I'll be there!"

When she told Jeff about the baby shower, he happily offered to look after Alana.

"Go and enjoy yourself. A break will do you good," he said.

• • • •

Although she'd miss Alana and Jeff, Rach couldn't wait to spend time with her old friends.

As the train pulled into Paddington Station, she felt excited to be in London again. She'd always been a city girl.

But as she stepped onto the platform, she was pushed. She only just stopped herself from falling. No-one apologised. She'd forgotten how rushed everyone was here, she thought, rubbing her shoulder.

Once in the taxi heading for Sebastien's, she drank in the familiar sights – the Royal Albert Hall, Harrods, Hyde Park – until they finally pulled up outside the restaurant.

"Have to let you out here, love. Traffic's a nightmare," the taxi driver said.

"No problem," she said, amazed at the blocked roads.

Was she already used to the slower pace back home in Devon?

As she paid her fare, she realised she'd just mentally referred to Little Fletcher as home. It jolted her. No doubt it was a mental slip.

She checked her reflection in the restaurant's window then pushed open the door.

"Rach! You're here!" She was ambushed by Sally, Vi and Akira who all rushed to hug her.

"We've missed you so much," Sally rubbed her enormous bump.

"I've missed you all, too! How are you? You look fabulous," she said to her friend.

Sally lowered herself into a chair around their table, decorated with pink and blue helium balloons.

"I'm not fabulous," she pulled a face. "I'm huge with swollen ankles, heartburn and endless cravings for boiled eggs and horseradish."

"Oh my – no wonder you've got indigestion." Rach laughed.

After chatting to Sally about the baby who was due next month, the girls asked Rach about her new life.

"You're so lucky, living on the coast," Akira said.

"I suppose so, but I miss London."

"Whatever for?" Sally laughed. "The air's dirty, everything costs too much and the traffic's at a standstill."

"But I love the life, the energy, the nightlife."

Vi agreed but added, "I love London but if I could live on the coast like you, I'd jump at the chance."

When their afternoon tea arrived on dainty stands, they started eating.

The conversation moved on to Akira's new boyfriend.

Rach listened, but their reaction to her move filled her thoughts. Was she missing something? Was the coast really a special place to be?

She looked out of the window, as people hurried by clamped to their phones, and thought of Little Fletcher where the locals had time to chat, like the woman with the dog who'd told her where to buy milk.

No, London was the best place in the world.

Devon would only ever be second best, she thought, biting into a delicious salmon and cream cheese finger sandwich.

• • • •

Going to London and meeting her friends made Rach feel better.

"Just knowing I can go back to visit makes all the difference," she told her mum when she popped in for coffee.

"Well, I love you living here. I see more of you, Jeff and Alana. This is something you couldn't do in London – drop in for a quick chat."

Rach smiled. Her mum was right.

"And the house is coming on. That will make you feel differently," Mum said, rinsing her cup under the hot tap.

"The Grange is definitely looking better," she agreed. "More home-like."

Scooping up Alana, she left her parents.

"Beach, Mummy," the toddler said when she put her in the car seat.

"OK – then we must go shopping." She smiled as she drove. Alana really loved the seaside.

"Look Mummy – birds! And sun! And the sea!" Alana laughed and pointed as they parked.

Rach smiled, lifting her out of the car. As soon as they stepped onto the sand, the toddler rolled over.

She laughed but as she watched her daughter, she couldn't help overhearing the family sat near her.

"I'd give my right arm to live here. Get away from the smoke," the man said to the woman laid beside him on a tartan blanket.

"I don't think I can stand another week living in our awful flat. That new family do nothing but row."

His partner nodded.

"The traffic gets on my pip," she said. "It's lovely to park here and only pay a few quid."

"And not get the car nicked or the tyres slashed."

Rach wanted to butt in, tell them city life wasn't that bad, but they did have a point.

She loved London but she'd been ignoring the downsides to living there.

As she watched Alana, she realised how much the little girl loved living here and glancing along the already familiar promenade, she began to see it through her daughter's eyes.

The sun was shining, glinting off the azure sea, as seagulls swooped, calling to each other.

They could be on holiday, but they were lucky enough to live in Little Fletcher.

In London, they'd only had a narrow balcony.

Here, Alana could play on the beach or maybe, like this morning, eat breakfast on the lawn. There was room for a sand pit, a paddling pool and the builders had now fixed many of the Grange's "foibles".

"Are you happy, Mummy?" Alana suddenly asked.

For a second she thought. Little Fletcher wasn't London, but it was beginning to feel like home. Jeff was happy. Alana was happy. Like measles, it was catching.

"Yes," she smiled, "I think I am."

Moments Like These

Kate missed spending time with her dear granddaughter . . .

BY MARIE PENMAN

SUMMER holidays meant different things to different people.

Children, for example, revelled in the endless weeks of freedom, with no school to attend.

Working parents, meanwhile, often worried about a lack of childcare and felt guilty about having to leave their children while they went out to work.

And grandparents were either dismayed or delighted to find that they were expected to rearrange their own schedules to accommodate the routine of caring for little ones.

Kate loved being a granny. She had enjoyed being a mum as well, of course, but the fun side of that had often been lost in the sheer, unrelenting stress and worry of looking after children for 24 hours a day.

That was all in the past, though, and her two little ones were now all grown up with babies of their own.

Dan had a ten-year-old daughter, Ella, and Louise had her hands full with two-year-old twin boys.

Kate had taken early retirement when Ella was born and in the pre-school years had shared childminding duties with Dan's mother-in-law, Nancy.

She'd cherished those years with baby Ella, but now that she was older – ten going on fifteen, as her mum described her! – there was less need for babysitting.

The twins, meanwhile, were a force of nature and came to her two days a week while Louise worked part-time. But this summer, Kate would have all three of the children at once!

Ella was supposed to be going to a full-time kids' club at the local sports centre but this had somehow fallen through at the last minute, and so Dan had called in a panic, begging his mum for help.

"I'm doing my usual shifts on the ward, but Lucy is scheduled for the same hours, plus she's on call as well!

"It's a nightmare, Mum, and poor Ella is left with nowhere to go."

Kate had smiled, happy to have her darling girl back.

With both Dan and his wife Lucy working as hospital doctors, Ella's week normally revolved around a variety of after-school clubs, childminders and sports lessons.

To be honest, Kate felt a bit sorry for her, never able to simply relax at home, but she wouldn't dare say this to Dan or Lucy.

She might have commented on it if Ella had been Louise's daughter, but there was no way you could criticise a daughter-in-law!

Despite her many offers to babysit, Lucy seemed to prefer using childminders who lived closer to their home.

"You have to let them make their own choices, love," her husband, Phil, said. "Remember how reluctant you were to ask my mum for help when the kids were small?"

"I suppose so . . ." she replied. "I just wish we could see more of Ella.

"Before we know it, she'll be a teenager and won't want anything to do with her granny and granddad."

But according to Lucy, she was already acting like a teenager.

"She's so huffy these days!" Lucy told her when she phoned to make arrangements for the summer. "She's constantly frowning.

"I keep telling her that if the wind changes, her face will stay like that!"

Kate laughed, to be polite, but was worried to hear that Ella wasn't happy, and was even more determined to make her week with her special.

Dan dropped her off the following Sunday afternoon, on a lovely sunny day, so Kate announced that they'd have dinner in the garden that night.

As they sat on the patio, eating Ella's favourite roast chicken, Dan spoke about the plans they had to have a new kitchen fitted.

Ella was a bit quiet to begin with, but Kate guessed she was just feeling shy. She asked about the twins, who she hadn't really seen since they were babies, and Kate told her she'd meet them the next day.

Then Dan headed off to drive home and as they cleared the table together and brought in the dishes from the garden, Ella seemed to visibly relax and was excited to unpack her things in the cosy little spare room.

Kate helped her hang up the summer dresses and tuck T-shirts into a drawer.

She watched as Ella placed a selection of books on the bedside cabinet and lay her faithful cuddly toy, Flopsy, on the bed.

Kate smiled and hugged her granddaughter.

"I'd forgotten about Flopsy!" she said. "I haven't seen him in years."

Ella patted the faded and worn rabbit.

"I wouldn't go anywhere

without him," she said solemnly.

She was a funny, quirky little girl, no longer full of the giggles of young childhood, but far from the moody pre-teen her mother had portrayed her as.

"How about a nice bubble bath, then a hot chocolate and a story before bedtime?" Kate suggested, remembering the old routine they'd had whenever Ella had stayed over in the past.

Her face broke into a huge smile. "Granny, I would love that!"

Despite the fact that Ella had brought a pile of books with her, she begged Kate to read aloud to her from the old book of fairy tales they'd read years ago.

The book, faded and very well-used, had actually belonged to Kate when she was a child, then she'd read it to Dan and Louise when they were little, before continuing with Ella.

She hoped to read it to the twins as well, though they weren't quite at that stage yet, still focusing mainly on breaking and destroying everything they came into contact with.

Kate reached up and got the book from the shelf, then asked Ella if she wouldn't rather have something more grown-up to read.

"Oh no, Granny!" she replied. "This is my favourite ever book.

"I still try to tell myself the stories when I'm lying in bed at night – they bring back such happy memories."

Kate frowned slightly, wondering if this meant that Ella was no longer as happy, but didn't want to press the issue.

Then, despite the fact that her granddaughter been reading confidently herself since the age of four, she snuggled in and waited for her granny to start reading.

The book was very much of a different era, heavy and wordy with long sentences and a noticeable lack of pictures compared to modern children's books.

Kate asked for the story of Cinderella and was engrossed, as always, from the opening sentence:

"Once there was a gentleman who married, for his second wife, the proudest and most haughty woman that was ever seen . . ."

The story went on for page after page, with only a single colour image to illustrate it and surprisingly no picture of Cinderella herself.

Ella had always loved the story.

Afterwards, Kate asked her why.

"I get to picture it all in my head," she said, "so I can imagine what Cinderella looks like and what style her dress is.

"She might look totally normal – like me, even."

She smiled at her granny.

"It's better like that, isn't it?"

Kate had to agree with her wise little girl.

The next morning, all peace was disrupted as the twins, Noah and Jake, arrived, barrelling into the house like an avalanche, knocking over anything in their way as Phil chased after them, trying to limit the damage.

Louise hurried in behind them, carrying backpacks and bottles, and looking exhausted, even though it was just after eight in the morning.

"It's a terrible thing to say, Mum," she said as she dumped all her stuff on the hall floor, "but I actually look forward to going to work, just to get some peace and quiet."

Kate laughed and hugged her. "Don't worry, sweetheart – it gets easier!"

Just then Ella appeared on the staircase and waved shyly at her auntie.

"Oh my goodness, look at you!" Louise shrieked. "Come and give me a cuddle, you gorgeous girl, or are you too big for that now?"

Ella grinned delightedly and ran into Louise's arms, and they hugged each other for a full minute, as the twins careered into them and pulled at Ella's arms.

"Who this?" they yelled.

Louise knelt down to her boys and formally introduced them to their big cousin, who they had met before but couldn't remember.

"You know you're to blame for this pair of horrors," Louise said to Ella. "You were such a perfect, adorable baby that I thought being a mum would be easy! And look what I ended up with!"

Then she kissed her boys goodbye, gave Ella another hug and disappeared out the door.

The rest of the day was a whirl of activity, with a trip to the playpark, a picnic by the river, and a visit to the toyshop in town, where the twins knocked down a display of LEGO and then destroyed a model train set.

Kate had to buy something just to make up for all the trouble they had caused.

Thankfully, they were able to strap the boys into their double buggy afterwards for a nap, then Kate and Ella got ice-cream cones and sat on a bench for a rest.

"Are they always like this?" Ella asked as she carefully licked her cone, avoiding getting drips on her finger.

"I'm afraid so!" Kate laughed. "They were sweet when they were babies, but as soon as they could walk, all hell broke loose!"

She smiled at Ella.

"Auntie Louise was right, you know – we were spoiled having you as our first baby. You made it seem so easy."

"They're so cute, though," Ella said, "even if they are a bit crazy!"

Then Ella looked down and said she felt a bit ashamed, because she'd kind of resented the twins a little bit, just because they'd replaced her and now spent so much time with Kate.

"They get to see you all the time and they're so cute and easy to love. I'm past that stage now, I suppose."

To Kate's dismay, a lonely tear tricked down Ella's cheek.

"Sweetheart, don't be silly!" she cried, sweeping Ella into her arms. "I'll never stop loving you!

"The boys might be cute but they're also horrendous! Haven't you heard of the terrible twos?

"Auntie Louise and I are always saying we wish they could be more like you!"

Then Ella spoke sadly about how she didn't feel like she fitted in anywhere these days.

Too nerdy at school, not sporty enough at the after-school clubs, and no longer cute and cuddly to anyone.

She also said she was dreading going to the "big school" next year.

So she wasn't huffy or moody after all – just worried and sad. It broke Kate's heart to hear this.

"Ella, my darling, you're my first ever grandchild – my only granddaughter and the absolute light of my life!

"I hate that you live too far away to see us so much, and I miss you all the time."

Then they hugged each other tightly, shed a few tears and felt a bit better.

For the rest of the week, Kate and Ella did all the things they'd done in the past – baking cakes, making glitter paintings, and watching Disney films.

And despite the intermittent chaos brought by the boy cousins, both agreed it was a perfect week.

"Can I maybe come again for another week later in the summer?" Ella whispered, as her dad packed her things into the car on the last day.

Kate wrapped her arms around her funny, beautiful, shy little girl, and suddenly realised how hard it must be to be the only child of such high-achieving parents.

"Ella, darling, you can come and stay with me any time you want, for as long as you like!"

And Kate knew for sure that her bond with Ella would last long even after the sunshine had gone.

Fit For Purpose

Could Sandra find a good swimsuit to wear?

BY HELEN YURETICH

SANDRA held up her swimming costume and tried to think of the last time she'd worn it. It must have been years ago when Gabrielle was still little.

It was as bad as she'd feared – the elastic had perished and the colour had faded. It was a limp rag, definitely not fit to wear.

When her daughter had rung recently to suggest the whole family get together for a summer holiday, Sandra had been delighted.

"A week at the seaside, Mum," Gabby had enthused. "Just like when I was a kid – sandcastles, donkey rides, fish and chips. Rosie and Max are so excited. Will you and Dad come? Say yes."

"It sounds wonderful, darling."

Sandra meant it sincerely and was really looking forward to it.

Now she sat on the edge of the bed and reminisced.

The seaside holidays had been the highlight of their year. They always stayed at the same small hotel in Rhyl with the famous sandy beach just yards away.

In those days, there was a fun fair and boating lake at one end of town, amusement arcades and bingo at the other, with miles of golden sand in between.

There were even donkey rides on the beach. She remembered the first time Gabby heard the donkeys.

Bells were attached to the harnesses and for a moment it sounded as though Santa's sleigh was coming.

Then half a dozen donkeys trotted round the corner, over the road and down on to the sand. Gabby's eyes were like saucers. She begged to have a go.

She lined up with the other children and the handler lifted her gently on to a donkey.

Every day for the rest of the week she listened for the jingling bells which signaled the donkeys' arrival.

A ride along the beach and back became a daily highlight.

It was a simple time when they were happy to play on the beach, swim in the sea then go home to their digs for a fish and chip supper.

Looking back, it seemed that the weeks they spent at the seaside were golden days filled with sunshine and laughter and love.

Those wonderful holidays only stopped when Gabby entered her teens and was too sophisticated to go away with her parents.

What a marvellous idea to start again with the next generation – fresh air, sunshine and simple pleasures.

Sandra looked at her swimming costume again. The sight of it made her heart sink.

She definitely couldn't wear it and the thought of going to buy a new one filled her with dread.

It was years since she'd stood in a changing room to try on new clothes.

Back then she'd been a slim young woman with no inhibitions. Now she was a grandma, what she liked to call matronly. She'd just have to accept that she wasn't going in the sea.

• • • •

Gabby made the arrangements.

"It's all organised, Mum," she told Sandra a few days before they left. "I've booked two caravans.

"They're fully equipped and I've ordered a delivery from the supermarket."

"You're the model of efficiency," Sandra teased.

"Is there anything left for me to do?"

"Have you still got the old picnic blanket? Bring that if you can find it; otherwise just remember to pack your cossie."

Sandra remembered the tartan blanket.

"Yes, I've still got the blanket," she said. "It's in the attic. But my old costume is headed for the ragbag."

"Everyone has to swim." Gabby laughed. "Treat yourself to a new one."

• • • •

The following day Sandra spoke firmly to herself.

She wanted to swim at the beach so she had to get a new costume.

She headed for a department store. There were racks of swimwear but it was nearly all bikinis.

There were a few one-piece suits but the legs seemed to be cut very high or the waist was cut away in a revealing manner or the front was plunging.

She looked at the mannequins; they were all long-legged and flat stomached. She didn't know anyone who looked like that but the swimsuits looked fabulous on them.

They were clearly not designed for the mature figure, though. She left without buying anything.

Back at home she thought about the men's swimwear – long baggy shorts.

It seemed unfair the men could be so comfortable while the women's costumes were revealing and uncomfortable.

Once again she decided that she would simply stay out of the water. She was a bit disappointed because it was years since she'd had a dip in the ocean and she'd been looking forward to it.

But she couldn't possibly wear her old costume and she couldn't possibly buy one of those modern ones.

• • • •

The caravans were next to each other.

Sandra and her husband settled in one while Gabby's

family settled next door.

The children ran in and out indiscriminately, beside themselves with excitement.

It was a glorious day – the sea was glittering in the sunshine, the sand looked pristine and the beach was nearly empty.

"Everyone into their swimming costumes," Gabby called when the unpacking was done.

Ten minutes later they were all trooping down to the water ready for a swim, all except Sandra.

"Where is your cossie, Mum?" Gabby asked.

"I'm not swimming. I'll just watch," Sandra said. "Have fun. I can get the picnic ready and guard the bags."

She indicated the tartan rug that she'd brought.

"Aren't you coming in, Grandma?" Rosie looked disappointed.

"I haven't got a costume, darling," Sandra told her with a forced smile. "I'm going to get the picnic ready."

The children ran off with their parents and were soon splashing through the surf, or climbing on their father and diving into the waves.

They dashed up the beach whenever they were hungry and wolfed down a sandwich or an apple.

"Will you come swimming tomorrow, Grandma?" Rosie asked as she gulped down a drink of water.

"I told you, darling. I haven't got a swimming costume."

"Just buy one, Grandma."

Sandra wished it was so simple.

"We'll see."

"Please, Grandma. Promise you'll come in tomorrow."

Sandra nodded reluctantly.

"All right, Rosie. I promise."

• • • •

By tea time the fresh air and exercise had tired everyone out.

Andrew went for fish and chips while the children showered the salt and sand off, ready for bed.

Once they were asleep, Gabby knocked and walked into her parents' caravan.

"What a great start to the holidays."

"Yes," Sandra said. "It was a beautiful day. The kids are having a wonderful time. It was such a good idea."

"But they want you to swim, Mum. We'll have to go into town first thing and get you a new cossie."

"Don't worry about me," Sandra replied. "I'm happy to watch."

"But Rosie said you promised."

Sandra shrugged guiltily.

"Yes, I did."

"Well, then that's settled. New cossie tomorrow. And anyway, I don't want the kids to see you sitting on the sidelines."

"It's important that you join in. You're a great role model for an active Grandma."

Sandra looked at her in surprise.

"It's true, Mum," Gabby said.

"I don't want Rosie to grow up thinking that the women step back while the men have all the fun."

Sandra was astonished. She'd never thought about it before.

• • • •

The following morning Gabby and Sandra set off as soon as the shops were open.

The rest of the family stayed behind playing cricket on the sand.

"We'll wait till you get back, Grandma," Rosie said. "Then we can all go swimming together."

Sandra crossed her fingers that she wasn't going to disappoint her little granddaughter.

They looked in several shops without success.

Once again all the costumes seemed to be designed for skinny teenagers.

Then Sandra spotted Mature Modes.

"That looks hopeful."

She pointed at the window display.

The mannequins looked almost normal. It was a good start.

Inside the shop they were greeted by a large woman. She certainly matched their target customer.

"Good morning, ladies. How can I help you today?"

"I need something to swim in," Sandra told her with a sigh.

"And I'm struggling to find anything suitable for a mature lady."

"You've come to the right place."

The assistant led them to a rack near the window.

"We have plenty of stock at the moment."

She assessed Sandra with a professional eye then flicked through the hangers.

"Try this."

She took a blue costume from the rack and offered it to Sandra.

It was nothing like the costumes Sandra had been looking at.

This one had short sleeves and a zip up the front. But the best thing about it was that the leg extended half way down the thigh.

Sandra was impressed that the woman had chosen exactly the right size.

"They are a nice comfortable fit," the assistant continued.

"The elastic is a little firmer than usual for extra support and they offer good protection from the sun."

"In other words," Sandra said, "they stop you wobbling and getting sunburnt."

The assistant laughed.

"Yes, that's about it. The fitting room is over there. See what you think."

This was the part that Sandra was dreading, but she took the garment and headed off to try it on.

She got undressed and wriggled into the swimsuit. It felt good.

She considered herself in the mirror. She should definitely lose a few pounds but she looked OK.

"How is it, Mum?" Gabby peeped round the curtain.

"It looks great."

Sandra sucked in her stomach.

"Better than I expected. It conceals a lot of bumps and bulges."

"It suits you," Gabby said. "And the kids will be thrilled that you can swim now."

They looked at a couple of other costumes but nothing was a good as the first one.

The assistant was pleased when Sandra said she'd take it.

"I knew that would suit you. It's a good quality swimsuit. It will last for years."

"As long as I control the spare tyre." Sandra patted her middle.

"Swimming is very good exercise," the assistant assured her as she handed over the package.

Back at the caravan Sandra wriggled into the swimsuit once more.

She had to admit that it felt comfortable but she was still a bit self conscious.

She hadn't worn a swimsuit for more than a decade.

She wrapped a big beach towel round her middle then braced herself to step out in public.

Down on the beach the children were making sandcastles while the men threw a Frisbee back and forth.

Rosie and Max jumped up when they saw Sandra and Gabby appear.

"I like your new swimming costume, Grandma."

"Can we swim now?"

"Yes," Sandra said. "I'm all ready for the water."

She tossed off her towel and headed for the sea, shouting that the last one in was a rotten egg.

But her grandchildren got there first and were waiting to splash her when she arrived at the water's edge.

She squealed with shock.

"Right, you little monkeys. You'll be sorry for that."

She chased after them as they ran off laughing.

Being doused with cold water had never felt so good.

"SEE that woman over there," Kaz said to her friends Jess and Maja on the first evening of their holiday.

They both twisted round in their chairs on the terrace of the hotel.

They were pleased with their choice.

It was in a charming old building in a quiet neighbourhood that also had a yoga retreat.

They had come to Ibiza for the natural beauty, which all of them had separately been told was sensational.

"What about her?" Maja asked, adjusting her sunhat to see better the woman Kaz was nodding at, a couple of tables along.

"I noticed her earlier," Kaz continued. "I think she's on her own. I wonder if she'd like to join us?"

They discussed it for several minutes until Maja said, "OK, I'll go and ask her. Only way to find out."

A couple of minutes later, she returned.

"No, she said she was fine. Very polite but, to be honest, I think she would've preferred not to have been bothered."

"Maybe she's waiting for someone," Kaz suggested.

They returned to enjoying their evening.

But Maja, a bit miffed at her invite being turned down, kept glancing over to the woman.

"No-one's turned up," she said eventually, "so I don't think she was meeting anyone."

"Maybe been stood up," Kaz said.

"Or maybe she didn't think we looked her kind of people," Jess said with a shrug.

"Why not?" Maja frowned. "She's about our age —"

"Your age," Kaz interrupted.

Aged forty-three, she was the youngest of the trio and never let the other two forget it — that was their opinion!

"She's very dressed up," Jess said, sneaking another surreptitious glance. "Proper

Intrigue In Ibiza

Who was this mysterious woman loitering around?

BY VAL BONSALL

shoes and all and here's us in our flip flops.

"And her dress wouldn't look out of place at a cocktail party."

"That's why I noticed her," Kaz said. "She's very smart for this kind of holiday."

The three friends speculated a while longer but then returned to their own gossip, admiring the spectacular sunset.

The next day, in the process of familiarising themselves with their new home for a fortnight, they came upon in their wanderings a hippie-style market.

"Ibiza's famous for them," Kaz announced.

Tie-dye T-shirts, jangly bangles and beads, long raggedy-hemmed skirts — it was all there.

Jess, into vintage, was enchanted.

"Well, you'll remember this sort of thing first time round in the 1960s," Kaz teased her. But then her face went solemn. "And see who else is here?"

Same as they had the previous evening at the hotel, Jess and Maja looked in the direction she was indicating.

It was the same woman Kaz had noticed then, immaculately dressed again.

"What's she after?" Maja said. "Nothing here to suit her style, I wouldn't have thought."

While Jess rummaged about, Kaz and Maja watched the woman.

She didn't buy anything but went round all the stalls, examining the offerings.

"Odd," Kaz said thoughtfully.

They kept seeing the woman as the day proceeded and her behaviour seemed to them to become even odder.

Passing a beach café after they'd finally dragged Jess away from the market, they saw the woman going inside.

She finished her drink and left even as they were still standing about outside wondering whether to go in.

They decided in the end not to.

"I think I saw somewhere nicer just along," Kaz said.

They went to check it out and the woman was now there.

Again, she finished her drink quickly and left, only for them to see her in yet another café on their way back to the hotel — always on her own.

"Something's going on," Kaz said.

"What d'you mean?" Jess asked.

"The way she's always gobbling her drink down which you just don't do when you're on holiday, with all the time in the world.

"You sit and look about you and send photos to your mates back home to make them jealous.

"I'm wondering . . . Do you think she could be a spy?"

She felt the other pair's eyes on her.

"I've just finished reading a book where the woman who was the spy out in the field had a regular meeting with her case officer — that's what they call the person who gives the instructions.

"Obviously it had to be secure and the way they did this was for there to be a list of possible venues.

"So if she went to the first one and the case officer wasn't there, it was because he was worried about being followed and she should go to the next one on the list, and so on until she located him."

The other two laughed.

They frequently recommended books to each other and Kaz's suggestions were always espionage thrillers.

Kaz briefly looked hurt but then joined in their laughter.

"OK, maybe not," she said. "But I do think there's something about her."

"Actually I agree with that," Maja said. "At the market – well, it was just so not her.

"I recently read a book about a jewellery thief using a junk shop to hide and pass on stolen gems. You know, mixed up with all the cheap bric-a-brac.

"Like that ring you bought, Jess," she continued. "It's rubbish, but a valuable one could've been substituted.

"And by prior arrangement someone comes to collect it . . ."

"Honestly!" Jess said in exasperation.

It was the case that all Maja's recommended books were crime novels.

With her Nordic heritage, they put it down to the success of the various Scandi noir series on telly.

"Yeah, you're right," Maja said, smiling at Jess. "It must be the sun, making me more imaginative."

"That'll be it with me, too," Kaz said.

Jess just shrugged.

Regarding books, she reflected, as she watched rather a handsome fisherman coming up from the beach, she liked a good romance.

That evening on the hotel terrace, they got chatting to a couple called Jan and Joe.

The next day Jan and Joe were going on a boat trip.

"If you'd like to come with us," Jan said.

It was something the trio had promised themselves so they eagerly said yes.

"Maybe you'd like to join us, too?" Joe said cheerfully to the woman, who was seated at the next table – alone, of course.

"That's kind, but no, thank you," she replied, before finishing her drink and disappearing into the hotel building.

"Well, just thought she might've enjoyed it," Joe said, as though he felt he needed to justify his offer.

"Maybe she's nervous in boats," Jess offered.

But the next day, as they were getting on to the boat they'd hired . . .

"Look who's there," Maja said, pointing, "and arranging a boat trip with someone else!"

"It's her," Jan said. "So what was so wrong with coming with us?"

But their theorising was abandoned as the trip got under way.

"The sea really is turquoise like it said in the brochures." Kaz sighed.

"Beautiful," Jess agreed.

The day after that, they hung out with Joe and Jan again and then it was time to say goodbye to them.

Jan and Joe were doing mid-week to mid-week and leaving early the next morning.

That evening at the hotel, watching another magnificent sunset, to their amazement the woman came over to their table.

"Excuse me, but have your friends gone?" she asked.

"Joe and Jan? Yes," Kaz said.

"I would like to have spoken to them properly before they went," the woman said, looking sorry. "To apologise.

"I know I must've seemed very bad-mannered to them about the boat trip.

"And to you as well," she added. "The way I turned down your offer to join you."

"It's OK," Maja said. "It's your holiday to do whatever you want on it."

"So can I join you now?" she asked.

"Of course."

Exchanging looks, they rearranged their chairs to make room.

The woman – Lynn, she introduced herself – followed their example and ordered a shot of the local traditional herbal liqueur.

The conversation was general at first.

"I brought all the wrong clothes," Lynn said, "but I wanted favourites that made me feel confident, I suppose."

She turned away briefly, looking embarrassed, then reverted to apologising.

"I don't know what you must've thought of me," she said.

"Well," Jess began, smiling. "First we had the idea you were a spy.

"Then a criminal mastermind, probably a jewellery thief. But, yes, we did find you . . . intriguing."

"The thing is," Lynn began. She paused, looking awkward again, but then shrugged.

"OK," she resumed with a half-smile, "but stop me if I get boring."

They listened as she explained how she'd married very young.

"Just out of school. So I never got used to doing anything on my own.

"Never had to – Todd was always there. Until then he wasn't.

"Last year he left our marriage and I was suddenly alone."

"You have family?" Maja asked. "Friends?"

"Yes. But I don't want always to be imposing myself on other people.

"I want to feel that I can do things – just ordinary things, like come on holiday or go in a restaurant and order a meal – on my own as well."

"That's why you were flitting about between all the beach bars?" Jess guessed.

"Yes, as a start. To get used to going into places alone. I know it sounds pathetic."

"No," Jess said, and the other two echoed their agreement. "So that's why you didn't accept our offer to join us?"

"Right again. You were friendly and nice, but if I'd just right away attached myself to your group, I wouldn't have proved anything to myself. Passed any of the tests I'd set myself."

"And do you now feel you have passed them and proved what you needed to?" Jess asked.

Lynn nodded.

"Also," she continued, "I didn't think it was fair to foist myself on you.

"Here you are, having a summer break together, three old friends –"

"Er, I'm younger than them," Kaz interrupted on cue.

"She's away again," Jess said as she and Maja rolled their eyes.

Lynn laughed.

"Whatever," she said. "It didn't seem fair for me to be gatecrashing your group.

"So how long have you been friends? You all seem very close. A long time, obviously."

"We met," Maja said, smiling, "just the year before last."

"When we were all," Jess added, "for various reasons in the same position you found yourself in, Lynn.

"Quite separately – because though we don't live that far apart we didn't know each other then – we all booked on a coach tour to Wales and got to know each other through that."

"I thought Wales was far enough for my first solo outing," Maja said. "You were braver than me, Lynn, coming here.

"But Wales turned out great. We had a grand time and have had many together since."

"How it goes," Jess said. "There're always new friends to be made if you're open to it."

"So, anyone want to do anything special tomorrow?" Maja asked, looking round the table but especially at Lynn.

Lynn smiled.

"Whatever," she said. "I'll go with you guys."

"How about a hike," Jess suggested, "up into the hills – fabulous views, I believe?"

"You reckon you're up to it?" Kaz teased her.

"Shall we go for that then?" Maja said.

"Yes!" they all agreed, as the sun sank over the sea raising their glasses to the future.

The Grass Is Greener

Would Mags have had a different life if not for that fateful summer party?

BY REBECCA HOLMES

"Is it really almost six months since we last got together?" Pete asked, helping himself to a prawn cracker. "I'm sure time passes more quickly than it used to."

"That's probably because we're always busy, as well as getting older."

Mags watched as Tash, Pete's wife, nudged him playfully.

As always, Tash was immaculately turned out, in well-cut jeans and a crisp linen blouse. Silver strands in her sleek, full-bodied hair only added an aura of sophistication to the overall image.

Mags's favourite floral cotton top, by contrast, looked washed-out and dowdy in the summer evening light, while her creeping grey felt like a wilful betrayal.

Her hair had always been awkward. When she was younger, she'd spend hours blow-drying it before going out of the evening, only for it to be flat again long before bedtime.

Her husband, Phil, practical as ever, said it didn't matter as she'd be going to sleep on it, anyway.

The four of them had met up for a meal in the Peak District village where Mags had grown up, not far from Pete's family's farm.

Now that they lived an hour's drive away, she loved to visit when she could, popping into the characterful, friendly bookshop, buying cakes

from the bakery and walking among the hills. The day always helped to recharge her batteries.

Even with their three children grown, life was busy. Grown children still had their share of problems; in some ways more complicated than when they'd been younger.

Tash, on the other hand, seemed to have unlimited energy. A physiotherapist at the "local" main hospital, 15 miles away, she had also brought up three children, as well as helping around the farm and running the home like clockwork.

Mags had fond memories of the cosy farmhouse kitchen, sitting at the scrubbed kitchen table and devouring home-made cake with her best friend, Emily – Pete's younger sister – and Emily's twin brother, Jake.

Much had changed since those days. Mr and Mrs Taylor senior had moved into a barn conversion to make room for Pete's growing family, while the village now had a new farm shop, art gallery and pottery studio, as well as the Chinese restaurant where they were currently eating.

"Well, maybe it's time we reclaimed our younger selves. Remember the summer parties we used to have at the farm?"

Everyone laughed and groaned in unison.

Perhaps it wasn't so surprising that Pete should bring up the subject.

He had originally come up with idea of a summer party 30 years earlier.

Countryside life had its good points, but it was a long way for locals, especially the younger ones, to go into town for a night out. At the party, they could let their hair down, dance to their favourite music in the open barn, with drinks and snacks supplied, and camp out in the field by the woods.

"Did anyone ever actually make it to the cooked breakfast in the farmhouse the next morning?" Phil asked.

"Some of us did." Pete smiled at Tash, who smiled back. "It was worth it. Mum always served up the full works, Derbyshire oatcakes and all. She still does. They were good times. Why did we stop?"

"Because most of the regulars settled down and started families. Including us," Tash reminded him. "In other words, life moved on."

"And now it's moved on again. Several of the old gang are still within hailing distance. What do you reckon? Shall we give it a go?"

It was agreed that the party would be revived, with grown-up children also invited.

"If only to show them we haven't always been as ancient as they assume we are," Phil said.

"Oh, we're going to have fun." Pete rubbed his hands together.

A date was set. Everyone would bring some food and drink, including soft drinks, to contribute.

Mags couldn't help feeling annoyed when Tash, taking charge, sent out a list detailing what they should bring.

She had to tell herself she would have probably done the same if she'd been organised enough.

When the "children" confirmed they would come, she thought she detected an element of amusement, as if sure their parents would retire early and leave them to it.

Only Dan, their youngest, hesitated, downhearted

because he and his girlfriend had split up.

"Come along anyway," Mags urged. "It's not a 'couples' thing and it'll do you good. Everyone mucks in and has a good time."

She crossed her fingers that that hadn't changed.

• • • •

Back at the first summer party, Mags, as Emily's best friend, had done her share of mucking in, helping with the preparations.

It was a time of excitement and promise for the future. Emily had finished training to be a veterinary nurse and had started work with a local practice, while Mags was getting to grips with her job at a mortgage brokers' firm.

She also had a serious crush on Pete and, according to Emily, might not suffer from unrequited love for much longer.

"He's definitely over his last girlfriend, and I know he's always had a soft spot for you. I wouldn't be surprised if he asks you out before the end of the night."

Mags felt butterflies in her stomach and hope in her heart.

She'd splashed out on a pretty new top and earrings which set off the blue of her eyes. Even her hair was almost presentable, thanks to liberally applied hairspray. It would probably collapse later, but should survive for a few hours yet.

Emily looked round as several people arrived, among them an effortlessly elegant young woman with long, glossy hair and a warm smile.

"Great. Jake's brought some of his friends along. We'd best introduce ourselves."

Emily's twin beamed.

"Meet the hospital gang. This is Karen, my girlfriend, and Steve, Tash . . ."

Mags didn't hear the other names, brought to a standstill as Pete's eyes lit up when he saw Tash.

Her hair did indeed fall flat before the end of the night, along with her hopes.

"They're completely mismatched. No way is Tash a farm type. It won't last," Emily asserted.

Something told her it would. It wasn't just that they only had eyes for each other from the very first moment. She sensed that part of them had met on another level.

Tired and despondent, she took refuge on fallen trunk in a quiet corner of the nearby woods.

Scents of moss and fern mingled with the sharp tinge of smoke from the barbecue, while the music and laughter made a mocking background.

"Sorry to intrude, but are you OK?"

She looked up into the concerned face of one of Jake's group. What was his name? Bill? Phil?

Afterwards, she wasn't sure what they talked about as the softly-spoken newcomer with brown hair and gentle, grey-green eyes that reminded her of the sea, kept the conversation going.

He coaxed her back to the party and fetched her a selection of food and a large glass of lemonade, vetoing her request for wine.

After bidding each other goodnight Mags assumed they wouldn't see each other again. The thought saddened her.

She never expected him to turn up at the office, a few days later.

"I'm hoping to buy a flat. Can you advise on the best mortgage deal?"

Emily's predictions were wrong. Tash did last, becoming as much a part of the farm as the flagstones in the kitchen.

Mags's heart, rather than being broken, found its perfect home with Phil.

The two couples were married within months of each other, attended each other's weddings and met up regularly over the next few years.

The summer party turned out to be the first of several, all run seemingly effortlessly by Tash. Mags, carrying food and plates between house and barn, felt herself pale in comparison.

"You play an important part, just in your own way," Phil told her as he did his bit, helping Pete set up the barn. "Never underestimate how important that is."

A famous footballer from the nearest Premier League team sang Tash's praises in the local paper for curing a hamstring injury where expensive private treatment had failed.

She was in the papers again, with Pete, when one of their rams won the top award at the county's agricultural show.

Readers loved the fact that she'd hand-fed "Ronnie" as a tiny lamb when his mother rejected him, and he'd become like a special pet, following her around the farm.

Mags's achievements consisted of arranging mortgages and adopting a cat from the local animal shelter.

"A prize ram doesn't curl up on the bed and purr in your ear," Phil reasoned. "Footballers' cured hamstrings don't help people buy homes where they'll raise their families."

Like everyone else, Mags grew genuinely fond of Tash, yet there was never quite the same warmth as between her and Emily, or indeed as between Emily and Tash.

There was something missing, although Mags couldn't define what it was. She wished she could make it different, but she didn't know how.

When a combination of busy lives, distance and the children growing up so that they no longer played together meant meetings dwindled, Mags wasn't sure whether to be sad or relieved.

• • • •

The date for the so-called "Summer Party: The Sequel" duly came around.

As she and Phil pulled up by the farmhouse, the first people to arrive, Mags felt a pang of nostalgia.

The gravelled area at the front was a far cry from the chaotic muddy patch she remembered from their younger days.

She and Phil had brought Wellingtons and reminded the children to bring theirs, as they'd be needed later, but gone were the days when they were needed to walk even a few yards.

Outhouses around the farmyard had been converted into holiday cottages, but the old stone farmhouse looked as cosy and solid as ever, as if it had grown from the ground, and the place still smelled of "farm", in the nice way that she remembered from her younger years.

A fresh breeze stirred from the hills that protected and watched over the land from time immemorial.

When it carried the tremulous calls of that spring's lambs followed by the deeper, stern responses of their mothers, she could almost believe that time had stood still.

The sight of Tash emerging from the house with a wave, and the sound of Phil opening the boot, complete with accompanying grunt as he lifted out their case, as they would be staying in the farmhouse's spare room, jolted her back to the present.

She waved back before hurrying round to retrieve the boxes of supplies they'd brought. If Tash could be organised, so could she.

Over the next hour, the two women ferried food to the open barn, arranging platters and covered bowls on old trestle and other sturdy, comfortably battered tables used at the original parties, dragged from their various lairs.

Phil and Pete sorted out "liquid refreshments" and shook their heads over the grandly named sound system.

More people arrived; long-ago friends with their partners, grown-up children. Everyone was greeted and new acquaintances made.

Mags was momentarily overwhelmed by a sense of déjà vu, as if her much younger self had stepped in, doing the same things older Mags was doing now.

What advice would she give to that younger version? Perhaps that life often didn't work out as planned but that, with an open mind and open heart, it would turn out mostly fine.

That didn't mean that everything would be smooth. There were always some details unresolved, she reflected as she made final touches.

That was then that she noticed Tash hadn't reappeared from checking on something in the farmhouse.

When more time passed, and with Pete and Phil busy with ladders, she decided to check.

The last thing she expected was to see Tash slumped at the kitchen table, head in her arms.

She rushed over.

"What's wrong?"

"I burnt the sausage rolls."

A glance at the baking tray on top of the range cooker confirmed that, while not black, they were definitely overdone.

"Oh, I'm always doing that. Scrape the worst bits off and serve them later on, when everyone's less likely to notice."

"That's not all. It's, well, everything."

Tash looked up. For first time, Mags saw, not the efficient career woman and farmer's wife, but someone else. Someone like herself after a trying day.

"Don't get me wrong, I love the farm and I love my job, but half the time I feel as if I'm running faster and faster just to stay on the same spot. And now this party. The summer party's always been special, it's where Pete and I met."

"I'm glad it's been revived, but it takes a lot of organising, and Pete's suggestion came out of the blue. It was one of his flashes of inspiration. He apologised afterwards and said we needn't go ahead, but everyone seemed so enthusiastic and I didn't want to let them down . . ."

"And then you felt that everything has to be just so, or people would be disappointed."

"You'd have sailed through it. I'm constantly in awe of the way you juggle work and family. I couldn't do your job to save my life."

Mags blinked.

"You're joking. It's the other way round. And you've been in the paper, which I haven't, unless you count my photo in the firm's adverts."

"I cope with the farm and family with help from Pete's parents. As for the rest, I simply eliminated the treatments which had already been tried with that footballer to find the right solution.

"Ronnie was one of many lambs we'd bottle-fed over the years. That's hardly rare on a sheep farm.

"The award was down to good breeding and Pete's expertise, more than anything."

The two women looked at each other in mutual astonishment.

"I think we both need a coffee break," Tash said after a moment.

"Agreed. And biscuits."

"Can I let you into a secret?" Tash continued, when they were each on their second cup and had made inroads into a packet of chocolate digestives.

"Before the party, I'd had a crush on Phil for weeks. I even hoped that would be the night he'd ask me out."

"As we know, things turned out differently."

Mags almost dropped her mug.

"I had a crush on Pete. Now, I can't imagine us together, never mind being a farmer's wife."

"But you grew up around here. You'd have been perfect."

"Heavens, no. I love coming back, and hopefully we'll do it more often now, but I love where I live."

As she said it, Mags knew it was true. Her and Phil's home may not be a charming farmhouse, but it was cosy and welcoming.

"It's convenient for getting to work. I'm not exactly the world's best driver. I'd dread commuting from here, especially in winter."

"Oh, it's not so bad. There are days when it can be grim, but there's nothing quite like seeming the light creep over the hills, and the land like a patchwork quilt, with the dry-stone walls as stitching between the fields.

"I enjoy being in the bustle of things, as well as the odd trip round the shops, but I also like coming home and feeling the countryside open out as I leave the city behind.

"Anyway, you and Phil are perfect for each other. It's funny, and maybe there's something in the air here, but the summer party always seemed to bring the right people together. I know at least two other happily-married couples who met at one of them."

She pulled a face.

"Imagine if I'd ended up with Phil. I love him to bits, as a friend, but he'd have driven me mad by now."

"Same with me and Pete," Mags agreed.

Soon they were soon imagining more and more ludicrous scenarios of how things might have been, with not-exactly flattering impersonations of their husbands.

They were both laughing so hard, they didn't notice when the subjects of their mirth came in, until Phil pointedly cleared his throat.

Pete, beside him, folded his arms and tried to look stern. The sight only set them off again, and it took more than a few minutes to get their breath back.

When they finally went outside, more people had arrived, including Dan, much to Mags's quiet relief.

Perhaps understandably, given recent events, he looked ill at ease, but that changed when Emily and her family arrived with her daughter, Catherine, among them.

After the women embraced, Emily nudged Mags and nodded in Dan and Catherine's direction. The two, chatting eagerly, were looking into each other's eyes as if they'd both been surprised by a sudden revelation.

"I said the party had a way of bringing the right people together," Tash whispered.

The rest of the balmy evening passed in a blur.

As Mags had predicted, the sausage rolls were fine with the burnt bits scraped off. The younger generation joined in the dancing with gusto, not even complaining about the "classic" music.

Mags felt warm inside as Dan and Catherine seemed to be getting along better and better.

And why not? After all, the magic had worked for her and Phil and Pete and Tash.

"Do you think we'll last out until Mum's cooked breakfast?" Emily asked as dawn crept over the sky.

On hearing the summer party was being revived, Mrs Taylor had insisted on also reviving her legendary repast.

Earlier, Mags would have been doubtful, but the thought of the delicious meal, and the fact that she'd never hung on long enough before, spurred her on, as well as the sight of several "youngsters" struggling not to yawn.

"We can start planning next year's party while we eat," Tash put in.

"You're on," Mags agreed.

She couldn't wait, either for the meal or next year's summer party.

Life At Smithy Cottage

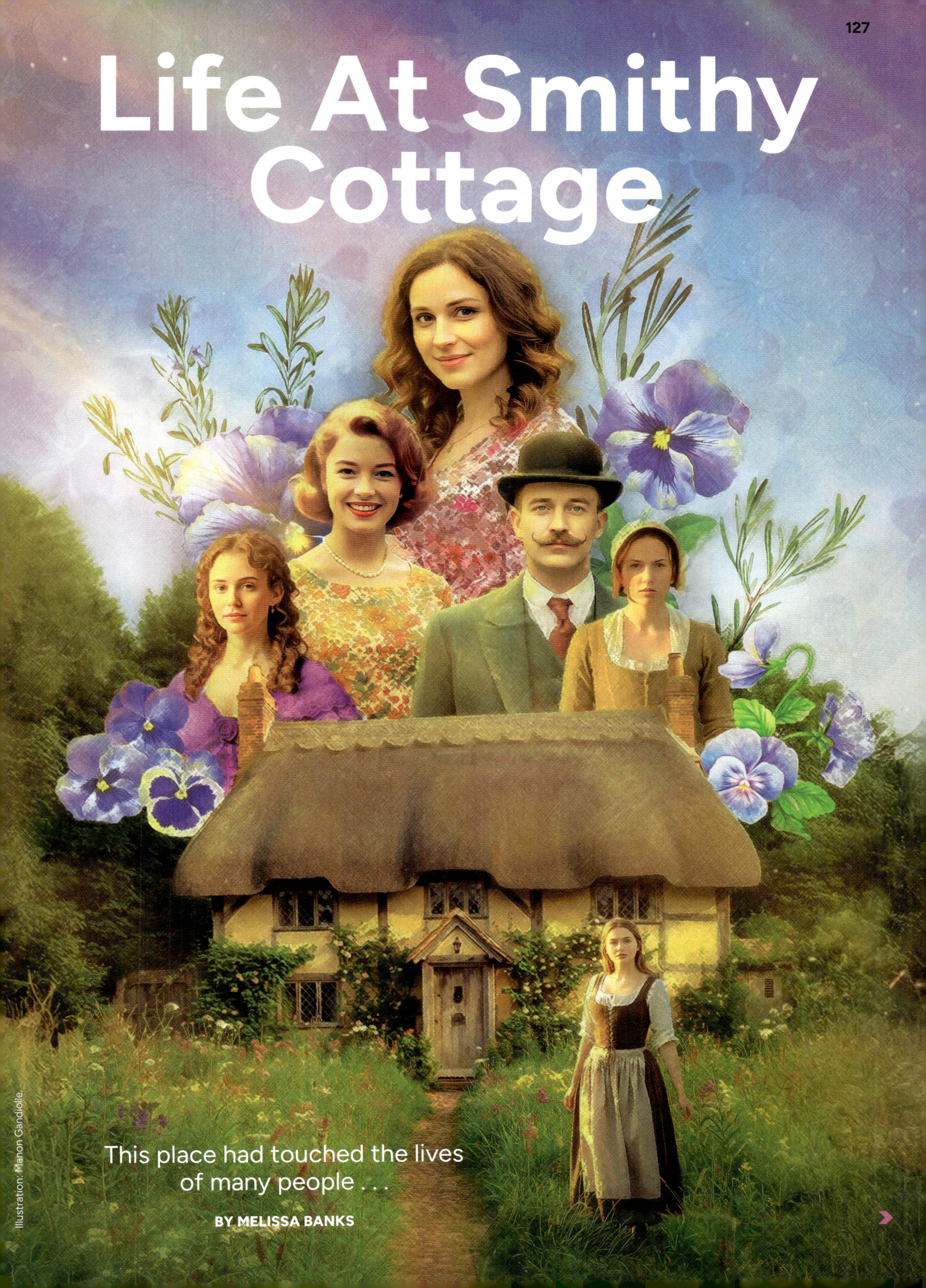

Illustration: Manon Gandiolle.

This place had touched the lives of many people . . .

BY MELISSA BANKS

THE sun was reaching its midday height. Elena Majewski dragged over the old deckchair the joiner had been using for his breaks and lowered herself into it.

There were just five weeks to go until her due date, and she was exhausted and huge.

Stefan was away, meeting their lender in London.

Normally she would be there with him, negotiating for loans.

Flipping houses was their joint project, their shared path to wealth.

Today she had given in and stayed home, in this remote spot in East Lincolnshire.

The site was quiet except for birdsong and she had been wandering inside, bored and restless.

The house was half-finished and smelled of planed timber and plaster.

Elena and her husband Stefan were both thirty-seven. They had come from eastern Europe 10 years before and had met while working in construction.

They were both bright and determined. Through hard work they had developed their "method", buying homes and selling them for a profit that increased with each project.

Number Four, Bendham Lane, between Bag Enderby and Somersby, was their latest.

It had been dilapidated when they'd acquired it.

The agent had admitted that since the 1950s, when it went on to the rental market, successive landlords had done very little work on the place.

Elena and Stefan had brought in skips and taken away rotted windows, bits of weird rockery, wall hooks, door plaques, old sinks.

The plan was to tart it up, decorate and add a pool or maybe a conservatory before slapping 30 per cent on top of the price they had paid, selling up and moving on.

Elena became ill during the work, sick and fatigued.

And as she lay in their caravan, their residence while they worked on each project, she found herself thinking hard about what they were doing.

"Is it long-term, though, Stefan?" she said.

Her husband was banging about in the kitchen while she talked from behind the barrier separating it from the bedroom.

"I get it, Elena," he said. "I've been irritable, too."

"This one is a real pain. I'm not sure we should have taken it on."

That was not what Elena meant, but she understood what he was saying.

Bendham Lane was old and too fiddly.

Before buying it, they had stuck to Victorian properties and younger.

This house had been cheap, but neither of them understood the implications of what was beneath the render and pebbledash.

"It's costing too much," Stefan said. "We need to finish up and move on."

• • • •

Then Elena discovered that she didn't have a bug.

She was pregnant.

Stefan stared at her when she told him the news.

Neither was interested in kids. They were both from large, struggling families.

On the day of the pregnancy test, they even argued about the loss of income.

Elena would have to stop work when the child arrived.

In the weeks that followed, as the summer warmed up, they avoided the topic.

They tried to agree but were tetchy, bound together only by their shared goals.

• • • •

In the deckchair, Elena considered fetching herself some water.

She thought back a few weeks, to a picnic she had been invited to. It had lifted her spirits while she worried about her marriage.

"It's a fundraiser, I warn you," the girl had said.

Her name was Emily and she was the daughter of Benny Hislop, the historic buildings expert.

"You'll have to buy raffle tickets and all that stuff."

The Hislops and their friends were fundraising for the church, for a sort of clean-up project.

Stefan refused to come, saying he was too busy.

Elena, propped up on cushions on the green, got into conversation with Emily's family.

Benny was talking about his "hobby horse" — a house he was building.

"People tell me it's whimsical," he said.

"It is," his wife said, "but we indulge you."

He was trying to build a house using the methods of the early 17th century.

The Hislop family had lived in the hamlet for centuries, and he loved its history.

Some of their ancestors, Emily told Elena, were from a certain non-conformist Christian group.

"Dour, but prosperous," Emily said. "Rumour has it that one of them was engaged to a man who went on the *Mayflower!* We can't be sure, though."

The Hislops didn't have much information on the family before about 1800, except that they'd owned property locally for long periods of time.

"Was our house among the properties?" Elena asked. "I mean, the house we're working on."

She and Stefan took care not to get emotionally attached.

They had a final destination in mind, a new build in London that would cost millions.

But she was interested, nonetheless.

"I don't think so," Benny said. "The only one mentioned in the papers we have was a smithy."

• • • •

In 1620, in the hamlet between Bag Enderby and Somersby where she had always lived, Penelope Hislop absorbed the news.

A ship had left London for Holland, and Gideon Nuttall, the man to whom she was supposedly still betrothed, was probably on it.

She might never know for sure.

The trip was perilous and the passengers were going into virtual hiding.

Penelope could not read or write, so she could not even send letters, if letters could ever be sent.

She looked around the room. The smell of new timber was strong.

On the wall opposite hung an eccentric wedding present from her uncle — an overly large pair of bellows, on a giant hook that still gave out motes of sawdust where it had been drilled into a beam.

She was alone now, owner of a new house, but husbandless and rejected.

Penelope's family were non-conformists, called "Separatists".

For more than a decade they had worshipped in

secret in a nearby manor house with permission from its sympathetic owner.

Penelope's father was a prosperous wool trader.

When she agreed to marry Gideon, her father had built a cottage for them.

It was on land once owned by the local smith, who had left the hamlet.

He had moved on to a busier area near Somersby.

The old smithy stood at a distance from the cottage.

Penelope had not questioned her father's unwillingness to have his daughters educated.

She had not questioned her destiny as a wife and mother.

She had moved in a month before her wedding to make the cottage a home.

Her mother had recently given birth to twins and the family home was overflowing with people.

She called it Smithy Cottage, and she was so proud of it.

The scrutiny of their beliefs and practices by church authorities had seemed a distant danger.

But then Gideon had announced that a group of the Separatists planned to leave Lincolnshire for Holland, where they could worship freely.

Penelope's reaction had been one of fear – of the unknown, of poverty and of enormous change.

She had looked forward to a contented, safe life.

"I cannot go," she said to her betrothed.

She had not expected to be so decisive, but as she spoke, she knew she was certain of it.

Gideon was horrified.

He talked of his principles, his faith and his need to take action, and then he left.

One letter came, written by him on the Dutch coast.

Penelope knew her father would read it for her, but she kept it to herself.

She did not want to know of the love she had lost.

Time passed.

Suitors did not come because she was seen as promised, and then she was seen as too old, and as an intimidating woman, what with the property she owned in her own right.

Her father did not take back the cottage – out of pity, Penelope supposed.

She gardened and learned how to grow fruit and vegetables in the fertile soil.

She took out the letter sometimes, and in her many quiet hours she began to compare the marks on the page with the letters and words in her Bible.

When Penelope reached thirty, she knew that she could read and write.

She wondered about writing to Gideon, gone now for 12 years.

But it was far too late and most probably the letter would not reach him, as the landing place of the group was unknown.

One day she took a small knife and carved two designs into the newel post at the bottom of the stair.

She carved a sprig of rosemary, for remembrance, and a delicate pansy – a flower that held the meaning "thinking of you, my love".

She had been told there was a French word, *pensée*, meaning thoughts, and wondered at how like the name of the flower that was.

• • • •

Penelope's father died the following year.

He had no sons to take on the wool business, which had been failing during the time that he was ill.

Penelope pondered for days what to do.

It was high summer.

She sat on a wooden seat in her garden, looked at her house and wondered how tied to it she was.

The scents of the flowers and the sound of larks would go with her if she moved; the sun would shine even if she went away.

She visited the warehouse and spoke to her father's men. Then she took a huge and terrifying step forward.

As well as being able to read and write, she knew arithmetic. She would see if she could run the business.

In 1627, she left Smithy Cottage and relocated the business to Lincoln.

• • • •

Anne Hawkes hoped that the ruins of a building at the far reaches of the land were safe for her small daughter to play on.

But Deborah's brother Job was thirteen now, and happy to mind his sister.

Her children looked hot – the temperature had risen on this cloudy summer's day in 1767.

Anne would go over there and let them peel off some layers of clothes, once she had cooled off in the shade.

William, Anne's husband, had said that the ruin used to be a smith's shop.

It seemed likely, because their own house was called Smithy Cottage.

They had been there for two years.

When she had asked why the rooms on one end looked so different from the rest, William explained that a previous owner had added them a few years before.

"And when was the smithy demolished?" Anne asked.

There was a sort of footprint of it remaining, the lowest parts of the walls, on which Deborah now clambered.

"That I cannot tell you," her husband said.

Anne had been reinstating the kitchen garden and guessed at what had been grown there in the past.

She liked the house and tried to feel settled.

Yet William's activities worried her constantly.

He was a bolster-maker by trade, but a restless soul and a taker of risks.

For some time he had been engaged in gin smuggling.

At their previous house, further inland, he had only stored barrels in their cellar.

Anne was no fool. She knew there was smuggling and she knew what the canvas-covered piles were.

In recent years William had joined in the smuggling with more enthusiasm.

He told Anne how much he liked the extra money and suggested that she should take part, too.

"But you like the excitement more, William," she said.

The extra money made her all the more nervous because she knew it had bought them Smithy Cottage.

She worried, but she loved the house, especially the carvings on the stair post.

"I wonder who made these," she said to her son Job one evening. "Do you think it's a man's work or a woman's?"

He gave the carvings a cursory glance and she realised that he had not noticed them before.

"Oh, a girl's," he said. "Flowers are for girls."

Her son was just like her husband, active and always on the move.

The chances of him not following William into the gin game were small.

She ran her fingers across the carvings.

One was definitely rosemary, but the other was less distinct, the centre of the flower damaged slightly.

• • • •

That summer, William became increasingly bold.

It was as though the season gave him bigger lungs and a larger heart.

He told Anne tales of carts being driven out into shallow waters to the waiting ships.

He described with relish the pale faces of horses being blacked up for disguise, their hooves wrapped in sacking to quieten their going, the iron rims of cartwheels wrapped in straw to the same end.

A feeling had been creeping into Anne's mind.

She was more and more sure that William should never have married at all.

He was a youth in a man's clothing.

The thought dismayed her, because she had fallen in love with his fierce enthusiasm for life.

She had thought they

were the same, but William was risking too much.

Anne kept a journal and in it she began to express her unease.

When the heat had calmed a little, Anne paid a visit to her mother who lived five miles away.

She took Deborah with her. The child sat happily on her grandmother's knee as the two women talked.

There was no need for Anne to reveal her worries to Mary Parkin, because a mother could see such things, etched into a son or daughter's face.

"It's your husband," Mary said, her words not even framed with a question.

Anne sighed.

"You know what he does when he's not at his work?"

"You have let enough of it slip, Annie. I think I know."

"The things they ask him to do grow more perilous."

Mary said nothing for a while, playing a clumsy game of cat's cradle with the child.

"You know that, in the end, you can take your children and get out of his way?" she said in a steady tone.

For a few seconds Anne did not understand.

"Leave him, you mean?"

She shook her head vehemently.

"No, I made him promises."

Mary nodded and set Deborah down on the rug.

"Your father, my husband, used his fists."

Anne stood still.

"You have never said."

"It didn't seem useful for you to know, my darling."

"You suffered violence at his hands?"

Anne's father had been dead since before she could remember.

"I called myself a widow," Mary said, "but the truth is that I ran from him.

"You won't remember the place we lived in, way over beyond Louth.

"I came here, took a new name, and prayed for forgiveness.

"In my soul I knew it was best, for you and for me."

It was as if she needed her child's forgiveness as much as God's.

"You had to go, then," Anne said.

The shaft of sunlight that had lit the floor was suddenly blocked.

A tall figure filled the doorway.

Deborah toddled away to play with her grandmother's old spaniel, which was lying in the corner.

"Peter," her mother said, and she got up quickly.

It was Peter Aquis, an old friend of her mother's and a man Anne liked.

Mary led him to a chair. Her face became more serious.

"Peter has offered to marry me," she said.

Peter Aquis put out an arm towards Anne.

"I have a home to offer your mother," he said.

"A good life in Stoke, I promise you."

Anne had no objection whatever.

She had long wondered why her mother had not married Peter Aquis before now, being widowed so long and he a good man.

Then she saw them look at one another and Peter gave Mary a nod.

"Your father . . ." Mary began, and she swallowed.

"Your father died only a few weeks ago, Anne, in a London prison. I got word only days ago.

"It was intention to write you a letter, but then you came and Peter arrived . . ."

Anne was trying to absorb her mother's words.

"So that is why you did not marry Peter?" she said.

"Now I am free," Mary said.

Her expression changed again.

She did not want to talk of the man who had made her suffer, about whom she had lied for so long.

"But I judged myself free of him a long time ago, and you should know that I would never judge another woman for taking her children away from –"

"You are thinking of Will," Anne said. "My situation is different.

"My husband has never laid a hand on me and never would.

"I wish you and Peter happiness."

• • • •

Anne was upset with her mother for suggesting she leave him.

She clung to Will and life went on. A full year passed.

Another summer was upon them when one evening, a glorious sunset behind the house, the Customs men came to call.

William was absent when the two men searched the house.

They stood in the main room – one mocking the great pair of bellows on the wall, the other saying that all the Hawkes family were criminals, by association.

"The boy's old enough to know what's going on," the second man said with scorn.

"Old enough to do his part, without a doubt."

He pointed to Anne.

"We know he's got a role, and you should know the danger you're in," he said, his voice a growl.

They left, and Anne made the supper.

As she wrapped the pudding in muslin, she imagined what leaving would be like.

Her heart thudded.

She had to protect her children – that was the chief purpose of her life, however much she loved William.

She thought of the smuggling and the men taken by officers already, all along the coast.

How could she bear it longer, waiting for him to be hanged or transported to those penal colonies in Australia? Waiting for Job to be dragged under?

• • • •

Soon after that, Peter and her mother visited together.

They had married quietly in their own church, and had both attended the speedy burial of Anne's father.

Peter made a speech, apologetic but firm, rehearsed but nervous.

He assured Anne that he and his new wife would make a good life for Anne and the children in the Midlands.

"Think of your mother's choices all those years ago," he said. "Think of your children."

Anne said that she would think on it. She seemed to spend all her life, these days, thinking on things.

A terrible night came, a night of thick summer rain and pitch black skies.

Anne awoke and realised the space in the bed beside her was empty. William had not come back at all.

She went to her nearest neighbour, a woman she trusted, to ask for the children to be minded, and then she went in search.

It was an hour before she found William, slumped, wet and chilled behind a barn owned by a man she knew was deep in illegal gin.

The man came out to the barn, his face like thunder, and told Anne that William had been lax and incompetent, taking risks in the middle of an operation.

"I lied for this man of yours," he said. "I told the crew I'd given him poor instruction and saved him from their wrath, and from worse – from the gallows!"

The next day, when her husband had gone to his work, Anne sat, weighing things up.

She came to a decision. She would leave Smithy Cottage with her children.

She would try not to picture life too far ahead.

Letters went back and forth between Anne and Stoke after that.

A night was fixed when Peter Aquis would come with a cart for her.

Anne wandered the house the afternoon before the appointed day, heartsick to be leaving but sure it was for the best.

She had always had a sense of the people who had inhabited the cottage before her – mothers, she was sure, and women who had cared for it.

She made wax impressions of the carvings on the newel post.

"Rosemary for remembrance," she whispered as she wrapped the impressions in a scrap of fabric and laid them carefully in her bag.

"I will remember Smithy Cottage and plan to return here one day."

She made a final entry in her journal.

She closed the book and packed it with the children's things.

When Peter drew up in the cart that warm night, Anne was outside the front door, wringing her hands.

He jumped down and took her hands in his, pressing them to stay their frantic movement.

"Job!" Anne cried out. "My boy is not here!"

The boy had never followed William before at night. She knew that was where he was.

She had seen looks pass between them, father and son, but she had chosen to ignore the possibility that Job was now involved.

They hunted for two long hours. Then Anne made a fresh decision: she must leave Smithy Cottage with Deborah.

William was more and more moody and irascible, the pressure of the dangers loaded upon him.

What would he do if he found her and knew her betrayal, before she fled?

The cart trundled away on the road above the cliffs.

Anne looked out and wept, Deborah sleeping already, her head on her mother's lap.

Once, looking at the sea in a gap between two hawthorns, she saw the figure of her son.

Job was the lookout, a slender, eager boy with his hand raised to his brow, keeping back the wind.

Below, the contraband would be on the move.

• • • •

The Gosse family had bought Smithy Cottage in 1849.

After tiring months of plaster dust and noise, the house was as ready for proper habitation as it was ever likely to be.

It was now the early summer of 1851.

"It's so very old," Marianne Gosse's mother said as she surveyed the back of the property from the garden.

She said it with distaste – it had been her husband's decision to purchase.

"Old, but venerable," Marianne said.

She adored the house precisely because it held a wealth of history.

Most Victorians were building stuccoed villas for themselves, over-stuffed with vases and drapes.

Marianne and her father understood the value of heritage and history.

She would often point out the bellows to visitors, picturesque and ancient, hanging on the wall.

She would laugh about the previous occupants who had carved things into the wood, and who had made all sorts of ill-advised alterations.

The Gosses had enlarged the property further, adding a long conservatory across the back and a small wing with a study, but Smithy Cottage was still quaint and it delighted Marianne.

• • • •

The Gosse family were Lincolnshire folk to the tips of their toes.

They had been acquainted with the Tennysons, during the time when Alfred Tennyson's father George had been rector of Somersby, Benniworth and Bag Enderby.

Alfred had been Poet Laureate for a year by 1851, and Marianne's family bathed in the reflected glory of having known him.

George Tennyson had now been deceased for 20 years, but his family had stayed on after his death.

George had been a man of superior abilities and attainments and well off, for a country clergyman.

It been some years since the Tennysons had moved to Essex, but the connection was still important to the Gosses.

They explained to anyone who would listen that they had socialised often with that great family.

Marianne was as cultured as she was aspirational.

Her fiancé Edward Moxon was taking a second degree at Oxford, and he was very clever.

He was also a poet in the Tennyson mould. Marianne was sure that he would make much of himself.

Sometimes she allowed herself to dream of being the wife of another Poet Laureate.

The Gosses had bought the land beside Smithy Cottage in the negotiation.

They had also decided to rename the house.

"I do think 'Smithy House' is better," Mrs Gosse said. "One can hardly call this a cottage, with all the bedrooms."

"I suppose it was once cottage-sized," Marianne answered.

Locals told them that the land had been used for horses, and before that there had been some sort of stone building on it.

Certainly it was stony ground.

The family had a rockery made about 40 yards from the conservatory with some of the rocks and added a fashionable carp pond.

Marianne showed off both these things to her single friends when they visited.

They were friends from her school days, and she was anxious about them.

All of them were less well read than she was and had less money, and so their prospects were more limited.

She gave them tours of the house and all its ancient features, always stopping at the bottom of the stairs to point out where she had added a carving to the two botanical carvings left there by some long-ago inhabitant.

"It is a foolish, girlish thing to do," she told her friends. "An indulgence, really."

She had carved the initials of her beloved Edward: *E.M.*

In June that year, disaster struck. It was an arrow to the heart of Marianne's hopes and dreams.

Edward Moxon was rusticated from Oxford, "sent down" in disgrace, a jape gone wrong.

He and his friends had painted a gargoyle on the outside of the cloisters, making it resemble the professor of Greek philosophy in so obvious a manner that punishment was demanded.

Edward, whose parents lived in nearby Wragby, came to Smithy House to see Marianne and ask for her forgiveness.

He was full of sorrow, but she was full of anger. This was not the young man she had expected to marry.

That young man had taken a first at Oxford and would do well for himself in any of a dozen fields of endeavour.

Edward kneeled before her in the conservatory.

"Look at the letter you sent me," he said, "telling

me that you love me, dear Marianne."

He took it from his pocket.

"Can you go back on the sentiments in it?"

It was her letter, sent four months before on St Valentine's Day.

At the bottom of the final page of five was a sketch.

"Your drawing of my initials in the wood," he said.

"You carved them and drew your carving for me.

"They are forever there as a sign that you love me, and you do love me, don't you?"

At that moment three ladies, entered, ushered in by Mrs Gosse, who did not know where the couple had gone for their tête-a-tête.

She was talking about the conservatory glass and how the architect had found a way to prevent overheating.

Edward leaped to his feet.

"Mrs Gosse. Ladies," he exclaimed.

He took the page out of Marianne's hand.

"See how my love carved my name!"

Marianne was mortified.

Before long, everyone in the villages would know about Edward and how he had brought himself low.

"I did no such thing, Mr Moxon," she said, looking at him as though she barely knew him. "The initials E.M. are common, are they not?

"I carved nothing. I have far too much respect for this venerable house to do such a thing!"

Mrs Gosse was puzzled.

She was trying to recall (Marianne knew) whether the "E.M." had been there when they moved in or not.

Edward was staring at Marianne, horrified and distressed.

As soon as the four ladies had closed the door and retreated into the house, he spoke in a small voice.

"Now I see to that you will deny me. This error of mine, for which another person might find it in their heart to forgive, is too much for a girl with your expectations.

"We are all fools sometimes, Marianne, but Edward Moxon is not good enough for you.

"Your husband must be perfection. Though he might love you deeply, he is not allowed one mistake!"

He left quickly and was not seen in the county all that summer.

In the summer of 1853, Marianne learned he had married to Frances Hindle, a schoolfriend of hers.

Frances's father was a clerk and in rather reduced circumstances.

Mrs Gosse thought that Frances Hindle's mama

might be doing dress repairs for extra income.

"But they tell me it's a love match," Mrs Gosse said. "I suppose it must be."

The Moxons had three healthy children and were said to be a kind family.

Edward was not a poet but an accounts clerk like his father-in-law. He worked for a Lincoln wool business.

"One of the few that still operate in Lincoln," Mr Gosse told Marianne.

"It was founded in 1627 by a woman, though some say the firm began earlier."

· · · ·

Marianne carried on with life at Smithy House.

She organised its modest library and laid on concerts.

She drank tea sometimes with a lady from church, Miss Richards, in the front garden.

For years she worked hard to keep the ponds and rockery looking nice, but her enthusiasm waned when her parents died.

One afternoon, she was with Miss Richards when a pale, sick-looking young woman passed by.

The girl glanced up at Marianne, lowered her head and walked on, but stopped when she reached the end of the wall and winced.

She was expecting a child and unmarried.

It was widely known locally; Marianne had heard it from the man who brought her milk.

"Goodness me," Miss Richards whispered. "I hate to sound coarse, but she looks very much as though she may enter her confinement any day.

"She's going to sit on your wall. I hope for your sake that she does not ask to come inside in this heat."

Miss Richards gave Marianne a look of horror.

"How would that look?"

It was a Damascene moment for Marianne. She stared at Miss Richards.

"How would that look?"

The question seemed utterly hollow and cruel, and against everything she had ever read in the Gospels.

Was this how she had lived her life?

She got to her feet.

"It's Kitty, isn't it?" she called out. "You must have some water. Come along into the house."

· · · ·

That day, Marianne ignored the roses that needed dead-heading. She ignored Miss Richards, too.

It was the start of a new life, from tea and cake for little Kitty Simpson to the following summer by which time the Smithy House offered many things.

It was a place to come for understanding and aid.

The building began to crumble just a little.

Marianne knew that such an old house ought to get more of her attention, but she had no time for that.

One day she had her maid pull off the rusting plaque that said "Smithy House".

"At least let's get that clean, so people can see the name," she said.

Under it they found a smaller plaque that read "Smithy Cottage".

"That's what we'll be," Marianne said.

"And help me unhook those enormous bellows from the wall.

"Last winter we never had enough fires going. And I mean to have far more, so this winter we'll need the bellows."

· · · ·

Harold Rutter had his doubts about Smithy Cottage, but it was cheap.

Harold had been forced to abandon the family's London home to save money, and now here he was with four boisterous sons, renting.

It was July of 1901, and the house was very much the worse for wear.

"The owner was a benevolent spinster," the agent said, "clearly not interested in maintaining its wattle and daub.

"The place has been empty for eleven years, since she left in her old age."

Harold's relatives were Lincolnshire people, hence his choice of the area.

His cousins in Bag Enderby disapproved of his lax child-rearing methods.

The truth was that Harold felt out of his depth with the children, but hadn't the money to hire a nanny or any other help.

He and his boys had a good feeling about the house.

"I think nice people lived here," his youngest said.

Harold missed their mother sorely.

She had died in childbirth

and only the oldest remembered her well.

He was an inventor, a brilliant man who understood a little of his own genius.

Yet he also knew how hard it would ever be to make money from his talents.

He earned a meagre living repairing traction engines, threshing machines and some electrical items.

The five of them lived in semi-chaos.

They took to calling the house Smithy Hole because it was always a mess.

The oldest boy, Graham, who was nine, had altered the plaque nailed beside the front door to read "Smithy Hole", and the second boy had pinned a cardboard sign beneath it that read, *Abandon hope, all ye who enter here.*

The boys were on holiday for the summer.

Harold was trying not to think about schools, having taken the boys who were of school age out of their London schools.

They were running wild in the sunshine, finding carp skeletons in the garden and asking where they might have come from, digging up rocks that didn't seem to be a natural part of the landscape, and building castles with them.

One day they even painted the stairs, thus covering the lavender that someone had carved there, and the pansy.

There were some initials, too – "E.M."

The boys never stopped mucking about with a pair of preposterous bellows they had found upstairs.

Harold found two of them trying to gather up dead spiders with the bellows, one rainy day.

"My goodness, would you stop?" he said.

"They're no good anyway," the oldest said. "I thought they'd suck, but they won't."

When they were all finally in bed, Harold found a large hook on the wall of the main room and hung the bellows from it, out of the reach of at least two of his sons.

He looked at the bellows and mused that they might suck up a spider, if their holes were repaired.

He had designed a few cleaning machines in his time, but all of them were supposed to blow or brush dirt away, not to suck.

It was still raining the following day and he had the boys test how much they could suck up bits of grit with their mouths, handkerchiefs between boy and dirt.

They had a lovely time and Harold was impressed by the results.

He had been building a small generator, oil-powered, and he attached it to a vacuum device that he'd cobbled together from bits and pieces, not unlike a pair of bellows.

It was huge, heavy and horribly noisy, but it worked.

"This may make our fortune," he told the boys.

They shrugged.

Cleaning was not one of their interests.

Harold and his sons lugged his vacuum device all the way to the London Patent Office, the children filling a railway carriage with noise.

At the Patent Office he learned that a certain Mr Booth had already filed a very similar device.

The Booth machine had the royal seal of approval and would be cleaning Westminster Abbey's carpets prior to Edward VII's coronation, come August.

Harold felt deflated.

He worried that he had wasted time when he should have been finding ways to support his children.

Resentment boiled within him. He should have gone earlier and got the patent.

"I've failed you," he said on the way home.

"I'm no good."

That silenced the boys. They looked at one another.

"But you're the best of men," the third boy said, surprised at his father's comment.

"Everybody knows that."

"The very best," Graham added firmly.

They sat closer to him as though protecting him, talked more quietly, and looked out of the window.

• • • •

Back in Lincolnshire, the boys delighted the wife of Harold's cousin by cleaning her house with the machine.

As the school year got underway, they began to take some responsibility for cleaning Smithy Hole.

Ten years passed.

Harold's oldest boy became engaged to a wonderful young lady.

Justina had fallen for the boy especially because he was domesticated.

When she found that Graham knew how to air linen and could make a pie, she declared herself in love.

Harold sat at their wedding breakfast and was astonished as he looked at his sons among the guests.

He appeared to have raised four good men.

Even his judgmental cousin said so.

The boys respected women; they could even see the world from a woman's perspective.

• • • •

World War I broke out. All four were called up and Harold lived in fear.

Two went to the Front, two to work in tank engineering.

All four come home alive.

The second boy had life-changing injuries but his adoring fiancée married him on his return.

Harold visited the couple one day and, arriving early, found his daughter-in-law using a vacuum machine on the rugs.

"I don't think about that invention of mine any more," he said to his son. "At least, not with any frustration."

His disappointment had gone.

His achievements were his sons and his good fortune was brimming over.

• • • •

Maureen Harper did not like Smithy Hole.

The name, she thought, should have put them off when they'd rented it earlier in 1958.

She scrubbed the plaque by the door and found that, under layers of paint, the plaque did in fact read "Smithy Cottage".

This was better, but what a place!

The ridiculous set of dusty bellows summed up a property that lacked most mod cons and was draughty and full of holes.

Brian, her husband, joked that he was fine with holes.

"I'm an archaeologist, after all!" he said.

Maureen had met her husband on a dig when they were students.

Luckily, they only had the house for 18 months.

Brian had been sent by the University of Nottingham to make a preliminary survey of Horncastle, five miles away, and this was the only convenient house available.

Nobody was sure why there were vestiges of Roman walls in Horncastle.

It did not lie on any major Roman road.

Brian wondered if it had been one of a line of 4th-century forts that ran from Hadrian's wall to Portsmouth.

The empire had come under attack from Saxons across the sea at the time.

Troops at Horncastle might have ridden to the coast when there was a threat, he said.

Or maybe the walls guarded an inland route for salt, which was then more valuable than gold.

They were in the little front garden one dewy July morning when a large car pulled up and a couple their own age got out.

To Maureen and Brian's surprise, the couple asked to look around the house.

Terry and Marie Wheatley had come from Brisbane on a quest to investigate Marie's English roots.

Smithy Cottage appeared in the scant stories they had of the family.

"Of course," Maureen said. "Come in."

▶

Terry and Marie poked about in each room. They made gentle jokes about the "Ten Pound Poms" currently flooding into Australia.

"We've gone in the opposite direction!" Terry remarked.

They'd never live in a damp old country like Britain, he added, describing the joys of Brisbane.

Marie told them she was a descendant of a man called Job Hawkes.

"I've got his dates here," she said, drawing a folder from her shoulder bag.

"Yes, circa 1753 to 1828.

"He was the son of a William Hawkes. His dates are unknown. Are you familiar with the name?"

Maureen explained that they were new to Lincolnshire.

Marie was clearly glad to be the expert in the room.

"Well, we want to find out what happened to William's wife, Anne.

"She's a gap in my records. All we have are some letters between Job and a young woman he was courting."

She took another piece of paper from the folder.

"These are copies. The letters paint a picture of a woman who abandoned her husband in his hour of need.

"William Hawkes was wrongly accused of smuggling and transported to Australia along with his boy, Job."

Brian peered over her shoulder at the copy.

"I'm a bit of a historian," he remarked.

"He's a professional archaeologist and an academic," Maureen added.

"Every source needs corroboration," Brian said.

"We can't say if Job Hawkes's assessment of his mother was fair or accurate."

Marie looked irritated.

"I guess not, but Job writes that his father barely helped in the smuggling.

"He was practically an innocent man. His mother was fickle and ungrateful.

"In one letter he suggests she had a lover, a fact that might explain why he and his father found themselves alone in Australia."

"Was Job a smuggler?" Maureen asked. "Does he admit to being one?"

"Oh no, Job had no part in it," Terry said.

Terry and Marie were staying in Lincoln.

Maureen and Brian asked them back, mostly for politeness' sake, and Terry gave an account of how well the Hawkes men had done in Australia after transportation.

Marie looked around her.

"This house is an antique," she said. "What are those?"

"Bellows," Maureen said.

By now she was keen to get rid of the Wheatleys and, shortly after, they left.

Maureen found herself thinking about Anne Hawkes.

She knew this was a smuggling area and wondered what it must have been like for the women.

As Brian got deep into his work, she began to spend time looking into the Hawkes family.

The name was reasonably common, locally.

She found baptism records for Job and a child called Deborah.

A marriage record came next, for William and Anne, and Maureen dug further.

She found Anne's mother in a damaged record, and her father, but no trace of him after that.

Beside the mother's name someone had scribbled in a second marriage.

The church mentioned was in Staffordshire, and the name was new to Maureen – Aquis.

• • • •

Maureen had caught the genealogy bug.

She asked the Horncastle librarian to help her look into the Aquis name, and it turned out to be rare.

"It really only pops up in Stoke-on-Trent," the librarian said.

It was a miserable summer, the temperatures low and the drizzle frequent, and Maureen spent her time on trains and in records offices and libraries.

Eventually she found her way to a journal written by an Anne Hawkes.

A curator agreed this was very likely the Anne that Maureen was researching.

The journal was housed in the collection of an industrial museum in Stoke.

"Yes, this is my Anne," Maureen said, showing a page to the curator.

"This is the house. My house – Smithy Cottage, Bendham Lane."

Maureen spent a week in Stoke, transcribing the journal and making diagrams of connections she found.

She wrote to the Wheatleys in Brisbane about Anne's character.

She didn't have a lover, she wrote. *Her husband was most likely a proper smuggler.*

I think she will have missed her son badly. It must have been a hard life.

The journal made many mentions of the house.

Back at home, Maureen cleaned the newel post, having read about the carvings in the journal.

Anne had written that she could not identify the second plant.

Maureen thought it looked a bit like convolvulus.

"Maybe we will never know," she told Brian.

He put his arm around her.

"My beloved assistant archaeologist," he said. He tipped his head to one side. "I think it looks like my mum's pansies."

"Pansy," Maureen said. "Its name means 'thinking of you', from the French, *penser*."

She wished she could speak to Anne about flowers, family and loss.

• • • •

Finally Elena hauled herself out of her deckchair and went inside to cool off.

Her hand brushed the big post at the foot of the stairs and found the carvings.

She paused, the baby hammering at her with its tiny feet, and looked more closely than she had before.

There were the flowers, or leaves, but now she noticed some letters.

"E and M," she said aloud. "Those are my initials."

They were old, filled with varnish and paint, and cleaned – layers of change.

She imagined moving into her first home.

Perhaps a woman had put her mark on her first home by making these carvings.

She tried to imagine the feelings of hope and pride such a moment might bring, and found they came easily.

She had never really had a home.

From a family flat in Bucharest she had travelled to a hostel in Kent, to a shared house with other women, to a mobile home with Stefan.

The baby had gone still. Without warning, a pain ripped through her.

"Labour," she whispered in the hot air of the hallway.

She staggered out to the garden, where Emily Hislop was strolling up the path.

"Got any old clothes? I'm collecting jumble," Emily began, before realising what was happening. "Oh! It's OK – my Mini is over there!"

They found Elena's phone and got her into the car.

Emily drove as fast as she dared to the hospital, while Elena called Stefan.

He came haring into the delivery room an hour later.

His daughter arrived half an hour after that, wife and child both healthy.

They were back at Number Four, Bendham Lane, the following morning.

"Have you got the key?" Elena said. She was walking painfully slowly, looking down at the car seat in which her daughter slept.

"Here," he said.

But Stefan was turning left, not towards the mobile home but the house.

"I've got guys coming with furniture later today," he said. "I made some calls while you were recovering.

"You're right – we need a home. Is this our home?"

"I think so," Elena said.

"It has a lot to say."

He kissed her cheek.

"I think so, too," he said.

At Close Quarters

There was something about Cloverdale Hall's history that nagged at me . . .

BY LOUISE MCIVOR

I FIRST visited Cloverdale Hall on a sultry July afternoon.

I was working for a magazine in London, my first job after university.

Folk struggled with my Belfast accent, and I struggled with juggling copy typing, answering a constantly ringing phone and the accursed fax machine.

One of the few perks was getting press tickets no-one else wanted.

Cloverdale Hall had just opened to the public after years as a private house. The girl managing the publicity was friends with the features editor.

I got the press ticket because, I suspect, none of the more senior staff wanted to work on a Saturday.

I was living in a two-bedroomed flat in North London. The other bedroom was occupied by a couple I had known vaguely at university.

There was no communal garden, so I jumped at the chance to get out of London, where everything was covered in a heat haze.

• • • •

The grumpy man at the entrance said he didn't know anything about a press ticket. I felt all flustered.

"Would you mind checking again?" I said.

I knew that I'd be in bother on Monday if I didn't turn in a few hundred words. I glanced at the entrance ticket prices. There was no way that I could afford them.

Just then, a woman in a polka dot dress strode over.

"You're looking for your press pack? Miranda's left it for you. They'll also give you a free coffee in the café," she said, handing me an envelope with the photographic transparencies and press release.

"Thank you," I said, feeling like I had overcome my first hurdle.

Now I just had to figure out what to see and write about.

"You can pick up your headset there. We're very proud of them, you know. Four different languages so far. Lord Cloverdale spoke at our opening, be sure to mention that."

"Of course," I said, feeling nervous and excited all at once.

I worried terribly about getting everything right and pleasing everyone.

The grumpy man pointed out the length of the queue building up behind us and the polka dot dress lady left me to explore on my own.

The headsets were like personal stereos and the tinny voice on mine kept cutting out.

"Excuse me, I don't think mine is working," I said to a woman who looked like she might be staff.

"I don't know why they insisted on getting those things. They're always going wrong," was all she said.

However, the woman didn't offer to get me another set, so I took my courage in my hands.

"Maybe you could tell me a little about this room?"

The room was lined with portraits of all shapes and sizes: children dressed as miniature versions of their parents, men who looked like Charles I, women in dresses that possibly cost more than the house did.

"Is there not information in your folder?" the woman snapped, indicating the press pack which I was holding awkwardly while trying to balance my notebook and work out the headset.

I felt like crying.

I thought I was doing so well, finding the place, which was 20 minutes' walk from the train station, along a traffic-choked road.

So often I felt out of my depth, and I wished I could summon up some of the steely confidence of my more senior colleagues, or even my friends from university who were busy in London newsrooms and court reporting in local papers.

However, the features editor would be expecting a feature on Monday, so I just had to get on with it.

The hair was sticking to the back of my neck, and I wished I had brought a scrunchie with me.

The woman turned to welcome a coach party with some tourists from overseas.

There was a seat that didn't look like an antique so while the woman answered the party's questions (much more politely than she had dealt with me), I took off the headset and left it discreetly on a bench.

I read through the press release and started to make notes, trying to think of ways to start off the feature.

I was always nervous that my shorthand wouldn't be up to the job, but I got chatting to two ladies from Winnipeg and managed to get a few words from them about how they didn't have anything like this near where they lived.

The Canadian ladies spent more time telling me how much they loved my Irish accent and how their grandmother came from County Cork.

Every tourist I met seemed to have a grandmother who came from County Cork.

However, now Dolores and Rita from Winnipeg had found a willing audience, they couldn't stop.

"It must have been awful ➤

for the poor maids!" Rita said.

"Imagine! Getting up in the dark on a winter's morning!" Dolores said. "Do you remember when I worked as a chambermaid in New York before I was married?"

"Oh yes, you always said that it made you study harder at secretarial college so that you could work in an office!"

I had stopped trying to take down what Dolores and Rita were saying.

I really had to get on and research my piece.

"Lovely to meet you," I said.

"Good luck with your writing, Carol," Rita said.

It was the first time that anyone that day had used my name.

None of the staff at Cloverdale Hall had bothered.

I wandered into the banqueting hall, its long table set with beautiful china and glassware, with a Russian samovar on a heavy oak sideboard.

I made a note of the bell pulls (still working, the press release said) to summon the servants and marvelled at the Minstrels' Gallery, wondering what it would have been like to be wealthy in days gone by.

I explored the old laundry, with milk white clothes hanging on pulleys, with a note about what the servants would have used for washing powder.

Apparently, they had to grate the soap. I wondered what that would have been like, standing grating soap, waiting for water to boil and hauling dirty linen into steaming tubs and coppers.

The stables were now a tea room and where I would have my free coffee. I'd decided to go for it at the end of my trip.

That way, I could give myself a chance to make any additional notes when everything was fresh in my mind.

I was just coming down from exploring the bedrooms – all decked out with beautiful sheets and embroidered counterpanes – when I started to feel a sense of misgiving.

It was a feeling I was familiar with. I had had the same feeling when I was going out with my first boyfriend at university (he turned out to be in love with one of the other girls in my Halls). Or when I was urged to do French A-Level instead of Music (I hated it and got a D).

It was the feeling that something wasn't right.

I walked purposefully to the tea room in the old stables.

I would have my free cup of coffee, and this nagging feeling would go away. I was just hungry, I told myself, trying to magic away that uneasy feeling.

The piece was already more or less done, I told myself. I had more than enough material. If I got in early on Monday morning, I could type it up before the phones started ringing and perhaps even finish it in my lunch hour.

I ate my lunch sitting on the lawns with a bottle of home-made lemonade.

That was anther thing which Miranda had highlighted in her press release.

I was too hot for my free coffee.

As I took in the beauty of the lawns, the exotic trees and bushes (imported as seeds by some Victorian ancestor), I tried again to reason this nagging voice away.

I looked through my messy shorthand, writing in longhand some of the more illegible words so I wouldn't forget.

I added a little bit about the beautiful grounds and the different accents and languages I had recognised from the visiting tourists.

I looked at my watch. I had about 45 minutes before I would need to walk back to the station.

After that, it would be an hour and a half before the last train.

I got up, thinking I would go back into the house, hoping this would satisfy the nagging feeling.

Ask the questions that everyone else is thinking but no-one wants to ask.

The words drifted through my head unbidden.

It was something our journalism teacher had said, a redoubtable man who had reported on the Troubles back home and was afraid of nothing.

I thought back to Rita and Dolores and their time as chambermaids.

There was no-one to ask the question I wanted to ask.

I hated having to "bother" people too much to make an investigative reporter, but I walked back to the ticket office to see if I could find any knowledgeable looking staff.

The queues had gone as there was no admittance after half past three.

The same grumpy man was at the desk.

I took a deep breath. Nothing ventured, nothing gained.

"Excuse me, where did the servants sleep?"

"No idea," he said unhelpfully.

I waited for a moment, trying to figure out what to do next. And then to my surprise, the man spoke again.

"That's the problem with these big houses. No-one ever thinks about the work that went into them."

Just then, a large church party got out of a minibus, and as he waved me away, started to explain in officious tones that they'd have to hurry as the last house tour had already started.

Despite my natural politeness, the bit was between my teeth now.

I knew, without a shadow of a doubt, that I needed to put something in about the long-dead servants, not just Lord and Lady Cloverdale and their ancestors and how the plasterwork on the banqueting hall ceiling was a particularly fine example of something or other.

I needed to know what it was like to be a servant, to give a voice to these folk who would never make it to a guidebook or a press release and certainly not to a portrait on the wall.

Otherwise, my feature would just be a "puff" piece, something my journalism teacher had warned us against.

"They may as well just pay for advertising," he had told us.

I flicked through the press pack again.

There was absolutely nothing about the servants, apart from the fact that an earlier Lady Cloverdale had made a particularly "generous bequest" to her lady's maid in her will in 1867.

While everyone else was pre-occupied with the late coach party, I made another quick exploration of the house.

Servants, from what little I knew, probably slept in attics or basements.

Unfortunately, any doors that looked like they might lead to a basement or attic rooms had *No admittance* or *Staff Only* signs.

I walked back up the stairs, past the bedrooms and the dressing rooms and found another door, with no sign on it.

I thought of the steely resolve of my colleagues at work, how they rang and rang until a theatre director or press officer would take their calls.

The door opened and it led me to another corridor. There were paint pots on the landing, boxes full of brochures for the house, and a very modern photocopier.

I felt disappointed that I hadn't stumbled across a long-forgotten servants' room.

"These rooms are just for staff."

It was the woman in the polka dot dress but her earlier breezy friendliness had gone.

"Oh, sorry, I didn't realise," I faltered, my earlier confidence melting as quickly as the frost on a spring morning. "I was just trying to find out where the servants slept.

"There's nothing about them in the press pack."

Still silence. I floundered for something to say.

"I've just been out to the laundry and I was thinking of how tough it must have been, washing all those big skirts and all by hand and then having to mend them..."

"And by candlelight or lamp light or if they were lucky, a seamstress's globe," the woman said, though I noticed that the tone was still imperious.

"It wasn't a glamorous job, it was badly paid, it ruined their eyesight, yet if you look at the stitching on the old clothes that survived, it is simply exquisite."

"Did the women not have hand sewing machines?" I asked, anxious to keep the woman talking, just to see if I could find out just a little more.

The woman looked at me with more interest.

"Not until well into the nineteenth century," she said. "Until then, everything was done by hand and they often worked day and night. There's a seamstress's globe in the housekeeper's room. They used them to reflect more of the candlelight back on to their work."

I realised then that the servants would probably have been too tired to notice where they slept.

The fact that the servants' quarters hadn't been considered important enough to be preserved told me all I needed to know.

The servants would never have merited their own picture, unless it was an idealised portrait of a rosy-cheeked maid.

I didn't realise it at the time but that was a moment I would never forget.

I had to learn to dig a little with my writing – to uncover things, to expose secrets, to ask the questions that everyone else was thinking.

On the way out, I took a last look at the room lined with pictures.

My perception was now coloured by wondering about who wasn't in the pictures.

I looked again at the portraits I had seen on the way in.

There were ladies in dresses so big that walking anywhere other than inside would surely have been impossible. Stern men with long hair. Children dressed in stomachers, wide skirts and elaborate jewellery.

What of the servants' children? Who looked after them?

There were no portraits of the women and men who cleaned the boots after the men hunted or helped excitable children into those impractical clothes or made sure the elaborate skirts looked perfect for the portrait artist. On this hot summer's day, it now felt chilly in the room with those portraits, as the sun had moved to the back of the house.

I thought about the maids who curled hair, who cleaned petticoats, who sewed until they had crashing headaches due to poor light.

What must it have been like, strapped into those uncomfortable clothes, sitting for hours, knowing that as a lady or a girl, you weren't permitted to run down the sloping lawns, paddle in the fountain, climb the beautiful old trees with their inviting branches?

What must it have been like on a day such as this, struggling in the heat, longing to be free?

It was now well after four and I went back out, hurrying to catch my train.

Families were packing up cars and picnics, drivers were counting visitors back onto the coaches, the grumpy man was imperiously telling some more late arrivals what time the hall would be open the following day.

I wondered what must it have been like on a busy summer's day during the hall's heyday, with horse-drawn coaches and the busyness of servants and delivery men.

How on earth did they keep things cool in the heat of summer?

I made my train with minutes to spare.

As I sipped the rest of my lemonade, I realised that the nagging feeling had gone away.

The piece was published a few months later. The features editor didn't tend to go in for high praise but the fact that the piece was published was a start.

I started it with the quote from Rita about the "poor maids" and included the fact that the headphones didn't work and how the servants were like ghosts, hardly meriting a mention in the hall's history.

I steeled myself from a complaint from the features editor but apart from taking out the bit about the headphones not working, the piece was published in its entirety.

I was so proud of that piece, buying extra copies of the magazine to send to my parents back in Belfast.

• • • •

Cloverdale Hall isn't open to the public anymore.

It's used for conferences now and I think the occasional wedding.

I learned a valuable lesson that day. I didn't learn to become a terrier of a reporter overnight – it's not in my nature, although sometimes I wish it was.

I moved more into researching and editing.

I learned never to take things at face value and to find a way into the story, the secret corridor that no-one had uncovered, the place you weren't meant to be.

I learned that trusting my instincts enough to ask the question that nags at me will usually lead me to the answer that unlocks everything.

I learned how important it was to find the place where the servants slept. ■

THE REMEDY

It's wet – it's hot,
It's always there,
It's just a cup away.
Why is it that
This brew should be
So vital every day?
It warms the hands
And soothes the soul,
Cures heartaches, too, they say.
Whatever life should throw at you,
Tea keeps it all at bay.

By Susan Batten

A New Chapter

Jackie wanted nothing more than to find the perfect place to open her bookshop . . .

BY KATIE ASHMORE

"P**ERHAPS** I should give up?" Jackie frowned, twirling the pasta around her fork.

"Don't do that. Not now you've found the perfect location," Wendy told her.

"But I haven't," she protested. "That's the whole problem."

Jackie sighed, gazing across the square, but hardly registering the beauty of the summer evening.

It was still 24 degrees at eight p.m., and the two were seated outside a charming restaurant watching the world go by.

A small fountain splashed in the centre of the stone-flagged piazza. To their left, the road dropped down to the sea and, behind them, pink and yellow houses climbed the hillside, their gardens bright with lemon trees, bergamot, and bougainvillea.

"I know you haven't found the premises you need, but the town is perfect."

"I'd love to live here, but it's no good if I can't find the right place to open my bookshop."

Wendy nodded.

"We've still got time. There's another week before we have to head home." She smiled and poured Jackie a glass of chill Chianti.

Once again, Jackie felt a wave of gratitude for her amazing friend. Wendy was so supportive, she wondered what she'd do without her.

It was six months since she'd been made redundant, and Wendy had been incredible throughout.

It wasn't the financial impact that had distressed Jackie.

She had saved a lot over the years and could retire early. The problem was that she had been happy as a career woman and now, having just turned fifty, she found herself without a job, a family, or a purpose.

"Come on, Jackie, buck up. You've never given up without a fight before. Look how hard you worked to achieve so much in your career."

That was true.

"I'm so proud of you finding a new dream to pursue now that the old one has run its course. Something will turn up."

Jackie grinned. Wendy was right. Tomorrow was a new day and this really was a stunning place.

"OK. We'll look again, but let's take a day off first and do some sight-seeing."

"Great plan." Her friend smiled, laughter lines creasing the skin at the corners of her eyes.

Wendy was an attractive woman with blonde highlights and wearing a green maxi dress.

They'd met at university and been firm friends ever since. The hunt for premises might be proving a challenge but it was fantastic to be sharing a month on the stunning Italian coast together.

• • • •

"Are you feeling better, *signora*?"

Jackie looked up to see a man leaning over her. He had tanned skin and a worried expression in his dark eyes.

She wondered where she was and tried to get up, but felt a restraining hand on her shoulder.

"Please, drink this."

Her head ached and she took the glass of water gratefully, looking around for Wendy as her eyes began to focus.

"I'm right here, Jackie." She heard her friend's voice and relaxed.

"You gave me quite a fright," Wendy continued, sitting beside her and taking her hand. "Thank goodness you're getting your colour back."

"I'm so sorry," Jackie felt the heat flood her face, as she remembered what had happened. "We should have taken a siesta as you suggested."

"Never mind that now. The main thing is you're OK."

Jackie felt embarrassed, but Wendy was right. She sipped her water and stretched her limbs grateful that everything seemed to be in working order. She hadn't fainted in years!

"I feel so silly. Queueing in the midday sun wasn't a good idea at all."

"Do not worry, *signora*. You are not the first to collapse in the sun."

The young man was still standing beside her. He was a tall, handsome Italian, probably in his late twenties, and wearing a linen apron around his waist.

"This is Luca. It was his restaurant that you fainted outside."

"Oh!" Jackie remembered passing an attractive *ristorante* nestled next to the museum.

"Thankfully, I was able to hang onto you until he rescued us."

"Thank you, Luca. I'm very grateful."

"It was nothing." He waved his hand dismissively, then gave them each a menu. "You must eat before you go on your way. It is on the house, as you would say. We must be sure you will not collapse again."

The women tried to protest, but he insisted and, not long after, a beautiful girl with dark, wavy hair appeared.

She was carrying a mouthwatering pizza and steaming bowl of rigatoni and was followed by a small child.

"Please, enjoy." She gave them a warm smile. "I am Luca's wife, Sofia, and this is our little girl, Chiara."

Chiara was a gorgeous child with huge dark eyes and a tumble of curls.

Wendy was soon chatting with her and admiring her toy unicorn, while her mother milled pepper and grated parmesan.

"This is so kind of you," Jackie repeated, thanking her once more.

"It's our pleasure. The summers are getting hotter and hotter. It is difficult even for those who are used to them. When I was expecting Chiara . . ."

"Christina, Christina, it is you!" A man in his fifties came rushing towards them, his face full of surprise and delight.

As he drew closer, however, confusion replaced it.

"I am sorry, I thought . . . Forgive me ladies."

He executed a bow and hurried towards the door.

Jackie's eyes followed him. He was an attractive man with greying black hair, tall and slim, and smartly dressed.

Who could he be and what was that all about?

Sofia shook her head.

"That was Luca's father, Emilio. I don't know what he was thinking. Please, enjoy your meal."

Sofia picked up Chiara and retreated to the kitchen, leaving them to savour the delicious food.

"Wow, this is amazing." Wendy tucked in enthusiastically. "It's turning out to be a great day after all."

Jackie had to agree with her. This must be one of the best restaurants in town. They'd enjoyed the cathedral, now they had fabulous food and, later, they were going for a swim.

Not a bad day at all, despite the fainting fit.

But who, she wondered, was Christina?

• • • •

The next evening, the two women made their way back to Luca and Sofia's restaurant.

They had bought some flowers to say thank you for their kindness and, this time, they wanted to order a meal and pay for it.

They opened the door and were greeted with the scent of basil and garlic and with a warm welcome.

"Ladies, you are back. Come in, come in!"

Luca ushered them to a corner table, with a starched white cloth and a candle flickering in a glass holder.

"What can I get for you?"

They drank wine and nibbled bread sticks while they waited for their food.

It had been another disappointing day, with no sign of suitable premises for the shop.

However, Jackie felt comforted by the cosy interior and the smiles of their hosts.

She sighed. She had been thrilled by her dream of living in this beautiful country and running her own business. She felt at home here, too, but it looked as though she would have to change her plans.

"Excuse me, *signoras*, but may I join you for a while?"

Looking up, she was surprised to see the handsome gentleman who had accosted them the day before.

"Of course, take a seat." Wendy smiled, clearly as intrigued as Jackie herself.

He pulled up a chair and spread out his hands.

"I wish to apologise for my abrupt behaviour yesterday," he began with a self-deprecating smile. "I don't usually shout at strangers, then disappear."

Jackie laughed and poured him a glass of wine.

"I'm sure you don't."

"I am Emilio, Luca's father. I once was owner of this restaurant."

"I'm Wendy and this is Jackie," her friend told him.

"I am delighted to make your acquaintance, signoras. I am afraid I mistook you for a dear friend I once had," he said, turning to Jackie. "You are remarkably like her."

"Christina?"

"Yes, Christina." His face took on a wistful expression and he sighed and shook his head. "She was from England, as I believe you are, and she was very special to me."

"What happened?" Wendy asked, with more interest than tact.

He smiled.

"I suppose it will not hurt to share my story with such a charming pair." He gazed at Jackie and she felt herself growing warm under his scrutiny.

"Christina was a beautiful woman and we fell in love. At least, I did." He paused and took a sip of wine. "We were planning a life together – a business, a home, but then her mother fell ill.

"She returned to England to nurse her. I was quite happy for this. I knew she would return when she could and family is important, no?"

"Oh, yes," Wendy exclaimed.

"However, she did not return."

Jackie felt a wave of pity. Poor Emilio looked so sad, but then he shrugged.

"She met someone else. It was not to be, but I have my family and my wonderful granddaughter here. There is much to make me rejoice.

"When I saw you yesterday, however, I confess I was a little emotional."

Jackie wasn't sure what to say. She was gratified that Emilio had shared this with them. She also admired his positive outlook and obvious love for his family.

"I'm sorry to have brought back difficult memories."

"It was several years ago and you have no need to apologise. I am delighted to meet you both."

"Have you lived here all your life? We love your town."

"Thank you, I have." He beamed at them. "It is a fascinating place with much history. Have you visited the old monastery or the *museo di storia*?"

The women shook their heads.

"We've not had much time for sight-seeing," Jackie told him.

"Now that is a shame. You must have a proper look round while you are here. Please, let me be your guide."

Wendy raised an eyebrow and Jackie protested.

"Oh, we couldn't let you go to so much trouble."

"It is no trouble," he reassured them, his eyes lingering again on Jackie's face.

She felt an unfamiliar sensation in her chest and wasn't sure where to look.

"Then that would be lovely," Wendy replied.

• • • •

The next day, Jackie dressed with more care than usual.

Emilio had arranged to meet them in the square.

She chose to wear her favourite dress, a pair of hooped earrings, and a little more make-up than usual. She checked her reflection and smiled ruefully – she wasn't thirty anymore, but she looked good.

Her dark hair contained little grey and her skin was clear. She couldn't complain.

She picked up her rucksack and made her way down to the hotel entrance.

"Wow, you look nice." Wendy grinned, eyebrows rising, but she said no more on the subject. "Have you put on sun lotion and got your hat and water?" she asked instead. "No more fainting, please."

"I'm prepared!" Jackie laughed. "Now, let's get underway."

They met Emilio outside the cathedral and spent a wonderful morning being conducted around the town, seeing the old walls, the monastery and other lesser-known gems.

"It's been wonderful," Jackie told him later, as they found seats outside a café in the shade.

"I am delighted," he replied. "It's an honour to share my town with you."

"We've seen things from a different perspective," Wendy told him. "It's great to have a local guide."

Jackie agreed. Emilio had been a fount of knowledge and great company, too.

She sipped her iced coffee and sighed with contentment. The small square that he'd brought them to was beautiful.

Water bubbled from a tiny fountain in the centre of a cobbled piazza and warm stone buildings edged the space, with arched doorways and shuttered windows.

An oleander tree, with stunning pink flowers, grew in one corner, whilst a vine climbed luxuriantly across the trellis above them.

"So, how is it that you have had so little time for sightseeing?" Emilio asked them now. "This is not why you came to Italy?"

Jackie shook her head and saw the expression of surprise on his face.

"I would like to live here," she told him.

"You have friends, family here?" he enquired.

"No, nothing like that." She took a deep breath. "I've devoted my life to a career in the IT industry but was recently made redundant."

An expression of sympathy warmed his features and Jackie hurried on. "I don't regret it and I'd do it again in a heartbeat. I loved my work and I achieved a lot."

"She certainly did – a managing director, no less." Wendy interjected.

"Now though, I want to pursue another dream – to live in this wonderful country and open my own business."

"Jackie has her heart set on this very town, but we've had no luck finding suitable premises for a bookshop."

Emilio looked struck, then animated.

"You also love books?" he asked.

"I do indeed.'"

"Thankfully I have more time for reading now. When I was young, my restaurant and family kept me busy – then, my wife, Federica, died."

"That must have been hard," Wendy said, concern writ large on her pleasant face.

"It was, but it was a long time ago. She was only thirty-five." His eyes clouded for a moment. "I had two wonderful children, however, and Mamma was wonderful. She helped with Luca, his sister, and the restaurant.

"Ten years later, I met and fell in love with Christina, but it was not to be." His eyes strayed again to Jackie's face and he shook his head. "What about you ladies? Are you married?"

Jackie laughed.

"Never have been. I was married to the job."

"I am. My husband Paul and I have three children and two small grandchildren."

"How wonderful."

Emilio and Wendy spent some time showing each other pictures on their phones.

Jackie watched them – they looked so happy.

She'd never wanted her own family, never had time to feel lonely, but maybe it would be good to have a relationship now life was changing?

Her eyes flicked to Emilio and away again.

• • • •

They spent the next couple of days sightseeing with their guide, and then a fruitless one looking for properties.

Soon, they would have to return home.

Jackie had enjoyed a wonderful month with Wendy, but her friend needed to get back to her husband and Jackie herself would have to take stock and decide what to do.

Would she try another part of Italy, another country? She didn't know. She loved this place and it would be a wrench to leave.

Today they would meet Emilio before going to a neighbouring town where they'd heard of a place to let – though Jackie held out little hope. Would it be suitable? What if she didn't even like the town?

It was her last option.

"Ladies, you came!" Emilio greeted them warmly, a kiss on both cheeks.

He seemed excited.

"I have a surprise for you." he told them.

"Really?" Jackie and Wendy exchanged glances.

Her friend clearly had no idea what he was talking about either.

"What is it?" Wendy asked him.

"I cannot tell you," he laughed. "I told you, it is a surprise."

He led them out of the restaurant and towards the main square.

It was a gorgeous morning. The sun was already hot, shining from an azure sky, high above the buildings. The scent of baking floated from an open window and, somewhere, a cicada began to sing.

He walked them past the cathedral and fountain to where a side street climbed its way up the hill.

"Now, you must close your eyes," he told Jackie.

"What, just me? But, why?"

"You must trust me," he told her. "I will guide you."

He linked his arm through hers and Wendy took the other side.

"Ready?" he asked.

Jackie nodded, a frisson of excitement knotting her stomach.

What was going on?

They walked her uphill for a while, then stopped. She heard a door being unlocked and was told to mind a step.

They went inside and the door closed behind them.

"You may open your eyes!"

Jackie blinked and, for a moment, couldn't see.

Then, when she was able to focus, she found herself in a large space with a wide glass frontage. There was a small office room to one side.

"What do you think?" Emilio asked. "It would make a perfect bookshop, no?"

"It would." Jackie swallowed. She and Wendy had passed this place before, but it had not been for sale or rent.

Instead, it was stuffed full of junk. She had even commented on what a shame that was, as it was in the perfect location and neither too large nor too small.

"I don't understand," she stuttered.

"It's yours, if you would like it." Emilio was watching her closely. "You remember that Christina and I were going to start a business together?

"When she didn't return, I was left with these premises. I have been renting them out for storage. I did not want to tell you about them until they had been cleared."

Jackie stared around open-mouthed.

"I could rent them to you. There's a small flat upstairs too. Or – or we could go into business together. Partners?"

"It's perfect, Jackie, you must. You and Emilio would be great together."

She stared at her friend. Then, she looked from Wendy back to Emilio's eager face and felt excitement spread through her stomach.

"Yes, business partners," she said.

And, as a grin broke out across his handsome features, she thought that, in time, she might even be ready for more.

Home Healing

Laura knew just the right property for Niki to start afresh . . .

BY JANE AYRES

FRAGRANT yellow roses bloomed in clusters along the path to the compact redbrick house, where Laura, the lettings agent, met her client, Niki, at the front door.

"These one-bedroom starter homes don't come up often," Laura said, unlocking the door. "Luckily, it's just come back on the market."

Like me, Niki thought bitterly, still fragile from her recent breakup with Greg, her partner of ten years. His betrayal still stung.

"I need somewhere as soon as possible," she said.

Her best friend, Mae, had offered her spare room when Niki left Greg, but Niki longed for her own space.

This little house, nestled in a quiet cul-de-sac a short bus ride from town, seemed ideal.

Stepping inside, sunlight poured through the lounge window, bathing the room in golden light.

The walls were a calming apple-white, and a cinnamon-and-mint striped rug warmed the oak floor. Everything was spotless, well cared for.

"It's fully furnished," Laura said. "Ready to move in."

Upstairs, the pine staircase led to a small landing with a boiler cupboard, neat bathroom, and spacious bedroom.

Niki noted the walk-in wardrobe could even fit her writing desk. It was everything she needed.

"I'll take it," she said. Two weeks later, she moved in.

Mae stayed over the first few nights.

"I never imagined I'd be living alone," Niki sighed. "I hate to admit it, but I miss Greg. Despite everything."

"Time heals," Mae said gently. "You might even enjoy your independence."

They shared a bottle of wine, and it was past midnight when Niki stood at the foot of the stairs.

"Night, Mae. Thanks for being here."

"Hey, what are friends for?" Mae grinned from her sleeping bag on the sofa.

"I have a good feeling about this place. It's like the house was waiting for you. Sounds weird, right?"

"A bit," Niki laughed. "But maybe."

When Monday came and she spent her first night alone, Niki was nervous – but surprised to sleep better than she had in weeks.

Bit by bit, things got easier. Not without bumps in the road, of course.

"Come with me to salsa class," Mae urged one evening.

Reluctantly, Niki went – and enjoyed herself more than she expected, especially after a kind-eyed guy named Ajay asked her for another dance.

As summer turned to golden autumn, her confidence bloomed. She asked Ajay out on a date. More followed. At Christmas, she invited him to her cosy home.

With the New Year came fresh energy, and by spring, Niki was offered her dream job – in Paris.

The old Niki might have panicked. But now, she didn't hesitate. She and Ajay decided to move and rent a flat together.

The future felt full of possibility. But best of all, Niki knew that whatever happened – good or bad – she'd be okay.

The past year had taught her that.

The day she handed the keys back, she paused on the doorstep, sad to leave the house that had helped her rebuild.

She hoped its next resident would feel its warmth as she had.

• • • •

Fragrant yellow roses bloomed again along the path to the redbrick house, where Laura waited to meet a new potential tenant.

Admiring the resilience of the flowers, she felt a warm glow at the thought of new beginnings.

She sensed the troubled young woman walking towards her had mustered real courage to be here.

"Hi, Chelsea. I'm Laura. This is the house we spoke about. Luckily, it's just come back on the market."

"I could do with some luck after the year I've had," Chelsea said nervously. "Your agency came recommended."

"We do our best to help," Laura smiled.

"I need a stopgap," Chelsea explained. "Somewhere safe. A fresh start."

"I understand," Laura said, meaning it. She once knew that feeling all too well.

"I think you'll find this place just right."

She turned the key in the lock and they stepped inside together.

"Wow!" Chelsea exclaimed.

"What a lovely room! So bright and welcoming. As if the house has wrapped me in a warm hug."

"It has that effect on people," Laura replied.

She recalled the happy years she'd lived there herself, the house providing much-needed sanctuary, eventually prompting her to take a leap of faith and set up her new business – a successful lettings agency that cared.

Chelsea was grinning, eyes shining.

"It's perfect. I'll take it. Sometimes you just get a good feeling about a place, if you know what I mean."

Laura smiled.

"I know exactly what you mean."

A Fair Bit Of Drama

A disastrous misunderstanding seemed to be unfolding at the village gathering . . .

BY JOANNE DUNCAN

LITTLE Mossop's annual summer fair was in full swing on the other side of the lane, when Grace, the vicar's mum, knocked on my door.

"Hello," I said, ushering her inside. "Aren't you meant to be helping with the cream teas in the vicarage garden?"

"I haven't the heart, Jenny," she replied. "Not after what David Pritchard said to me this morning."

And she burst into tears.

"Sit yourself down," I said. "I'll put the kettle on."

Like me, Grace was a relative newcomer to the village, having arrived from London to visit Simon, her son, and not yet departed.

As for the Pritchards, they owned Mossop Manor and were both professional actors. David had a regular part in a TV soap and Tamsin frequently appeared in police series and the like.

One thing I'd quickly learned about Grace was that she loved to name-drop, so I hadn't been surprised to find them topping the list of people in the area she was eager to network with.

"You know, Jenny," she said when I returned with the tea tray, "I've tried to fit in, I really have.

"Involving myself in parish affairs, volunteering for things. But it's no use.

"The villagers just think I'm pushy and now I'm being shunned by the folk up at the big house as well."

"You did have one success," I said, unable to resist. "Everyone agreed that St Oswald's looked magnificent on Pentecost Sunday."

I caught her eye and she smiled rather wanly.

Having put her name down for the church flower rota, Grace had been horrified to learn from Simon that her allotted slot, scheduled for early June, coincided with one of the key festivals of the Christian year. That was the day on which the bishop came to carry out the confirmations.

She could have simply requested help from someone more experienced, of course, but that wasn't Grace's way.

Walking home from the May meeting of the local bat group (to which David Pritchard also belonged), she had happened to notice a van parked in a layby off Church Lane.

"It was only yards from the vestry door, half-hidden by trees," she'd told me the next day, in strictest confidence, "and the name on the side was Flowers by Charlotte.

"That's the answer, I thought – I'll hire a professional florist!"

I'd had to laugh. It was so typical, somehow.

"I called her first thing and it's all arranged.

"I'm to let her into the church at around seven p.m. on the Saturday and she's agreed to park in the layby again, which means that, with any luck, none of the neighbours will spot her.

"I was so pleased with myself after that evening," Grace said now wryly.

"Not only had I found a solution to my flower rota problem, I'd also had a proper conversation with David for the first time. First and last, as it turned out . . ."

"There's one thing I don't understand about him," I said. "How come he's always here in Little Mossop?"

"I've heard he plays the fiddle for the morris dancers now, as well as being a member of the bat group.

"Don't most soap stars spend weeks at a time away from home, filming?"

Her eyes widened.

"Haven't you heard? His character went to visit an estranged daughter in Australia and died over there. They've written him out."

"Goodness."

This was news to me but then I wasn't much of a soap fan.

"Hence my suggestion," she said, "that he should present the prizes at the fair. Keep himself in the public eye."

"That was you?"

I'd seen David's name on the publicity and assumed the parish council had invited him.

"I thought it would be a real coup for Simon," she said. "You know it's his first summer fair since coming to St Oswald's? Of course, the plan's backfired now."

"David will still do it, though, won't he? I mean he's around today anyway."

"I doubt it, Jenny. He's far too angry with me. Although he seemed keen enough when I first broached the subject.

"Gave me his number or rather the number of the PA who organises their diaries, but she never got back.

"I did try again this morning and she put me straight through to him but, before I could say anything, he'd accused me of invading his privacy and threatened to take out an injunction."

"That's ridiculous," I said indignantly. "Makes you wonder if Tamsin wouldn't have been a better bet."

Grace stared at me open-mouthed for a moment, a joyful expression spreading over her face.

"Jenny, you're brilliant. Can you see any sign of the morris men yet?"

My binoculars, a retirement present from my colleagues, were on the windowsill.

I picked them up and panned from left to right across the sunny field opposite, past the merry-go-round and the various stalls and tents.

"Yes," I said.

"I can definitely see handkerchiefs waving near the tombola and there's a man standing there with a violin under his chin. That'll be him, won't it?"

"Yes, which means the coast should be clear for me to try the PA again." She began to rummage in her bag. "I'll call from the kitchen if you don't mind."

While she was out of the room, I zoomed in on David Pritchard. He looked to be in his fifties and was extremely handsome.

A youngish woman stood by his side.

"Good news," Grace said from the doorway.

"Who's that, standing next to David?" I held out the binoculars and she took them. "They seem very friendly."

"It's Charlotte." She handed them back with a slight frown. "I wasn't aware they knew each other but perhaps she supplies the flowers for the dancers' hats."

Sure enough, as I watched, Charlotte reached up on tiptoe and gently adjusted the roses nestling in the brim of David's bowler.

"The PA has no more idea than us why he's behaving so strangely," Grace was saying, "but is pretty sure Tamsin will be happy to oblige with the prizes if it's put to her.

"She's already left for the fair, in fact, and should arrive within the next five minutes. I'd better let Simon know so he can roll out the red carpet."

By now, Charlotte had finished tweaking and was removing a stray petal from David's jacket. I saw her hand brush, not quite accidentally, against his.

"Those two are definitely more than acquaintances," I said when Grace had ended her call. "Has it ever occurred to you to wonder why Charlotte's van was parked in Little Mossop so late in the evening?"

"Not really. An urgent delivery, perhaps?"

"Those bat meetings, taking place outdoors at dusk – someone could easily slip away without attracting too much attention.

"When you think about it, they're the perfect cover for an assignation."

"You mean she was waiting for David? I don't believe it!" Grace said.

"If they thought you'd rumbled them, his accusation would sort of make sense.

"Think about it," I said. "Charlotte deliberately parks in the least public place she can find and yet, within twenty-four hours, you're on the phone making it quite clear she's been spotted.

"Not threatening her exactly – just coming out with an unlikely-sounding spiel about church flowers.

"An excuse to probe further, perhaps, before offering the story to the press."

Grace looked horrified.

"She did seem a bit subdued when she came to the church. Wary, even. And now his wife's on her way over.

"Oh, Jenny, what if it's true and Tamsin knows? What if her sole purpose in coming to the fair is to create a scene and I've just sent my son to intercept her . . .?"

"Well, it's too late to worry now," I said as an elegant figure came into focus. "She's here and appears to be chatting to David and Charlotte quite normally.

"And Simon's also approaching, presumably to welcome her.

"They're walking off in the direction of the dais so the prize-giving must be about to commence."

A male voice reverberated through the public address system.

"That's Simon introducing her," Grace whispered.

After some applause, Tamsin herself began to speak but it was quite difficult to make out what she was saying.

At one point, a kind of shocked murmur from the audience made Grace gasp.

"I think she may have just announced the end of her marriage," she said. "It's either that or . . ."

"Or what?"

"Simon did mention there might be some controversy over the winning marrow."

Finally we heard more clapping, followed by a cheerful tune played on the fiddle as the morris display resumed.

"It's over," I said, "and it sounds as though everybody's happy so stop worrying. Go home now and have a lie down. If you want to pop back later, I'll cook us some pasta and we'll plot a way to get you back into David's good books."

• • • •

"So," Grace said as we sat down to eat, "would you like to hear the whole story as divulged to me by Tamsin? It's to go no further, mind."

"I'm all ears," I said.

"Towards the beginning of this year," she began, "the Pritchards agreed on an amicable parting as they'd both met other people."

I shook my head.

"Honestly, these show-business types. But why the secrecy? And why has neither of them moved out of Mossop Manor?"

"Because, within a week of the decision, word had come via their agent that they were being considered as a couple for a certain televised dance competition which, contractually, Tamsin isn't allowed to name.

"Obviously this presented a quandary. Should they risk sabotaging a wonderful opportunity by telling the truth or should they keep schtum?"

"Tricky," I commented.

"Then this morning, Tamsin overheard David shouting at me on the phone and decided that, in his present mood, the person most likely to let the cat out of the bag was him.

"Rather than wait for this to happen, she contacted their agent and asked her to break the news to the television people without further ado."

"And?" I pressed.

"They're over the moon at the thought of all the additional human interest the story's going to generate. That's why Tamsin immediately set off for the fair, to put David out of his misery."

"Well, I'm glad it worked out OK," I said. "Although I don't suppose we shall be seeing much of them in Little Mossop once the summer's over. There'll be all the training and the interviews and so on.

"I'm surprised you're not missing London yourself to be honest," I went on, my curiosity getting the better of me at last. "Your nice little flat you've told me so much about? All your friends?"

She smiled sadly.

"It wasn't until after my husband died that I realised they were actually his friends rather than ours.

"I could sense that even the ones who stayed in touch were only doing it out of a sense of duty.

"Eventually, I made up my mind to start again somewhere else. Build new networks, as they say."

Ah, the networking.

"Well, you never know," I said to cheer her up. "Maybe the Pritchards will sell Mossop Manor and then you can network with the new people."

Grace looked surprised.

"I'm past the networking stage, Jenny. I'm consolidating now.

"The next items on my agenda are: one, sell the flat and two, find a cottage as nice as this one. Oh, and I must take my name off the church flower rota.

"It's just not me at all and I don't know why I ever thought it was!"

The Whole Picture

Hazel's husband had always praised her artistic talent...

BY MARGRET GERAGHTY

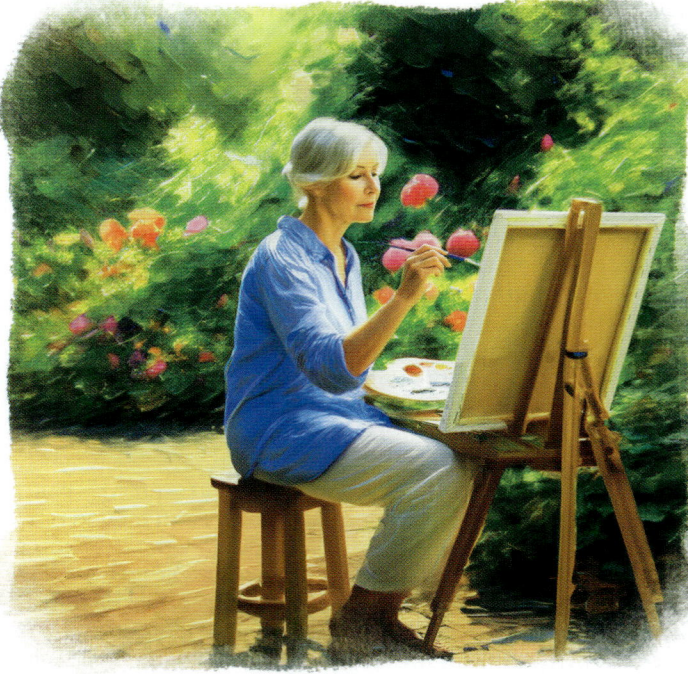

"My goal for today is to clear out the loft," Hazel told Merlin. "No ifs, no buts."

Merlin stopped chewing the fringe of the carpet and pushed his nose on to her lap.

He was so called because of his magical ability to clear tables with a swish of his tail.

Hazel grabbed her teacup just in time.

Merlin was the most lovable dog, but a complete menace where free-range crockery was concerned.

Hazel patted his silky head. She wondered how Merlin would cope with a move.

Since being born at the rescue centre, all he'd known in his short life was her cottage, nestled at the edge of a large grassland common where he went for his daily exercise.

It was a popular place for dog-walkers and Merlin loved a good run off his lead.

But as her daughter Nina was fond of pointing out, Hazel must think of herself, too.

"You're not getting any younger, Mum," Nina warned on one of her sporadic visits. "And without Dad, you're kind of isolated up here, aren't you?"

"Oh, I wouldn't say that, dear," Hazel said. "I like the peace and quiet."

While it was true that her tiny ivy-clad cottage was secluded, its tranquillity had been part of its charm for her and her late husband, Bob.

They'd moved here when Bob retired, after years of living on a busy road overlooking a petrol station.

The minute they'd stepped inside and seen the views through the windows, the sunlit green of the common and the big sky above, they'd known it was their dream home.

While no-one could ever replace Bob, Merlin was a sociable companion, even if he did knock over the bins instead of taking them to the gate.

Besides, she had a telephone and a broadband connection. Although, as Nina also pointed out, it wasn't as reliable as one in town.

It was funny how role-reversal crept up on you, Hazel thought.

It seemed only yesterday that she'd sat on the floor with Nina, showing her how to spin a top.

Now Nina was worried she'd turn into a recluse.

Hazel felt that if Nina was that concerned, she might think of visiting a little more often, but she already knew what Nina's answer would be.

"I'd love to, Mum, but my diary's so chock-full I don't know whether I'm coming or going."

But Nina meant well and Hazel had agreed to think about moving back to town.

Clearing out the loft was a first step.

"Yes, Merlin," she said in as firm a voice as she could manage. "Today is the day."

Hazel couldn't remember the last time she'd been in the loft.

Bob had installed a ladder and he was the one who usually went up there, to check for leaks in the roof and – once a year – to bring down Christmas decorations.

Now, as she gazed around, it all seemed a bit "Miss Havisham" with cobwebs dangling from the beams and surfaces thick with dust.

There were enough boxes piled up to rebuild the Berlin Wall.

Hazel opened one and found it full of Nina's old toys – jigsaws, board games, a doll with a scarecrow haircut and a teddy with a missing ear.

Why on earth had she kept them?

Of course, she knew why. They held precious memories.

She was about to open another box when there was a crash and a yelp from the far side of the loft.

Merlin ran towards her, tail between his legs.

"Merlin!" she cried, after checking that he wasn't hurt. "How on earth did you climb that ladder?"

Merlin just shook himself and yawned, while Hazel went to look at the pile of items now lying in an untidy heap across the boards.

They were canvases – paintings she'd done at an adult education class when she and Bob were first married.

There was a box of acrylic paints, too, all now solid as lumps of toffee.

"Well, these can go," Hazel said, putting the shrivelled tubes into a bin bag.

But the paintings, mostly landscapes, featuring hills and valleys with wildflowers in the foreground, were not so easily discarded.

They, too, brought back memories, although not particularly pleasant ones.

Hazel remembered the art class tutor, a young woman who was always careful to make positive comments about everyone's efforts, but whose taste was clearly focused on the avant-garde.

"Conceptual art," she had enthusiastically explained at the first session, "is art for which the idea is more important than its finished appearance."

That seemed a bit bonkers to Hazel but most of the other students climbed on the bandwagon, and the room was soon full of images of trains coming out of ring doughnuts and umbrellas on lobsters.

Despite stylistic differences, Hazel had enjoyed the classes, but things changed at the end of term display of everyone's work.

To Hazel's dismay, her painting of trees at the edge of a ploughed field had been hung in a corner, almost hidden behind the fire extinguisher.

In pride of place, the tutor had chosen a rather smudged drawing of a kitchen pedal bin, overflowing with chips and a half-eaten burger, entitled "Lost Appetite".

The snub had hit Hazel's confidence.

She took her picture home and didn't enrol for any more classes.

Bob tried to persuade her to continue but then Nina was born and, as often happens with the arrival of a baby, everything else took second place.

Looking at her paintings now with a more critical eye, Hazel could see that while they had a certain rustic charm, and were nicely composed, there was something missing.

They were dream pictures of imagined landscapes. They needed life.

Well, that could be fixed and there was no time like the present.

Hazel went down to an art shop in the valley and bought new paints, brushes, a new sketchbook and lots of paper suitable for acrylics.

Back home, she carried her easel into the garden and set to work.

Her fingers trembled with excitement as she laid out the plump tubes of new paint alongside her brushes and a jam jar of water.

It was a warm day and the coconut scent of gorse filled the air.

A girl riding a dappled grey pony, smiled a greeting.

The pony danced sideways, scaring a few rabbits, who scattered like children playing tag.

Hazel had tried drawing horses but they were tricky, especially the feet which ended up looking more like saucepans than hooves.

She needed something more familiar, something she could study, something like . . . Merlin.

Merlin was busy chasing butterflies, so Hazel grabbed her phone.

Click, click, click. And there he was, caught in mid-air, ears flying, body twisting. A dog in action, just what she needed.

As the hours passed, Hazel was delighted to find the painting coming to life.

After painting Merlin into the foreground, she added shadows beneath the trees and a woman in a retro-style crimson frock coat, striding across the grass with another small dog at her heels.

When she finally laid down her brushes, Hazel was surprised to find that she'd lost track of time.

Exhilarated, she went indoors to make tea.

When she came back out, there was an elderly couple at the gate and Merlin was desperately trying to interact with their blue whippet through the fence.

The whippet looked bored, but the couple was studying her painting with interest.

"Forgive us for being nosey," the woman said with a smile, "but we wondered if you accept commissions?"

"Commissions?" Hazel was thrown.

"Well, you've caught your dog's character so perfectly well, and we thought you might be able to do the same for Rocky here.

"He's our son's dog," she added, "and we need a present for his birthday."

Hazel was flattered, but a touch apprehensive.

"Well, I have to warn you I'm not a professional," she said cautiously, "but if you're sure you like my style of painting, I'd like to give it a go."

"Wonderful." The woman clapped her hands. "We're not local but we'll be here for a couple of weeks, staying at the Golden Eagle, if you know where that is?"

Hazel did. It was a traditional inn on the far side of the common.

She and Bob had popped in there occasionally for lunch or supper.

A commission! Hazel kept repeating that delicious-sounding word to herself.

Was she up to it? She'd soon find out.

As the days passed, Hazel found her confidence returning in leaps and bounds.

It had been a long time since she'd felt so exhilarated.

She remembered Bob's encouragement all those years ago.

"Sweetheart, you have talent," he'd said. "Why waste it, just because some hoity-toity tutor prefers something whacky?"

She hadn't listened at the time, but now painting the scenery they both loved seemed in a strange and wonderful way to keep him close.

Best of all, she knew he'd be proud of her.

She began to paint every day.

When rain and wind kept her indoors, she found that looking through the cottage windows allowed a different perspective.

And by arranging vases of flowers on the ledges, she created rooms with views.

On one such drizzly day, she was enjoying her first cup of coffee when a businesslike woman in a tweed skirt strode up the path and knocked on her door.

"I'm Isobel Harding," the woman said. "My husband and I have just taken over the management of the Golden Eagle Inn."

Hazel invited her in and offered her a seat.

"I believe you recently sold a painting to some guests of ours?" Isobel Harding said.

"Yes, of course – a little blue whippet. Is there a problem? They seemed pleased with it."

"Very pleased indeed. That's why I'm here. My husband and I have plans for the inn.

"Right now it's a little tired and frumpy. We want to refresh it, give it more of a distinctive flavour. And that includes displaying paintings from local artists."

"What a lovely idea," Hazel said.

"The plan is that if guests like the pictures, they'll have the option of buying them. Would you be interested?"

Before she could answer, Merlin wagged his tail and swept Hazel's vase of flowers off the window ledge on to the quarry-tiled floor.

"Oh dear, I'm so sorry," Hazel gasped as water splashed the hem of Isobel Harding's long coat, but Isobel just laughed.

"My, he's a live wire," she said, and ran a hand through Merlin's fur in a way that instantly endeared her to him.

"I tell you what," she added. "If you're free for lunch tomorrow, come across to the inn.

"There'll be a couple of other local artists there, too, and we can discuss details. How does that sound?"

For the rest of the day, Hazel walked on air.

"Merlin," she said as the two of them relaxed that evening in front of a glowing log fire. "I'm a real artist now.

"You don't know what that feels like, but I can tell you it's wonderful."

Merlin just wagged his tail, put his head on his paws, and nodded off, lost in his own dream world.

When Hazel's daughter Nina phoned later that week, wanting to know if she'd put the cottage on the market, Hazel knew exactly what to say.

"No, dear, I'm afraid haven't. My calendar's so chock-full I don't know whether I'm coming or going."

STEADY SAILING

I launch our toy yacht into the breeze,
Joining in with the fun in the park.
The sail flaps low, then steadies itself,
One last voyage as dusk turns to dark.

She bobs along on her zig-zag route
Among this fine, motley flotilla.
Seeking my son, a little weighed down
With a prize cargo to deliver.

Eager, Sam waits at the other side
Willing the wind to whip up to gust.
But slow and sure, I know, wins the race,
A sudden rush, and all might be lost.

My walk with God is calm and steady,
He never leads me into drama.
I hold his hand, always trust his will,
As he shields me with divine armour.

Sam raises his arm in victory,
As the yacht steers into the harbour.
Secured on the deck is a pack of sweets,
Which he receives with gleeful laughter.

By Emma Peterson